JACQUI ROSE

Tak

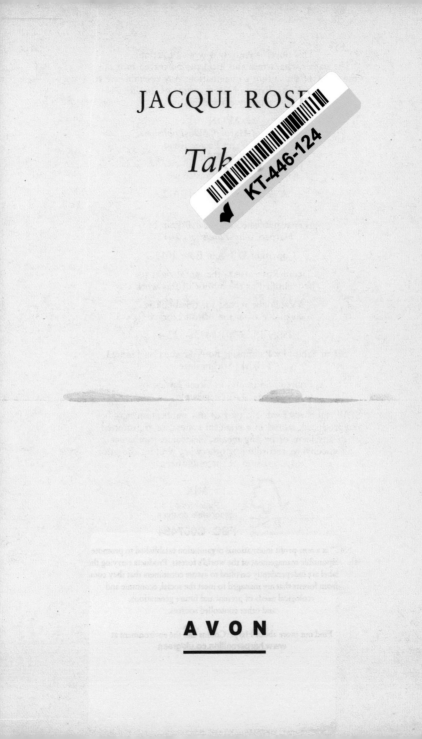

AVON

AVON
A division of HarperCollins*Publishers*
77–85 Fulham Palace Road,
London W6 8JB

www.harpercollins.co.uk

A Paperback Original 2012
1

First published in Great Britain by
HarperCollins*Publishers* 2012

A catalogue record for this book is
available from the British Library

ISBN-13: 978-1-84756-322-4

Set in Sabon by Palimpsest Book Production Limited,
Falkirk, Stirlingshire

Printed and bound in Great Britain by
Clays Ltd, St Ives plc

MIX
Paper from
responsible sources
FSC
www.fsc.org
FSC C007454

FSC is a non-profit international organisation established to promote
the responsible management of the world's forests. Products carrying the
FSC label are independently certified to assure consumers that they come
from forests that are managed to meet the social, economic and
ecological needs of present and future generations,
and other controlled sources.

ACKNOWLEDGEMENTS

My name might be on the cover but without the people behind me who've believed in me, encouraged me and saved me from falling I could never have made it here today. So in order of appearance I'd like to acknowledge my mum, Patricia, for the sacrifice she had to make all those years ago – we made it back together. Love to Lisa, Lee and Darren who I know have always loved me no matter how far away we've been. Love too to my other mum, Hilda who bandaged my knee when I fell, tucked me up in bed at night and told me I was special, and of course my dad, Gordon who is the kindest man I've ever known. A big love to my sister, Rosemary, who let me use half her name and whether she likes it or not is on this crazy journey with me. And of course, not forgetting my other dad Phil, who came out of the wings not because he had to but because he wanted to.

I want to send my deepest thanks also to Sanja, for everything she did to help me free myself of the life I had. But a special eternal thanks must go to Fatima, who lifted me up when I thought I couldn't go on, took my hand to guide me through the darkness and showed me how to live, without you I wouldn't be here. Thanks to all my friends who over the years I had held away at arm's length but when I could finally let you in, you were still all there to meet me with your friendship and love. To all the people who've ever showed me kindness, whether for a fleeting moment or for a lifetime, you'll never know how much it meant to me.

And lastly, thanks once more to Judith, my agent, Keshini my editor who is amazing – we had so much fun with our editing notes didn't we, I'll never be able to look at a pair of 501 jeans in the same way now, and to the whole wonderful team at Avon who gave me such a warm welcome I was truly overwhelmed. Thank you everyone from the very bottom of my heart; I didn't think I'd make it, but I did.

For my three wonderful children who are the air I breathe and the heartbeat of my life.

And for my wonderful agent, Judith Murdoch, who saw something in me I didn't see in myself – thank you.

And finally for Keshini Naidoo, who was my editor before she stopped being my editor, but best of all, she then became my friend.

'Soho' – derived from a 17th-century hunting cry

CHAPTER ONE

'Dean Street please.'

Casey Edwards sat in the back of the black cab and sank her body against the grey faux leather seats. She was exhausted but knew it was pointless trying to get some sleep; she was too wired and decided after she'd settled in, she'd dump her bags and go for a well-needed drink.

'Here on business or pleasure, love?'

It was a simple question from the cab driver, who stared intensely at her with his watery blue eyes in the driver's mirror, but it was one Casey didn't know the answer to. She wasn't here on business and she certainly wasn't here on pleasure; the driver was as much in the know as she was. Not being put off by Casey's silence, the cabbie continued to talk whilst weaving in and out of the traffic on the invariably busy Euston Road.

Casey gazed out of the window, watching the passing cars absentmindedly as she thought about the events of the morning.

Casey opened her eyes and looked down, wondering who the naked man fast asleep on her leg was. She moved her

1

body slightly to the right and groaned audibly as her head began to pound and the sticky residue of semen between her legs betrayed the fact that once again, she'd had sex with a complete stranger.

Her life had become a series of alcohol-fuelled sexual encounters and now for the first time last night she'd added cocaine to the mix.

Getting off the small double bed, she took a second look at the man, who momentarily opened his eyes before turning over and letting out a loud fart. Casey grimaced, trying to remember the events of the previous night, but her head hurt and trying to think made it ache even more.

Vaguely she recollected getting ready; unwashed skinny jeans, a white Gap t-shirt and black leather jacket, before heading to Luigi's wine bar on the corner of Station Road. She recalled ordering an overpriced scotch on the rocks – the first drink was supposed to give her the courage she needed, but instead it became the first of many. The taste of the burning whisky on her lips was as far as her memory took her; she couldn't think how she'd ended up in a shabby hotel room having had sex with a man who had a clear case of flatulence.

Going over to where she'd thrown her clothes, Casey saw the remaining cocaine cut neatly into lines on the tatty brown dresser. Picking up the rolled-up twenty-pound note, she bent over, greedily snorting up the fine white powder and feeling the coke immediately cutting the back of her throat, leaving an acidic taste followed by a tingle as the buzz hit her head and body.

Looking round the room, Casey noticed her suitcase was slightly open and her eyes were immediately drawn to the battered red journal which lay amongst her crumpled clothes.

'Any left for me?' The unidentified man came up behind her and put his hands round Casey's naked waist. He leant *forward and kissed the back of her neck, sending shivers of disgust down her body. She could feel his erect penis pushing hard onto the back of her legs as she bent down again to snort some more cocaine, hoping to numb herself from what was about to happen.*

'How do you want it, baby? Slow and hard or quick and rough?'

He was laughable; did he really think any woman would be turned on by him sounding like he'd just stepped out of a cheap American porn movie? What she really wanted to do was tell him to fuck off, but instead she sighed and answered him in a slow drawl, mirroring his cheap and corny line.

'Anything you want, honey; as long as it's quick, baby. Just make it quick.' She knew this would be the last time; it had to be. There could be no going back now, and somehow she needed this feeling of self-loathing; this debasement of herself to remind her if she didn't make it, couldn't make it, this was what was waiting for her. With tears stinging her eyes she'll let the man's rough hands wander over her body.

After it was over, Casey dressed and walked out, leaving the man hungrily finishing the last of the coke. All she wanted to do was get out of there. Get on a train and head for London, the place she'd been avoiding going for so many years. But it was finally time.

'I didn't know they let blind people drive,' the taxi driver yelled as he overtook a white Fiat, jolting Casey from her thoughts. After getting blocked in by three double-decker buses outside the fire station in Shaftesbury Avenue, the cab driver finally managed to turn right – after much hand gesturing and swearing – into Wardour Street.

'Do you want me to drop you here or go right round, love? It's one way so I can't go down.'

'Here's just fine.' He pulled over without signalling, causing the cyclist behind him to swerve onto the other side of the road, very nearly hitting an oncoming car.

After handing over a ten-pound note for the nine-pound fair and watching the taxi drive off, beeping the horn violently, Casey made her way down Dean Street. She caught glimpses of her stooped, tired looking reflection in the windows of the bars she walked past. She was only thirty-two, but felt much older – each passing day seemed a lifetime. She continued down the street, noticing the mix of Georgian houses once occupied by aristocratic families, and the contemporary shop faces and restaurants, feeling the knots of anxiety in her stomach.

The flat she hadn't seen yet but had agreed to on the phone was next to a pub being refurbished and almost opposite the Soho Theatre. In front of the communal front door Casey saw a Turkish couple arguing violently, and her heart dropped as she wondered if they were to be her new neighbours.

It was just gone five thirty when the landlord, who'd agreed to meet Casey at four o'clock, showed up.

'Hope I haven't kept you waiting.' Bernard Goldman spoke in such a manner it was apparent to Casey he didn't care if he had or not. He continued to talk in a bored voice as he took out a large set of keys from his brown leather briefcase.

'So, like I said on the phone, its one month's rent in advance and one month's rent as a deposit. Each month I'll come and collect the rent in cash and if you can't pay, then it's out. Okay?'

Casey nodded and followed him up the bare staircase to the battered white door at the top of the building. The landlord paused and it took a second for Casey to realise what he was waiting for. Quickly she scrambled in her bag and took out a large envelope, handing it over to him.

After taking several minutes to count the money twice, the landlord was eventually satisfied it was all there.

'Here's your keys; flat, building and utility meters. If you've any problems you've got my number.'

'What about an agreement?'

'What about it?'

The landlord sighed and scratched his flaking head, answering Casey in a sardonic manner.

'Okay. I agree and you agree. Happy now?'

He turned and walked down the stairs and Casey heard the slam of the bottom door close as he hurried out. She stood on the top landing wondering what she'd let herself in for and after a deep breath she put the key in the lock.

It was worse than she'd expected – and she hadn't expected a great deal. The paisley brown wallpaper was visibly peeling off the walls, exposing a multitude of wires. The furniture was non-existent and the floors were bare boards, though Casey thought that was probably a blessing; the idea of having to live with a carpet, riddled with god knows what, might take some doing. The kitchen was really a kitchenette, built as if an afterthought on the far right wall of the L-shaped room. The stove was filthy and Casey reckoned it was a good thing she hated cooking. Surprisingly the kettle was new; so at least she'd be able to have a cup of coffee in the mornings without fear of electrocution.

She opened the door to the bathroom to see what horrors awaited her and immediately shut it closed again. The last door was to the bedroom; in it was a double bed with a mattress still covered in plastic wrapping, a side cabinet with one of its legs being propped up by a pile of yellowing porn magazines, and a large curtainless window overlooking the street.

Even though she wanted to pick up her bag, leaving the

squalid flat to its crawling inhabitants, she'd no other choice but to stay there now. The rent with the deposit had worked out to nearly three and a half grand which had totally wiped out all her savings and she certainly couldn't afford to lose it, plus, unlike most landlords, Mr Goldman only insisted on hard cash and not references and Casey knew it'd be hard to come by a flat in London whose owner didn't require all the proper paperwork and, for that, being extorted by ruthless landlords was the price she'd have to pay. Not wanting to open the bathroom door again, Casey washed her face and brushed her teeth in the kitchenette sink. Pulling out a beige sweater from her bag, she touched the tattered red diary lying at the bottom of it. She'd started writing it when she was fifteen and had only kept it up for a couple of years, but the idea of throwing it out had never even crossed her mind. Over the years she'd moved around the North of England and the first thing she ever packed was her diary, always unable to throw it away, but always unable to open it. Now she had no choice. If she wanted to reconnect with the girl she once was, she had to remember. That girl had had hope, ambition, but more importantly she'd been innocent – and when Casey thought about who she'd once been, it was if she was thinking about another person.

Opening it, Casey read the first entry – written in red capital letters and two lines long.

Sat 15th July 1995
OH GOD – I'M PREGNANT!!!! MUM AND DAD ARE GOING TO KILL ME.

Casey slammed the diary closed and threw it back in the bag. She needed a drink; preferably several. It was the end of a long day and she refused to let herself feel guilty about needing to take the edge off. She could start her good intentions tomorrow. For now, she was going to let her hair down.

Looking round at her new home, she realised how utterly alone she was; moving round so much had given her few opportunities to make friends but this was different and the loneliness frightened her. There was no hiding from the truth either; she'd hit rock bottom and if she was going to ever climb out of this hole, she needed to find the courage to do what she'd come here to do.

Unable to stay in the flat for a moment longer, she hurriedly pulled on her jumper, brushed back her long auburn hair and grabbed her jacket before heading out and down the stairs, just in time to see a woman from the flat below being dragged out into the street by a man who was clearly a junkie.

Walking up Old Compton Street, Casey stopped to read a board outside a comedy club; she could do with a laugh. But tonight she really needed to have a quiet drink and think about what she needed to do. After all, there was a reason why she'd come here, and she didn't want to get distracted by anything else. She continued to walk into the heart of Soho, not noticing the stare of the man across the street.

CHAPTER TWO

Alfie Jennings hated tarts. He didn't mind fucking them but that was as far as it went. He'd certainly no wish to exchange small talk with them – he got enough of that at home with his wife, Janine, without some big-breasted brass talking shit in his ear. All he'd wanted was to get his cock sucked in peace and now he was being forced to listen to a brass talking ten to the dozen.

'Bleedin' hell it was cold outside last night; I nearly froze my tits off and it'd been so sunny during the day. Apparently the rest of the week is going to be rainy but I'm . . .'

The shoe missed, which was Alfie's intention – it wasn't really his scene to hit women, not unless he really had to, but he was certainly coming close to it now; the brass was jangling his nerves with all her yacking.

'Ow! What was that bleedin' for, Alf? You could've hit me on my boat race!'

'If I'd wanted to shag a flippin' weather girl, I'd have given Ulrika a call. And if I was trying to hit you, believe me darlin', I wouldn't have missed.'

'Oh that's nice ain't it? If that clump of a shoe *had* hit me, it would've split open me fucking lip and then how would I give blow jobs then? It'd take at least a week to heal and that'd be a whole week's money lost, not to mention . . .'

Alfie walked into his en-suite bathroom and slammed the door closed; hookers weren't what they used to be. He could remember the time they fucked, sucked and kept their mouth shut. Now they all wanted to talk; thought it was their right to; and that pissed him off no end. He wanted a whore not a fucking wife.

Still hearing the complaints on the other side of the door, Alfie Jennings leant his muscular body on the edge of his black marble sink which had cost him a small fortune and no end of grief.

The men who'd delivered it had tried to tell him it was so heavy that they couldn't bring it up the stairs due to health and safety reasons, so they'd no other option but to leave it on the pavement outside. He'd offered them a score each and asked them politely to make an exception, but they'd given him a point blank no, before starting to get lippy with him.

'Sorry mate, I'm not hurting my back or getting a parking ticket for you; you'll need to get some other mug to lug it up the stairs.'

Alfie had given the men time to grin triumphantly at each other before he'd grabbed hold of the sweaty fat one, pinning him up against his newly decorated hallway whilst noticing the man's yellow-stained teeth as he grimaced in fear.

'You better shut yer north and south you paki cunt otherwise I might do something I regret.' The look of fear on the two men's faces had amused Alfie no end, making it more entertaining to watch them later struggling up his stairs with blood streaming out of their broken noses, carrying the handcrafted sink.

The whole country was changing; nobody wanted to do anything for anyone else unless there was something in it for them. Alfie knew no one should really have to go to those extremes just to get some bellends to help him; not that he didn't enjoy a ruck. Violence to him was like a good wine you savoured and took pleasure in any time of the day.

Sighing, he opened the smoky glassed bathroom window, enjoying the sound of West End life and taking in the cutting cold air on his bare chest.

His flat looked out over his favourite street in London and was directly opposite his club. Old Compton Street was in Alfie's mind the heart of Soho; he'd even argue it was the heart of the capital: he never tired of it. He could still remember the excitement he'd felt as a boy when he'd jumped on the number 8 bus with his father on a Saturday night, heading away from the gloom of the East End and towards the heaving streets of Soho.

His father regularly visited an old brass at the Soho Square end of Greek Street, leaving Alfie outside no matter what the weather. Far from seeing this as another spiteful torment from his bullying father, Alfie had always relished the time, taking the opportunity to explore the smells and sounds of the Soho streets. Even on the coldest of winter nights the lights and the vibrancy of the people had made Alfie feel warm.

He'd got to know the bouncers of the clubs and the toothless toms with their vulgar jokes and stale breath touting for business outside the peep show doors in Brewer Street. He'd seen the pimps and the gangsters hanging out on the corner of Wardour Street and the small time crooks and drug dealers in the numerous side alleyways, and Alfie had loved every moment of it.

It was worlds away from the East End, where each street seemed to Alfie to be made up of drab grey houses, the smell of poverty lingering on every corner.

'I'm going to get myself a club here when I grow up. That one there is the one I'll buy.'

He was twelve years old when he'd pointed out the club painted black with the silver double doors and the silver lettering on the sign. His father had looked at him with so much scorn on his face Alfie had wondered how it'd all managed to fit on.

'You've more chance in going to the moon. You'll come to nothing, you little bastard.'

'Then I'll be in good bleedin' company won't I?'

Alfie had got a battering from his father leaving him with a broken rib and a long walk to the Whitechapel hospital. Even with all the pain, Alfie had thought it'd been worth it; he'd got to tell the old fucker the truth.

On the day Alfie turned twenty-three he'd bought the club with the black sign and silver lettering in Old Compton Street. He'd dragged his alcoholic father from his filthy Mile End council flat into his car, hauling him out at the other end and depositing him in front of the silver double doors of the newly bought club which was to be the start of Alfie's empire.

'There you miserable fucker; have a look at that. That's mine, every fucking last brick of it. Now try telling me I'll come to nothing.'

The scorn hadn't changed on his father's face but the fear was new, and Alfie had enjoyed seeing it.

As Alfie continued to stare at his father he watched the fear turn into a sneer. 'I don't care if you've got bleedin' money pouring out of yer fucking arse, it won't change the fact yer a useless little prick; as useless as a third sleeve on me fucking vest.'

Alfie had kicked his father in the head, sending him reeling backwards into the path of passersby. He'd continued the attack; stamping on his father's ribs, twisting his foot on his face and hearing the breaking of cartilage in the nose of the man who'd beaten and humiliated him, and laughed as he'd come home drunk and forced Alfie to get on his hands and knees whilst he urinated on him.

It wasn't until a tall black man with dreadlocks had pulled him off his father that the assault had stopped, leaving Alfie Senior in a pool of blood, covering his face in agony. Alfie had felt the tears rolling down his face, partly from anger, partly for his mother, but mainly for himself.

Some years later, Alfie had been doing some business off the Mile End Road, when he'd seen an old tramp outside the Nag's Head pub. He'd been about to put his hand in his pocket to hand him a pony – feeling flush after winning on the dogs – but when he'd looked again at the tramp, underneath the heavily unshaven face, the long straggly hair, he'd seen the familiar grey eyes, the cold blank stare, and he knew it was his father. They'd locked eyes for a moment, neither of them saying a word, staring at each other with steely hatred, then Alfie had turned away and walked back to his car.

He'd sat there for countless hours, his head filled with painful memories, but as the sun had begun to rise over the grey houses of the East End, he'd put his keys into the ignition and driven away; away from his past and away from his pain. Alfie Jennings never laid eyes on his father again.

Alfie didn't know why he loved this street so much – after all it was full of nancy boys and tourists and he wasn't partial to either – but it was where he felt at home. Over time Alfie had secured other properties in London; flats in Docklands, shops in East Ham, and he'd bought a large eight-bedroom family home in Essex for his wife Janine and his daughter Emmie, but it was always this street he came back to, although he never allowed his family to come. At home he was Alfie the husband, Alfie the father; but here in his own apartment he was just Alfie the man.

Although Janine hadn't been to the flat it hadn't been for want of trying; she never missed an opportunity to nag his earhole off to ask to stay. 'Why can't we come up West with you, Alfie? It'd make a nice change for me. Oh come on Alf, what do you say?'

His wife had looked at him over the large breakfast table with egg yolk spilling down her chin. He wondered what had ever possessed him to marry her. When he'd first met her she was a tiny pretty thing who found it hard to say boo to a sparrow, let alone a goose. Fast forward twenty-two years and she'd morphed into something unrecognisable; a fat nagging moaning bitch of a wife who'd too much to say about everything.

One thing Alfie had never done was raise a hand to her; he wasn't sure why, because he'd no problem using violence on anyone else, whether it was a mouth full of knuckles to a man who owed him money or a slap round the face to a brass who'd given him too much cheek: as long as it wasn't his family it didn't matter.

The thought had crossed his mind that the reason he didn't hit Janine – though god knows every time he was with her more than an hour, he longed to put his fist in her mouth – was because he'd watched his own father beat the shit out of his mother on a daily basis.

Living with Alfie Senior had eventually become too much for Annabel Jennings, and Alfie had come home from school one day to discover her lifeless body in the outhouse at the bottom of the garden, lying in a pool of blood, still clutching the garden shears she'd used to stab herself in the neck with.

Alfie had sat with his mother until the next morning holding her cold hand, sometimes screaming, sometimes

13

crying silently; hoping a miracle would bring her back to life.

As soon as his father had come home and the doctor had been called, Alfie had gone out and battered senseless the first kid he'd come across.

Alfie couldn't remember how many diets his wife had been on and none of them ever seemed to work; if anything, with each coming year she'd got bigger, though ironically, her tits, the part of her body he'd been most drawn to, were the one part of her body that'd lost weight. Now they were sagging, empty sacks and when she lay on her back in bed, they'd hang over each side of her body, almost touching the mattress.

'Why don't you touch me any more?' Janine would complain. 'I bet you've got some skinny tart up Soho and that's why you don't want me to come up.'

Most of the time Alfie was able to convince his wife there was no one else and his lack of sexual interest in her was down to tiredness, but sometimes words didn't cut it, and he was forced to show her with actions. Shagging his wife was like shagging the Mersey Tunnel Alfie thought – large, cold and passionless.

When he did fuck her, he always struggled just to get semi-erect, which Alfie thought said a lot about his wife; even with the oldest and ugliest of old brasses he'd no problem getting a boner, but Janine Jennings, with her big fat mouth and her just as big fat pussy, had a flaccid effect on his poor penis.

Alfie had kept the black sign of the club for nostalgia and as a reminder not to allow himself to fail. The fear of failure was a legacy from his father who had constantly told him he'd never make it; that he'd amount to nothing. So each

14

day when he went into the club and put the key in the imposing door, it was his vindication to himself he'd proved those words wrong.

He'd had the club since he was twenty-three and had given it a facelift, renaming it Annabel's Whispers, though everyone called it Whispers Comedy Club or Whispers for short; but to Alfie it would always be Annabel's Whispers – named after his gently spoken mother. Having her name there was a way of keeping his mother alive to him – it was important to Alfie because he couldn't remember her face any longer, causing him to feel a deep sense of shame and sadness. When he tried to remember, all he could see was the blood, and all he could hear were his childhood screams.

Whispers had evolved over time and it'd become useful for his other businesses. It was a place where he could hold his meetings with the biggest faces in London, a place he stored the countless numbers of stolen goods which came in and out of his possession and a place to launder money, but for all Alfie felt he had achieved, the one thing he was proudest of was the public face of Whispers. He'd turned it from just a drinking bar into a successful comedy and nightclub. He regularly attracted the biggest acts in the business; sometimes pulling in favours from the cigar-smoking promoters and sometimes resorting to what he knew worked best; bribery and threats. Whatever it took, Alfie made sure Whispers was the place to be.

Often Alfie took to the stage himself, supporting the acts but securing the biggest laughs; it was one of the perks to being him, being a face, being someone everyone was scared of; even if he wasn't funny, they were all too damn scared of him not to laugh.

Not that he wanted it to be that way. He longed for the applause and laughter to be genuine; he really did love doing stand-up, but his problem was the nerves.

'You're all wound up and tight like an Irish nun's fanny. What you need to do is relax, Alf – enjoy it instead of bleeding worrying about what everyone else will think and being terrified you'll be crap,' Janine would say to him constantly.

'Thank you bleeding Oprah. When I want your flipping input, Janine, I'll ask for it – until then, keep your big fat mush shut.'

Annoyed, he'd storm off, slamming the front door behind him because what she said always hit a nerve. It was true he worried about what people would think of him and it was true the word failure loomed large in his head. And the more he worried about it, the worse it got; moments before he was due to go on stage with the solitary spotlight hitting down on him as the audience looked up in anticipation, the nerves would get the better of him; his palms and brow would begin to sweat, the well-rehearsed lines would disappear from his mind, leaving only panic and dread in their wake.

He wished he could confide in his friends but he knew he could never admit it to anyone; he'd a reputation to keep and it wouldn't do for people to know that the great Alfie Jennings, the man so many men had feared, was crippled with stage fright. He'd be a laughing stock, and the fear of that was nearly as great as his nerves. He'd secretly gone to a hypnotherapist in Harley Street and paid through the fucking nose to try to conquer his fear but it hadn't helped, nothing seemed to.

Up until five years ago Alfie's hideaway flat had been above his foundling club, but when he'd started branching out into other business he'd decided to buy the penthouse across the road and it was now his second home. Not that the penthouse had been for sale – the owners had no intention of moving out until Alfie had sent round three of his

16

henchmen with a stark warning and an offer. Six months later, he'd moved in.

The club had survived the nail bomb in Old Compton Street, though The Admiral Duncan, a pub a few doors along, hadn't been so lucky, and neither had some of its punters. But Whispers Comedy Club had survived and as Alfie looked out at the club opposite, he felt a pride in his chest like the one he'd felt when he'd seen Emmie for the first time.

His thoughts were interrupted by banging on the bathroom door.

'Alfie, let me in love. I need a wee.'

Alfie Jennings could feel his temper rising. Not only was she a mouthy brass, but she also expected to go for a piss in his expensive marbled bathroom. Swinging open the door, Alfie took in the state of the woman in front of him who an hour ago had been giving him a blow job and sticking her tongue in his arse. She stood naked, jigging about with her huge tits uncovered, pulling her face into a scowl.

'Christ, about bleedin' time. I'm going to burst like a dam.'

The scream from the young woman's mouth was one of shock as Alfie picked her up and carried her through the doorway of his bedroom and out of his flat.

'Put me down yer fucker.'

'You want a piss? Piss here where the dogs do, it should be like home from home for you.'

Ignoring her effing and blinding, Alfie unceremoniously dumped the naked woman outside in the street before catching sight of a stunning looking woman across the other side, reading the board outside his club. He took in her curvaceous yet slim body, her long auburn hair and full red lips and for a moment he just stood there, forgetting about the tom he'd just thrown out, forgetting about the show later on that night; for one of the first times in his life, Alfie Jennings was mesmerised. He willed the woman to go into the club, but she turned away in the other direction. He contemplated going after her, turning on the Jennings charm, but he needed to get showered first and wash off the brass; it wouldn't go down very well if he had the smell of another woman all over him. Besides, it wasn't as if his dick would go hungry; Soho was always full of top class pieces of pussy waiting to get laid.

CHAPTER THREE

It was already six o'clock and Oscar Harding needed to get ready. He'd been trying to get ready since this morning but had found it impossible after waking up to the scene of carnage next to him. It was the second time it'd happened and although it hadn't shocked him as much as the first time, it'd still fucked up his day.

He'd called Billy a few hours ago and had left a message but he still hadn't arrived and that was really winding him up. He paid Billy a lot of money to be at his beck and call and on the few times he did call him, the little prick was nowhere to be seen.

It was his own fault though; his mum had always warned him about trusting coons. That thought pissed him off even more; knowing his mum had been right about anything.

'Boss? Boss?'

Oscar watched Billy swagger into the bedroom of his large executive flat and then freeze as he took in the sight; his black skin blanching. 'Fuck me.'

'Are you trying to be an Anthony Blunt? I called you over

three hours ago and the first thing you come in and say is fuck me. Where's my fucking apology?'

'Sorry Boss, it's just a shock.'

Oscar looked at the horror on Billy's face; he was short and stocky and his skin was black as a hole. And had a naked woman tattooed on his neck. Oscar decided that he needed to get rid of him as soon as possible. It was no good having a henchman who was shocked at the sight of a little bit of blood.

'I need you to clear this up; I'm meeting Alfie Jennings down at the club later and the last thing I need is him moaning like a cunt because I'm late. I'm going to have a shower and I want it gone by the time I'm finished.'

Oscar stood feeling the hot water of the power shower beat down on his chest and as he opened his mouth to let the water bubble into it, the events of the night before came rushing back.

He'd spent the first few hours of the evening listening to Vaughn Sadler talk about his holiday trip to Marbella. It'd been excruciating and Oscar was sure if he was forced to listen to any more holiday anecdotes, he'd end up comatose at UCH.

He'd no interest whatsoever in travelling or in listening to Vaughn pretending to be a page out of the *Lonely Planet*. He'd tried to look at his watch discreetly but Vaughn had spotted him.

'Somewhere else you'd rather be? I'm not boring you am I, Oscar?'

'Not at all, Vaughn, it's fascinating. I could listen to you all night.'

'Glad to hear it. Now where was I? You've made me lose me train of thought.'

'You were about to tell me about your new swimming pool.'

He'd wanted to bury an axe in Vaughn's head to stop him talking, like he'd done to the Albanian guy last week who'd tried to rip him off, but he'd continued to smile through gritted teeth as he listened to the multiple ways of aerating the water in a pool.

Oscar doubted he'd be able to sit and listen to anyone else spouting shit like this but it was, after all, Vaughn Sadler – and even though he'd 'retired' and been out of the business for the last couple of years, Oscar didn't know any sane man who would fuck with Vaughn. He hadn't just heard about his reputation, he'd seen it first hand, and he was one man he never wanted to get on the wrong side of.

He'd known Alfie and Vaughn since their early twenties when they all hung around the clubs of Soho desperate to make a name for themselves. It was Vaughn who'd shot up the ranks first with his fearlessness; never shying away from anyone or anything. When everyone else including himself had been reluctant to go to certain places, Vaughn had gone in controlled and precise, his presence as menacing as the weapons he carried.

Vaughn had taken on the older faces, people like Mad Boy Collins and Leroy Andrews, who even by Oscar's standards were merciless in their quest to get justice for anything they saw as disrespect or wrongdoings.

Rumour had it Mad Boy Collins had been owed less than two grand by Eddie Williams – a small time crack dealer with a big time gambling habit – but Collins had taken exception to the fact he'd had to wait for the money whilst Eddie had gone on a weekend trip to Amsterdam. Pissed off by what he saw as disrespect, Collins and his men had stormed into Eddie's house while he was away and raped his wife and two teenage daughters, before chopping them

21

up into tiny bits – but not before Mad Boy Collins had made himself a cup of tea and a ham sandwich.

Taking on men like Collins without fear had gained Vaughn respect and he'd earned his place amongst the top faces. He'd stayed at the top ever since.

Along the way Vaughn had earned vast amounts of money; everyone had wanted to do business deals with him, knowing they'd never be turned over by Vaughn, who had a reputation not only for being an untouchable but for having integrity; a rare and strange quality in their world.

Oscar had never done any business with Vaughn, although he'd have liked to – he'd heard whispers that Vaughn thought of him as untrustworthy. It'd fucked him off no end to think Vaughn Sadler went around thinking he was better than him, but not nearly as much as it fucked him off to have to sit and listen to him recount his tedious tales of his latest trip abroad. It was either that, though, or risk getting on the wrong side of Vaughn – and no one wanted to do that.

Finally, he'd been able to make his excuses when his phone had rung and he'd pretended it was his mother.

'You know how it is, Vaughn, got to go and see me old mum. She's on her own now and she hasn't been very well.'

'That's what I like to see; sons looking after their mothers.'

Thankful to get out of the bar on Glasshouse Street, Oscar had thought about his mother. There was no way he ever wanted to lay eyes on her again or even speak to her; moreover, if he ever saw her lying in the street he'd cross to the other side. She was nothing more than a drunken slag and if it wasn't for the fact he'd promised his father before he died that he'd look after her, he would've put her in the ground a long time ago.

Thinking about his mother always brought on one of his headaches so he'd decided to do the five-minute walk to Whispers to see what was going on. The club had been empty besides a few nervous and very bad comedians. He'd watched as they took their turns at the open spot and he'd struggled to raise even a smile. Oscar couldn't see the point in a comedian's existence; to him, it was a fucked-up kind of life if you needed to spend it trying to make other people laugh.

He'd heard Alfie's stand-up routine many times and by far he was the worst comedian he'd ever seen; it verged on the embarrassing. Oscar guessed owning the club was the only way Alfie would ever have the chance to go on stage; nobody else in their right mind would let him. But however bad a comedian Alfie was, Oscar had to admit he was a savvy businessman and the club was a perfect smokescreen for their projects; especially the one they were just buying into.

As Oscar had stood eyeing up the barmaid, he'd felt one of his migraines coming on, making him doubly grateful Alfie wasn't performing. It was one thing listening to Vaughn talk about his holidays but an entirely different one listening to Alfie Jennings on stage.

Oscar had left the club when a female comedian had come on stage talking about periods and the menopause. He'd headed back to his flat in Holborn, feeling the pain in his head travel down behind his right eye and the taste of metal on his tongue.

He'd picked up the phone when he'd got home and spoken roughly to the person at the other end.

'Bring me one.'

'Which one Boss?'

'Any. I want to have some fun.'

The girl had stood looking at him nervously and Oscar had guessed she was about twenty, though it didn't really matter how old she was; he'd no interest in knowing anything about her. She was very slim with dark hair but when she'd taken her clothes off, he'd been annoyed at the size of her tits; they were huge and it'd made him feel sick; it reminded him of his mother.

She'd lain back on his clean slate-coloured sheets, naked, and as his headache had got profoundly worse, Oscar had heard her mutter something inaudible, then she'd leant forward and started massaging his penis; first softly and then hard, using her tongue in rapid motion on his shaft.

Nearly blinded from the pain in his head, Oscar had stared down at the woman working away on his limp penis. He couldn't remember the last time he'd had a hard-on and the useless bitch with her colossal tits certainly wasn't helping.

With a lunge of his arm he'd thrust his hand between her legs; she'd screamed loudly, accentuating the pain in his head. He'd punched her; hard enough to daze her but not hard enough to knock her out.

Grabbing hold of her hair, Oscar had dragged the girl further towards him; manoeuvring her underneath him, ready to show her he was a real man. He'd prised her legs wide open and attempted to enter her but he hadn't been able to get an erection.

The humiliation and frustration he'd felt had turned into anger, and in a flash he'd started to kick out at her in a frenzy.

Oscar had looked down at the slate-coloured sheets which had turned into a pool of crimson blood and suddenly he'd felt very tired. It was then that he'd realised his headache had gone; and his pleasure at being pain-free was only slightly marred when it dawned on him he now needed to sleep on the couch, rather than in the blood-soaked bed.

Stepping out of the shower, Oscar hoped Billy had finished cleaning up. He was happy now he remembered what'd happened; all day it'd troubled him. Not what he'd done;

she was only a cheap whore anyway and he doubted she'd ever be missed; it was the not remembering he hated.

Whistling, Oscar continued to get ready for his meeting. He was in a good mood and even Alfie performing his stand-up act couldn't change that.

CHAPTER FOUR

Emmie Jennings sighed as she looked in the mirror for the umpteenth time. Her room was dusky pink with cream silk wallpaper – ordered from America – bordering the bottom part of her walls. Her mother insisted on her having Ralph Lauren silk bedding at all times and her new fifty-inch flat screen TV sat on the far wall with MTV on mute.

There was a pile of clothes on the floor and a walk-in closet full of designer outfits, but nothing she'd tried on so far looked right. Her friends at school had always complimented her on her tiny figure, but no matter how many times they told her she was slim, Emmie always felt fat.

Her dad, Alfie, was up in town and her mum Janine was going up to North London to see some of her friends so it gave Emmie the perfect opportunity to go and meet Jake.

Justin Bieber was blaring out on her iPod station when her mother opened the door and walked in. Emmie had put a sign on the door last year saying *No entry without knocking* but neither her mum nor dad had taken the slightest bit of notice of it since it'd been there.

Emmie watched her mother eating a king size Mars Bar as she sat on the end of her white leather double bed. There was no denying how much she loved her mother but she couldn't help feeling ashamed of her; and having those feelings made Emmie feel ashamed of herself.

She was always mortified when her mother turned up at school and it'd been especially difficult when the other kids had started teasing her.

'Your mum's so fat when she stepped on the scales it said to be continued. Your mum's so fat even God can't lift her spirits. Your mum's so fat I thought she was a solar eclipse. Your mum's so fat she has to wake up in different time zones.'

The hurtful jokes had continued until Emmie, not being able to take any more of the taunting, had told her dad – and after a little coercing and the bribe of a new Chloe handbag, she'd pointed out the kids to him.

Her dad had paid a visit to each of the children's parents with a couple of dodgy looking friends and overnight the teasing stopped, but Emmie had continued to carry the guilt of her own thoughts. She loved her mum, but Emmie's biggest fear was she'd become like her; she spent many hungry hours worrying about it, and hours after that feeling wretched for thinking such horrible things.

'What are you going to get up to tonight, Em?'

'Mr Lucas has given us a ton of biology homework; I swear I'll die doing it.'

Janine Jennings smiled at her daughter; she was always so dramatic and had been since she was a toddler. She would bet her Prada handbag the homework Emmie was complaining about was probably no more than one page of revision. Even though Alfie paid over eighteen thousand a year in school fees, it was hardly a school of great academic achievement.

'I'll be back late. Don't wait up, but I'm on my mobile if you need me. And eat something, Em; there's food in the fridge. You'll be nothing but skin and bones if you're not careful.'

Her mother gave her a huge hug before heading out of Emmie's bedroom, leaving the empty chocolate wrapper lying on her bed.

Emmie waited until she heard the purr of her mother's Range Rover driving away, and as soon as she'd gone, Emmie went to the back of one of her closets and pulled out a shoe box which was well hidden under clothes. Taking the lid off, she stared down at the letters. She'd read them so many times she knew them all off by heart. She should really put them back where she'd found them but she couldn't quite find it in her to do that yet. It had become a ritual; every time she knew she was alone, she'd open the box and just stare at the letters without taking them out. Feeling a surge of anger rising in her, Emmie put the lid back on and placed the box safely away from prying eyes.

Turning on her iMac, Emmie scanned the screen to see if she had any messages. Not that she was really expecting any; the few friends she'd had she'd pushed away when they'd started to show concern over her eating.

'Oh my days, Emmie, you've lost *so* much weight, you look like one of those lollipop girls; head too big for their body. You'd give the skeleton in the science lab a run for its money.'

Emmie hadn't appreciated them sticking their noses into her business; she got enough of that from her mother. So she'd slowly backed away from their friendship and eventually they'd stopped calling. She saw them at school but she didn't sit with them in lessons or at lunch as she used to; she preferred to keep herself to herself.

And so that only left the *OMG* girls, or as Emmie liked to call them, the bitches. She'd always been selective with her choice of friends and had deliberately kept away from the girls with their loud mouths and cruel comments. She'd never liked being mean to people and the thought of being friends with girls who spent their time bitching about other people made her shudder. No, she was happy being on her own – though she wasn't really on her own any more was she?

Unable to resist, Emmie logged onto her Facebook account and with a smile she changed her status from 'single' to 'in a relationship'. That would give them something to talk about when they saw it. It would stop them calling her 'Skelly Emmie'. It would show them that someone thought she was nice, someone thought she was pretty and someone wanted her.

Smiling and sitting back on her bed, she took out her white Swarovski crystal iPhone and dialled a familiar number.

'She's gone. Where shall I meet you?'

The journey into London took Emmie longer than she thought it would. The traffic was terrible as they hit Upper Street in Islington and with the cab driver playing bhangra music complete with a deep bass the journey seemed even longer.

She'd decided to wear her black leather skinny VB trousers with a pink cowl neck top from All Saints but she wondered if she should've just put on her new Rock and Republic jeans with a plain black t-shirt instead; she didn't want Jake to think she was overdressed.

She hadn't really wanted to come up to the West End but Jake had told her he was going to have to work later, so if she wanted to see him, she needed to come to him.

Emmie could feel the butterflies in her stomach; she knew she was taking a risk by going so close to her dad's club but she was desperate to see Jake, and the thought of not being able to see him for another week was more than she could bear.

* * *

It was another twenty-five minutes until they made it to Chinatown and Emmie got out of the cab looking round nervously in case she saw her father, whose club was only a few streets away from where she was standing.

The area was packed with people; a colourful mix of tourists, revellers and Chinese residents all milling round. The sounds and smells blasted Emmie's senses and looking at the array of roast duck, crispy pork and char-siu hanging up in the various windows of the Chinese restaurants made her feel hungry. She'd already had some soup and an apple earlier on in the day and it'd made her feel like a pig and she'd ended up sticking her fingers down her throat, desperately hoping her body wouldn't have absorbed any of the calories, so any thought of having a Chinese meal was totally out of the question.

Outside the dim sum restaurant she saw Jake standing with a long sour expression on his face. He was twenty-two; six years older than she was, but he was one of the few people apart from her father who made her feel good about herself.

He worked part time for her dad and she'd met him when he'd delivered a package to their house in Dagenham. Her father had been out and by the time he'd arrived back home an hour later, Emmie and Jake had already swapped telephone numbers and email details.

Of course, there was no way that she could tell her father about Jake; he was so protective of her, no boy could even look at her without her father threatening to 'put brains on walls'.

When she'd had her fourteenth birthday, her father had hired out Sugarhut nightclub in Buckhurst Hill for her and her friends. She'd invited her friend, Paul, a sixteen-year-old sixth former with wandering hands. She'd spent the evening dancing with him and thought she was in love when he'd bent down to kiss her on her neck.

Emmie didn't see Paul for a whole week after the party but when she did eventually catch up with him, she discovered he had two broken fingers and flatly refused to speak to her. In turn, Emmie refused to speak to her father until she came home from school one day to find a gorgeous Chanel suede jacket on her bed and a note from her father saying sorry.

Emmie so far had only managed to see Jake when he dropped off the packages each week to their house, and she had thought it best if she ignored Jake on these occasions in case her mother or father suspected anything. They'd spoken on the phone every day, sometimes twice a day, and Facebooked each other – but tonight would be her first chance of being on her own with him.

'You're late. I've been standing here looking like I'm touting for fucking business. My mate's lent me his flat and I was supposed to be picking up the keys.'

'I'm sorry, we were stuck in traffic.'

Jake scowled and marched off not saying another word, leaving Emmie to run behind him, trying to keep up with his long strides.

Vaughn Sadler happened to be walking out of Wong Kei's – a Chinese restaurant in the heart of Chinatown – at the same time as a lanky looking man with bad skin barged past him. Vaughn, who'd always been a stickler for manners, was about to grab hold of the ill-mannered youth and teach him a lesson in etiquette, when he saw he was being followed by a very pretty blonde-haired girl; a blonde girl he'd know anywhere. It was Emmie, his goddaughter.

He didn't imagine for a moment Alfie knew Emmie was wandering around Chinatown semi-clad, chasing some toerag, and if he did, Alfie would have him to answer to; he took his godfathering duties very seriously. Vaughn pulled out his mobile as he followed the star-crossed lovers across Shaftesbury Avenue.

'Alf, it's Vaughn.'

Alfie slammed the phone down. He was just about to go on stage and do his set when he'd taken the call from Vaughn informing him that not only was Emmie in London without his permission, but she was chasing some guy like a bitch on heat.

If it'd been anyone else phoning to tell him, Alfie doubted he would've believed it, but Vaughn was Emmie's godfather. If he said it was Emmie, then make no bones about it, it was Emmie.

He attempted to get through to Janine to see what the fuck she was doing letting Emmie out, but it went straight to voicemail. He was grateful his wife wasn't standing in front of him right now, as the promise he'd made to himself to never raise a fist to her might have been sorely tested.

'Tell Oscar to wait for me, I've got some personal business to attend to.' Alfie barked the order at his cousin, who was leaning back on a chair, drinking a bottle of Becks at the back of the busy club.

As Alfie raced past the bar, situated by the entrance of the club, he caught sight of one of the new bar staff who'd been giving him the eye earlier in the week. He'd planned to take her back to his place but now instead of feeling lips round his dick, he was going to have to go and find Emmie and deal with the fool who thought it was okay to date Alfie Jennings's daughter.

Knocking several customers into the wall by the cloak-room, Archie marched out into the cold of the Soho night, ready to put brains on walls.

* * *

32

'They're in there.' Vaughn looked at Alfie sympathetically, thankful he'd only himself to worry about rather than an unruly daughter. He could see the beads of sweat under Alfie's thick fringe of black hair on his forehead.

'You want me to come with you, Alf? Maybe I could stop the situation becoming too heated. Go easy on her and him. You know what kids are like.'

Alfie just looked at Vaughn; he didn't want to use any more energy than he had to.

The stairs leading up to the flat looked like they were never swept. Alfie could hear a baby crying from another landing and the sound of televisions coming from the various flats. It was a shithole and a perfect place to do what he was about to do.

'It's that one. I watched them go in.'

Vaughn pointed at the door and then proceeded to grab hold of Alfie's arm, feeling the tension in it.

'Alf, remember what I said. Keep your head, pal.'

Alfie didn't bother answering or knocking; he raised his right foot and kicked hard, using the momentum of the kick to put enough force behind it to boot the door open first time.

'What the . . .' Jake bellowed as he walked into the hall, clad only in a pair of off-white boxer shorts, ready to confront the intruder, but he was met by a fist slamming into his face, knocking his front teeth out before he managed to finish his sentence.

Jake's blood sprayed over the damp walls of the hallway as he was sent sprawling across the floor by the punch. As Alfie raised his foot above the boy's head ready to bring it down, he recognised who it was; Jake Bellingham, one of his employees, who he'd thought he could trust, had been trying to bang his daughter. The realisation made Alfie bring his foot down hard as he ignored Jake's pig-like squeals.

Alfie looked up quickly as he heard a scream directly in front of him. It was Emmie.

'Daddy no! Don't! It was my fault. Daddy, please leave him alone!'

Alfie stared at his daughter, noticing she was in her bra, though thankfully she still had her trousers on – unless of course they'd already . . . Alfie stopped his thoughts. It was too much to contemplate, so instead of picturing what might have happened to his precious daughter, he dug his heel deeper into Jake's face, twisting it into his nose; shattering the bones and making it bubble with blood.

'Go and put some clothes on, Emmie. Now.'

As she ran back to the front room to get dressed, Vaughn looked at Emmie but turned his head quickly. He didn't like to think of her with the pitiful piece of scum squirming on the floor; she was far too good for that.

'Take her to the club for me, Vaughn. I've still got a few things to do here.'

'Leave it now Alf. You've made your point.'

As Vaughn led the hysterical Emmie out of the flat, he grimaced as he saw Alfie take a pair of pliers out of his pocket.

Vaughn squeezed Emmie hard to him; all this violence wasn't good for her to see. He'd have a word in Alfie's ear when he'd calmed down.

As much as Vaughn had been born into the arms of London gangland and he'd been good at what he'd done, his heart had never really been in it; unlike the other men he'd known over the years, he'd never lived for the violence.

His dad had been a face, as had his granddad and his father before him, and from a very early age he'd known that there was only one option, and that was to go into the family business whether he liked it or not.

He knew over the years he'd gained a fearsome reputation,

but mostly that'd come from the early days when he'd been young and over the top with his fists; trying to compensate for the fact the aggression didn't come as naturally to him as everyone presumed it would. The reputation had suited him well; it'd meant a lot of men only needed to see him walk into the room before that look of fear crossed their face and they told him what he needed to know.

He was pleased he was out of the violence, but that didn't stop him missing the excitement of the life. He'd thought when he retired he'd step away from the people as well, but after a few months he'd gone back to his old haunts – to the old faces, to the men he'd shared drinks with and the men he'd shared fights with. It was who he was through and through; it was the core of him and there was no other place he'd rather be than the heart of Soho. And then of course there was his promise; the promise he'd made to Alfie's brother all those years ago.

It was an easy job – or it was supposed to be: break into the old warehouse down on the Canning Town dock. Everyone who needed to be paid off had been: the onsite drivers, the night security, even the cleaners had been bunged a few grand to keep their mouths shut tight and their eyes shut tighter.

The prize in the warehouse was worth paying the hush money for; 300 kilos of the finest brown, shipped in from North Africa and stored in the old warehouse by the McKenzie brothers, a rival South London gang. The brothers had left it there thinking no one would be foolish enough to touch it, but Vaughn and Alfie's brother Connor were impervious to the fearsome reputation of the McKenzie boys.

The brothers had hidden it at the back of the warehouse where the fish and meat traders kept their goods and went about their daily business, not realising they were in touching distance of nearly half a tonne of heroin which was like powdered gold. The people who worked in the warehouse didn't know either; all they were aware of was that they were being paid to look the other way.

Vaughn stood up and watched Connor sitting tensely over in the corner of his front room; he was worried about him. He'd known Connor since his late teens and nearly eighteen years later he was as close to him as ever.

The first time they'd met, they'd got into a fight with each other after Vaughn had accidentally knocked a cup of tea onto Connor's cheap looking suit. Connor's strength and height had been no match for Vaughn's, but he'd squared up to him nevertheless in the back of Johnny's All-Night Cafe on the corner of Greek Street.

'Bleeding look where you're going, mate. You've gone and ruined my whistle.'

Vaughn had looked at the red-faced Connor and had smiled apologetically before walking towards the gents. A moment before he'd reached the door, Vaughn had felt a hand on his shoulder and then a fist to the back of his head.

It'd been an easy fight for Vaughn; he'd grabbed hold of Connor's arm, twisting it round expertly before dragging him effing and blinding into the men's lavatories, dunking Connor's head into the bowl of the stinking unflushed toilet.

Far from being enraged like Vaughn had thought he'd be, Connor had rolled backwards and spluttered and spat out the offending toilet water, prior to bursting into laughter; they'd been inseparable ever since.

It was Vaughn who'd brought Connor up the ranks with him; his friend was too hot tempered to be running any turf on his own but he was loyal and funny and Vaughn enjoyed having him around. He especially admired the way Connor looked out for his younger brother Alfie, never letting anyone disrespect him or harm him and always making sure his brother had money and a decent roof over his head; it was touching to see.

Connor had once confided in Vaughn how guilty he'd felt for not being there for Alfie when his mother had committed suicide. He'd been banged up in a boys' reform school at the time for breaking and entering. On the day he'd been let out, instead of going on the piss and shagging a hooker he'd gone straight home and cooked a meal for Alfie. He'd looked after him ever since; mother, father and older brother all rolled into one. Connor tried his hardest to give his younger brother the stability he needed and which, Vaughn suspected, Connor had always longed for himself.

Connor never talked about what had gone on inside the reform school but from what Vaughn had heard from other people over the years, it became clear Connor had been abused more on the inside of the grey stone walls of the East End school than he'd ever been on the outside by his violent alcoholic father.

Vaughn also had a sneaking suspicion that Connor had not only been abused physically in the reform school but also sexually, although he'd never dream of saying anything to him about it; not for fear he was wrong, but for fear he was right. Vaughn couldn't bear to know too much about the pain his friend had to carry around with him, so he stayed silent and tried to make it up to him in his own way, by keeping him by his side and making his life as easy as he could.

One thing Connor did talk about with him – and one of the legacies of being in the reform school – was his fear of small spaces, and over the years Vaughn had done everything he could to stop Connor getting banged up: paying other people to fess up to the crime; framing people; even doing a small stint himself for Connor; but the last time he'd been *fingered by the law, Vaughn hadn't been able to get him off and Connor had served thirteen months in Belmarsh Prison for GBH.*

When Connor had been released, Vaughn was there to meet him at the gates; but the person who greeted him was a shadow of the person who went in. To see him through the months and to take the edge off his fear of confined spaces, Connor had turned to smack. He didn't manage to shake the habit once he got out, making him unpredictable and unreliable. Looking over at Connor now sitting in his chair, Vaughn could see he was either clucking for some brown or coming off some.

'Why don't you stay here, Connor? The job's all neatly wrapped up – we can manage without you.'

Vaughn watched as Connor bounced his knee up and down agitatedly.

'Are you trying to push me out, Vaughnie? I've heard rumours you're trying to get me out. If you've got a problem with me just say so and we'll have it out here and now.'

Vaughn looked at his nails absentmindedly. He knew Connor and he knew he was looking for a fight, but he wasn't going to indulge him. The smack was addling Connor's brain and Vaughn knew he had to get some help for him once the warehouse job was over. He spoke with slight annoyance in his voice.

'Fine, Connor. Just saying, mate. You want to come along that's fine with me – you won't see me objecting. I'm not your keeper.'

Those words would come back to haunt Vaughn Sadler.

Emmie sniffed loudly, breaking the intensity of Vaughn's thoughts as he continued to lead her down the stairs. At the bottom, he noticed a woman with long auburn hair, swaying from side to side, struggling to pick up her keys. Smiling, he bent down to get them for her. 'I think you're trying to get these.'

'Thank you.'

As he gave her the keys, he hesitated, taking in her face. She was beautiful, one of the most stunning women he'd ever seen; but also there was a familiarity about her face. He was about to speak to her again when Emmie let out a huge wail, making both him and the woman jump in fright.

As Vaughn walked down Dean Street and back towards Whispers Comedy Club, attempting to hold up the lamenting Emmie, his mind started to wander back to the woman and where he knew her from; but as he turned the corner into Old Compton Street, any thoughts of her were forgotten when he saw an animated Janine Jennings, causing mayhem outside the club.

CHAPTER FIVE

Weds 16th Aug 1995
Told Mum and Dad last week. Dad refusing to talk to me and Mum walking round with a glass of vodka stuck to her hand as if she's an old drunk. Anyone would think I killed someone rather than just being pregnant. Dad came into my room last night trying to make me tell him who the father is. When I didn't tell him, he got mad and started to call me names. Then he got really angry and started chucking my stuff round the room. He broke the china doll he got me last year. An hour later he came in to say sorry. Wouldn't talk to him. I hate him but not as much as I hate myself.

Thurs 7th SeptNov 1995
Mum and Dad sat me down and told me they'd made a decision. I thought they were going to tell me they were getting a divorce, seeing as they're both so unhappy with each other but they think nobody knows. Everyone knows!! Especially Dad's friends; they all cover for him when he goes to meet some woman. He's ~~an idiot~~ a prick. Instead of talking about a divorce, Dad said

Mum thinks I should get an abortion, couldn't believe it. Told them I was five months pregnant, so there was no way. Mum started to cry, Dad started shouting as usual. Mum managed to stop crying enough to tell me if that was the case she was going to arrange for my baby to be put up for adoption!(bitch) Ran out of the room and won't open bedroom door to Dad's stupid knocking on door. Anyone would think this is the 1930's not 1995. So much for parent support. Don't know what to do. Very, very scared.

Fri 22nd Sept 1995
Woke up in hospital. Everyone thinks I want to kill myself. I don't, I just wanted to tell my side of the story to someone who might listen. I wanted to tell them I love my baby and want to keep it but no one seems to be listening. Ugly social worker came to see me (she had big wart on side of nose) She seems to agree with Mum about giving baby up for adoption. Says drinking the vodka and taking Mum's sleeping tablets shows that I'm not emotionally mature. What does she know? Says I might have harmed the baby. Devastated. All I want to do is love my baby. I can't believe I might have hurt him or her. Sorry, sorry, sorry. I love you. Still scared might have to run away but I have nowhere to go.

Thurs 18th Jan 1996
Think I'm in labour!!!!!!!!!!!!!!

Casey closed the diary and sat motionless on the bare floorboards of the flat. Her head was spinning from all the excess alcohol she'd drunk, but reading the extracts seemed to have a sobering effect on her. The writing was immature and there was a tragic innocence about it; she didn't recognise the naive girl who'd become the woman she was today, but she still felt that pain as if it had happened only yesterday.

The diary looked unremarkable on the outside with the dog-eared corners and faded cover, but the pages inside told a different tale: they grasped on to her past, refusing to let go, like a dying man wanting to hold on to his last breath.

It held the key to who she used to be, even though she hadn't been able to read it for years; it had been a hot piece of coal burning into her, making her hurt all over again. She didn't want to hurt any more.

She was tempted to go to the off-licence she'd seen on Shaftesbury Avenue to buy a bottle of scotch, but that would only make her a casualty of the situation again; something she'd fought so hard over the years to avoid. She'd come to London to try to find out the truth, she'd found out so little over the years but from the one lead she'd managed to find, she hoped finally she was in the right place and drowning herself in alcohol – which she'd done for too long now – had victim written all over the label.

Wiping away a tear, Casey decided the best thing she could do was try to get some sleep; she'd a busy day ahead of her. Undressing rather unsteadily and checking there weren't any nasty creepy crawlies wanting to share the bed with her, Casey lay down and closed her eyes. But within a moment the unwanted memories came running into her head.

'It's best this way, Casey, you'll see.'

'Best for who, Mum?'

'For everybody.'

'But it's not. It's only best for you and Dad. Please, I know I'll be able to look after it, just give me a chance. Let me keep my baby.'

'Casey, you don't know what you're talking about. A baby

42

isn't something you can put away in a drawer once you get bored of it. I know it seems hard at the moment but later on you'll thank us and realise we were just doing what's best. You'll be able to go on and make a life for yourself, get a career and get married. You'll have the chance to have more children one day and put all this business out of your mind. I doubt you even know who the father is.'

'Of course I do, but I'm not telling you.'

Her mother snorted in disgust. She wasn't going to tell her who it was; she could think what she liked. Granted, Paul was just a boy at school – he hadn't been the love of her life, but he wasn't the one-night stand her mother thought he was. They'd dated for a few months until he'd moved to Swansea with his parents. She hadn't bothered to keep in touch with him and when she found out she was pregnant, she certainly had no desire to complicate anything further by adding him to the equation. So her mother could continue to think she spent her time jumping into bed with strangers; Casey knew whatever she said she wouldn't be believed anyway.

She spoke with as much hostility as she could conjure up between the painful contractions.

'I'm not like you, Mum; I'm not going to pretend things aren't happening because it's easier. Maybe that's what you can do with Dad but I can't.'

'What's that supposed to mean, young lady?'

'You know exactly. Dad's been shagging about for as long as I can remember. And you know something? I don't blame him one little bit.'

The pain of the slap on Casey's cheek from her mother stung less than the pain from the hurt and humiliation it caused. The midwives rushed forward and started to usher Casey's mother out of the room.

'No Mum, please stay! Can you let her stay please?'

43

The Chinese midwife first looked at Casey and then her mother before speaking.

'You can stay if she wants you to.'

'Mum?'

Casey watched her mother's eyes narrow and a stony expression appear on her face as another contraction began to take hold.

'It's fine. My daughter's made her feelings abundantly clear. I'm sure she'll manage just exceptionally on her own. She always does.'

'Mum please, don't go! Mum! Please, I'm scared!'

The banging of the labour room door reverberated round the little room. Less than an hour later Casey's 9lb 8oz baby was born.

'Can I see? Is everything okay?'

'Everything's fine, Casey, you did really well.'

'Please can I see?'

The midwife looked sympathetically as she spoke.

'It's probably best you don't; it'll make it easier.'

The tears poured down Casey's face as she begged the midwife in charge to listen to her.

'Please, at least tell me if it's a boy or a girl.' It was the second time the labour room door had banged shut but it this time the noise sounded even louder to Casey as it hung in the air, mixed in parts with her scream.

Casey jolted herself up out of bed. She refused to lie there all night being melancholic. Moving back to the living room she started to search in her bag, hoping there was still some vodka left in the bottle she kept tucked away in case of emergencies.

CHAPTER SIX

'I'll give you fucking strict orders, mate.' Janine Jennings's face was red with anger as she pushed the bouncer in his chest, using the full force of her weight.

'Let me fucking past, you great big lump of cunt.'

Vaughn smiled at Janine's foul language. He'd known her for as long as he'd known Alfie and even though most of the time she tried to behave like an Essex princess sitting in her eight-bedroom mansion, the real East End girl came shining through when it mattered.

'Now what's all this?'

Janine turned at the sound of the familiar voice and saw Vaughn Sadler standing there with a bedraggled Emmie.

'Where the fuck have you been, young lady? You've had me worried out of me bleedin' mind. I drove up here like a bitch out of hell when I got your father's message. You've got some explaining to do.'

'I'm sorry Mum, I thought . . .'

'You thought? Fuck me, Em, that'll be a first.'

'Don't be too hard on her Jan; she's had a bit of a rough evening.'

'Hard on her, Vaughnie? She don't know the meaning of

45

it. Her father treats her like her shit's made out of gold. I nearly choked on me fucking biryani when I got the message she was up West, and then when I got here this cunt said I can't go in my own husband's club!'

Vaughn saw Emmie start to cry again and he gave her a big hug, feeling sorry for her. He loved spending time with his goddaughter and he found her to be a sweet girl who was often overshadowed by Janine's loving, but domineering personality.

Vaughn looked at the bouncer, who shrugged apologetically at him. He guessed Alfie had given him strict orders not to allow Janine in and it was probably worth more than the bouncer's life to go against them.

It was a comedy club open to the public but he also knew it was a front for Alfie's other business dealings. No doubt he didn't want his wife poking around upstairs where he stashed a lot of his stolen goods.

Vaughn felt Emmie shiver and he brought her in closer to the warmth of his body. Alfie had asked him to take Emmie back to the club but now Janine had arrived he wasn't quite sure what to do. He looked first at Emmie and then at Janine and decided to take matters into his own hands; as long as he kept an eye on Jan, it wouldn't do any harm to take her inside. They could sit in the back room together until Alfie came back.

'It's fine; she's with me, you can let her in.'

The bouncer didn't get out of the way immediately and Vaughn not only noticed this but saw it as a blatant sign of disrespect. He grabbed hold hard of the bouncer's crotch, making him double up in pain.

'Don't be an arsehole; get out of my way, shit-for-brains, otherwise your missus will have something else sliced up in her egg and bacon sarnie in the morning.'

*　*　*

Oscar had been wrong. When he'd left his flat he was certain nothing could've wiped away his good mood. Billy had done a good job cleaning up the bedroom, leaving it spotless and without any trace of the night before, and he'd been looking forward to the meeting to discuss the new business venture he and Alfie had branched into – but that had all changed after he'd been kept waiting. The only thing he felt like doing now was putting a knife in somebody's head; preferably Alfie's.

He'd been waiting nearly two hours, and as his good mood had been drained away by the passing of time and the countless comedians rehashing old jokes and expecting applause, Oscar's head had started hurting and he'd been forced to take one of the migraine tablets he'd been given by one of his associates who dealt in pharmaceuticals.

The only part of the two-hour wait Oscar had enjoyed were the abusive heckles he'd shouted at the comedians. When Alfie went on stage, the audience were always pre-warned not to heckle. If anyone did, one of Alfie's heavies would have a quiet word in their ear. Oscar remembered with a smile a man who thought he'd play tough guy and ignore the warnings; he was found later on in the evening outside Ronnie Scott's with severe concussion and *'funny cunt'* written on his forehead in black marker pen.

Oscar was about to get up and leave when he saw Vaughn walking into the club accompanied by an anorexic looking teenager and a woman who would put Ten Ton Bertha to shame. He quickly stooped down in his seat, not wanting to be spotted by Vaughn and having to engage in any more talk about fucking holidays.

Janine hadn't ever been inside her husband's club and she was impressed by what she saw. In the back of the large room was a stage, lit up by four huge disco balls with a dance floor in front of it. A DJ was on the stage playing a mix of classic soul tunes. Thick purple velvet curtains, which matched the velvet sofas and chairs placed round the room, hung down from the high ceiling framing the stage. There were different-shaped mirrors everywhere, and the long bar on the side wall was heaving with punters waiting to be served. It had everything. There were high-tech private booths at the back of the massive room complete with their own television and music players, and it looked to Janine as if business was doing very well. With that in mind, she continued to follow Vaughn into the back, making a mental note to ask her husband for a larger monthly allowance.

Half an hour later, Alfie walked into the back room, still wound up from the events of the night. He stopped dead in his tracks – causing Oscar to bang into the back of him – when he saw Janine sitting there eating her way through a large bag of crisps. He placed the pair of pliers, still stained with Jake's blood, on the side and spoke angrily to his wife.

'What's the point in you having a mobile phone if you never answer it? You're a fucking disgrace, Janine.'

'Me? What about Emmie? It wasn't me that sneaked out on heat chasing some guy.'

'No, but pity the bloke if you were. Fuck me, you're her mother! You should've been watching her.'

'Stop it, both of you! I hate you! I hate you!'

Emmie screamed hysterically as she ran out of the room, leaving her parents open mouthed.

Oscar sat quietly watching this display; he'd known Alfie was married and had a kid but he'd never seen either of them until now. The daughter was pretty enough although she was evidently underweight, but the idea the handsome, womanising Alfie was married to the woman in front of him, whose right arm alone would feed the starving millions, took some believing.

Janine Jennings was about to open her mouth and chastise Alfie for upsetting Emmie but she saw the look in his eye and decided not to say another word.

She was furious with Emmie. Not just because her daughter had snuck off with a boy – she'd done that herself when she was the same age, and Emmie was no different to any other teenager – but she'd given her a fright, and when she got frightened she got angry; she'd always done that. The thought of something happening to her beloved daughter was unimaginable. Recently though, she'd noticed a change in Emmie; she'd become much more secretive and sullen, and Janine Jennings had a feeling there was more to it than just teenage love.

Alfie banged his hand on the table giving Janine a fright and made her jump out of her thoughts.

'I'll get one of my men to drive you both home and we'll talk about it tomorrow, but tell Emmie she should count herself grounded.'

It was another hour before Alfie and Oscar arrived in Redchurch Street, a scruffy road full of office blocks behind Shoreditch High Street. He hadn't had the opportunity to talk to Oscar properly yet, as Vaughn had insisted on having a drink with him; reminiscing about jobs they'd done together and trying to calm the hyped-up Alfie down. Then, when Vaughn had heard they were heading towards the East End, he'd jumped in the back of Alfie's BMW and got a lift to an illegal gambling house in King John Court, a few streets away from where they were now.

As Alfie followed Oscar up the stairs of the empty block of offices Oscar owned, he wondered why he'd been so guarded about speaking in front of Vaughn. He'd always been open in sharing the ins and outs of his other businesses with him: the protection rackets, the counterfeit money, the stolen electrical goods and hundreds of cloned bank cards he'd kept above the club; even the copious amounts of drugs he shipped into the country each year from China: Vaughn knew about it all. But this venture, with Oscar, Alfie wanted to keep close to his chest.

The passage along the top floor was lit with a low-watt light bulb, making it difficult, but not impossible, for Alfie to see the rubbish strewn everywhere. At the end of the hall sat a large Albanian looking man sitting on a hard chair, staring at nothing in particular. At his feet lay a large machete and an empty bottle of water.

The man stood up, nodding an acknowledgement to Oscar as he approached, and opened a door to the side of him. Alfie trailed in silence through it and up another flight of steps. At the top, Oscar opened another door.

Inside Alfie saw five young women, aged from around sixteen to twenty-five. They stared with wide anxious eyes and expressions of fear as he walked further into the room. Alfie briefly thought of his schooldays as the girls stood to attention, scared to make a movement.

'They're no trouble, not like the brass here. They don't talk much English, if any, but the guy downstairs speaks their language so communication's no problem. They'll do anything I tell them; they're too scared to say no.'

Oscar grinned at Alfie then leered at the smallest and youngest looking woman, who quickly put her head down.

'Want to test the goods, Alf? We need to start breaking them in, so you might as well start now.'

Alfie shook his head, feeling strangely uncomfortable. At the back of his mind he realised this discomfort was probably the reason he hadn't confided in his long-term friend. Over the years he and Vaughn had owned brothels, but the brasses had come and gone as they pleased. This was different; this was trafficking, and even people like him had a conscience.

'What's up, Alfie, getting cold feet? Are you going soft on me in your old age?'

One thing Alfie Jennings prized highly was his reputation. He hated anybody thinking that he was weak, and looking at Oscar with that mocking glint in his eye pissed him off. What was he thinking? Business was business; there was no room for sentiment. Storming out, Alfie put the haunted faces of the girls in the back of his mind.

'So are we going to keep them there?'

'It's not ideal. We could maybe move a couple above your club tomorrow morning.'

'How many have we got?'

'Ten; well nine now.' Alfie raised his eyebrows, waiting for an explanation.

'It's a long story, I'll tell you on the way back.'

With all the temporary road traffic lights on the blink, the drive through Shoreditch and through the Angel into Soho would have usually frustrated Alfie but instead he sat listening to Oscar recount his tale of the previous night in stunned silence.

When they arrived back at his club, Alfie was still lost for words and it was Oscar who turned to look at him.

'So you know everything now; my darkest little secret. There's no backing out now.' Oscar chuckled, rubbing his pulsating temples. 'You're well and truly in now, Alfie.'

As Oscar stepped out of the car, Alfie realised he'd let himself in for a whole lot more than he'd bargained on. There was no backing out now; Oscar had shared his secret with him and Alfie knew that in Oscar's mind they were now both implicated. If he tried to walk away from the deal,

Oscar would think he couldn't be trusted and would bring him down. One thing Alfie was certain of was when Oscar got jumpy he was a dangerous person, and the last thing he needed right now was any more shit, especially when it came to Oscar Harding.

Oh yes, Alfie Jennings knew he was over a barrel, and a very large fucking barrel at that.

CHAPTER SEVEN

Casey Edwards didn't know if it was the thumping of her head which had woken her up or the loud scratching noise in the far corner of the room. After she'd discovered her emergency supply of vodka was empty, she'd taken herself out to a late night bar, but she had no recollection of getting home. As she opened her eyes, the noise got louder – she supposed in her intoxicated state she must have picked up yet another stranger with hygiene issues. Raising her head with a slight amount of difficulty, Casey stared in horror as she saw a large rat – of the four-legged kind rather than two – scratching away.

Her loud high-pitched scream didn't do her head any favours as she ran into the lounge, barricading her body against the door. She felt the bile rise as she rushed to the toilet, forgetting for a moment about the filth awaiting her in the windowless bathroom as she violently emptied the contents from her stomach.

A black coffee and a half a Kit Kat later, Casey was on the phone to the landlord, frustrated at the lack of alarm Mr Goldman was showing.

'What do you want me to do, love? Start charging him rent?'

'I want you to do something about it. Come and take a look.'

'It needs poison, not an audience. This is London love; weren't you ever told the story of Dick Whittington? What you need is a cat.'

'I thought pets weren't allowed.'

'They're not.'

He laughed and carried on joking. This infuriated Casey, causing her to break down into floods of tears. Within a moment of her emotional outburst he agreed to take a look, preferring it, Casey supposed, to female hysterics on the phone so early in the morning.

After the call, Casey hurriedly went through her packed bag of clothes and discovered that apart from two pairs of lilac lace knickers, her only other clean item of clothing was a low-cut grey mini dress more appropriate for a night out than an overcast Thursday morning or a pair of jeans with a stubborn red wine stain on them.

After fifteen minutes of trying to get the stain out, Casey decided it wasn't going to shift, no matter how hard she scrubbed. She felt faint and realised she needed to eat something other than chocolate; she had a busy day ahead.

Pulling on her jeans and putting on the least crumpled top she could find in her bag, she left the flat and wandered the short distance down Dean Street, doing a right into Bateman Street and walking into the first cafe she came across.

The runny egg on the chipped white plate and the overdone piece of fatty bacon were just two of the culinary delights of Lola's Night Cafe. Casey stared at what was in front of her, feeling her stomach turning over once again.

'Not hungry love? Never mind.'

Casey tried to smile at the woman who was speaking to

her in between breaking out into short bursts of 'Fly Me to the Moon', which was being played on the radio. Contrary to the toothless woman's belief, Casey was very hungry, just not for what was on offer on her plate.

Getting up to pay, Casey saw the scrawled sign behind the counter: 'Waitress wanted'.

'Are you still looking?'

'For what? My prince in shining armour? Bleedin' hell, he's already been in; took one look around and fucked right off again on his white charger.'

The woman opened her mouth wide and cackled loudly, causing Casey to draw back from her rancid breath.

'I meant the waitressing job.'

'I know what you meant, love. You'll be no good to me if you can't crack a smile.'

'Sorry, I'm just a bit tired, that's all.'

The woman stared hard at Casey, looking her up and down and pausing at the top of her head; as if the job depended on Casey's height.

'You'll do. I'm Lola by the way. Now take off that fancy jacket of yours and grab an apron.'

By the time four thirty had arrived, Casey's feet were killing her and she was certain there were much easier ways to earn minimum wage. The stifling heat of the cafe, with its smells of old cooking oil, greasy fry-ups and countless bowls of watery tomato soup, combined with the lack of food in her stomach meant Casey needed to step outside on occasion into the busy street to get some fresh air.

'I'll dock your wages for that.' Lola had glared at Casey for a moment but almost immediately had broken out into a smile. 'You won't have to mind me, Casey love; you'll get used to me jokes. Keep smiling is what I say; helps your heart keep beating.'

Casey had warmed to Lola and found the woman's open honesty about her past life refreshing but startling at the same time.

'I was a brass for nearly twenty-five years. Don't look so surprised! I didn't always look like this. I use to have to put ear plugs in from all the wolf whistles I got.'

Lola laughed again and then her face went serious. 'I would've carried on being a tom if it wasn't for my last husband; been married five times and all of them were a waste of bog paper; but the last one, he was something else. You'll probably see him in here from time to time, but take my advice, love – don't be drawn in by his gift of the gab. Do yourself a favour and stay clean away.'

Casey nodded, taking in all the information.

'What's his name?'

'Oscar Harding.'

Old Compton Street was packed with tourists with London guide maps in their hands and puzzled looks on their faces. It was nearly six o'clock and Casey wanted to sleep, but she'd no intention of going back to the flat until it was absolutely necessary. She thought about Lola and what she'd said, but for all she was and did, Casey suspected she was probably a darn sight happier than she was.

She could do with a drink to pep her up but she'd made a decision and for now she was at least going to try to stick to it. She sighed as she carried on walking. It was so hard to live in the present – her mind was always full of fading memories; but it was all she had and her reason for getting up each day.

The bus journey down towards Notting Hill Gate had taken longer than expected and Casey had been ready to get off the overheated bus and go back to the flat in Dean Street, but she'd seen a woman and a little boy sitting quietly at the back of the bus holding hands, saying nothing, just content in each other's company. They reminded Casey what she had to do.

Portobello Road was dark and deserted, unrecognisable from the bustling market road it became during the daylight hours, and Casey wasn't sure she'd come to the correct place. She looked down at the address she'd hurriedly written on a torn-off piece of newspaper and realised she was standing right outside where she needed to be.

The red door pushed open and Casey walked up the narrow stairs to the first-floor landing. There was another door to the left of her and she could hear voices coming from inside the room. Taking a deep breath, Casey opened the door to walk into a well-lit room.

'Hello, please come in and take a seat.'

The red-faced man greeted Casey with a warm smile, gesturing for her to come and take the empty chair next to him.

'We've just finished introducing ourselves. Perhaps you'd like to say who you are.'

Casey glanced at the man with his enthusiastic manner and smiled shyly.

'Hello, I'm Casey and I'm an alcoholic.'

'Hello Casey.'

The group greeted her in monotone unison, making Casey smile as it reminded her of being back in school.

'I'm nearly one day sober and I need to get clean so I can find my son and tell him I'm sorry.'

The applause of the group made Casey blush and unexpectedly brought tears to her eyes as she was handed the white keyring of twenty-four-hour sobriety by a tall woman in her early twenties.

Sitting down in her chair she could feel her heart racing; she hadn't thought she'd be nervous, after all it wasn't the first time she'd been to a meeting. In Newcastle she'd been to a few and in Liverpool and in Birmingham as well, but maybe it was different because this time she was determined to get clean; she knew it was her last chance.

She'd never wanted this life but somehow it had invited her in and she'd stayed in its clutches. Living this way certainly wasn't going to help her find her son, and even if she did, he'd never want her if she was a drunk. The meetings were her only way to keep steady on the tightrope she was walking.

Looking round the meeting in the small room above the designer clothing shop in Portobello Road was like flicking through the pages of a society magazine. There were models and actors both from film and from screen, musicians and old-time rockers, and sitting next to her was an infamous aristocrat holding on to his keyring of twenty-four-hour sobriety.

For the next forty minutes Casey sat listening to tormented stories about the struggle to stay sober, and as far removed as her life could possibly be from most of the people in the room, the sentiments by and large were the same.

In the remaining moments the serenity prayer was read out, as it always was at the end of any meeting, and even though Casey knew it off by heart she chose to stay silent. The words were so poignant to her and as she listened to them with closed eyes, she hoped they'd see her through the following days.

'God grant me the serenity to accept the things I cannot change; courage to change the things that I can and wisdom to know the difference.'

CHAPTER EIGHT

Casey groaned as she looked at the clock; her next shift at the cafe started in less than twenty minutes. She didn't know if it was going without alcohol or the fact she'd never really worked in her life before, but she was knackered. She'd drifted in and out of work and never really had to worry about money till recently, having had a conservative but steady flow of money from her family who were only visible in her life through the money they'd put in her account.

Eighteen months ago she'd closed her bank account down, deciding it only served to rubber stamp her feelings of worthlessness; it made her feel her family were paying her to stay away. So now if she wanted to eat, drink or pay the rent, she only had herself to rely on; it was both frightening and liberating in equal measures.

Casey washed herself quickly and pulled on yesterday's clothes. It was pointless putting on anything clean; within two hours of working in Lola's she'd smell as if she'd taken a plunge in chip fat, and besides, if she was honest, she could just about make the effort to get dressed let alone bother to do herself up.

The cafe wasn't open for another hour but Lola had asked

Casey to come thirty minutes before opening time to help set up. She was early, which would give her half an hour to sit down with a cup of coffee, hoping it would help her wake up properly. The cafe door had a sign saying 'closed' but the open door said the opposite.

'Lola? It's Cass. Hello?'

There was no answer so Casey put her bag down and went to switch on the large urn to make some much-needed coffee.

Taking her coat off, she walked into the cloakroom and was stopped dead in her tracks by what she saw. Lola sat on the cold cracked tiles of the bathroom floor with a belt around her left arm, the other end of it between her teeth. In her right hand was a syringe, half full with a cloudy liquid which Casey guessed was heroin.

On seeing Casey, Lola paused for a moment before pulling the belt even tighter with her teeth, then plunged the needle greedily into her waiting vein.

Almost immediately Casey could see the heroin taking hold of Lola; her eyes rolled back and her head started to loll against the grimy walls of the cloakroom. Slightly incoherently, Lola spoke.

'Don't look like that, lovie, who did you think I was? Mother bleeding Theresa?'

Lola cackled and the force of her laughter against her drugged-up body threw her head forward to rest on her chest.

Casey was shocked and her stomach tightened as she watched the abandoned needle still stuck in Lola's vein. The blood trickled down Lola's arm and for a moment Casey didn't know what to say. It was Lola who broke the silence.

'He did this,' Lola slurred, pulling out the syringe and lifting up her cream polyester blouse. Casey's eyes widened as she saw a vast scar running diagonally from underneath

60

Lola's breastbone, across her stomach and finishing off at her hip.

'My god, what happened? Who did this to you?'

Casey knelt down by Lola and touched the old but still raised angry scar gently.

'I don't really remember much of that night; me and the old man were watching some shit on the telly; usual Sunday night crap. He turned and stared at me as if I were a stranger in me own home; like he'd never seen me before. Then he blinked a couple of times and started cutting.'

'Who did, Lola? Who?'

Casey watched Lola's eyes roll when she tried to focus on her.

'Oscar.'

'Jesus, how long did he get?'

Lola burst into more high-pitched cackling. 'He didn't, I'm old school, love; we don't grass on our own.'

'But . . .'

'But nothing, girl. I did alright; he got me this place as a way of compensation.'

Casey stood up and looked horrified.

'Money's money, love; it's an expensive habit I've got. Most of what I earn goes up my arm and if I didn't have this place I'd be back on the streets. So you see, Oscar did me a favour in a way.'

'How can you say that? What he did was shocking.'

'What he did was life, sweetheart. I'm happy like this, I like it, never wanted to give up . . .'

Lola just managed to finish speaking before she suddenly jolted and turned her head to the side to vomit. Casey curled her face in disgust and backed away. What the hell was she doing in a place like this?

'I'm sorry . . . I've got to go.'

Lola wiped the side of her mouth and looked up. Casey

could see the tears in her eyes and the pain on her face but she had no idea what she was supposed to do.

'Don't go, Casey. Stay and keep me company . . . please.'

Lola raised her shaking hand towards Casey and the stench of the vomit and the misery of the situation suddenly hit Casey.

'I'm sorry, Lola, I can't.' Turning quickly and grabbing her bag from the chair, Casey ran out of the cafe to the cool of the morning air and immediately felt very ashamed for running out on someone who'd asked for help. She put her hand on the door to go back inside but something stopped her. The desperation of the situation was clear to see and it was as if she was looking at herself in the mirror – but all Casey wanted to do was run.

CHAPTER NINE

It was four thirty the following Wednesday and Casey had slept most of the last few days away. Walking in on Lola and going to sobriety meetings in the evening had taken it out of her, and as much as she hated being in the flat, she'd rather sleep than watch the minutes slowly tick by emphasising her struggle to abstain from drinking. What she really needed was to try to take her mind off it. She remembered the club Whispers had a comedy spot on most nights and even though she knew she'd have to stay strong not to drink, Casey decided having a laugh would be more helpful than lying on her bed staring at the ceiling. The sign said it didn't open until seven o'clock, so Casey settled on the cafe four doors away. It was in these quiet moments she found the unwelcome memories came knocking; today they also had her reaching for her mobile phone. The phone on the other end rang twice before it was answered by a man with a deep voice.

'Hello?'

Casey didn't speak for a moment but held her breath, trying to calm the pounding of her heart. The silence on the phone caused the person on the other end to repeat their question.

'Hello?'

'Hello Josh.'

'Casey! Oh god it's good to hear from you. How are you? Why haven't you called before?'

'I'm sorry.'

'If it wasn't for the postcard you sent me I wouldn't have known you were alive, eighteen months is a long time, Cass. Are you sure you're okay?'

'I'm doing okay. I've been to a meeting.'

'I'm glad. Wow, sorry it's just such a shock to hear from you. Where are you?'

'In London.'

There was an awkward pause before Casey heard Josh tentatively speak again.

'Have you done anything about it yet? About . . . well you know.'

'No not yet. Funny, I've waited all this time but now I can't quite find the courage to go.'

'Be careful Cass; I don't want you to get disappointed . . . or hurt. It was so long ago, they might not even live there now. I don't think you should Cass. Maybe you should let sleeping dogs lie.'

'Anyone would think you don't want me to find him.'

'It's not that . . . It's just . . .' Josh trailed off and Casey spoke impatiently wanting to find out what he was going to say.

'Just what?'

'Nothing, listen forget I said anything.'

'I know you're worried but for all the tourists and the craziness Soho is a tight-knit community; if they're not there, I'm sure someone will remember them and even know where they've gone.'

Casey listened to Josh breathe on the other end of the phone. She knew him well, but then she should do; after all, she was married to him. She knew his silence was that of a person with a difference of opinion, but he was too diplomatic – or too sensible – to say anything.

They'd met at a wedding but it hadn't been love at first sight; if she were truthful she hadn't thought much about him at all. They'd spent the evening sitting next to each other in a huge draughty hall as they toasted the happy couple who she knew through her cousin. Josh had talked about his work and asked her polite questions which she gave the shortest of answers to. She'd been civil but aloof, but Josh had persisted.

'Would you like to dance?'

She hadn't, but she'd been unable to think of a good excuse before he'd got up and put out his hand for her to take. Even though it'd been their first dance, Casey couldn't recall what song had been played – she'd stopped being sentimental the day she'd given birth; there was no room in her heart for it. What she had felt was a feeling of safety as he held her in his arms. For the first time in her life she'd felt secure. Three weeks later he'd asked her to marry him and she'd not hesitated in saying yes, hoping saying, 'I do' would fix the gaping hole in her heart and fill the void from losing her child.

'Casey? Are you listening? I think you should be careful.'

Josh interrupted her thoughts and she returned her focus to the conversation on the phone.

'Thanks for your concern; I'll be fine.'

She could hear the tightness in her voice although she didn't mean it to be there; she had no quarrel with Josh; he'd done nothing wrong. He was a kind, warm, sensitive man who'd tried to look after her and heal her wounds. She shouldn't have married him and he was better off without her.

'Bye Josh.'

'Keep in touch, Cass, and think about what I said.'

Casey clicked off the phone and was suddenly startled by a man standing in front of her.

'Can I get you another one; or maybe something stronger?'

Casey quickly wiped away her tears which seemed to spring to her eyes all too easily these days for her liking; she felt embarrassed being caught at a vulnerable moment.

Her answer was delayed as she looked at the tall well-built man with a wind-tanned complexion, dark brown hair with slices of grey running through it and intense green eyes. He was undoubtedly very handsome. The prospect of something stronger than her lukewarm coffee was also tempting, but she declined the offer.

'My name's Vaughn by the way.'

'Casey.'

She gave him a small smile and Vaughn was knocked sideways by her beauty.

'Did you manage to get in safely the other night?'

Vaughn Sadler watched as a blank expression came over her face. It was still niggling away at him – he was positive he knew Casey from somewhere, but hopefully it'd come to him.

He could tell she had no idea what he was talking about and he contemplated explaining how he'd helped her pick up her keys, but quickly he decided against it, in case the boy Alfie had given a seeing to had opened his mouth and talked to the hospital. That was of course if he was still alive.

If the filth *were* sniffing around, it would be foolhardy of Vaughn to admit he'd been anywhere near the building. He didn't want to get fingered for something he didn't do; and if he did get collared, it wasn't as if he'd squeal on Alfie. With his form, they'd throw the book at him before you could say Jack The Hat McVitie.

66

'Let me get you another coffee then.' Casey nodded and wished she hadn't given up smoking.

Whispers Comedy Club was starting to get busy by the time Casey and Vaughn had arrived. They'd talked for over an hour, with neither one of them divulging anything personal.

'Tell me about yourself; I'm intrigued why a young lady like you is on her own.'

'There's nothing really to tell; and I'm not that young. What about you?'

'Oh, I lead a very dull life.'

It was apparent to both of them that they were each hiding things but neither said anything, and neither pushed any further.

Alfie watched Vaughn chatting away from the stool at the bar; he recognised she was the woman who'd been looking at the board outside the club the other day. He never forgot a face; especially one that had distracted him from his show-night nerves. She was laughing, obviously enjoying the attention of his friend, and for some reason it fucked him off no end that Vaughn had beaten him to it. Not that he minded having his cast-offs – he slept with hookers most nights, so second-hand pussy wasn't a problem for him – but it rankled his ego.

On the way across to join them, Alfie grabbed a bottle of cheap house red from behind the bar; if her pussy was already taken for tonight, he wasn't going to bother breaking open a bottle of the expensive stuff, though from what Alfie could make out, so far she'd stuck to drinking water.

'Vaughn!' Alfie slapped Vaughn hard on his back, a little harder than usual; something which wasn't missed by his friend.

'Alfie; let me introduce my new friend, Casey. Casey, this is the friend I was telling you about who owns the club.'

Alfie smiled tightly as Vaughn quickly turned his attention back to Casey.

She waved as way of a greeting and Alfie sat down to join them to watch the show. It was gong night at Whispers, the most popular night of the week, and Alfie could feel the whole club buzzing with anticipation. Would-be comedians, old timers and members of the public had three minutes each to get on stage and keep the crowd laughing. Members of the audience were given red cards on entering the club, and if for any reason they found the person on stage unfunny or just took a dislike to them, they could lift up their card; three red cards in the air and the master of ceremonies would bang the gong, much to the crowd's amusement.

Since he'd been running gong night, Alfie had seen very few people actually get through the three minutes, and the drunker the crowd got, the less chance anyone had of getting to the end; unless of course they were him. Not one card had ever gone up when he took to the stage on gong night – no one dared.

'So are we going to get you up on stage tonight, Casey?'

'I think I'd need something stronger than spring water if I was going up there.'

Casey smiled at Alfie, who gave her a discreet wink: another indiscretion which didn't go unnoticed by Vaughn. The lights went down and the spot went up as the master of ceremonies amused the crowd with his opening set.

'Ladies and gentlemen put your hands together for our first victim . . . I mean contestant.'

From the left hand of the stage, Casey watched a nervous looking man walk towards the mike; before he'd had the chance to even get there, three red cards went up one by one, much to the hilarity of the crowd. The master of ceremonies loudly rang the gong, to the annoyance of the comedian as he turned to leave the stage with the sound system playing 'Hit the Road Jack'.

Casey roared with laughter, enjoying the atmosphere of the club along with everyone else. As the next anxious contestant walked on the stage, a loud commotion was heard at the back of the club, and pandemonium quickly spread through the audience. The clubbers started to scream and run towards the emergency exit as a handful of men came charging in, brandishing various weapons. A slap to the side of Casey's head sent her flying backwards off her chair. She stood up to run but her path was blocked by a small fat man, who grabbed her and tried to drag her towards the back room – but his grip wasn't tight enough and he let go, giving Casey the opportunity to run through a door marked 'Staff Only'.

The tallest of the men jumped on top of Alfie and yelled angrily as another grabbed hold of his hair, bringing down a cosh and smashing it into his face; it took Vaughn only a nanosecond and a resigned sigh to get into action.

'Lock the fucking doors!' Vaughn boomed out his order, simultaneously smashing the bottle of red on the side of the table, and lunged across to the man who was holding a dazed Alfie in a neck lock.

Vaughn drove the jagged bottle into the man's face, not as hard as he could, unwilling to do more than was necessary. The man fell to the floor, releasing Alfie as he dropped on his knees.

Vaughn stepped back, not wanting to continue with the violence now all Alfie's men had run to step in to get things under control. Managing to recover, Alfie bellowed loudly as his foot pounded a dark-haired man on the floor.

'You motherfucking cunt. Who sent you?'

The man didn't answer and Alfie bent down, grabbing hold of the man's arm and twisting it round as the bone threatened to snap at the shoulder.

'You've got some brass fucking neck coming into my fucking club. Who sent you?'

'Bellingham.'

'Bellingham?'

'Jake's uncle, he's a face from East Ham – he heard what you did to his nephew.'

Alfie would've laughed if his face hadn't been hurting so much and his front veneer wasn't broken. He'd been shitting himself when the men came in; he'd thought it was the Russians after the mess-up with the heroin last month, or even the Davidson brothers from Stratford, who were fucked off with him over the fake credit cards he'd been selling on their turf. But Jake's uncle? It was fucking laughable.

'Give Bellingham a message; tell him Alfie Jennings says his nephew's a useless cunt and if he ever sends his men to my patch again, I'll come looking for him and he won't be as lucky as his nephew was.'

Alfie paused whilst he touched his nose, wincing at the pain. He turned his attention back to the man. 'I want you to take him something back for me.'

Alfie put his hand into his back pocket and pulled out the pliers he always carried. He nodded to two of his men who came forward and pulled the man up from the fall. One held him up and the other prised open his mouth, leaving Alfie to teach him a lesson the Jennings way. 'Now say "ah".'

As Vaughn turned away from the violence, a thought struck him.

Where's Casey?

Casey ran through the back room hoping to find a way out. The exit door was locked but there was another door slightly ajar, and she could see a flight of stairs behind it. Rather

70

than stay in the back room or head back into the chaos, she decided it'd be safer to head up the stairs.

At the top, Casey saw crates of wine and boxes stacked up neatly against the wall. She walked cautiously down the corridor hoping to find one of the doors open and a room she could wait in. The first door she tried was locked but the second opened and led to a storeroom full of large boxes. Almost unconsciously, Casey continued to look around. There were televisions, computers, Blu-ray players, iPods and iPhones, all boxed, plus a huge selection of Romeo y Julieta cigars.

There was a door at the back and Casey, letting her more inquisitive side take over, quickly opened it to see what was behind it. It was a tiny bathroom.

About to walk out of the storeroom, Casey heard voices coming down the corridor. She felt panic rise within her and she stayed motionless and waited for the voices to go past.

The voices didn't pass. Casey could hear them directly on the other side of the door. She saw the handle turning and immediately crouched down behind the largest box, hoping whoever it was wasn't coming in to take the plasma TV she'd just hidden behind.

The voices Casey heard were foreign. One belonged to a man and the other was female. Casey peeked around the box. She got a glimpse of the man, and saw that there were two women with him, not one as she first thought.

She continued to watch, terrified she might make a noise. She saw the man push one of the women hard in the back as he opened the door to the bathroom. The woman let out a tiny squeal and was given another shove to stop her cry. Casey felt as if she should be doing something but she didn't know what, so she stayed hidden and watched as the man leaned on the doorway of the bathroom, not letting the women have any privacy as they used the toilet.

Crouching behind the box, Casey noticed the women were dressed in tracksuit bottoms and thin short-sleeved tops and their feet were bare. As they were coming out of the bathroom, the light was bright enough for her to see the smaller woman's arm was covered in bruising and marks. The man opened the door to the storeroom, leading the women out behind him. Casey listened to the footsteps disappearing down the corridor.

In the darkness of the tiny storeroom Casey could feel her whole body shaking; she was terrified and she knew she couldn't be caught hiding. She took some deep breaths to try to calm her racing heart and listened to see if she could hear anybody else coming. It was all quiet and she decided it was probably safe to go back downstairs.

Casey cautiously walked down the corridor. She wasn't sure what she'd just seen but whatever it was she certainly didn't want to get involved; she was here in London for one reason only and all she wanted to do was get the hell out of there.

Coming down the stairs Vaughn was standing at the bottom.

'Where've you been? I was worried sick. You alright? You look a bit pale.'

'I'm fine; thought it was best to wait on the stairs.'

Vaughn looked to the top of the stairs.

'That's where you've been all this time?'

Casey nodded her head and couldn't help but think Vaughn was looking at her suspiciously. She was feeling very unsafe and it dawned on her how stupid she'd been to agree to have a drink with Vaughn in the club alone. She didn't know the first thing about him, but after what she'd just seen happen, if he was a friend of Alfie's he was part of something very dangerous.

She wanted to go home but she didn't want to raise

Vaughn's suspicions any more than they seemed to be raised already. She needed to be careful; she didn't want him guessing she'd seen the girls. Mustering up some courage which she didn't feel, Casey spoke, hoping her voice would sound light and be relieved of any tension.

'Anyway, Alfie was right; gong night is certainly something not to be missed.'

Casey grinned up at Vaughn who grinned back, with neither of their smiles reaching their eyes.

CHAPTER TEN

'For fuck's sake, woman, can't you be a little gentler? You've got hands like a fucking gorilla.' Alfie pushed his wife's hands away as she tried to clean the hardened dried blood off his face with a ball of cotton wool.

He knew he should've washed it off last night but by the time he'd got home to Essex, his face had been hurting so much, he hadn't wanted to look at it in the mirror, let alone touch it.

He'd taken some sleeping pills, but he'd been rudely awoken a few hours later by Janine's piercing scream directly in his ear, after she'd turned over in bed and seen him asleep next to her with his face covered in blood.

'What the fuck are you screaming about, woman?'

'I thought you were bleeding dead.'

'And if I was, how the hell does screaming make it better? You nearly fucking gave me a heart attack.'

'Well what was I supposed to think?'

'Nothing, like you usually do. Christ almighty, Janine, if I was going to cop it, I hope my dying hours wouldn't be lying next to you snoring your head off.'

Janine had laughed and waddled off to find some cotton wool and TCP to bathe Alfie's face.

Alfie had been driven home by one of his men, which had given him time to think about the situation with Jake. He hadn't actually known he'd been connected to the Bellinghams in East Ham, not that it would've made a difference; in fact, he might have enjoyed dishing out the punishment all the more.

He still hadn't spoken to Emmie any more about the matter; the last thing he wanted to listen to were wails of hysteria from his lovestruck daughter. He'd leave her to stew for a few days and then he'd pick her up something special from Selfridges to cheer her up.

It still pissed him off when he thought about it; he couldn't get the image of his daughter with that scumbag out of his head and as he put on his shoes, the image of Emmie in just her bra got larger and he felt the rage start to enter his body. He stood up abruptly, throwing the bowl of hot water Janine had brought onto the floor.

He stormed along the marbled landing, kicking Emmie's cat out of the way, and marched down the elegant curved staircase to the front door, slamming it behind him as he banged out of the house.

'Fucking hell, Alfie, has Janine been knocking you about again? There's helplines you can ring for that sort of thing you know.'

As they sat in the large back office, with crates and boxes piled at the far end of the room, Oscar grinned at Alfie. He'd heard about the showdown at the club from one of his informants and he'd been annoyed he hadn't been around to see it; he'd had one of his headaches and had needed to sit quietly in the dark of his flat for over an hour to let it

75

calm down. When it had, he'd taken a phone call and rushed down to Shoreditch.

'You'll understand why I'm not in the best of moods, Oscar; I still have to go to the dentist to get me veneer fixed, so if you wouldn't mind I'd like to get on with our meeting.'

Oscar grinned and was rewarded by a scowl from Alfie, which made him laugh out loud as he spoke.

'You weren't the only one who had a bit of a problem last night, Alf. I got a call from Nesha, the Albanian guy looking after our girls down in Redchurch Street. One of them managed to open the window when she went for a piss and . . .'

Alfie sprang up from the chair, sending waves of pain through his face, and the suppressed anger he'd tried to contain earlier broke through.

'What the fuck? Oscar, I thought you said you had them all under control?'

'I did; I do. Nobody, not even me could've guessed the little whore would've jumped out of a sixth-floor window.'

'What?'

'Yeah, silly bitch decided to jump.'

'What, do they have rubber bones in Albania? How did she think she'd survive?'

'She probably thought it was a better option to jump.'

'Jesus.'

Oscar grinned, his eyes dancing with amusement.

'I know, fucking waste of money.'

Alfie shot a stare at Oscar. 'You haven't got a heart have you?'

Oscar put his hand on the front of his chest, pretending to try and feel the heartbeat. 'No, not even a pulse. You need to stop getting fucking soft on me, Alf; I didn't think you're the type.'

'I'm not, and I don't like you thinking I am, because I

might have to show you what sort of heart I've got if you carry on taking the piss.'

Oscar looked at Alfie; pleased with the reaction. He didn't need to do business with a pussy.

'Of course, Nesha moved the body quickly; put her in the boot and then threw it in the canal at the Hackney end; it'll be a while before she's found. Obviously the car wasn't registered, but he left it on a nearby estate so it can be burnt out by some little fucker who gets his kicks that way.'

'What about the girls?'

'Moved them to Bow, but it's only temporary, it's too small there. I thought maybe you could keep some more above the club for a while. I'm going to speak to Lola and get her to break them in.'

'I thought you hated your ex-missus?'

'I do, she's a hard bitch who'd sell her own grandkids for money – so she's exactly what we need.'

It'd been a week since Casey had walked in on Lola, and every day since, she'd regretted the fact she'd walked out on her. Yes, it'd been shocking for Casey to see Lola like that, but the most shocking part of it all was how much Casey had seen of herself in Lola – and it was for that reason that Casey had run away from the situation. It wasn't Lola she'd seen on the bathroom floor vomiting on the cracked tiles, it was herself. The similarities between herself and Lola frightened her.

Taking a deep breath Casey opened the door of the cafe, which was jam-packed with mud-clad builders, all looking for a fry-up after their morning's work on the building site in Manette Street. Over the steam of the cafe, Lola and Casey locked eyes. Lola broke out into a big grin.

'Bleeding hell, what kept you? Your shift started a week ago.'

Lola threw Casey an overall and with a wink, turned back to continue taking the overly large woman's breakfast order in the far corner.

Casey had been working the morning shift and was expecting to finish at noon, but the rush of people made it necessary for her to stay on for the afternoon shift.

'You don't mind do you, Casey?'

Even though Casey was exhausted she was happy she could help out; anything to try to make up for walking out like she had.

'No problem. And Lola, I'm . . .'

Lola put up her hand to stop Casey saying any more.

'There's no need to say anything girl. It should be me saying sorry. Now we'll hear no more about it. But Casey?'

'Yes?'

'I'm happy you came back.'

By four o'clock, the lunchtime rush was over and Casey sat down for a cup of tea; the first she'd had all day.

'Want me to put some whiskey in that, love?' Lola cackled as she sat down with *The Daily Star*. Casey wasn't sure if she was joking or not; there was a strong possibility she had smelt like a brewer's daughter the day she'd discovered Lola's cafe but since the sobriety meeting she hadn't touched a drop, though it was killing her. She'd found a miniature bottle of whisky tucked away in one of her boots this morning and she'd sat staring at it for over twenty minutes before she'd finally poured it down the kitchen sink. Her addiction was still holding her as tightly as ever.

Sipping her tea she thought about the club. She still felt shaken by what had happened, and the women she'd seen had troubled her; they'd more than troubled her, they had frightened her; but she was doing her best to put it to the back of her mind. She didn't want to get distracted by anything – she needed all her energy on getting well and finding her son.

She hadn't bothered asking Vaughn about it. To a certain extent it was through fear, but mainly she wanted a simple life, without any complications; she'd had enough of those to last her a lifetime.

Vaughn had insisted on walking her home, but he hadn't spoken much and had seemed rather distracted. When they'd been out on the street, the fear she'd had of him in the club had slightly diminished; he'd seemed so much less threatening, and even though he'd been in his own thoughts, she'd picked up something else from him: something warm, caring even; but then what would she know? She wasn't the best judge of character by any means, and besides, it didn't really matter what he was or wasn't; she didn't want to get involved.

He'd asked to meet up with her the following Saturday for a drink and she'd accepted his invitation, just to be polite, just to humour him, but now she regretted it. She was a fool; her own worst enemy.

Casey took a sip of her tea as the cafe door opened and both she and Lola looked round; two tall men walked in, bringing with them an air of confidence. Casey recognised one of them; it was Alfie. His face was swollen and shockingly bruised.

Lola stood up and hurried over nervously to the men, who sat down at the far table.

'Bring us some teas, Casey love.'

Casey got up and went across to the large silver tea urn, sensing she was being watched. Putting the teas on the Princess Diana tray to take over, Casey glanced up and immediately locked eyes with Alfie, who was staring at her intently.

She placed the tea in front of them without saying a word and without wanting to listen to anything being said; it was obvious to her something was going on, and she was determined to know nothing about it.

Alfie couldn't help staring at Casey; he'd no idea she was working with Lola. Casey looked so out of place: no matter how stained her clothes were and unbrushed her hair looked, there was no hiding her beauty. Lola on the other hand blended into the greasy walls of the cafe like she'd crawled out of the walls with the cockroaches.

Alfie decided he was going to ask Vaughn if he'd finished with Casey. He could do with a treat after the week from hell he was having, and she was just the treat he needed. He imagined her sitting on his cock, riding away with her tits bouncing up and down. He was about to continue his fantasy, when Oscar's voice threw cold water onto his thoughts.

'Alfie?'

'What?'

'I think that blow you took to your fucking face must have hit your brain as well.'

Alfie glared at Oscar. He didn't like the fact he was disrespecting him, least of all in front of a rat's arse like Lola Harding. He'd have a word with Oscar later, but for now, he'd keep quiet and listen to what he was saying.

'We want you to show them how it's done, Lola. I thought they'd be like lambs but they're still wanting to think for themselves. Your job is to get them smacked up; get them *so* used to the taste of brown they can't do without it. That shouldn't be too hard for you.'

Lola cackled, taking a sip of the hot, milky tea in front of her, and continued to listen to Oscar.

'The other thing is the pill; I don't want them knocked up when the punters ride bare back, so you need to get hold of some. Plus, show them how to use the sponge when they're on their periods; a lot of the punters will be put off by the

80

blood and I don't want to lose money because of bleedin' bitches.' Oscar laughed loudly at his own joke. 'It's easy money for you, Lola. It'll be like home from home, as long as you keep your mouth shut of course.'

'Haven't I always, Oscar?'

Lola paused for a moment, looking first at Oscar and then at Alfie; choosing her words carefully.

'Listen, I appreciate the offer and all but you know I don't do stuff like that any more. A bit of handling and selling I don't mind, but not this, Oscar; left it all behind a long time ago, you know that. Besides, I'm trying to get off the stuff. I'm slowly weaning myself off it.'

Oscar looked at his ex-wife. It never ceased to amaze him how old she looked; they were the same age, 44, but anyone guessing, would've thought she was at least twenty years older.

He stretched over to Lola and squeezed her hand very hard thinking how much her toothless grin was akin to his fat whore of a mother's. Oscar watched as Lola's mouth trembled. He was sorry he hadn't actually killed her that night; she gave him nothing but grief. He leaned in to Lola and spoke quietly across the table.

'The smack's fucking up your brain, Lo. I'm more likely to turn into a fucking black man than you give up that shit. So do me a little favour sweetheart; stop fucking mugging me off. I've never been the sort of person to give you a choice and I'm not about to start now.'

Oscar squeezed even harder on Lola's hand, making her let out a tiny squeal.

'So we have a deal?'

Lola nodded quickly, her eyes full of fear. Oscar let go of her hand and leant back in the chair, very much aware of the waitress with the auburn hair staring at him with a mix of hatred and fear in her eyes.

CHAPTER ELEVEN

If it wasn't for his broken fingers, Jake Bellingham would've given Emmie a hard slap in the face. He was lucky to be alive, and all she could do was give him a headache with her crocodile tears while her fat mother sat eating her second bar of chocolate, keeping an eye on them.

They'd given him painkillers but he was still in agony. Alfie Jennings had delighted in breaking four of his ribs, the fingers on both hands, and extracting five of his teeth – and all because he was going to bone his frigid daughter.

The last person he thought he'd get a visit from was Emmie. The minute she'd walked in and seen him lying at the end of the four-man ward, she'd run and grabbed hold of his broken fingers and buried her face in his body, right on top of his broken ribs. When he'd yelled out, his mouth had started to bleed again and Emmie had screamed for the nurse before sitting down on the chair crying; something she'd now been doing for the past ten minutes.

He couldn't even talk to tell her to stop as his mouth was too sore, so all he could do was wait for her to shut up and stare at the faded green curtains around his hospital bed.

Finally, Emmie stopped crying and spoke. 'I'm sorry Jake,

I had no idea you were this bad. Dad doesn't know I'm here, he'd kill me.' Emmie hesitated for a moment before adding, 'Well, kill *you* really.'

She smiled apologetically and Jake squirmed.

'I wanted to come and see you before but it took me forever to persuade Mum to bring me. I thought I'd die before she'd agree.'

She smiled at her mum and Jake scowled, turning his face away from them. She was so dramatic and obviously thought she meant something more to him other than a quick fuck – not that he'd even got one. He hadn't even got a whiff of her pussy, which made the whole situation even harder to accept.

The next half hour was torturous for Jake as Emmie chattered away about her school friends who sounded as pointless as she was, so he was more than grateful to hear the West Indian nurse come into the ward, letting his unwanted visitors know it was time to go.

'I'm afraid I'm going to have to ask you to leave; visiting time's over.'

He was less grateful however, when he heard the rest of the conversation.

'Mr Bellingham, you need to open your bowels for me, the doctor wants to see if you've got any blood in your stool. Shall I help you get on the bedpan, or would you like your pretty girlfriend here to help?'

Without giving Jake a choice, Emmie piped up, 'It's alright, me and my mum will help him, won't we Mum?'

As Jake watched Emmie come towards him holding the bedpan and her mother rolling up her sleeves, Jake felt his humiliation was complete. Somebody was going to pay dearly for it.

Back at the Jennings house in Essex, Alfie wondered where Janine and Emmie were. He'd tried calling, but as usual both his wife's and his daughter's phone went straight to voicemail. It infuriated him when they didn't answer their phones and it wasn't doing anything to help his current mood either. When they *did* finally find their way home, he'd certainly have a lot to say to them; and he was sure they wouldn't like it. Alfie Jennings would be turning the air a deep shade of blue.

'Are you using this house as some sort of drop-in centre? Where the fuck have you two been?' Alfie roared, striding up to his wife's white Range Rover as it came down the pebbled drive.

Janine looked at Emmie, trying not to look guilty. They'd decided to tell Alfie they'd been to Lakeside shopping centre, giving them the excuse to stop off and buy a couple of new tops in Karen Millen on the way home.

Janine wasn't a good liar – she always felt guilty – but there was no way she could ever tell her husband where they'd been; she was sure if he ever found out, it wouldn't be just Jake who was lying in a hospital bed.

Janine had listened to Emmie beg her to take her to the hospital to see Jake. She'd listened to her daughter's hysterics turn to pleading and then into quiet sobs in her bedroom. Eventually she'd caved in, remembering how she'd felt when she'd fallen for Alfie twenty-odd years ago, and how she'd wished she'd had an ally in her own mother. She also hoped by letting her go and see Jake, Emmie could see that she was on her side, and then perhaps she might start opening up to her about what else was playing on her mind. Janine felt Emmie was slipping further away from her and she'd do anything to stop that happening, even if it meant going behind Alfie's back. And she guessed if it was a lie for the greater good, what harm was there?

*   *   *

After the showdown with Janine and Emmie, Alfie made a few phone calls and left the house. He was going to meet up with Oscar again and get formally introduced to the head of the Albanian gang, Zahir, who spoke the English language far better than he did. It was important for him in business to know every link of the chain; that way, Alfie knew exactly what he was dealing with.

He and Oscar were going to discuss the possibility of bringing some more girls into London from Albania, but first they needed to discuss the costs. The girls they had in their possession now had been exchanged for kilos of heroin, so only drugs, not money, had been involved.

The Albanians had wanted to flood the streets of Manchester with heroin so they could become the main supplier of brown up there, but their drugs supply had been compromised after the cargo ship carrying it had been searched at Bilbao docks and consequently, the smack had been seized. They'd been desperate to get hold of a large amount of gear quickly to keep their finger on the market up North, so they'd put the word out they were looking to buy.

When Oscar had first come and put the idea to him about the exchange of goods Alfie had been uncertain, even though they'd been in possession of an excess amount of heroin, following a gangland killing of a main dealer in Holborn. The dead man had worked for Todd Wakeman, the leader of the EC1 gang. Alfie and Oscar had been owed money by the deceased and as Todd hadn't wanted any more trouble, he'd let them take the dealer's supply of heroin by way of payment.

When Oscar had explained the returns and showed him the sums, Alfie hadn't been able to say no. As he and Oscar had owned the heroin 50/50, they now owned the girls in the same split.

Sitting in his car and waiting for the traffic light to turn green at Piccadilly Circus, Alfie knew it was vital to get their numbers up if they were going to make a real go of it. They were already two girls down but he was feeling better about the whole situation now; he'd gone over it in his head and he could see what a great opportunity it was. He'd had a twinge of conscience but then he'd thought some more and realised he wasn't a social worker – the world wouldn't be healed overnight if he didn't do this. There was a market for it and why give it to someone else when he could have it? That would be like giving a stranger a bag full of money. After all, he was Alfie Jennings, and if there was anything which was going to make him feel he was doing the right thing, it was making money. Lots of it.

CHAPTER TWELVE

It was the following Saturday morning and Casey was relieved she wasn't working in the cafe. She'd even managed to sleep till eight, which was unusual as her troubled mind usually woke her up.

Up until that morning she'd only been able to have a wash using a flannel and a bowl of hot water in the lounge as she refused to go into the bathroom apart from to use the toilet, so she'd taken herself off to the swimming baths in High Holborn, where she'd been able to have a shower for the cost of the three-pound entrance fee.

She felt fresh after spending ages scrubbing her skin and washing her hair. She'd carefully blow dried it so it now hung down in tousled shiny auburn waves to the middle of her back.

On the way home she'd treated herself to a new light blue top from Berwick Street market and washed her clothes at the launderette in Romilly Street. For a moment she'd felt happy; the late winter sun on her face and the unseasonably warm breeze on her skin reminding her of the time she went on holiday to Sardinia with Josh.

She hadn't wanted to go and had refused at first, crushing his boyish enthusiasm. She was worried he'd be watching her every move, her every drink, and she wouldn't have the freedom she needed to sneak off when she wanted to as she did at home. Though when she thought about it, she didn't actually need to hide – she had hours on her own to do as she pleased, to go where she liked and to drink as she saw fit.

On some days she and Josh would be like ships passing in the loneliness of the night. The long hours he worked gave her the opportunity to live her life as she wanted to without having to see the disappointed look in his eyes.

She stood her ground, refusing to go and refusing to look at the brochures of the upmarket hotel he'd booked them into, but after a week of him looking forlorn over the breakfast table, Casey had reluctantly agreed.

'You won't regret it, Cass. It'll be wonderful, I promise.'

Casey smiled knowing the sentiment of the moment didn't really hit either of them as it should've done.

Sardinia was a jewel; bathed by turquoise seas and surrounded by ivory white sandy beaches, and for a moment Casey forgot her pain and was able to live in the moment of the seductive beauty of the island.

Josh picked up the hire car – an open-top white Mercedes – and drove them both away from the busy seaside resort of Santa Teresa di Gallura; along winding roads, past citrus groves and velvet green pastures, up towards the rustic blanket of forested mountain peaks and just beyond to Bosa, the impossibly picturesque medieval town with pink and white buildings flanking the swirling river.

'It's beautiful, Josh.'

'I told you you'd like it,' Josh said, grinning.

And he'd been right. Casey had loved every moment. She hadn't stopped drinking but it didn't have that desperate *edge to it and Josh had said nothing, just held her hand as she walked unsteadily along the mountain paths. He sat by her side as she slept off the lunchtime bottle of wine, and when the day was finished, he carried her to bed after the town's evening festivities.*

It was all going so well – the simple things were being let back into her life; and then on the second week when Casey wasn't looking her world came falling in again.

'Why don't we have a baby? Our baby. It might help you.'

Casey had looked at Josh, taken in his face and the naive excitement in his eyes before speaking, the distance between them becoming wider than it was already.

'Take me home, Josh. I want to go home.'

Within four hours they were on a plane heading back to England.

When she got back to the flat Casey remembered she'd promised to meet Vaughn later; annoyingly she couldn't call him to cancel their drink as she didn't have his number.

Sighing, Casey absentmindedly picked up her diary and started flicking through it. For a two-year diary it had surprisingly few written entries. It was mainly full of doodles, and scribblings of homework.

Partway through the journal, Casey came to a familiar page which made her catch her breath and the tears swelled in the back of her throat. Stuck neatly in the middle of the page was a lock of hair.

Fri 15th January 1996
Nurse brought me a tiny lock of hair from baby. I will keep it forever. Feel so, so sad, can't stop crying. Think I'll cry forever.

'I'm sorry Casey; it's more than my job's worth.'

'Please, just take me to see my baby.'

'I'm sorry; you know I can't do that. Sweetheart, you've got to try to stop thinking of it as your baby; it'll only make it harder for you. I know it's tough but eventually it'll get easier.'

Casey looked at the midwife who'd been so kind to her; she thought she might have been able to convince her to take her down to the neo-natal unit but Casey could see from the look on the midwife's face it was pointless trying to persuade her.

The feeling of isolation was crippling; no one would tell her anything about her baby. Her mum had come to see her twice, both times with a sullen look on her face. She hadn't seen her dad at all and had only received a telephone message from him wishing her a speedy recovery.

'Then if you can't do that, just tell me what I had. Was it a boy or girl?'

Before the midwife could answer, Casey's mother drew the bed curtains back sharply.

'Casey, stop pestering the nurses. If it's so important for you to know, I'll tell you. You had a boy.'

The midwife glanced at Casey's mum and scuttled away with her head down, leaving Casey to bury her head in her hands as her mother stood motionless at the side of her bed.

It was well past midnight and Casey was drifting off into a restless sleep when she felt someone at the end of her bed.

'Casey?'

Casey sat up to see the kind nurse smiling at her. The nurse spoke in a whisper.

'Casey, I brought you this but it's only between you and me; I'll lose my job otherwise.'

The nurse took Casey's hand and placed a tiny curled lock

of hair in the middle of her hand. It took Casey a moment to realise what it was.

'Is that from . . . ?' Casey was unable to say any more but the nurse smiled again and nodded her head as she watched the light come into Casey's eyes for the first time.

Casey stood up, making sure the lock of hair was still secure in the pages of her diary. She was about to throw it back in her bag but she stopped and instead put it inside her jacket pocket. Maybe it was silly, but sometimes she needed to have the diary close to her. Knowing the lock of hair – the only reminder of the child she had – was next to her was the only way she got through the day.

She *had* to go to a meeting; the urge to drink to take the pain away was beginning to overwhelm her and she was afraid if she didn't make it this time, it would be the end.

CHAPTER THIRTEEN

Alfie was feeling refreshed. With all the tension from the week, he hadn't bothered going back to Essex after the meeting with the Albanians, instead picking up two toms who he knew through Vaughn.

He was going to throw them both out in the next half hour, but not before he'd got another blow job from the blonde. He wanted to be relaxed before his big night. He was due on stage at nine and as long as there were no more dramas, Alfie was certain he was going to knock the audience dead.

He was hoping Vaughn would come in and he'd be able to ask him about Casey. With that thought in mind, he grabbed hold of one of the sleeping women's backsides and pulled her towards him on the leather super-king-sized bed, ready for some more action.

Vaughn Sadler couldn't understand it. Leaning over the pot in his vast hothouse, he poked the dying buds of the climbing Altissimo rose he'd been trying to grow. He'd thought by the summer it'd be creeping up the far glass wall, vigorously climbing with rich, slightly scented bright scarlet flowers, which eventually would turn a deep crimson. Altissimo in Italian meant 'in the highest', and so far, Vaughn thought, it was hardly living up to its name.

Sometimes he had to laugh at how totally absorbed and wound up he became over his gardening; if anyone had told him a few years ago he'd be spending hours on end tending to his roses he'd have thought they'd been too long on the old crack pipe. It also amused him when he thought about what Connor would've said if he could see him elbow-deep in flowers and fertiliser, but maybe if his friend had been here, he wouldn't have had to find something to try to distract from the raw pain he felt when he thought about Connor Jennings.

'Connor; you okay?' Vaughn turned round in the car and watched in dismay as his friend took a swig from a bottle of whisky. 'What the fuck are you doing? I need you clear-headed, Connor, not bleeding three sheets to the wind.'

'I'm just taking the edge off a little. Have you got a problem with that?'

'Too right I have. I want you staying in the car when we get to the warehouse; I'm not having you fuck up this job for us.'

'Don't try to fucking tell me what to do, Vaughnie, never tell me what to do. Some of these goons might think you're some big fucking hot shot, but I'm not one of them.' Connor Jennings sneered at his friend before taking another gulp of the whisky, whilst the other men in the car watched with interest the fall out of their boss and his best friend.

Vaughn was aware of the other men's eyes on them; usually arguments between him and Connor were kept behind closed doors to help retain the respect from the other men but, as usual, the whisky had made Connor obnoxious.

Some men were able to drink but Connor wasn't one of

them. No drink suited him; vodka made him cry, brandy made him want to entertain the masses and whisky made him sullen and aggressive. The last thing Vaughn needed now was to try to tolerate a pissed-up Connor Jennings.

If anyone else had spoken to Vaughn like that, he would've given them a reason to go to the dentist, but this was Connor. He loved him as if he was his own flesh and blood, and in Vaughn's book that meant never hurting him; even if it meant having to put up with crap he'd never normally put up with.

Vaughn knew the other men were waiting to see what he'd do about the lip he was getting, but they'd have a long wait because he wasn't going to do anything apart from give Connor a good talking to later in private.

He saw the driver 'Doc' Phillips give him a sympathetic raise of his eyebrows. He liked Doc; he was a man that could be trusted and relied upon and he'd used him on a lot of jobs over the past couple of years.

He'd had met Doc when he was on remand for handling stolen goods and Doc was serving five years for supplying morphine. Doc had already been struck off by the medical board a few years earlier for self-medicating on hospital drugs, but that hadn't lessened his enthusiasm for opium or narcotics in general, though his drug use had never interfered with the jobs he did for him. Vaughn knew Doc was reliable and would never arrive to do any smile and smirk eyeballed up like Connor had.

Arriving at the warehouse, Doc turned into the side yard and turned off the ignition, signalling to the van behind them to do the same. Vaughn could see the tall fenced gates of the warehouse had been left open as arranged and the night lights turned off. He couldn't see the security guards; another discreet arrangement which his money had bought. It looked like it was going to be an easy job; he hoped it would.

Although the warehouse was a working one, at night it

was dark and deserted and the smell of blood from the dead carcasses hung in the air. It was freezing; on the verge of sub-zero; the combination of the harsh winter's night and the temperature needed to keep the fish and meat cold made it feel unbearable even to Vaughn's gloved hands.

'Fuck me, it'll freeze me bollocks off. This'll put paid to me having kids.' Vaughn spoke quietly and grinned whilst gesturing to the other men to follow. They had to be quiet. He didn't think there was any immediate danger but he still liked to be cautious just in case any of the warehouse staff had decided to grass them up, or worse, the McKenzie brothers had got wind of it.

A few minutes later they were at the back of the warehouse and standing in front of the metal door where the brothers had stashed the heroin. Vaughn turned to the men, his eyes adjusting slightly to the dim night lights of the warehouse which were never turned off.

'Okay, behind here is our just reward, gentlemen; you know what the plan is. Doc, you go . . .' Vaughn stopped and looked around quickly. His senses suddenly became on heightened alert and when he spoke the anxiety in his voice was evident to the men.

'Where's Connor?'

The other men gave a quick glance round and a shrug, not wanting to say anything which might make them culpable for Connor's absence.

'Stay here, I'll go and find him.'

'I'll come with you.' Doc Phillips followed him.

The walkway in the warehouse was clear and as deserted as it was when they came in, which meant Connor must have gone back outside or he'd gone through one of the back ways. Vaughn cursed out loud; he knew he shouldn't have brought him; he should've insisted at the very least he stay in the car.

Doc and one of the other men were still a few feet behind him and in the very far distance Vaughn could hear dogs barking. The shadowy gloom of the light made it difficult to see properly and as Vaughn hurried down a corridor he realised they were now in the derelict part of the warehouse; it seemed to creak with hidden noises and was filled with unfamiliar smells; the remains of pipes and tubing lay abandoned on the floor making it precarious to walk. From the eerie silence of the darkness, Vaughn heard a faint sound; a cry.

'Connor!'

Vaughn bolted forward in the dark to where the noise was coming from, stumbling and tripping over unseen objects. It was pitch black and getting colder by the moment and when he stopped to get his bearings he could feel water dripping on his face. A torch light was shone from behind him; it was Doc with another one of the men. Vaughn grabbed the torch and shone it round the room, startling a rat which scurried quickly away from the beam.

'Connor!' Vaughn's voice was layered in worry. Another cry came but this time it seemed closer as if it was coming from above. Vaughn shone the torch upwards and recoiled as he comprehended: the drips of water were drips of blood, slowly trickling through the broken floorboards of the ceiling.

Vaughn ran towards the far stairwell, knocking Doc and Jimmy out of the way. The wooden stairs groaned with the heavy weight of his urgency as Vaughn took them two by two. At the top, he shone the torch again and in the middle of the room he could see Connor lying on his back; he looked strange and Vaughn couldn't make out why until he moved closer; Connor had fallen through the hole in the ceiling, becoming impaled on the two-foot-high pane of glass which was now sticking out of his stomach.

'Help me.'

Vaughn ran to Connor at the same time Doc and Jimmy made it into the room. From behind him he heard Doc scream, 'No, don't! Stop!' as he yanked the glass out from Connor's stomach. The blood spurted up into a fountain, pumping everywhere. Vaughn fell to his knees, holding Connor as he shook and started to convulse.

'Oh my god!' The blood continued to pour out of Connor, saturating them both and pushing Vaughn to yell at Doc for help.

'Do something for fuck's sake!'

Doc Phillips stood motionless. 'I can't.'

Vaughn scrambled to pull out the hand gun in his pocket and pointed it at Doc as he screamed at him again.

'I said do something!'

Doc shook his head slowly and as Connor trembled in his arms, it suddenly hit Vaughn why Doc had yelled at him to stop; he'd instinctively pulled the glass out of Connor and had inadvertently signed his death warrant by causing him to bleed to death.

'Connor! Oh my god I'm sorry, what have I done?'

Vaughn pressed his head against Connor's and he felt the staggered breath on his face.

'I'm cold, Vaughnie.'

Vaughn looked at Connor under the torch light now held by Doc; his face was pale and waxy and with every trickle of blood coming out of his body, his life was draining away. Vaughn felt Doc kneel next to him.

'Say goodbye, Vaughn; he won't have long. It's time to say goodbye,' Doc said gently.

The cry from Vaughn met with the look of terror in Connor's eyes.

'I'm not ready to die. Don't let me die, Vaughnie.'

'You're not going to. You're going to stay with me. Do you hear me?'

Connor nodded weakly and arched his body as he started to cough mouthfuls of blood and Vaughn felt a squeeze on his shoulder from Doc. He looked down at Connor and saw he was trying to say something.

'Alfie. Look after him for me.'

Vaughn couldn't see through his tears but he picked Connor up towards him and held him tight, rocking him against his body.

'I won't need to, Connor, because you'll be there.'

'Promise me. Please Vaughn, just say you will.'

'I promise, I promise.'

Connor's head began to loll to the side as he mouthed a silent goodbye; his eyes stared out into the darkness; blank, void, unaware of his surroundings.

Frantically Vaughn shook him and Connor's eyes refocused for a moment, locking with his.

'I love you.' And then the glaze came back into Connor's eyes; and stayed. Connor Jennings was gone forever.

Vaughn took a deep breath and tried to focus on the dazzling buds and colours of the other roses instead of his thoughts but it was so hard once the box began to open.

They'd tried to make him leave Connor's body at the warehouse but he couldn't; not there in the dark, not on his own. He'd taken him home instead of the smack and the McKenzie brothers had never known how close they'd been to losing their fortune.

They'd driven Connor's body to the hospital where the staff had been suspicious and called the Old Bill, but within a week they'd released the body and they'd been able to give Connor the East End funeral to beat all funerals.

Alfie had taken it hard at first and had either not spoken or been on all-week benders. Eventually he'd managed to get his life back on track, but he rarely spoke about Connor.

Vaughn imagined the suicide of his mother when he was a kid and the death of his beloved brother a few years later was too painful to put into words.

As for himself, he'd been left with the guilt of killing his best friend. Doc Phillips had tried to assure him Connor would've died anyway even if he hadn't pulled the glass out, but no one would ever know or could tell him that for sure.

'Vaughnie, I know you feel bad but you've got to give yourself a break. No one told him to get pissed and wander round an old warehouse as if he was on a bleeding sightseeing trip; Jimmy said he'd been shooting up only an hour before we went on the job. If anyone's to blame he is. Stop giving yourself a hard time.'

It hadn't made a difference what anyone said; he knew Connor was bang on it and he knew he'd been drinking. He alone could've stopped him coming on the job but he hadn't done it and no one understood how that made him feel. No one understood how every moment of every day he missed his friend.

Fuck. He had to stop thinking. Flowers were meant to relax him, according to the guy who'd introduced him to them. When he'd served his last stretch inside, he'd walked into the cell and it'd been plastered with pictures of flowers.

He'd assumed wrongly the lag was a shirtlifter but he turned out to be a father of four who was serving life for stabbing his missus twenty-six times in the neck and face, having come home early from work to find her shacked up in bed with his own father. The prison shrink had told the lag he had anger issues and for therapeutic reasons he'd been allotted the job as gardener in the prison garden, and there he'd fallen in love with nature.

Vaughn had used his connections on the outside to get the screws on his wing sent a box of champagne along with cigars and an iPod each, and in return, he'd been able to join his cellmate in the garden, learning about the rights and wrongs of growing roses and getting out of the twenty-two-hour lock-up regime Strangeways had in place.

Vaughn had served three years out of an eight-year sentence he'd got for his part in dealing in counterfeit banknotes. When the judge had sent him down he'd decided enough was enough and he was going to retire, and when he'd walked out of prison two years ago, he was as good as his word.

He'd always been careful with money and he'd enough put away in offshore accounts to live in luxury for the rest of his life. He had no family or kids to look after and apart from his sister, who he always made sure was alright by sending her money each month, the money he had was all for himself, to do what he liked with.

As tough as he was it had never really been in his nature to enjoy hurting people for the sake of it and he'd become tired of looking over his shoulder.

He'd spent over a hundred grand on the hothouse and like his cellmate, found it therapeutic growing flowers. So now he found himself tending to his roses, knowing that he had to be calm when he went up West later.

Vaughn had two good reasons for going to the club later. The first was to meet Casey; he'd been looking forward to seeing her for the past couple of days, which was unusual for him; women usually came and went without him giving them a second thought.

He'd never bothered to even think about having a relationship before; it'd suited him and his lifestyle to be on his own. He liked his freedom and he usually got bored of a woman after a couple of days, which was why hookers were perfect for him. Apart from liking the company of hookers, life was simple with them; fuck them and then fuck off; they weren't offended and they didn't nag. Life without relationships was uncomplicated, which was why he felt so pissed off about Casey; she'd got under his skin.

The one thing that did bother him about her was her secrecy; when he'd tried to talk to her about herself he could almost see her clam up in front of his eyes. Vaughn hoped she'd open up: he wanted to get to know her in the good old-fashioned way; but if that didn't work, he could always get some of his old connections to dig about to see what they could find out. He hoped there would be no surprises; one thing he'd always hated was surprises.

The second reason he was going to the club was to speak to Alfie. He'd heard some rumours about a new business venture he and Oscar where setting up and if what he heard was true, he was going to have to slap some sense into his friend; some things you didn't deal in – especially with the likes of Oscar Harding. The man was a nut job and he wouldn't trust him with his late mother's ashes – or with his prize roses for that matter. Oscar Harding spelt nothing but trouble.

Lola stretched out and farted; a loud smelly stench of a fart.

'Jesus woman, haven't you any manners?'

'No, I lost them when I lost me virginity.'

Oscar pushed his ex-wife away and was thankful he was at her flat and not his, or he would've needed to call on the services of Billy again to clean the place up.

He'd gone round to Lola's the previous evening to drop some smack off, which he was going to make her feed to the girls whether she wanted to or not. His head had been hurting him so badly he'd insisted Lola give him a massage to see if the headache would ease off; he could tell she hadn't wanted to by the face she'd pulled but he'd been too weak to give her a clip. The massage hadn't done any good and he was unable to drive back home because of the intense pain.

He suspected he'd blacked out, because the last thing he remembered was lying down on his ex-wife's uncomfortable bed.

His headache was completely gone and he was eager to get out of the flat; he'd some business in Kennington he wanted to finish before going to the club later.

'Come here and give me a kiss, Oscar.'

Lola's breath was sickly sweet and her mouth was caked with dried white spit at the corners. She was high, having just finished chasing the dragon. Oscar brushed her off angrily.

'What's the matter O? Still can't get a hard-on?'

The moment Lola said this, she knew she'd said the wrong thing. A flash came into Oscar's eyes followed by a dark hatred she'd seen on his face many times before.

Oscar lifted Lola up by her hair. She screamed, trying to fight off the frenzied attack, and kicked, her legs knocking over the tea-set which she only used on high days and holidays. Oscar pulled her through to the tiny kitchen and with one hand lit the gas hob. He yelled at the top of his voice, salivating as he shouted.

'Are you still laughing now, Lola? Do you still think it's funny now?'

Lola tried to shake her head but Oscar had her hair in a tight grip, making it impossible for her to do so. With a yank of his arm, he lifted her up and pressed his other hand on the back of her head, pushing her down towards the flame. Lola managed to turn her head to the side, pleading.

'Please Oscar, I'm sorry, please don't!'

'I can't hear you!'

He pushed her head the small distance to the flame and held it there as the fire seared into her cheek, melting away her skin. Lola fought hard, trying to push away and making desperate pleas the whole time.

After a few seconds, Oscar released her as the strong smell of torched flesh hit his nose. Lola dropped to the floor writhing in agony, with Oscar crouching down to poke her head.

'I'll be here tomorrow at five as arranged. Make sure you get that seen to, Lola, it looks nasty.'

He stood up, smoothing down his hair and wiping away the blood from his lips. 'Oh and Lola? I think you've wet yourself.'

Going to the sobriety meeting in Great Titchfield Street had made Casey feel better; able to put things into perspective. She had renewed energy as she walked through the West End and a feeling of hope which was all too rare in her life.

She thought of Josh again and how they'd stumbled through their few short years of married life. He'd been the ideal husband in every way – it'd been her who hadn't been able to commit. She'd tried, but there was something inside her which wouldn't let her. The only person she'd ever wanted to commit to had been taken away.

Josh had constantly been there to pick up the pieces. He'd been there waiting for her at home, worried out of his mind on the occasions when she hadn't bothered to come back after a night out. There'd never been any recriminations; only tears and pain with Josh begging for assurances that it wouldn't happen again, but it always had. The more it did, the worse she'd felt about what she was doing to him, and the worse she felt, the less she wanted to come home. After they'd come home from Sardinia, Josh hadn't mentioned having another baby until the day she'd found him sitting out in the garden on his own. When she'd walked up next to him, he'd taken her hand and asked her again.

'Casey, won't you even contemplate it? Wouldn't you like to have another child of your own?'

She'd wanted to scream; she didn't understand how he couldn't see having another child to her would be like replacing her baby; it'd be like she was trying to forget – and she could never forget. Equally, she didn't want to hurt Josh, because she could see his pain written on his face, so she'd agreed, but stayed on the pill thinking it'd all be fine; and it had, until their six-week road trip to the States for Josh's birthday when it had all gone wrong. It became the beginning of the end for their marriage.

Soho captivated anybody who walked through it and Casey decided to take a long detour, enjoying blending into the vibrant streets. She walked through Dean Street and into Soho Square, trying to spot the media types and the ones who thought they were. She walked through the green and into Frith Street, marvelling at the social fusion of people; hookers, tourists, restaurant goers, tramps and of course the sex shop connoisseurs; they were all out in force on Saturday night.

After the brawl in the club and after what she'd seen, Casey had been wary about going back there. She hadn't said anything to Lola about the girls but when she'd mentioned the fight Lola had picked up on her apprehension.

'Christ girl, if it's not in Whispers it'll be somewhere else. Wherever there's men, lovie, there's trouble; thought you would've learnt that by now. Just get yourself down there, have some fun; don't let your head get carried away with you. What you going to do if you don't go? Spend the rest of your days alone in your flat playing that bleeding sudoku? Fuck me; I'll have to finish you off meself if that happens. Look, you'll be fine, and besides, Vaughnie

104

wouldn't let anything happen to you. He's one of the good 'uns.'

Lola had winked at her and she'd felt herself blush at the mention of his name.

Perhaps Lola was right and it was all in her head. Taking a deep breath and wondering if she'd been right to let Lola persuade her to come to Whispers, Casey smiled at the formidable looking bouncer and left her jacket with the female cloakroom assistant before heading to the bar.

'Iced water please.'

'I'll get that.'

Casey turned and saw Vaughn behind her. Although the smell of alcohol was heavy in the air, she could still smell the strong, crisp aftershave Vaughn was wearing.

She'd forgotten how handsome and tall he was. Usually, she would've scoffed at the sight of a man in a silk shirt, but the charcoal grey one he was wearing was expensive and well cut; it clung to his body enough to show off his muscular build without looking ridiculous and any doubts she had about him started to slip away.

'It's getting to be a habit, you sneaking up on me and offering to buy me a drink. How about I buy you one?'

'I can't have a woman buying me a drink, goes against my moral code; and especially when she's such a beautiful one. You look exquisite, Casey.'

The lights were too dim for Vaughn to see Casey blush but the way she put her head down, he guessed she was uncomfortable with compliments. He'd known she was stunning but now her hair was freshly washed and her clothes were clean, he couldn't take his eyes off her. Smiling, he touched her back and nodded to the barman for service.

* * *

Alfie peeked out from behind the curtain; it was filling up quickly. On most occasions he would've been pleased to see so many punters come into the club but he was set to go on stage in the next half an hour and he was feeling rather ill at the thought of it.

His tendency to suffer from stage nerves was always bad, but tonight it'd been made worse by the fact he hadn't rehearsed his set. The crazy week had made it impossible to do so, and the two whores he'd picked up had stayed longer than he'd anticipated.

He saw Vaughn sitting down with Casey near the front and the hunched-up figure of Oscar Harding sitting right at the back. Other business associates were dotted round the venue and he could see his henchmen taking their seats at the side walls, making sure that they could keep an eye on any cunt who thought they'd put him off his stride by heckling.

The first open mike act of the night went on and Alfie could hear the laughter, which only added to his stomach flips. He contemplated having a double vodka to steady his nerves but it was a double-edged sword; his nerves would be calmed but he would forget his routine completely.

Each time he stood in the side wings before going on stage he swore he'd never put himself through the trauma again, but then he'd start missing the rush of it; it was like a drug but a whole lot better. He'd dabbled in his fair share of illegal substances and still had a nose for cocaine, but nothing beat the buzz of stand-up, though he was thankful that no one was allowed backstage to see how frightened the mighty Alfie Jennings really was.

Oscar saw Vaughn sitting at one of the front tables with an attractive woman. He recognised her face from somewhere but couldn't think where, but then he wasn't surprised; he saw so many whores every day he never really took much notice of any of them.

He didn't really want to go across but etiquette required it, and as always, Oscar Harding wanted to be on Vaughn's good side. Oscar walked across to the table, ignoring the inexperienced but cocky comedian who was on stage. As he stood in front of Vaughn's table Oscar spoke loudly.

'Good to see you V, how are your roses?'

As Oscar carried on talking, the comedian, cheesed off with the loud interruption and the poor response from the audience, decided to make his feelings known and try to get a laugh.

'Oi, excuse me mate, I was wondering if that was a line in the middle of your forehead, or just the scar where they removed the dick? Do me a favour and shut the fuck up.'

Vaughn looked at Oscar and then at the comedian before sitting back and putting his arm round Casey, ready to watch the drama unfold.

Oscar wasn't sure at first if he'd heard correctly but when it sank in that the guy on stage was trying to make him a laughing stock, he decided to teach the cocky prick a lesson.

Grinning menacingly and winking at Vaughn, Oscar jumped on stage and quietly started to do his best Robert De Niro impression to the guy, with the audience unaware what was going on.

'You talkin' to me? You talkin' to me? Cos I'm the only one here. Who the fuck do you think you're talkin' to punk?'

Vaughn watched in fascination as the comedian stopped smiling and suddenly looked very scared as Oscar went to grab the comedian by his jacket, narrowly missing. Within a moment Alfie ran on stage, not wanting unnecessary trouble in the club after the other night.

'I'm afraid, ladies and gentlemen, it's the end of the show, but we've DJ Spooz on in half an hour, playing classic eighties soul taking you into the night. Thank you and goodnight!'

Alfie threw down the microphone and left the stage; he saw the comic surrounded by the other performers.

'Call the police; I want you to call the police; that man tried to attack me!'

Alfie ignored him and flashed a glance at Oscar, feigning anger but in truth very much relieved he'd got away with not performing his set. For once, Alfie Jennings was thankful for Oscar Harding's erratic behaviour.

CHAPTER FOURTEEN

'You know I'm working in the cafe with his ex-wife?'

'With Lola? God, that place is a hygiene hazard. Last time I was in there, I heard one of the cockroaches phoning health and safety.'

Casey smiled. 'She showed me a scar on her body, told me Oscar had cut her up.'

'Her and hundreds of others.'

'What do you mean?'

'I mean, you best stay away from him.'

'You're the second person who's warned me off.'

'Well then, both of us can't be telling a lie. Come on, I'm starving.'

As Vaughn strode on ahead Casey watched him and wondered, not for the first time, what she was doing agreeing to go out with him. It was obvious there was more to Vaughn than he was letting on, but in a strange way he made her feel things would be alright. She wanted them to be alright, and more to the point, she wanted *him* to be alright. Anyway, what harm could a meal do?

* * *

The restaurant in Chinatown was packed to capacity. Each table was covered with red paper tablecloths and untouched pots of green tea. It was gone midnight and Vaughn had devoured a plate of special fried rice, roast mixed barbecued meat and a large bowl of prawn crackers. He was in the process of eyeing up the Peking duck Casey was pushing round her plate, not having touched any of it.

'How about I order you something stronger than water, and you give me your food? That way we'll both feed our hunger.'

Casey answered him tightly.

'No thanks.'

'Not drinking?'

'Something like that.'

Vaughn carefully scrutinised Casey's reaction to the question; he watched as she fidgeted with her empty glass, putting her finger in it to stir round the ice and stealing a glimpse at him before looking back down again.

'So why are you here, Casey? What's the big secret?'

'No secret; nothing to tell. I just fancied a fresh start.'

'It's hardly a fresh start working in a place like Lola's.'

'Suits me fine. It's uncomplicated. I had a bit of a hard time when I broke up with my last boyfriend; knocked me sideways a bit. Pretty usual stuff really; sorry to disappoint you – there's no mystery I'm afraid.'

Casey smiled, and as she put her head down she hoped the answer she'd given Vaughn would be enough to satisfy his curiosity.

Vaughn walked the short distance from Chinatown back to Soho telling Casey about his roses, still trying to place where he knew her face from. For some reason he could hear an alarm bell ringing even though what she'd said made sense, but throughout his criminal past, he'd rarely ignored his gut feeling and on the few times he had, he'd found himself well and truly stitched up.

The problem also was, he was desperate for there not to be a problem because he liked her; liked her a lot. In the past, he'd never bothered with full-time relationships; he'd enjoyed having his pick of women without the emotional responsibility of them; he wasn't good with matters of the heart.

He'd loved his mother, but not his father particularly. His younger sister, who now lived on one of New Zealand's beautiful coastlines, he also loved; and he loved his goddaughter Emmie, and of course he'd loved Connor. Four people. In all his years, he'd only given his heart to four people, and he knew two of them were by default.

When it came to intimate relationships, once the woman had picked up her Alan Whickers off the bedroom floor, he never gave them a second thought. But like he'd heard them say on the movies he'd hated watching but his mother had always loved, she was different. Casey was different and he was struggling with it.

'You can leave me here. I'm going to have a walk round before I go back to the flat.'

'Here?' Vaughn knew he sounded worried. 'Why don't I walk you back to your flat, Cass? Then if you want to go walkabouts at least I'll know I've done my job and dropped you to your front door. Humour me.'

Casey turned her head away from his warm eyes. She didn't want to get involved; she had too much to worry about without adding more complications.

He twisted her towards him and only for a moment did she find herself resisting. He caressed her face and she leant into his hand, closing her eyes and enjoying the closeness she hadn't realised she was missing.

'Come back home with me, Casey.'

Casey shook her head; she didn't want her old life back, having sex with people she didn't know or care about; but if she were honest she knew that wasn't the real problem. The problem was she liked Vaughn; she liked him a lot, and that meant she needed to keep away.

She couldn't be distracted by Vaughn or by anyone else; it would be all too easy to let herself forget what she was here to do by being with Vaughn, but Casey knew all she'd be doing was burying her head and hiding away as she'd always done, scared of being hurt again. But this was probably her last chance to sort her life out and find her child, and as painful as it might be, this time round Casey was determined nothing would get in her way of doing that.

'Then let me come to your place.' He put his hand under her chin and lifted it up, placing a gentle yet passionate kiss on her lips. Casey could feel the hardness of his body against hers.

'No Vaughn.' She pushed him away and saw the look of confusion on his face.

'What's the matter, Cass? I thought you wanted to?'

'I do, but I can't. I have to go. Goodnight.' She turned and left Vaughn standing on the corner of Brewer Street, confused.

It was four thirty in the morning and the streets were still full of people. Drunks, spurned lovers and disgruntled club goers, left out in the cold. Casey saw them all. She hadn't gone inside when she'd left Vaughn, instead walking through to Piccadilly Circus and down towards Trafalgar Square, and had found a late night bar behind the National Portrait Gallery.

She'd stood outside the bar for a while before walking in. Looking at the array of hard liquor behind the bar had made her involuntarily lick her lips and it'd been on the tip of her

112

tongue to order a whisky chaser, but instead she'd ordered only a juice, to the raised eyebrows of the bartender.

She'd have stayed happily through till sunrise watching Sky News on mute, but the barman had had other ideas.

'Ladies and gentlemen, the bar will be closing in five minutes. Drink up please.'

He'd spoken to Casey as he collected the empties.

'No home to go to?'

'Yes, but not one I'm in a rush to get back to.'

It was getting chilly now and Casey pulled her jacket around her tightly. She'd forgotten to put any money on the key meter and she didn't fancy the walk down Shaftesbury Avenue to the twenty-four-hour newsagents to top it up. The flat would be icy when she got back.

She walked past Whispers Comedy Club, which was all locked up, and stopped as she passed the silver double doors, hearing a noise down the tiny side passage which led to the back door fire exit.

Curiosity got the better of her and she cautiously went to the entrance of the passageway. Craning her neck round the corner she squinted to see who or what it was. As her eyes adjusted to the darkness of the alley, Casey was able to make out the sturdy frame of Alfie. She raised her hand to wave, about to call hello, but she stopped as she made out the outline of three women.

Deciding it was best not to say anything, Casey turned to walk away – and jumped with fright as she stood inches away from Oscar Harding. Fear kicked in and for a second Casey thought about screaming. The sneer on his face was full of hatred and Casey couldn't help picturing Lola's scar. In panic Casey started to explain her reasons for being there.

'Err, I heard a noise; thought it could've been a burglar.'

Oscar continued to stare at her, his face twisted with rage. He grabbed hold of the top of Casey's arm, making her yelp out. He pushed her roughly down the alleyway and through the fire exit into the back room. Once inside, Casey caught a glimpse of Alfie with the three young women slightly in front of him, disappearing down the corridor.

'What the fuck is she doing here?' Alfie glared at Oscar, shutting the door behind him as he came back into the room on his own five minutes later.

'Found her sneaking round the back.'

Casey shot a stare at Oscar and directed what she was going to say to Alfie, trying to keep her voice steady.

'That's not entirely true. I wasn't round the back, I was passing and I heard a noise. And as I said to your friend here, I thought it was a burglar.'

'And you decided to investigate? Seems a little odd.'

'No more so than being bundled in here.'

'Touché.'

Alfie glanced at Oscar, thinking what a prick he was. What the fuck he thought he was doing dragging people off the street, he'd no idea. He was too paranoid.

'I'm sorry Casey; I think Oscar has taken his Robert De Niro impression a step too far. We're cashing up and he gets jittery; thinks all the takings are going to be robbed. Then bang goes his dream of retiring to the Costa Del Sol.'

Casey could feel the tension in the room and she knew Alfie was lying but she didn't know why. She was curious to know about the women and if they were the same girls she'd seen upstairs, but she wasn't so stupid as to ask.

'Why don't I get Oscar to walk you home? Make sure you get there safely.'

The last person Casey wanted walking her home was Oscar, and she certainly didn't want him knowing where she lived.

'No, it's fine, really.'

'I insist.'

Casey could hear the underlying threat in his voice and the way Alfie said it made her aware she had no choice. Without thinking, she spoke. 'I can't because I'm waiting for Vaughn, that's why I'm here; I said I'd meet him outside the club. He's just left me to go and get his car.'

'Vaughn doesn't drive into town.'

'What can I say? It's what he told me. Maybe he's gone to look for a cab.'

Casey looked round nervously at Oscar as Alfie spoke with a wry smile on his face. She could tell he didn't believe her.

'I tell you what, Casey, why don't I give Vaughn a call to clear up this misunderstanding?'

Casey wanted the ground to swallow her up. Why had she said such a stupid thing? All she could do now was hope that Vaughn would back her up. But then why would he? He was Alfie's friend, not hers.

As Casey watched Alfie pick up his phone to make the phone call, she felt her legs start to tremble.

Vaughn Sadler felt the phone ring in his pocket but he didn't have any intention of answering it. He had a good hand and he wasn't about to take a late night phone call in the middle of a card game.

It was after the fifth time that Vaughn, more annoyed he was ten thousand down than by the persistent ringing, answered his phone.

'This better be fucking good.'

'Vaughn, it's Alf. I've got someone here who says they're waiting for you.'

'What are you talking about?'

'Says you were going to get your car.'

'I don't fucking drive my car into town, you know that.

115

Congestion charge; daylight fucking robbery – and I won't drive if I'm drinking.'

'That's what I told her.'

'Her?'

'Casey.'

Vaughn blanched and threw his cards in, gesturing he was out of the game. What the hell was going on? And why the fuck was Casey with Alfie?

'So I take it she's telling me porky pies then, Vaughn? I thought so.'

'Actually Alf, I *was* going to meet her but I decided to give her the big shrug off. Didn't have the heart to tell her. I'm going soft.'

Vaughn listened to the silence, almost able to hear Alfie deciding whether to believe him.

'So what shall I tell her? She thinks you're coming back for her.'

'Tell her I'm sorry but I got held up.'

'I'll get Oscar to take her back.'

'Oscar?'

'Yeah; always the Boy Scout.'

'On second thoughts, I'll be there in ten.'

Sunday lunchtime came and went. Casey was still asleep and Vaughn stroked her hair, kissing her gently on her forehead as she slept. He'd picked her up from the club and they'd jumped in a taxi. He'd insisted she came home with him.

Vaughn had never been the most patient of men and it'd taken him all his willpower not to demand to know what the hell she thought she was playing at sneaking around the back of the club at nearly four in the morning. But all he'd done was keep his mouth shut, show her to one of his numerous spare guest rooms, and let her go to bed.

He'd waited and made sure that she was fast asleep before

having a rummage through her bag, but there was nothing to give anything away. Her mobile phone was devoid of any stored numbers and her purse was almost empty, but he remedied that by slipping in a fifty-pound note. Maybe she had been telling the truth after all, and she was exactly who she said she was. He hoped for his sake she was.

As he sat on the edge of the bed, watching her sleep, Casey stirred and opened her eyes, taking a moment to remember where she was.

'Good morning, or should I say good afternoon, sleepy head.'

'What time is it?'

'Time to tell me exactly what you were doing last night.'

'Why does everyone think *I* was doing something? I went to a bar after I'd left you and on the way home, I walked past Whispers. I heard a noise and before I knew what was happening, Oscar was dragging me into the club.'

Casey gave a half smile but Vaughn scowled; this was the first time he had heard this part of the story and he could feel his jaw tightening.

'Did he hurt you?'

'It's no big deal. It's just a misunderstanding.'

Vaughn got up from the bed and started to pace around the pastel-coloured bedroom furiously. One thing guaranteed to make him come out of retirement and break somebody's legs was scum who pushed women around, especially when it came in the sinister form of Oscar Harding.

'Vaughn, sit down. Really, it's no big deal.' Casey said this knowing she wasn't fooling either herself or Vaughn, but she could see what she'd said was making him angry, and she certainly didn't want to make an awful situation worse. What she needed to do was to try and placate him.

'I'm not a china doll; I'm much tougher than you think. Perhaps it was all a misunderstanding.'

117

Vaughn spoke roughly but not harshly to Casey, his eyes blazing with fury.

'Misunderstanding? Are you for real? Get dressed, I'm taking you home. I've got somebody I need to see.'

Casey pulled on her clothes as Vaughn left the room and worried about what she'd started.

Another person who knew about misunderstandings was Lola Harding. But what her ex-husband had put her through was no misunderstanding. He'd meant every single second of her agony, and as she looked in the mirror at the weeping sore on her cheek, she wished she could pay him back somehow.

Standing in the tiny bathroom with the 1970s avocado bathroom suite, Lola attempted to re-dress her burn with the lint and gauze the hospital had given her.

She'd kept her mouth shut about how it'd happened when she'd gone to the emergency outpatients' in Charing Cross Hospital. The Indian doctor on duty had tried to grill her about the injury but she was used to keeping schtum, and in the end the doctor had given up trying and had sent her home with dressings and antibiotics.

She could feel the tears and she didn't like them; she knew she was feeling sorry for herself but some days her life hit her like a runaway train; her kids were gone, taken from her and put into care, and now they were grown up she knew they wouldn't give her the time to spit on her. She'd tried to be a better mother than her own, who'd introduced her to her pimp at the age of thirteen. A year later Lola was not only a fully-fledged brass but a drug addict as well.

She'd tried so many times to turn her life around, but for some reason she could never quite manage it. She pretended she liked being on the gear – even to herself – but her habit

118

was like a parasite inside her which could never go hungry and always needed to be fed.

A tear running down her face brought Lola back from her thoughts. She looked in the mirror once more and spoke out loud.

'You daft cow, Lola Harding, when did you get so soft?'

She smiled but it hurt like hell. What she really wanted to do now was to get stoned, but Oscar was coming to pick her up and the last thing she wanted to do was to piss him off any more.

Looking again in the mirror at her ravaged face, Lola smiled sadly. It was only in moments like these she saw herself how other people must; a washed-up junkie whore.

If someone came along to show her the way, to teach her how to turn her life around, she wouldn't think twice about grabbing on to them with both hands, but there was more chance of her being seduced by Elton John than that happening. She chuckled at the thought and the more she pictured it the more she laughed. Then she pulled back her shoulders, arranged her top and continued to get ready; single-mindedly making the most of the life she had.

CHAPTER FIFTEEN

'Who was that?' Janine Jennings frowned at her daughter suspiciously as she walked into her overheated bedroom.

'Who was what?'

Ever since they'd come back from the hospital, Emmie had become more secretive than ever. She hoped her daughter had been speaking to one of her friends, but by the way she'd swiftly put her phone behind her back Janine Jennings had a strong suspicion it'd been Jake on the phone.

'Can't you knock, Mum?'

'Yes, and I'll start by knocking your bleedin' head in. I want to know who you were on the phone to, Em.'

'None of your business.'

Janine bit her lip. She really wanted to give Emmie a bit of verbal for speaking to her like that but she knew it wouldn't do any good, so she lowered her voice and spoke softly to her daughter.

'But it *is* my business. I'm worried about you; what's going on?'

'Too late to be worried now isn't it?'

'What's that supposed to mean.'

'It means *none of your bloody business*!'

The last part was shouted, and without thinking Janine stepped forward, slapping her daughter hard on her face, instantly regretting it. She watched as the red welt appeared on Emmie's cheek and the tears ran down her daughter's face.

'I hate you, Mum, you know that?'

'Emmie, I'm sorry, I didn't mean it. You can be a cheeky madam and you know I've a temper on me when I worry.'

'What have you got to be worried about? Running out of chocolate?'

The hurt in Janine's eyes was evident and Emmie hated herself for saying it, but she was furious with her mum. And rather than say sorry and tell her what was really on her mind, she screamed at the top of her voice, angry at her mother, but more angry at herself for her cruel words.

'Get out of my room . . . NOW!'

Within a few seconds of Emmie's outburst, the door opened; it was Alfie.

'What the fucking hell is going on?'

His voice boomed, making Emmie's tabby cat run off her bed in fright. Alfie turned to his wife, then to his daughter for an explanation.

'Will someone please answer me? What is going on in my house? I want to know why I was lying next door hearing you screaming like a frigging banshee, Em.'

Emmie glared at her mother. 'Ask her. Ask her where she took me the other day.'

Janine shot round to face Emmie. She knew her daughter could be a little bitch when she wanted to but she hoped Emmie wouldn't say another word. Surely she could see it was in both of their interests to keep her mouth shut? Janine watched as her husband narrowed his eyes.

'What's she talking about, Jan?'

'I don't know, Alf. Beats me.'

Janine looked at her daughter pleadingly. For a moment she thought Emmie was going to spill the beans, but she picked up her jacket and marched out of the room, much to the relief of Janine Jennings.

'Have I missed something, Jan? Because you know I don't like secrets, especially when it comes to my fucking family.'

'No babe, she's just at a difficult age.'

Janine smiled weakly at Alfie, hoping it was only her who could hear her heart racing.

Emmie squatted low down in the bushes until her dad had driven past. If he saw her, he'd tell her to get into the car and she'd have no option but to go with him. She was going to show her mum and dad she wouldn't be treated like a fool.

She was running late after the run-in with her mum and she'd promised Jake she'd be there now. She'd been both surprised and pleased when he'd called, because she'd got the distinct impression he wasn't too happy to see her when they'd visited him in the hospital.

He'd been due to be discharged but he'd insisted she went and saw him before then. When she'd tried explaining it might be tricky getting out, he'd become annoyed with her.

'Listen Em, if you don't want to bother coming, tell me now and I'll find myself another girlfriend.'

'You know I want to come, Jakey.'

One of Jake's pet hates was anyone calling him Jakey, but he said nothing and let her whine down the phone. She was a spoilt little bitch, but one who was going to be worth something to him – and to Jake Bellingham that's all that mattered. He had very big plans where Emmie Jennings was concerned.

'Well if you want to come, what's stopping you, Em? I thought you loved me?'

122

'I do.'

'Then be here on Sunday. Oh and Emmie, one other thing; I need you to do something for me.'

'Anything Jakey.'

When Jake had told her what he wanted, she'd been reluctant at first and a little afraid.

'I can't Jake. What if Dad finds out? We'll both be dead.'

'But you know where he keeps them?'

'Yes.'

'And you trust me don't you, Em?'

'Yes.'

'Then do as I say and everything will be alright. If you do this, we'll be able to be together without anyone telling us we can't.'

Emmie felt the brown package in her pocket and watched the tail lights of her dad's car disappear into the distance. She wasn't so sure if everything would be okay once her dad did find out but she didn't care. She loved Jake and he'd told her he loved her too, and it was certainly more than her mum and dad did. Every time she started to feel guilty about what she was going to do, Emmie reminded herself of the letters she'd found and instantly her guilt turned to anger, making it easier for her to justify her actions.

'Fucking hell Lola. If you wouldn't mind, I'd like to get there today.'

Oscar took the stairs two steps at a time, turning round as Lola caught her breath. Alfie had called him to say he was running late, something about problems at home; so it was left to him and Lola to deal with the girls.

'Wait up Oscar, I can't breathe.'

Ignoring her, he continued up the stairs in the back of the club. He had a feeling her inability to walk quickly was partly due to her not wanting to be here, but she wasn't fool enough to say no to him and it wasn't as if she could hide; she had nowhere to go. Even if she did, she'd be back in Soho before you could say Old Compton Street. Lola knew nothing but the West End life; she'd be nothing without it.

Oscar walked along the short, dimly lit corridor to the middle door, which was closed and had three newly fitted locks. He knocked.

'Nesha, it's Oscar.'

The sound of the locks being unbolted echoed round the corridor and the few moments it took Nesha to open the door gave Lola enough time to catch up.

Inside it was dark and the room had been divided into two parts. A light shone from under the partition and Nesha showed them through. The two Albanian women stood up from their small camp beds in terror as they saw their captors come in.

'Nesha, tell them we've got a little treat lined up for them. It'll help make their stay more enjoyable.'

Oscar laughed over Nesha's translation while Lola took out her tools of the trade wishing with every bone in her body she didn't have to do it. As she arranged the drugs paraphernalia on the floor ready to prepare the fix, one of the women started to cry and spoke to Nesha, begging him to release them. Lola tried to stay completely unmoved by the display of tears, recognizing she was just as much a prisoner as they were. She spoke to Oscar matter-of-factly.

'I need you to hold them for me; I don't want to pop their vein if they struggle.'

Oscar and Nesha held the women, who didn't put up any resistance as Lola tied the belt tightly around one of their arms. Next she lit the candle and started to heat the drugs on the spoon. The heroin started to bubble and sizzle. Quickly and expertly Lola drew the brown liquid up with the syringe, pulling the belt on the girl even tighter. For a fleeting moment, Lola locked eyes with the frightened woman, before she plunged the needle deep into her vein.

She repeated the procedure on the other girl and almost right away, Oscar could see the heroin taking effect; their eyes started to roll back into their heads, which lolled against the wall, their mouths hanging slackly.

'Leave them now but watch they're not sick later, Nesha; otherwise you'll have dead whores on your hands.'

Lola coughed and the pain from her cheek made her wince.

'What have I missed?' Alfie strode into the room and saw the two women spaced out on the bed. He turned to Lola, about to praise her for a job well done, when he saw the huge dressing on her cheek.

'Bugger me, what happened?'

'Burnt herself cooking, didn't you love? I tell my ex-wife all the time she needs to be more careful; she's no Nigella Lawson.'

Oscar smiled – and Alfie thought it best not to ask any more questions.

CHAPTER SIXTEEN

Casey sat on the wooden chair in the middle of the room looking round at all the expectant faces. She was in an old church hall in Paddington and the draught from the ill-fitting door was chilling all the assembled people, forcing everyone to hunch down in their chairs over their weak cups of tea.

The age range in the room varied from a girl who looked no older than eighteen to an old man who Casey suspected was well into his eighties. All brought together by the realisation alcohol had become their lifeline. She wished she wasn't there, but it was the only way she was going to have a chance of finding her son.

The chair of the group was a well-dressed woman in her early fifties who spoke with a soft Black Country accent.

'I'd like you all to welcome our sharer today, who's bravely agreed to tell her story as part of her twelve-step programme.'

Casey smiled as the group said their hellos.

'Thank you. My name's Casey and I'm an alcoholic. I came down from Birmingham to find my son. The journey to get here hasn't been easy, and I've still got a long way to go, but I refuse to be a victim.'

126

Casey paused, rather embarrassed as a few people clapped.

'When I was fifteen my son was taken away from me before I even had the chance to hold him. I felt powerless, and that's the overwhelming feeling I carry round with me today. Over the years my life has become unmanageable.'

Casey stopped talking but felt a hand on her arm as the chair of the meeting reached over to show her support; letting her know everyone in the room had been on a similar journey.

'Maybe you could share with us why you came to London now, after all this time.'

Casey put her head down, aware of the group watching her.

'I don't usually talk about this to people.'

'Of course you don't have to, but it might help. And you know you're in a safe place, Casey; nothing you say here will be repeated or judged.'

Casey gazed round the room and nervously clenched her fingers together. She was hesitant for a moment and then she spoke in a quiet voice, making those present lean slightly forward to hear her. Fleetingly, it crossed Casey's mind not to say any more but she suddenly realised she needed to talk; needed to let them know she hadn't been a good person. She put her hand in her pocket and felt the diary containing the lock of hair from her son, giving her the courage to talk like Dumbo's feather had given him the courage to fly.

'My husband wanted us to have children and I didn't. I know it sounds selfish but there was no way I could have another baby after my child was taken away from me; it was as if I was trying to replace one with another. Anyway I thought I had everything under control, and then I discovered I was pregnant.'

Shit, shit, shit. Rushing to the bathroom to be sick, Casey tried to ignore Mother Nature's giveaway signs. It'd been ten weeks since her last period but she'd tried to put it down to her drinking, because she was too scared to face the truth.

Casey stared at the pregnancy kit and the smiling face on it telling her the test was positive. Her heart dropped.

She was nearly three months pregnant and they weren't due to fly back to England for another six weeks. Josh had arranged the road trip along the famous route, determined to celebrate at least one of his birthdays in style.

'I want to go home.'

'Casey, you're not doing this to me again, not after the trip to Sardinia. I'm not going to jump when you say jump, especially as you won't tell me why. Can't you just try to enjoy this – or if you can't, at least pretend you are?'

He was putting his foot down to her which he never usually did, and Casey saw he was at breaking point with her. He was angry and hurt and she could tell he was desperate for the holiday to work; so they could work.

She hadn't been able to tell him why she needed to go home and she hadn't been able to convince him to fly home and apart from the four hundred dollars she had after Josh had taken her on a shopping spree, she had no money; she never needed it. Josh always took care of everything, but without an explanation he wasn't going to hand over the price of the airfare. Not now anyway.

She couldn't leave it; by the time they got back home she would be over four months pregnant and she couldn't do that; not that late.

Quietly she got out of bed, leaving the note telling Josh she'd just gone to explore the local town and would be back later, leaving him to sleep off the excess food he'd eaten the night before at the Amarillo Festival.

She'd phoned around and found a clinic who charged only five hundred dollars – the other hundred dollars she'd had

128

to take out of Josh's pocket when he'd gone to the bathroom – and they'd told her matter-of-factly that she'd be done by lunchtime.

The gown the clinic had given her to wear had seen better days. The whole clinic could do with a spruce up, but then people who came here weren't coming to look at the state of the decor; like her, they were looking for a five-hundred-dollar lunchtime solution.

'Mrs Edwards, can you come with me, ma'am?'

The clinic nurse's voice, heavy with a Texas drawl, spoke through the frayed curtained cubicle. Casey closed her eyes for a moment and placed her hands on her stomach.

'Mrs Edwards, if we don't get you in there now we won't be able to do your procedure today.'

'I'm sorry, I'm coming now.'

Casey drew back the curtain and gave a weak smile, catching her reflection in the mirror opposite and wishing she could feel as if she was doing the right thing.

'Cass? Cass? Wake up. Are you okay, honey?'

Casey heard Josh's voice. She had a vague memory of leaving the clinic and making her way back to the hotel, where she'd got straight into bed and had fallen asleep. She remembered hearing Josh come in and speak to her – something about the three-day festival – but she'd been too tired to answer, and sometime later she'd heard the hotel door shut and had fallen back to sleep.

But now she was hot; burning hot; and she could hear Josh's voice speaking to her but she felt unable to answer him.

'Cass, you look terrible. Jesus Casey, you have to lay off the booze. I don't want to give you a hard time but . . .'

Casey heard Josh's voice fade into the distance; she couldn't focus on it. All she felt was heat, and a slicing pain in her

129

abdomen; an unbearable pain which was stopping her moving.

She felt the covers being pulled off, the cool of the air on her bare flesh, but then she heard a shout; Josh was shouting and she couldn't make out why or what he was saying.

'Oh my god Casey, you're bleeding. Oh my god. Hello? Hello? I'm in room 379, I need an ambulance.'

The flashing lights of the ambulance came and went, and the drawl of the Texan voices asking her to open her eyes, asking her if she was alright, asking her to tell them what had happened, filtered through Casey as she fell in and out of consciousness.

Casey's eyes opened and first she saw the lights in the ceiling of the side room and then she saw Josh sitting by her looking worried and perplexed.

'Cass, you're awake. How are you feeling? I was so worried. I've been sitting here out of my mind. They've been trying to tell me some shit, trying to tell me you've had an abortion and that you picked up an infection from it, but I told them they had to be wrong. I told them they must have made a mistake; that perhaps you had a miscarriage because we were trying for a baby, and there's no way you'd terminate our child – because why would you if we were planning a baby? I told them they were wrong . . . Tell me they were wrong, Casey?'

The words rushed out of Josh and his voice quivered with emotion. The pleading look in Josh's eyes to tell him they were wrong made Casey look away. The shame and the guilt she felt made it impossible to look at him. What had she done?

'What have you done, Casey?' He echoed her thoughts and she just managed to speak.

'I'm so sorry.'

Josh didn't move for a few minutes, nor did he say anything; and then he'd spoken words which had felt alive in the savagery of their meaning.

'The doctors think it's probably unlikely you'll be able to have any more children. You got what you wanted, Cass.'

The tears rolled down Casey's face.

'I am so sorry; you have to believe that I didn't want this. I just . . . I can't explain.'

She wanted to scream and tell him she felt unworthy of having another child, she wanted to explain how she was too afraid to bring herself to love another child after spending most of her life disabled by the pain of being without her son, for him to understand the loss inside her was still as great as it was on the day they took her child away from her – but what she wanted to do more than anything was to let him know she was sorry and she'd never set out to hurt him. Except she didn't; she couldn't find the words. So Casey said nothing and stared at Josh, unable to speak.

He'd looked at her with so much hatred before walking away, leaving her passport and an envelope of money. She hadn't seen him again until she'd flown back home, where he'd barely been able to look at her.

Casey stopped and took in the faces of the group; none of them seemed to be judging her and apart from the man who'd fallen asleep on the end, their eyes were full of empathy. She smiled back gratefully. 'I just want to know that my son is alright and that he's happy. That's the most important thing; he's happy.'

As Oscar drove through the city and on to Mile End he decided to stop at his office in Whitechapel. As he pulled up he saw Vaughn standing outside with his face looking like thunder.

131

'This is a pleasant surprise. What can I do for you, Mr Sadler?'

'Don't play fucking games with me, you cunt. I want to know when it became okay to put your hands on Casey?'

Oscar looked round quickly to see if anyone was watching. He didn't want a scene outside his office; he liked to keep a low profile and it was important he was seen as a respectable businessman.

'Shall we go in, Vaughn? We can talk inside.'

Oscar unlocked the brown door of the office with shaking hands. He'd known Casey was going to be a problem the minute he'd seen her in Lola's cafe, and now she was spitting trouble his way.

The moment the door was open, Vaughn pushed Oscar hard, sending him flying into the desk piled with paperwork. He put his hands out to stop him from falling. Vaughn gave him a forearm punch to the back of his head, then twisted him round before driving a clenched fist into his face. 'Vaughn, please, I would never have done anything to hurt her.'

'No? But you pushed her about and that fucks me off big time, Oscar. I've never liked men who bully women. You've made me come out of retirement and that doesn't make me happy.'

'I'm sorry; no harm done.'

'You've mixed me up with someone else because in my eyes, I see a lot of harm done.'

Oscar's speech came in short bursts as he struggled to speak through the pain of his broken nose.

'How can I make it up to you?'

'You can't. I'm toying with the idea of breaking your legs and letting someone stick their fist up yer fucking arse.'

'Come on Vaughn; we're friends.'

'Oscar, let me make something perfectly clear to you. I don't like you; not one little bit. You're the sort of shit I wipe off my shoes every day and if it wasn't for Casey not wanting me to do anything I'd be feeding your dick to my dogs right now. If I ever get wind of you even looking at her the wrong way, I'll be burying you in your own shit.'

Vaughn gave Oscar a final kick on the side of his body before turning and walking out.

As Oscar lay there getting his breath back, he felt enraged; who the fuck did he think he was treating him as if he was something nasty the dog had dragged in? And all over a red-haired piece of pussy. Vaughn Sadler may have the upper hand now, but his time would come. Oscar hoped it would come very soon.

'And you'd tell me if you were?'

Alfie looked Vaughn straight in the eye and lied, 'Yeah, we're friends aren't we?'

'What about Oscar?'

'Oscar? No, I would've known.'

Alfie was trying to hide his irritation at the fact that Vaughn was questioning him. Anybody else would've got a good battering and been thrown out, but Vaughn was one of his oldest standing friends, as good as family. He could trust him; a rare quality in the circles he hung round in, and he wasn't willing to give that up.

Nevertheless, Alfie could feel his fists clenching. It was hardly any of Vaughn's concern what he did and didn't do in his business. Admittedly, he'd struggled to get his head round the girls at first but if it wasn't him who was doing it, it'd be someone else.

The problem was, now Vaughn had retired, he was out of the loop. Business was changing and what people wanted was changing too. There was a demand and he was going to supply it; better than some other cunt reaping all the rewards.

Nobody went round telling Vaughn how to grow his fucking roses, so Alfie expected the same respect back. Of course, he wasn't going to say that, but he *was* curious to know how Vaughn had got to hear about his new venture.

'So who's been talking then? Even if it is shit, I'd like to know, V.'

'I can't say, Alf, but if it isn't true, I wouldn't worry about it.'

'But that's the thing; I do worry, Vaughn.'

Vaughn looked at Alfie and thought it best to change the subject. He'd got the answer he'd needed by Alfie's reaction. One thing he always knew was when Alfie was irritated or lying, and at this moment he was doing both.

He wasn't quite sure how he felt about Alfie lying, or about the situation. There'd been so many times he'd wanted to walk away from Alfie, but he'd made the promise to Connor all those years ago. But surely there was a line? He needed time to mull it over and decide what to do.

It was Alfie who spoke next, trying to lighten the mood.

'How's Casey? You serious about her?'

'Serious enough to break Oscar's legs for him.'

Alfie looked at Vaughn in surprise.

'Oscar?'

'Yeah, funny how you neglected to mention your business partner was a bit free with his hands the other night,' Vaughn spoke pointedly. 'But I had a little chat with him – ruffled his feathers a bit. Though it might be a bit awkward Casey seeing him go into Lola's cafe looking like a fucking poster campaign for disabled Britain.'

Alfie looked down sheepishly. 'You know what he's like. No harm done eh?'

'He's a nasty fucking piece of work, Alf, he's always spelt trouble. It's no skin off my nose, but take my advice and stay well clear mate, otherwise you'll end up regretting it.'

Alfie said nothing, but had the horrible feeling his friend was probably right.

'Is that alright?' Casey smiled at Lola and hoped she wouldn't mind her getting off early. After the meeting she'd decided to pluck up the courage to go round to the address Josh had given her, and she felt she needed to go before she lost her nerve.

'Okay then, but I'll be working you like a dog tomorrow because of it.'

Casey hugged Lola. In the short time she'd been at the cafe she'd become very fond of her boss; she understood her and Casey guessed that Lola understood her too. As she released her from the hug, Casey accidentally banged Lola's face.

'Ouch! Do you want me back in hospital, girl?'

Casey lowered her voice and a look of concern crossed her face.

'Who did it to you, Lola? I can't understand why you won't tell me.'

'Because it's none of your flipping beeswax; it's part of life and part of who I am.'

'But it shouldn't be – I know it's not really who you are. Tell me who it was, Lola, and we can go to the police together. I know some people who might be able to help.'

Lola let out a painful laugh, full of hardness and bitterness. 'Love, this isn't a movie where everything turns into a fucking pink fairy cake at the end. Oh and don't look so worried; everything *will* be alright; if I keep my mouth shut. I've told you before; put up and shut up.'

'But . . .'

'Casey love, there's a lot you don't know about me and a lot of things I've done I'm ashamed of. I try not to be like that any more but maybe this is my payback time. Some things you just can't change, no matter how hard you try. So don't you fret about me; just concentrate on yourself.'

The sound of the cafe door opening made Lola stop talking as both women turned round at the same time to see Vaughn come in. Casey smiled and Lola nudged her, knowing Casey was becoming soft on him but was fighting her feelings.

'Cup of tea, Vaughn – or have you just come to window shop?' Lola chuckled and went to get Vaughn a cup of tea before he'd had a chance to reply.

Casey, slightly embarrassed, pushed back her hair and spoke.

'I wasn't expecting you.'

'I'm actually here to see Lola, but I'd rather be seeing you if I'm honest. It's funny to see you work in here, you look so out of place.'

'I don't really know how long I'll stay; I'm thinking of maybe moving on.'

'Casey, I don't know what you've heard about me, if anything, but my past is my past. If you're in trouble, you know you can always come to me; maybe I can help.'

Casey blushed and looked down at the floor, noticing a line of ants making their way under the table.

'You've got me down as this mystery woman. I'm really not very exciting I'm afraid, I just like to move on that's all. I think it's because my father was in the army and we were always moving. It's in my blood.'

'I thought you said he was a teacher.'

Vaughn stared at Casey, frowning, but before she could answer, Lola came across with a steaming mug of tea.

'Here you are, Vaughn love, get that down you.'

'Can I have a word, Lola?'

'For you Vaughnie, I'll give you the world. And if you're a very lucky boy, I might give you something else.'

Lola winked cheekily and cackled loudly as she sat down

136

with Vaughn, but not before he'd glanced in the direction of a tense looking Casey.

'I'm not asking you to grass, Lola, fucking hell, that'd be like asking you to give up the gear. All I want to know is if it's true; and if it is, where the girls are. Nobody will know you've said anything. I don't know if I'll even do anything with the information, but it'll be worth a bit to you.'

'What's a bit?'

'How about a couple of grand?'

Lola raised her eyebrows and whistled, feeling the soreness of her cheek. What harm would it do? She knew Vaughn well and she knew if he said nobody would know, it was the truth. The only reason she was loyal to Oscar was through fear, nothing else; but what she really wanted was for him to have his comeuppance. Touching her burnt cheek made her decision all the easier, but she didn't want to look too eager.

'Let me think about it, Vaughn.'

'Here's my number; don't leave it long.'

Vaughn wrote down his number on a piece of paper. A moment later the cafe door opened and Oscar walked in, just in time for him to clock Lola taking the number from Vaughn and putting it away in her apron pocket. Vaughn turned and saw Oscar. He stood up and walked across to him. It was the first time he'd seen him since their chat.

'I hope you won't forget what we discussed?'

Oscar spat out his reply not looking Vaughn in the face, angry and humiliated he was being dressed down in public.

'As if I could, Vaughn. You made your feelings perfectly clear.'

'I'm glad I did.'

Vaughn patted Oscar on his chest menacingly before turning to Casey.

'I wondered if you fancied going for a meal tonight?'

'I don't know if that's a good idea.'

'Casey, I'm not asking you to marry me; I'm asking you to come out for a meal with me as a mate.'

Casey softened. 'I'd like that very much.'

'Great, I'll pick you up at eight.'

Vaughn waved goodbye to Lola and Casey, and as Oscar stared after him he was already planning a way to wipe the cheesy fucking grin off Vaughn Sadler's face.

CHAPTER SEVENTEEN

The restaurant in Greek Street was deceptive from the outside; it was unadorned with a drab blue and white painted exterior, but once inside there was opulent splendour everywhere. Magnificent hand-carved wooden panels went along the full length of the walls, and the red velvet sofas in front of the burning log fire were trimmed with gold. The music was playing softly and each alcove was lit by candles, making it feel peaceful – in stark contrast to how Casey was feeling.

After leaving Lola's cafe she'd gone back to the flat and got ready, changing her clothes several times and breaking down into tears when the zipper on her skirt had broken. Her immediate thought had been to have a drink, but she knew herself well enough to know when she'd probably end up hitting the self-destruct button to avoid facing up to her problems. She'd had to sit with her head in her hands for the craving to pass and eventually it'd gone.

Twenty minutes later she'd found herself standing outside a tall grey tower block on the outskirts of Soho, just behind Drury Lane. It was on a rundown estate, and the thought of her baby son being brought here sixteen years ago to live with strangers made Casey experience the same sense of desperation she'd felt all those years ago.

The people Casey wanted to see were a Mr and Mrs Simms; foster parents to her son and hopefully a gateway to more information. She needed to know if he was well; if he was happy; if he was even alive. Her last thought startled her and she quickly rang the buzzer, which was engrained with dirt. There was no answer so she tried again, giving up after half an hour.

What had she expected? She'd been so busy building up the courage to go there, it hadn't once crossed her mind they might be out; and as Josh had reminded her, they might not even be living there any more.

Maybe Josh had been right about everything. She'd been a bitch to him and she hadn't liked herself for it. After they'd got back from the States she'd found him crying late one night. Casey had looked at him and in that moment she knew he deserved to be loved so much better. He was a good man and he shouldn't have to suffer because of her. Shortly after, she'd packed her things and left without saying goodbye.

For the next eighteen months she'd drifted from place to place drinking, picking up men and trying not to think; then she'd seen the date on the calendar: it was her baby's sixteenth birthday. She knew she had to do something about her life; to try to make up for all the mistakes she'd made – but first of all she had to find her son.

Subdued, she'd walked past the club on the way to the restaurant and seen Alfie head to head in deep conversation with Oscar sitting at a table outside. Seeing them together made her feel on edge; it brought back the memory of the women she'd seen in the club, which left her with a sinking feeling each time she thought of it.

* * *

As Casey sat in the warm atmosphere of the restaurant she couldn't help thinking more about the women. There was something not quite right but she wasn't quite sure what it was, and as much as she didn't want to get involved in anything, she also couldn't ignore her unease at the situation. She didn't know if she was being foolish but she decided to try to talk to Vaughn, albeit very carefully.

'Can I talk to you? It's probably nothing and I'm probably being silly, but I saw something at—'

'Oh god, that's all I need,' Vaughn interrupted Casey as he waved to a group of women coming up from the basement.

'Janine, what you doing here? Does Alfie know you're up West?'

Janine chortled and slapped Vaughn on his back. She spoke loudly, making the other customers turn round and stare.

'Eh, what the eye don't bleeding see, then the heart won't mind.'

Vaughn smiled, knowing it wasn't a case of Alfie's heart minding, more a question of him not wanting Janine to catch him with his dick up some hooker's arse. But of course he didn't say anything.

'I came up here to celebrate my mate's birthday, but he thinks I've gone to see me Auntie Nan in Chigwell. You know what he's like.'

Vaughn nodded; he knew exactly what Alfie was like. Suddenly realising he was being rude, Vaughn introduced Casey to Janine.

'This is my friend Casey, Casey this is Janine; Alfie's wife.'

Casey offered her hand, but Janine looked at it with so much disdain Casey had to take a quick glance to see she didn't have something on it. Janine continued to talk in between shooting Casey icy glances and laughing raucously at her own jokes. Eventually she said her goodbye to Vaughn and waddled off with her friends.

'Sorry about Jan, she's like a tiger. She probably thinks you're just a . . .'

Vaughn trailed off as Casey stared at him. She decided to ignore what Vaughn was going to say; there were more important things to discuss than Alfie's wife thinking she was a whore. Before Casey could speak, Vaughn's phone rang.

'Sorry Cass, I should get this. Hello?'

Vaughn listened to the familiar voice of the caller on the other end of the phone.

'It's Lola, I'm on my way to the cafe. Can you meet me in half an hour?'

'That was quick; I got the impression you wanted more time to think about it.'

'Not me, sonny Jim, I'm a fast mover; thought you'd know that by now.'

Vaughn smiled but moved the phone away to stop the cackle of laughter hurting his ear.

'No problem, I'll be there.'

Putting down the phone, he watched Casey take a large bite of her bread roll; he'd wanted to try to get to know her and he felt genuinely apologetic as he spoke.

'I'm sorry Cass, I have to go. Can you tell me tomorrow what you were going to say?'

She was surprised how upset she felt at his leaving and hoped it wouldn't show on her face or in her voice.

'Do you want me to come with you? I can tell you on the way.'

'No, it's a bit of business I have to sort out. You stay here and finish munching and I'll call you tomorrow. I'll leave some money with them for the bill on the way out. Feel free to have whatever you want.'

He went to kiss Casey on her lips but she turned her face slightly to receive it on her cheek instead.

* * *

142

Bateman Street was dark; two of the street lights had been vandalised and the place was deserted, save for a wino drinking from what looked to Vaughn like a bottle of turpentine.

Vaughn put his collar up, feeling the cold of the London air, and continued down the road with the distinct feeling somebody was watching him.

As he approached the cafe, Vaughn turned round at a noise and was relieved to see it was a dog going through the black bin bags left out for the early morning collection. He smiled at how jumpy he was becoming in his retirement. Quickly taking another look round, he knocked quietly on the cafe door.

'Lola, it's Vaughn; open up.'

The two grand sat in four neat piles on Lola's rickety kitchen table. It was the easiest money she'd ever made. All Vaughn had wanted was the nod and the whereabouts of the girls. He hadn't asked for anything else so it hadn't felt as if she was grassing anyone up. Hopefully Vaughn would do something about the girls locked up like canaries in a cage.

Pleased with herself, she walked into the bathroom and ran the hot water in the bath. Lola put the radio on full blast and started to hum the tune to a club mix of Rhianna's 'Umbrella'.

She hadn't been on holiday in a long time; maybe she'd go and visit her mate in Wilmslow in Cheshire who was serving a six-year term for firearms offences in Styal prison. She'd been up there before and as much as she was a city chick, a few days amongst the hedgerows might be good for her. If she played her cards right she might be able to pull one of them posh country blokes. She chuckled out loud at the thought of her being a lady of the manor.

'Care to share the joke?'

Lola nearly wet herself in fright as she heard the voice right behind her.

'Oscar! Fuck me, you pretty much turned me skin inside out. What are you doing here?'

'Maybe I should start off by asking what *you* were doing with Vaughn Sadler.'

Lola swallowed hard and felt her heart racing. She'd thought she'd been careful; made sure no one was around. It crossed her mind for a moment that Vaughn had said something to Oscar, but it was probably the least likely explanation. She didn't think Oscar had seen her take Vaughn's number when he came into the cafe, but he must have done. The only thing left for her to do now was something her mum had always drummed into her; deny bleeding everything.

'I don't know what you're talking about, O.'

Oscar glared at Lola, who looked guiltier than a kid getting caught with their hand in a biscuit tin. Living with her, he'd learnt to read the signs when she was lying to him; she folded her arms as she was doing now and she'd unconsciously bite her bottom lip. As Oscar Harding stood in the bathroom, which was filling up with steam, he knew right away his ex-wife was hiding something.

He was starting to get a migraine and he could see the specks of white in front of his eyes. He could feel the anger towards Lola and he was struggling not to smash her face in and let the blood run into her mouth as it choked her.

He wanted to show her the consequences of disloyalty, but first he wanted answers. Oscar was determined to know what exactly she'd told Vaughn.

'I saw you, Lola; I saw you take his number.'

'That was nothing; he said he knew someone who could get me a deal on meat for the cafe. Save me a few bob.'

'And that was all?'

'Yes.'

'I don't believe you. Funny that.'

Lola wasn't finding anything about the situation funny; in fact she was downright scared.

'You see Lola, I couldn't get the image of you and Vaughn out of my mind; so I came to pay you a visit to discuss things. I waited outside for a while and then I saw you coming out of the flat and I followed you. I saw you go into the cafe, Lo, and then when I was coming away fuck me, what do you know? A few minutes later I saw Vaughn and I followed him and guess where he went? To the cafe. Now don't try to insult my bleedin' intelligence and tell me your late night meeting was about sausages and fucking bacon. And I for one know old Vaughnie values his dick enough not to shove it up your rancid fanny, so he wasn't looking for a taste of pussy. So tell me, what was it all about eh?'

'I don't know what to say; it was nothing.'

'Nothing. Is this nothing?' Oscar grabbed hold of her face and he brought his knee up to the side of her skull. Lola screamed and started to talk.

'Okay, okay. He just wanted to know about the girls. He knew about them anyway.'

'What did you tell him?'

'I told him you had a few girls, that's all, I swear.'

'That's all?'

Oscar smiled and as Lola nodded, he brought down his fist and smashed her hard in the face. Picking her up under her arms, Oscar threw Lola head first into the burning hot bath and watched her struggle. He pushed her down with his booted foot. Lola's mouth filled with water as her face slowly submerged. He wanted her to feel every last moment of a snitch's punishment. He smiled to himself and rolled up his sleeves; he was going to enjoy this.

* * *

145

Walking through Lola's kitchen ten minutes later, Oscar stopped to pick up the money, seeing it as payment for his trouble.

Even though she'd eaten alone, Casey had enjoyed the meal in the restaurant. It'd been the best meal she'd had since coming to London and it was certainly a welcome change from Lola's greasy meals. Her mind had been racing, but she'd been able to decide what she needed to do next. Casey walked home and was about to turn into Dean Street, when she suddenly remembered she was supposed to be opening up the cafe in the morning and had rushed off without taking the spare set of keys.

'Shit.'

Sighing, Casey pulled out her phone to call Lola. It rang several times, and Casey cursed again as she willed Lola to pick up the phone, hoping she'd agree to do the early morning opening instead. It was no good; she'd have to go round there. Annoyed with herself, Casey turned round and headed off to Lola's flat on the east side of Soho.

CHAPTER EIGHTEEN

'I need you to bring me one more packet, Em – this isn't enough.'

Emmie looked at Jake, sitting smoking a large spliff on the Dralon couch which was making her skin itch, and she decided she wanted to go home. She'd been excited when he'd discharged himself from hospital, thinking they'd spend some quality time together cuddling up watching movies, but Jake had had other plans and Emmie was starting to think he was using her, as well as thinking it'd been a mistake to get involved. If it hadn't been for her finding the letters she would never have betrayed her dad like this, but it was her way of getting back at him; she wanted to hurt him like he had hurt her.

'Jakey please, I told you I won't be able to bring you any more. I don't know why you want them anyway.'

Emmie leant in to kiss Jake but he pushed her away roughly; she repulsed him. Her spoilt behaviour and her whining had put paid to the idea of screwing her but for the time being, he still needed her.

'Do you want me to blow you, Jake?'

Jake looked at Emmie's pouting lips. She was trying to look sexy but it wasn't working; all it was doing was making her look stupid. He wasn't even sure she knew how to give

147

a blow job, she was always so frigid and uptight; but his mind was on better things anyway.

He'd only have to put up with her moaning for a little while longer and then he'd be rid of her, but in the meantime he'd have to try and keep his cool with the silly bitch. He was so close, and all he needed was for her to bring him one more package.

He was planning to take over from Chris Wardale, who'd been the main dealer for the Stonebridge area of Wembley. Chris had just been banged up and was looking at a nine stretch for supplying class As, and Jake had seen it as an opportunity for him to stop being a nobody and become a face.

He was sick of being pushed around and although he was a Bellingham, he was so low down in the ranks he hardly got the respect he felt he deserved. If all went to plan, the likes of Alfie Jennings would be sorry they ever messed with him.

He'd been to see Johno Porter who was the number one clinch of the whole of Wembley and a cousin of his mother's, to ask permission to start dealing on his turf. Johno had laughed at him at first and seen him just as a spotty kid, until he'd showed him some of his supply.

'And you can get hold of more of this?'

'Yeah, I told you I'm good for it and it's quality stuff.'

'I had been thinking of putting Wardale's number two in charge,' Johno said. 'He knows the area, the customers and what to look out for. It'd be less hassle all round. But I guess family comes before everything else.'

'I won't let you down, Johno.'

Johno had grinned, showing his crooked teeth in a menacing smile.

'That's right you won't, otherwise they'll be fishing pieces of you out of the Thames and I'll have to explain to your mother what happened. And what's all this shit I hear about you and Jennings's daughter? I can't have you bringing any trouble to the area for a bit of cunny. I can see they did you over good and proper.'

Jake squirmed; he didn't like to be reminded of what had happened. His body still ached. His ribs were still strapped up, as were his fingers; and by the end of the night, his mouth usually ended up bleeding, causing him so much pain he needed to pack his spliff with extra skunk to dull the throbbing.

'That's all finished, she's out of the picture now.'

'Glad to hear it. So if we're going to do this, you need to know what I charge. It's important for you to understand what my cut is; we don't want any misunderstandings.'

Jake shook his head and hoped one day he'd be able to exude as much power over people as Johno Porter did.

'For every three kilos, I expect one.'

Jake was shocked. He was expecting it might be over the top, but one kilo of heroin for every three sold was by anyone's standards excessive. Without thinking, he spoke.

'Fuck me, bit steep isn't it Johno?'

Jake Bellingham saw the sour look spread across Johno's face, and it was a few moments before it spread into a smile.

'I like your honesty, Jake. You're right, it is a bit steep, but when *you're* a face, you can make the rules. Until then, family or not, that's the deal. Show me all the goods by the end of the month, give me my share upfront, and you've got yourself your first piece of turf. Welcome to the firm.'

Johno had leant across the table and shook Jake's hand. Finally he was going to become someone.

'Jakey?'

Jake's thoughts were broken by Emmie's whining and her attempts at trying to undo his G-Star jeans. Jake clasped hold of Emmie's hand and spoke, trying not to let his irritation show in his voice.

'No thanks Em, I told you what the doctor said; no

149

excitement. I was lucky not to have internal bleeding after what your dad did.'

He looked at Emmie and saw her cheeks flush; he knew she felt guilty and he was happy to play on it. She was a spoilt brat trying to play the sexy grownup when really she was just a child; but she was also needy and seemed pretty fucked up, and that suited Jake Bellingham down to the ground.

'Maybe I could see if I could get another packet. I'm sure he won't miss it, and anyhow, he'll never guess it was me.'

'That's my girl. How about you run along and try to get it and then we can concentrate on us? Perhaps when you do come back, maybe you could try that blow job you were talking about.'

'What about the doctor's orders?'

'What about them?'

Jake winked at Emmie, amazed at her stupidity. Couldn't she see the only reason he was being nice to her was to get his own back on Alfie? He was going to enjoy using Emmie to help him get his revenge.

Alfie counted the packages for the sixth time, crouching on the floor of his office. He couldn't have made a mistake. it was hardly rocket science to count up to thirty. But it wasn't thirty he was counting, it was twenty-three. Twenty-three packages of heroin when there should've been thirty.

It'd only been two weeks ago he'd taken five out from behind the fake fireplace and sold it to Scottish Charlie, and he was certain there were thirty left. Seven packets missing was equivalent to nearly seventy grand.

Alfie chewed on his thumb, spitting the skin out of his mouth and onto the wooden floor. He knew he wasn't losing his mind, so he wanted to know how the fuck they could've done a disappearing act.

However, Alfie knew *how* they came to vanish was the

150

least of his worries at the moment. He was supposed to be handing the packages over to Oscar today and now he was well and truly fucked unless he came up with another seven packets – or seventy grand.

It was useless even trying to stall Oscar. He knew he wanted it today. Oscar had told him it was going to be couriered to Newcastle by some of his men and distributed up there, so everything had already been arranged.

This heroin had been separate from the stash he and Oscar had owned together, which had already been given to the Albanians in exchange for the first lot of girls. This batch had been his and his alone, therefore it was his responsibility and he had no business partners to turn to now it had started to go wrong. The only way of replacing it was to buy some more from his contacts or give Oscar the money back he'd already paid for it. Either way, it meant coming up with some money, and Alfie knew that was impossible.

His money flow had been tight recently. He'd ploughed a lot of money into the club, bought some flats in Stratford which had been going for a song with the money he'd got from selling the smack to Oscar, and the remainder had paid for his share of more girls and that had completely wiped him out after he lost nearly five hundred grand on a bad money deal. The money situation was tighter than it'd ever been since he'd started out. Once upon a time he'd have sneezed away seventy grand in a day, but things were different now. Seventy grand might as well be seven million. He owned a lot of properties but most of them were re-mortgaged up to the hilt.

The only person Alfie knew with the sort of amount he needed was Vaughn. Picking up the phone, he dialled his number.

'Vaughn. It's Alf; I've got to pull in a favour. Can you shoot over to me? I'm at the house in Essex.'

* * *

151

After the phone call from Alfie, Vaughn had jumped in his car to make his way down to Essex. The phone call had been tense, with Alfie sounding worried but pretending he wasn't. Vaughn had known him long enough to know when he was under pressure.

Vaughn always enjoyed going to the Jennings household and seeing the family. He had a soft spot for Janine and even though she was a loudmouth, he couldn't help but like her. Emmie had always been in his heart from the moment he'd seen her. Sometimes when he looked at her it made him regret not having children of his own.

Today was going to be the exception to the rule, however. Today Vaughn knew he wasn't going to enjoy his visit; and once he'd finished, he doubted Alfie would either.

Janine opened the newly painted cream front door and greeted Vaughn with a welcoming hug. 'Alright Vaughnie, how's it going?'

'Fuck me Jan, you'd put a grizzly bear to shame, nearly broke my ribs. Where's the old man?'

'Moping about in his office. He's been like a skunk without his stink all morning. I dunno what's wrong with him.'

'How's Emmie?'

Janine smiled at Vaughn. She always appreciated the way he asked after Emmie and treated her like his own; not that the little cow deserved it – she was turning into a little minx and it was starting to get on her nerves.

'Out, ain't she. But I'm telling you V, she's winding me up like a bleedin' jack in the box. I swear I'm going to swing for her. There's something going on in that girl's head and by Christ I'm going to get to the bottom of it.'

Vaughn gave Janine a loving squeeze of the arm. She never changed; whenever he saw her she was either moaning about

Alfie or Emmie, but Vaughn knew she loved them both ferociously.

'Go through, he's in his office. Maybe you can cheer him up.'

Vaughn Sadler doubted that very much.

The mahogany office wasn't to everybody's taste, and it certainly wasn't to Vaughn's. It always reminded him that people who had money didn't always have taste. He knew a lot of it was down to Janine buying *Country Living* magazine and trying to emulate the lifestyle, thinking having a panelled office in a mock Tudor Essex mansion somehow made her part of the landed gentry.

Vaughn yawned; he was only half listening to Alfie explain about the smack, and about Scottish Charlie.

'I reckon I must have counted it wrong and somehow Charlie did me over good and proper, but how? That's what I can't get me head around. I had my eye on the ball every moment, but what other explanation could there be? He's the only one who's been near the stuff – but fuck me Vaughn, I'm sure I never left the room. But the more I try to think about it, the less I can remember anything.'

Vaughn looked at his friend; he really didn't give a shit who took it, whether it was Scottish Charlie or Welsh fucking William, it meant nothing to him.

'So Vaughn, look, I'm short of the readies at the moment and I need a loan. We can say twenty per cent on top. I can't have Oscar on my back.'

Vaughn finished off the expensive brandy and put the glass on the small table next to him. He looked at his brown suede brogues and saw they needed a clean. Sighing, he spoke.

'I'm afraid I can't do that, Alf.'

Alfie's face dropped and Vaughn saw the panic on it.

153

'Okay, let's say thirty per cent interest. Christ, you drive a hard bargain.'

'It's not the interest; I'd be happy to give it interest free.'

'So what's the problem?'

'The problem's you, Alf. You lied to me.'

Alfie was puzzled; he'd no idea what Vaughn was talking about. 'You've lost me.'

'I asked you about the girls, Alf, and you looked me straight in the face like I was a cunt and told me you weren't farming. I did a bit of digging and I found out you are. And now you expect me to give you a loan. No chance.'

'It's business. For fuck's sake, Vaughn, the only reason I didn't tell you was I knew you'd be like this. Since you've retired you've lost your balls.'

Vaughn stood up and faced Alfie, standing over him in height and menace. 'I'd watch what you say if I were you. I haven't lost anything. I'm old school; pimps and brass is one thing, been around forever and always will. But what you're doing is bang out of order.'

'You're kidding yourself; it's exactly the same. Buying and selling flesh. The strong and the vulnerable. In our game there isn't room to be fucking soft, you know that.'

'It isn't my game and it will never *be* my game, Alf, because I won't deal with nonces and I won't deal in this.'

'A hooker's a hooker, no matter where they're from.'

'They are, but there's a big fucking difference between toms and traffic. Okay, you've got the pimps, but you and me both know the majority of toms choose that life. Granted sometimes life chooses them out of need, greed or fuck knows what else, but they've still got their freedom to come and go – they haven't got cunts like you and Oscar locking them up and choosing their life for them.'

'You're a fucking romantic, Vaughn. The brass here are as trapped as the rest of us.'

'Maybe so, but I've told you my point of view and I won't play any part in it.'

'But you're not playing any part in it. I'm asking you for a loan.'

'You don't get it, Alf; whilst you're doing what you're doing, I don't want any part in you.'

Vaughn ignored the desperation in Alfie's voice as he pleaded with him.

'You can't do this to me! We're mates and we have been for years. And what about the promise you made my brother? What about that?'

Vaughn headed for the door but stopped in his tracks. He didn't know Alfie knew about that – but then why wouldn't he? Years ago he'd told Janine about it and telling her anything was like reporting it on CNN. Angrily he turned round to face Alfie.

'Don't you dare use that against me, Alfie. I promised to look out for you, but that didn't include you being able to do exactly what you wanted and I stand by like a fucking noodle and foot the bill. So like I say, stop doing what you're doing and then we can talk.'

'But it's none of your business what I do.'

'I know, but it *is* my business who I give my money to.'

'And what the fuck am I supposed to do once Oscar finds out his gear is missing and I haven't got the money to pay him back?'

'One word, Alfie. Run.'

Oscar sat in his car behind the coach full of kids giving V signs out of the back window. What he really wanted to do was pull out the gun which was safely hidden in the panel under his seat and give the little fuckers the shock of their lives when he shot one of them through the window. He didn't fancy serving a life term for a

155

snotty-nosed kid though, so instead he tried to ignore them as best he could.

He was off to meet Alfie at his house in Essex. He usually met him in the club or at one of his other properties but this time Alfie had insisted on him coming to Essex. He'd never been invited to the family house before but Oscar suspected the reason for that was because Alfie had been trying to hide his whale of a wife.

As the traffic crawled forward, Oscar's mind moved to Lola. He reckoned it'd be a couple of weeks or more until anyone discovered her. The cafe would of course be shut, but he hoped people would see it as a blessing in disguise – or at least their stomachs would. She was the only one who lived on the top floor of the block, so the neighbours wouldn't complain of the smell for some time, and she'd no family to speak of. She had three kids but they'd been taken into care a long time ago. They were all grown up now and no doubt popping out unwanted kids of their own.

He thought it best not to tell Alfie about Lola; let everyone think it was some punter or pissed-off drug dealer. As long as he kept it to himself, he was sure everything was going to be fine; he was hardly going to grass on himself.

The traffic started moving and Oscar sped off, overtaking the coach and moving into the fast lane of the motorway. The only other problem was Vaughn; he wasn't sure what he was going to do about him. If it was anybody else he would've taken his men and put a hammer to his head, but with this man it was different. He was going to have to think very carefully what to do with him.

Oscar drove along the motorway towards the Jennings house. He hated the countryside, though he suspected not everyone would call Essex the countryside. As he slowed down behind another queue of traffic, he noticed the flowers on the verge moving hypnotically in the cool breeze. He saw the cows in the lush green fields and he smelt the manure of the farmer's field – and he detested everything about it.

Parking in the large white pebbled stone driveway of the Jennings's Essex mansion, Oscar saw Alfie's anorexic daughter walking into the house. He beeped his horn and waved but she turned round and scowled and continued to go inside. Oscar was annoyed, and he could feel a slight throb to his head. Even if she didn't remember him from the club, it was still disrespectful to ignore him, and one thing Oscar hated was bad fucking manners.

Getting out of the car he stretched his legs, admiring the house and the grounds they stood in. It was located within an exclusive private estate. He remembered Alfie had told him it had eight bedrooms and the same number of bathrooms, as well as four receptions and a conservatory which at first he hadn't got planning permission for, but he'd given a large backhander to one of the men on the board and the next day he'd got the green light.

Oscar reckoned it must have cost at least four million plus. He knew Alfie had always done alright for himself and was a shrewd businessman, but he'd no idea just how alright. This house was very nice indeed.

Oscar noticed the two empty glasses on the table next to the chair and wondered who Alfie had been entertaining. He doubted he'd been cosying up to his wife, not from the way he'd spoken to her when she'd shown him through.

'Thank you Janine, you can piss off now.'

'Do you want me to bring you some biscuits through? Or I could always rustle you up a bit of dinner.'

'What the fuck part of "you can piss off now" don't you understand?'

She'd said nothing else and quickly closed the large panelled door.

'It's a pukka place you've got here, Alfie.'

'It suits us.'

Oscar noticed how edgy Alfie looked as he spoke. He was pacing up and down and had poured himself two large brandies in the space of ten minutes.

'A bit jumpy aren't we?'

'There's been a little bit of a problem,' Alfie spoke quickly as Oscar stared at him. 'Nothing that can't be fixed mind, but a problem nonetheless.'

'Go on.'

'The packages. There are a few less than expected.'

Oscar continued to stare hard at Alfie. He couldn't quite believe what he was hearing. He didn't think Alfie was the sort of man to try and rip him off; he wouldn't be so stupid.

'When you say "a few less", how few?'

'Seven. Fuck knows, for the life of me I don't know how. I can't understand it.'

'But you took the money; you nearly chewed my fucking hand off to take it. I paid you because I thought you were good for it.'

'I know you did, Oscar; but you know me, I wouldn't try to pull a fast one on you, I wouldn't do that.'

'You better not, Alf, because it doesn't take a lot for me to think someone's taking advantage of my good nature.'

'Give me till the end of next week and I'll come up with the money or the goods.'

'Too long I'm afraid; I want the money by Friday.'

'But I won't be able to get it by then.'

Unblinkingly, Oscar spoke coldly.

'That's not my problem, it's yours.'

* * *

Emmie leant on the door and listened to her father talking. She was terrified both for herself and for him. She'd no idea he would discover the packages were missing so soon; they'd been there for ages behind the fake fireplace and she really hadn't thought he'd notice. But now it sounded like her dad was in trouble.

She'd been stupid, and she didn't know what she'd been thinking; she'd wanted to please Jake because she'd thought he'd loved her, even though nothing she seemed to do made him happy, but mainly she'd wanted to get back at her mum and dad. Why hadn't they told her? She loved them so much, but when she'd read the letters she realised she didn't know them at all.

Emmie could feel her legs shaking; there was no way she could tell her dad what she'd done and why. Perhaps Jake might give her the packages back if she told him her dad was in trouble.

The door was opened and Emmie jumped back. Alfie looked surprised to see Emmie but he said nothing and introduced her to Oscar.

'You met my daughter at the club; this is Emmie.'

'Nice to meet you, Emmie. I'm Oscar, a good friend of your dad's.'

Oscar glanced at Alfie and gave a tight smile.

'You've got till Friday. I'll let myself out. Nice meeting you, Emmie.'

CHAPTER NINETEEN

Casey was cold with sweat. She'd fallen asleep in the chair and had a bad dream, with images of the past whirling round in her head. When she'd woken up she hadn't known where she was until she heard the beeping of the monitors and saw Lola lying unconscious on the hospital bed in front of her.

She'd gone round to Lola's to try to get the keys but she hadn't got an answer. Casey had been ready to give up but a man had come out of the block of flats leaving the security door unlatched, and she had taken the opportunity to slip inside.

When she'd got to Lola's landing Casey had hammered on the door, hearing the sound of the radio blaring out from inside the flat.

'Lola, open up, it's Casey.'

Guessing Lola wasn't able to hear her over the sound of the music she'd looked through the letterbox. In front of her Casey had seen the bathroom door slightly ajar, with the body of a naked woman lying motionless on the floor.

'She's lucky to be alive. You probably saved her life. Any longer I doubt she'd have made it.'

Casey turned round to the voice of the nurse coming into the room to check the monitors.

'When do you think she'll come round?'

'I'm not sure; it's early days yet. You should go home and get some sleep.'

The nurse smiled at Casey and left the room. She hated hospitals but she was loath to leave in case Lola woke up. From what she'd seen she didn't have anyone who cared for her, and Casey wanted to be there for her when she regained consciousness. Taking out her phone from her bag, she dialled a number.

'Vaughn, it's Casey.'

'Hello you, what do I owe this wonderful pleasure to?'

'I'm in the UCH, the hospital on Euston Road.'

'Are you okay?'

'I'm fine but Lola isn't. She's been attacked.'

There was a long pause on the phone before Vaughn spoke.

'I'll come over straight away.'

'No, really it's fine, I . . .'

The phone was put down at the other end and Casey guessed he was on his way.

'Jesus, Cass. How can you live in this dump?' Vaughn spoke as he walked into the front room after picking Casey up from the hospital. She wasn't sure if she should be insulted or not. Vaughn's question just echoed what she thought every time she came back to the flat in Dean Street, so she guessed it'd be hypocritical to take offence. *She* knew why she was here, but she wasn't about to start telling her life story to Vaughn.

'I can't afford to be choosy, and it won't be forever; but do yourself a favour, don't use the bathroom.'

'Why not?'

'Just trust me. Can I make you a cup of tea?'

'Thank you. I didn't mean to be rude.'

Casey smiled at Vaughn. Each time she was around him, he made her feel good about herself; safe even. It was stupid because she hardly knew him, and the small amount she'd heard about him through the gossip in Lola's cafe would usually have her running a mile.

'She doesn't look good does she? The nurses said she's lucky to be alive.'

Casey talked as she made the tea, and saw her diary lying on the top of the work surface. She quickly hid it behind the torn wallpaper, making sure Vaughn hadn't seen her do it. She knew it was silly but the idea someone would read her thoughts frightened her.

Finished with the tea, Casey turned round to speak to Vaughn seriously.

'I wanted to talk to you about something else. You'll probably think I'm stupid, but it's been playing on my mind – and after what's happened with Lola, well . . .'

Casey trailed off, wanting to be careful how she approached it. 'The night of the fight in the club, I know I told you I was waiting on the stairs but I actually went up them to keep out of the way. Anyhow, I tried one of the rooms and it was locked, and then I tried another,' Casey rushed out her words as she spoke, not knowing what his reaction would be, 'and admittedly maybe I shouldn't have gone in the storeroom but . . .'

Vaughn laughed nervously. 'You saw a whole lot of televisions and electrical goods which would put Comet out of business.'

Casey's face stayed serious and Vaughn started to get a bad feeling. 'Yes, but that's not it. When I was in there I heard some voices and I hid and I saw a guy with two women.'

162

Vaughn interrupted, trying to make light of it. 'So you saw a guy and two women. No big deal, Cass.'

'It *is* because the guy they were with was pushing them about and they looked frightened. I can't explain it, but I know something wasn't right. Then the night Oscar bundled me into the club, I saw Alfie with some women as well. I don't know what it is but something doesn't feel right.'

Vaughn stayed quiet for a while. There was no way he was going to tell Casey what was going on, but he wasn't quite sure what to say to persuade her what she saw was harmless. He didn't know what Casey would do if he didn't convince her there was nothing to worry about. It was doubtful she'd go to the police with just a feeling something wasn't right, but it was as well to be cautious. As much as he didn't want to, he needed to warn Alfie and tell him to move the girls. He didn't agree with what his friend was doing but he didn't want to see him banged up either.

'Alfie's a bit of a player when it comes to women; always has been. Keeps his wife and family in the dark about it though. It'll be something like that. He's a bit shady is our Alfie when it comes to ladies. Just forget it.'

'I know what I saw, Vaughn. I know my instincts.'

'Casey, listen to me. Whatever your instincts are telling you, don't listen to them. Take my advice and steer clear.'

She tilted her head and looked at him. 'You know something don't you?'

Vaughn sighed, wondering why women always thought he was hiding something. Granted he was, but she wasn't to know that. What was it about the female sex that grasped on to something and wouldn't let it go?

He remembered this was one of the reasons he'd always sidestepped long-term relationships; women's perverse ability to incessantly flog the same subject until you gave them the answer they wanted. When you just fucked them and left, they hardly had time to catch their breath, let alone talk.

'I don't know anything about it, Cass, but I do know Alfie and Oscar, and they wouldn't appreciate it if they thought you were snooping in their business.'

'Oscar? Why did you say Oscar? I didn't say anything about him. What's he got to do with it?'

'Christ woman, Oscar was there with Alfie wasn't he? He was the one that grabbed you. What is all this?'

Casey quickly put her head down and flushed, becoming embarrassed by her own persistence. Vaughn watched her and wondered if the woman he'd fallen for was about to cause trouble.

It was one thing him beefing up to Alfie about it and disapproving, but it was another thing altogether someone from the outside, albeit Casey, poking around; it made all his defences go up and made him shut off. Old habits died hard and no matter how much he liked her, if she started to ask too many questions, he'd have to forget her.

It was well into the morning, and Vaughn and Casey had spent the last couple of hours talking and laughing about everything apart from the club, which they were both avoiding talking about.

'Have you decided if you're going to stick around yet?'

'I guess I'll have to now with Lola in hospital. I want to keep the cafe going for her and then she'll have something to come to when she gets better. After that I'll probably move on.'

'You don't have to do that. I'd like you to stay.'

'Vaughn please, it's complicated . . .'

'Only if you make it.'

Vaughn stood up and walked across to Casey in the small lounge of the flat. He crouched down and lifted up her chin, gently kissing her on her lips. He was expecting her to push him away again but she kissed him back and closed her eyes.

'Let me make love to you.'

Casey nodded. She wanted to feel loved, so she let Vaughn lead her to the bedroom, trying to blank out everything else as he gently started kissing the nape of her neck.

Vaughn slowly pulled off Casey's top, exposing her perfect breasts. He picked her up effortlessly and laid her on the bed, taking her clothes off slowly and admiring her body.

'You're a beautiful woman, but a mystery to me.' He smiled at her and started to take his own clothes off, exposing a tanned muscular torso.

Vaughn bent over to kiss Casey's body, making her relax and helping her not to think how she might be making a mistake. He slipped the rest of his clothes off and lifted her naked body up towards his; she kissed him passionately, feeling loved and letting herself fall into the moment.

His tongue circled her nipples, biting and sucking her breasts gently and making her gasp. He moved his body down hers and buried his head between her legs, using his tongue expertly.

'Are you alright?' Vaughn moved his head up and looked at her tenderly, stroking her hair as she opened her eyes and nodded. He held her gaze and Casey caught her breath as his penis entered her slowly. She responded in rhythmic motions and she bit down gently on her lip as he started to make fervent love to her; taking her body to a place it'd never been to before. She let out a cry as he held her tight, gripping hold of her hand as they climaxed simultaneously.

'Shit, I've left my phone. Pass me your keys and I'll be back down in a minute.'

Vaughn prayed the phone, which hadn't really been forgotten and was actually in his pocket, wouldn't ring. He

165

left Casey watching the in-car television in his Porsche 4x4 and went upstairs to her flat.

Inside, Vaughn quickly looked round; he only had a few minutes as he didn't want to arouse Casey's suspicion. He went into the bedroom first and glanced round, seeing nothing apart from the rumpled bed.

He went back into the lounge and saw her black zip bag thrown onto the bare floorboards. Vaughn looked in it, not quite knowing what he was looking for but hoping he'd find some sort of a clue to who she was and where she'd come from. He was falling for her and he'd no intention of getting a nasty shock. He needed to know exactly who she was before he allowed himself to fully trust her – he wasn't good at being hurt and if she wouldn't tell him, he'd have to find out himself.

Again, there was nothing, apart from clean and dirty clothes all mixed up together, and three empty bottles of scotch. Vaughn stood up perplexed. He couldn't understand it. There was nothing, literally fucking nothing, which gave him any clues to who she was, which was odd in itself. It was if she'd erased her whole life – or never really had one in the first place.

Still, he hoped he'd persuaded her there was nothing to worry about in Alfie's club. He knew Lola wouldn't say anything when Casey went to visit her. He really wanted to have another talk with Lola, but he'd leave it until she got home; there was plenty of time to talk later.

Having a last glance round, Vaughn was about to leave the flat but turned back to use the bathroom.

'Casey?'

Casey looked up absentmindedly at Vaughn; she'd been watching *Masterchef* and had got quite submerged in it, marvelling at how a few tins of tomatoes and a few herbs could transform a plain meal into something special. She looked at Vaughn, whose eyes were twinkling with mischief.

'Casey, I did something stupid.'

'What?'

'I opened the bathroom door.'

Casey's laughter was heard all the way down Dean Street.

His day was going from bad to fucking worse, and it'd started off so well after the phone call. Alfie kicked the back tyre of his car. How he'd got a flat, Christ alone only knew. He was supposed to have left by now but Emmie had had a hissy fit with Janine again and he'd been left to sort it out.

He didn't want to take the Audi; there was something wrong with the catalytic converter in it and he hadn't had an opportunity to take it into Epping to get it fixed. There was nothing to do apart from take Janine's Range Rover.

'I'm taking your car.'

'Alfie, I need it.'

Throwing the can of Pepsi cola he'd just opened into the sink, Alfie turned on his wife fuming.

'Tell me what the fuck for? What the fuck are you doing which is so important you need your car today?'

Janine Jennings had been planning to go shopping in Bluewater shopping centre. She was after the new Prada handbag which she'd spotted in *Vogue* on the arm of Paris Hilton, but by the looks of Alfie's face she wasn't going to be able to go today. Without saying a word, she handed over her keys to him.

En route to the club, Alfie went over the short conversation he'd had with Vaughn.

'Alf, it's me. We need to talk; I'll meet you at the club at five.'

167

'It's good to hear from you, Vaughn, I'm happy you changed your mind.'

'Just be at the club.'

He'd put the phone down and immediately the feeling of panic in his stomach disappeared. He wasn't sure why Vaughn had changed his mind and actually he really didn't give a shit why; all that mattered was he had.

What had irritated him had been the constant squabbling of Emmie and Janine. He knew his wife was a moody bitch and he accepted that, but now his daughter was turning into one. She'd been sulking for the past day or so, since the day he'd seen Oscar, and it was starting to get on his fucking wick. If he had some time later, he'd try and stop off at Harvey Nicks and pick her up a new Chloe handbag or something; that way she'd have nothing to moan about.

Parking in Soho was a nightmare as usual, and predictably the NCP car park in St Martin's Lane was full. Alfie drove round and round hoping to get lucky with a car park space not too far away from the club. In the end he found a space in Bloomsbury Square, a good ten minutes' walk away from Whispers.

'For fuck's sake.' Alfie raised his voice at the ticket machine, causing passersby to turn round and look nervously at him. It wasn't taking credit cards and he knew for a fact he only had a couple of pounds on him, and he certainly wasn't going to leave the car without a ticket to go looking for some change, only to return to see some cunt who was working for Camden council towing it away.

Alfie opened the glove compartment and saw it was full of empty chocolate bar wrappers and crisp packets. His wife was a slob, no question. Alfie remembered the mess at home when they'd first got married, but he'd soon put a stop to it and had hired two cleaners. Now it seemed she was still a slob, but only one in the confines of her own car.

There was no change in the glove compartment or in the money holder, which would've been the obvious place to put it in, but Alfie guessed too obvious and too organised for Janine.

He bent down and looked under the front seats and saw a couple of fifty pence pieces and a few coppers – no good to him. Stretching his hand further, he pulled out a piece of paper which was stuck underneath the runner of the seat.

Alfie glanced at it nonplussed until he saw what it was. It was a ticket dated from a couple of weeks ago and it was for Whipps Cross Hospital car park. He didn't know Janine had been to visit anyone in hospital, or she hadn't said, and that was unusual for her as she liked to spell out in tedious detail what she'd been doing every day. Unless, of course, she was hiding something.

Alfie carefully folded the ticket up in his pocket and got back into the car. When he got home later he would find out exactly what was going on, but for now he needed to go and find a space. Putting the car in drive, he set off with the ticket very much on his mind.

'Sorry Vaughn, motherfucking car park spaces. I tell you the guy I've just left was lucky I didn't smash his head in. He was fucking with me, trying to tell me it was his space. I asked him to show me where his name was written. The cunt came back with some cheeky comment about looking up my arse for it and I tell you, Vaughnie, I had him out of his seat and on his bonnet before he could say "yellow line".'

'I take it he gave you the space.'

'Of course; it went to its rightful owner. I see why you don't drive in. Have they sorted you out a drink?'

'I'm fine. I actually drove in today, ironically. Shall we go into the back?'

The back room of the club was chilly. Alfie switched on the heater and grabbed himself a packet of peanuts out of one of the boxes in the corner.

'What changed your mind, V? Not that I'm complaining. I appreciate it. I was well and truly up Fuck-up Street with Oscar, he was giving me till Friday. Christ. All the times I've helped him out. He wouldn't be anybody without me, and he treats me like a cunt.'

Vaughn looked at Alfie's swagger and wondered how long they'd remain friends in the long term. He didn't miss the violence of his old lifestyle and he sure as hell didn't miss the arrogance and bravado which went with the people. He was too old for bullshit; he could smell it a mile away, and Alfie Jennings's stench was getting stronger by the minute.

'I haven't changed my mind, Alfie: I meant what I said.'

Alfie's face dropped and a look of bewilderment came over it.

'I thought that's why you arranged this meeting.'

'No, you assumed it was, and I didn't like to talk on the phone. Casey's been asking questions.'

'Casey? What the fuck are you talking about? What the hell does that cock tease know?'

'Watch your mouth, Alfie.'

Alfie looked at him and sneered. 'That bitch has messed up your brain.'

Vaughn launched at Alfie and dragged him over the table.

'I said watch your mouth; you're walking a fine line.'

Alfie's face was aglow with anger; he couldn't believe what he was hearing and he certainly couldn't believe he was lying flat on his back with one of his oldest friends threatening him in the back room of his own club.

'Get the fuck off me,' Alfie growled at Vaughn who let

go and stepped back, dusting down his expensive suede jacket.

'I don't know why I bothered, but my better judgement told me to warn you. Casey saw your little arrangement upstairs.'

'What the fuck was she doing snooping around?'

'This is like déjà vu. She wasn't snooping; the night of the fight she went upstairs and that's when she saw them. I told her it was nothing and the reason they probably looked rough was because you have extraordinarily bad taste in pussy.'

Alfie rubbed his head. He appreciated that he hadn't broken the code of honour, though he wasn't going to admit that; he was too pissed off about not getting the money. He knew he was being unreasonable because he'd always known Vaughn would never approve of the women, but at this moment he was too angry to care.

He had to get the girls out of the club. Alfie looked at Vaughn and wished he'd never got involved with this venture. As Vaughn turned to go he spoke, feeling sad at the way things were turning out between him and Alfie, but there was nothing he could do until he started seeing sense – and the way things were going that was looking more and more unlikely.

'Did you hear about Lola?'

'Lola?'

'She's lying tubed up in the UCH. I don't think it's very hard to guess who did it.'

Alfie didn't say anything as Vaughn walked out of the door, suddenly feeling as if he'd been abandoned. His bad day was quickly turning into a nightmare.

CHAPTER TWENTY

Sun 14th March 1996
Back at home after staying in hospital for what felt like ages. Caught a bug and they kept me in; it was miserable but not as bad as being here. Mum is walking round like nothing has happened. I want to shout the word 'Baby' in her face but I don't think it'll make a difference. Nothing touches her. Dad has hardly come home. I want my baby back!!!!!!!!!!!!

Sun 12th May 1996
Dad has gone. Moved out and left me with Mum who seems to be drinking herself to death. I hate Dad for going but I actually don't blame him, I'd go myself if I could. Found a stash of Mum's vodka. Was going to throw it away but decided to drink it myself instead. Felt better for a while then was sick everywhere. Mum went mad. Stupid cow.

The buzzer was just as dirty as before, but this time somebody answered, making Casey's legs nearly give way underneath her. The voice was a woman's and it sounded harsh.

'Yes?'

'Mrs Simms?'

'Who's asking?'

'Casey Edwards, I just wanted a word.'

'What about?'

'My baby.'

The flat was overcrowded with mismatched bits of furniture. There were photos all over the walls and huge boxes with 'shipping' written on them.

Casey followed Mrs Simms into the lounge, and as she did so she noticed her hunched back and strong body odour. The flat was on the eighteenth floor, and standing in the middle of the room Casey took in the stunning views of the rooftops of Soho.

'Sit down love. You're lucky you caught me – I'm off tomorrow to go and live with my sister; she lives in Australia would you believe. Been pestering me for years to go over there. I wasn't bothered before but now my husband's dead there's no reason for me to stay here on me own. I've never even been on a plane but here's me packing up to emigrate down under. You don't mind if I busy myself; I've got so much to do still and the moving people said they'll be here in a couple of hours to take my stuff.'

Casey tried to force a smile as Mrs Simms laughed. 'Thank you. I was hoping you'd be able to help me. I'm looking for my baby; well he won't be a baby now, he'll be sixteen. I know you fostered him when he was born, and I wondered if you might have an address or still keep in touch with whoever took him.'

Casey stopped and watched as the old woman put in her false teeth, taking them from a tissue on the side.

'I don't keep in touch after they've gone and I've long given up fostering. Ill health and too many rules; I used to say they'll make you have an assessment just for going to the toilet. I got into fostering because I was good with kiddies but when they started making you take tests for this and for that and turning up to check on you, then giving you a bollocking if you were having a fag, I called it a day.'

Casey nodded feigning sympathy and attempted to turn the subject back to the matter at hand.

'My son was born January 1996, and he came to you in the same month. Apparently he was here with you for nearly a year.'

'I don't want to know how you found out where I lived – like I used to say to my late husband, spare me the gory details. But I'm afraid you've had a waste of a journey; I didn't foster your son in 1996, or '97 come to think of it.'

'How can you be so sure?'

'I might look like I haven't got my wits about me, but I remember all my foster children like they were my own.'

'Maybe you've made a mistake though.'

The woman looked at Casey over her rimmed glasses and frowned.

'I'm so sorry lovie, I know it must be hard, but there's no mistake.'

The woman shuffled over to the far wall, where she took a photo down and showed it to Casey.

'January 1996 you say? Well January 1996 to the end of 1997, I had this little one, gorgeous little thing.'

Casey took hold of the black and white photograph to see a little baby smiling up. She watched the warmth come into Mrs Simms's face as she spoke.

'Took my heart this baby did – she was like a china doll. Her name was Emmie.'

CHAPTER TWENTY-ONE

It hurt when he laughed, but he couldn't help himself. He leant back on the reclining leather chair as Emmie stood in front of him in floods of tears, begging him to give her the packages back. She was a fucking joke.

'Please Jakey, I need them. Dad's going to be in so much trouble if I don't get them back.'

This last statement made Jake laugh even more. Was she so fucking stupid to think he'd give a shit about the man who'd nearly killed him? In fact, it was music to his ears.

He watched as she collapsed, wailing onto the faded brown couch in the middle of his friend's council house. He felt nothing but scorn for her. He picked the dirt out of his nails as Emmie continued to cry.

'Stop that snivelling, Em, it's doing my nut in.'

'But you don't understand; I heard Oscar tell Dad he only had till Friday.'

'But that's exactly it, I do understand. I understand perfectly. And when they come looking for Alfie, it'll take the police a week to find all the pieces of his body.'

Jake leaned forward towards Emmie and spoke very softly.

'And when you bury him, Em, remember you have no one to blame but yourself.'

Emmie let out a hysterical cry.

'You said you loved me! You told me you did, that's the only reason I gave them to you.'

'You're having a laugh aren't you, mate? A piece of piss schoolgirl like you; who in their right mind could love a fucking skeleton like you? Now do me a favour, get out of my flat.'

Emmie looked at him and wiped away the dripping snot from her nose. She raised herself up to her full height and spoke defiantly.

'Don't think I won't get you back, Jake Bellingham. Nobody messes with the Jennings and gets away with it.'

Jake roared with laughter and threw the television controls at her head, only narrowly missing her. Who did she think she was, fucking Al Capone? She was a comic story, just like her dad.

'You're frightening me. I'm shaking, Em, look.'

Laughing again, Jake held out his hands and shook them wildly. Emmie turned and ran from the flat. She'd been so stupid, and now her dad was in danger because of her. She needed to sort it out, but there was no way she could tell her dad; she had to do it alone. She was the one who'd messed everything up and now she was the one who had to put it right. Jake Bellingham was going to pay and Emmie knew exactly how.

Oscar sat in his parked car on Caledonian Road, waiting for his headache to pass. He watched a woman with a Sainsbury's shopping bag cross the road and her bulbous frame put him in mind of his drunken mother. He hated to think about her, but sometimes the memories came flooding back, whether he liked it or not.

Oscar's mother was called Violet. She was from Cork in Ireland and even though everyone agreed her she had a pretty name, they also agreed god should never have blessed her with the ability to have children.

Oscar couldn't remember the bruises and the cigarette burns the first time they happened, but he suspected they started after his father had left. Oscar had been devastated when he'd watched him walk out the door with only his coat and battered trilby hat. He'd said goodbye to his son, telling him he'd had enough, and the young Oscar had been left standing on the doorstep watching his father go and willing him to turn round and come back.

His first vivid memory of Violet was when he was about three years old and he'd come downstairs to discover her semi-naked on the living room carpet in a drunken stupor, one of her numerous boyfriends lying in a similar state next to her.

'Mum? Mum, wake up.'

'What the hell do you want?'

'I'm hungry.'

'You grubby little bleeder, get out me sight before I give you a hiding you won't forget.'

It'd been another day before his mother had decided to give him anything to eat and when she had, it'd been a bowl of cereal without milk.

Thinking back, Oscar remembered his childhood to be nothing more than a succession of beatings and abuse, but his mother had been a sly bitch, always careful not to mark his face so she could continue to send him to school without them informing the welfare. Not that they ever did a lot of good – the one time they'd come round they'd asked him in front of his mother if she'd been knocking him around and all he could do was stand motionless, unable to even shake his head. When they'd gone she'd given him the beating of his life and he still had the scar above his eye to prove it.

Oscar hated his mother more for the fact she let her drunken boyfriends batter him whilst she just sat and watched, and when they'd got bored of him being their punch bag, his mother would either lock him in his room or make him wander the streets. He'd left home as soon as he could and left her to drink herself to death, but it hadn't worked. She was still alive and kicking as much as ever.

The man beeping his horn broke into Oscar's memories, which he was grateful for. Rubbing his temples, Oscar thought about Alfie. He hadn't heard from him since he'd seen him, but he imagined he was running round like a blue-arsed fly, trying to get the money together.

He hoped he was able to; he quite liked him as a business acquaintance. Even if he'd wanted to, he couldn't let him get away with ripping him off; whether it was intentional or not. If he let Alfie off, then everyone would start to take the piss and he'd not only lose face but he'd lose his repu-tation as well, and reputation was everything in this business; it made people want to work with you. If you didn't have reputation, you didn't have anything.

Casey sat in her flat and opened the bottle. She stared ahead in the dim light of the evening as she put the glass rim to her lips, tasting the burn of the whisky. It'd all come to a dead end. For so long she'd thought of Mrs Simms as the one connection to her son, and now it was over just as quickly as it had begun. In less than fifteen minutes all hope had disappeared; and if there was no hope, then there was no point in trying. Closing her eyes to stop the tears, Casey took another large swig of whisky hoping it'd take away the pain.

CHAPTER TWENTY-TWO

'Hello?'

Casey spoke down the phone in a hoarse whisper. Her head was throbbing and her mouth tasted stale as a jarring hangover kicked in. On the other end she heard Josh sounding very cheerful.

'Hi, it's me.'

'What can I do for you, Josh?'

Casey knew that Josh would know she'd been drinking from her voice, he'd seen it all before; but she didn't have the energy to pretend otherwise.

'I've got to come down to London later; stuff to do with work here in Birmingham. I was hoping we might be able to meet.'

'I don't think that's a good idea, Josh. Perhaps some other day. It's not a great time for me.'

'No, you don't understand, I need to see you.'

'Josh, please. We've been through this.'

'Casey, listen, you know I'll always love and care for you but . . .'

There was a long pause and Casey knew in her heart what

was coming; she could've filled in the missing words and made it easier for him.

'Cass, I've met someone else. The reason I need to see you is because I want a divorce and I need you to sign some papers.'

She paused for a moment, taken aback, but at the same time not surprised. She answered Josh, hoping to sound calm and reasonable, but as she spoke even to her it sounded brash and cold.

'Fine.'

'Is that all you can say?'

Now Casey was on the defensive: she knew she had no right to feel hurt and she was angry at herself for being so, and the more angry she felt the more unreasonable she sounded.

'What do you want from me, Josh? I said I'll sign them; just don't make a big deal out of it.'

'Are you okay?'

She snapped, annoyed at the concern in his voice.

'If you mean have I been drinking, the answer's yes.'

'That's not what I meant.'

She was annoyed at the way she was behaving; he didn't deserve it. Softening her voice she spoke again.

'I went to the address.'

'And?'

'Right woman, wrong baby.'

The pause of the phone seemed eternally long before Josh spoke.

'I was afraid of this. I'm sorry, Casey.'

'Me too.'

Casey had tried on everything twice and decided nothing was right. She'd no idea what she was supposed to wear to go and see somebody she'd left without warning and hadn't seen for over eighteen months. Sighing, she sat down defeated in the middle of the pile of clothes. What she needed was a drink instead of worrying about her clothing. She pushed the guilt of breaking her sobriety away, took the bottle of whisky out of her bag, and drank a large mouthful.

She sucked back hard when the heat of the alcohol hit the back of her throat. She was back in her dark tunnel and was starting to feel sorry for herself again; she hated that she was turning herself into a victim: something she swore she'd never become.

It was almost time, and Casey wanted to get to the station before him. It was important for her to seem composed, even though her stomach was doing somersaults. She was annoyed she was so nervous, and gulped down another large mouthful of whisky to steady herself.

As it turned out, Casey was late. When she'd finished getting ready, she was so much on edge she'd poured herself another drink and half an hour later was splashing cold water on her face to try to sober up.

She walked up Dean Street and as she turned onto Oxford Street she missed Vaughn waving to her from the other side of the busy road.

Casey stood outside St Pancras station, the traffic on Euston Road rushing by, and took a deep breath. Looking up at the towering neo-gothic building it dawned on her she was scared.

Casey saw him before he saw her. He hadn't changed; he still had the goatee which he'd grown to try and make his youthful face look older, the slicked-back brown hair curled to the side as it had always done, and his eyes – his blue eyes – were as piercing as ever.

She willed him to look up, but he carried on drinking the

steaming coffee and reading *The Guardian* as he sat outside Costa Coffee.

'Josh.'

'Oh my god Casey; it's so good to see you.'

Josh Edwards jumped up from his seat, sending the metal chair he'd been sitting on clattering to the floor. He held Casey in a tight hug, then pushed her back, holding her in a firm grip at arms' length.

'Let me look at you. You've lost weight, Cass.' He looked at her worriedly, trying not to pay attention to the strong smell of alcohol which couldn't be disguised by the overzealous spraying of perfume.

'Sit down. Can I get you a coffee?'

Casey wasn't sure if Josh was asking out of good manners or because he could smell the cheap alcohol on her breath.

'I'm fine, thank you.'

She looked at Josh and saw he was lost for words now the greeting was over, so she thought she'd help him out.

'I'm sorry.'

'For what?'

'For walking out on you and not coming back. The problem was, time goes by, and then it's harder to go back.'

Josh raised his voice and Casey placed her hand on his to soothe him. 'Go back? Jesus, it wasn't Monopoly you were playing, Cass. You were my wife, and one morning I woke up and you'd gone.'

'I'd gone a long time before that day, Josh, you just didn't know it.'

'You could have talked to me.'

'It wouldn't have made a difference; I couldn't stay – not after what I did to you – and I had to come to look for him. It was time.'

'So you thought you'd run? What about me, Cass? Didn't

you think about me for one minute? Didn't we mean anything?'

'Of course we meant something. I thought about you every day, but it wasn't going to be enough. I lost a part of myself back in that hospital when they took my son and I've been searching for that part ever since. I needed to do this.'

Casey stopped and looked at Josh, seeing the hurt in his eyes; there was no point in talking about the past. Trying to lighten the moment, Casey leant back on her chair, feigning a smile.

'Anyway, you've done alright. Met a new woman. What do they say? As one door closes, another one opens.'

Casey held the smile but felt her throat tighten as she struggled not to cry. Josh glared at her angrily.

'This is a joke to you isn't it?'

Ignoring Josh's outburst, Casey spoke in a calm manner, sad for the pain she'd caused a man who loved her, but she could never love him back in the way he wanted her to.

'Now where are those papers you want me to sign?'

Casey bit her lip as Josh pulled out the papers and gave her the pen. They held each other's gaze for a moment before she put her head down and signed on the dotted line, with her hand visibly shaking.

'I better go now.'

As Casey spoke she stroked Josh's face, saying nothing as she saw the tears in his eyes. He hugged her again and she wished she was capable of loving him like he loved her.

'I am sorry; you know that don't you? I hope you have the happiness you deserve.'

As Casey turned to leave, Josh grabbed her arm.

'Wait. I didn't know if I should give it to you. I thought it might make things between us worse and maybe I should've given you it before now, but I thought if I did I might lose you and we wouldn't stand a chance if something or somebody got in the way, but looking back I can see we never stood a chance in the first place.'

He handed her an envelope with simply her name written on it in familiar handwriting. Casey stared at Josh in puzzlement.

'It's from your father. Before he died he asked me to give you this when I thought the time was right. He explained a little bit to me but he was worried it might hurt you too much and neither of us wanted that, he wanted me to wait until you were strong but I can't justify holding onto it, not now, not when perhaps it might help.'

'I don't understand. What does it say?'

Josh shrugged his shoulders feeling uncomfortable by his own guilt for not giving Casey the letter when he'd first got it.

'I don't know. I never read it, your father asked me not to but I know vaguely what it's about.'

'Wait Josh.'

Wanting to get away, Josh backed away not wanting to talk any longer.

'Just read it. Goodbye Casey and please look after yourself. Be careful.'

Casey held the letter tightly in her hand as Josh walked away. When they'd got married, Josh, wanting to do the right thing, had insisted on inviting her parents; but they hadn't come. Part of her had been glad, but another part had been hurt and angrier with them than she was already. When her father had become ill, it was Josh who'd gone to see him, not her, and over the months prior to his death it was clear Josh and her father had formed some sort of a bond, which she'd seen as a betrayal. On the day of her father's funeral, Josh had stood solemnly by her father's graveside, whilst she'd been miles away getting drunk with a nameless stranger.

Casey sighed; she would read it later. Whatever was in it, she was sure she'd need to sit down when she did. Quickly she headed back towards the tube station, passing a Paul's bakery on the way, and not seeing the two men leaning on the pillar watching her.

'Yes? Who the fuck is it?'

Oscar's phone manner was as charming as ever as he answered the phone, but he got the surprise of his life when he heard who the caller was. In actual fact, he'd have been less surprised to hear his newly deceased ex-wife Lola on the other end.

'Leave everything with me and I'll call you back as soon as I can. Don't worry; you've done the right thing.'

Oscar put the phone down and roared with laughter. It couldn't be any better. It was so good, in fact, that he was sure this is what it would feel like if he'd just heard his slag of a mother had just died.

Three hours later, Oscar was parked in Huntley Street, a quiet road running parallel to Tottenham Court Road. He was listening to *The Golden Hour* on Magic FM and was uncharacteristically humming along to 'Black Velvet' when his car door opened.

'Glad to see you could make it. Don't look so nervous; if anyone can help, I can. Now, how about I take you for a cup of coffee, and then you can tell me all about it?'

As Oscar drove off, he glanced quickly at his passenger and wondered what he'd done so right to have luck like this.

Thursday night, and Alfie knew it wasn't good. He'd been everywhere to try and sort out the money but no one was willing to help. It'd crossed Alfie's mind it wasn't a question of people not being able to help, but of them not

185

being willing to, hoping to see him fall. He knew the underground rumour mill had been in overdrive, and all the important players knew why he needed the loan and were happy to watch the mighty Alfie Jennings take his punishment.

Outside his world, Alfie knew owing money only meant debts and humiliation and maybe the odd sleepless night, but in his world, if you owed money and didn't pay it back – especially when you owed it to people like Oscar Harding – it only meant one thing; sooner or later you were going to be brown bread. Simple as.

He'd even gone to see Max Donaldson, a notorious loan shark and dealer who ran his business empire like he did his own family; with an iron bar and bucketloads of fear and intimidation.

Max was a cliché of his upbringing; a prostitute for a mother and an unknown father. He'd been in and out of reform schools before graduating to adult prisons as his reign of terror and bank balance grew. Alfie thought Max had small man syndrome: he stood no taller than five foot five, but his aggression and violence befitted twenty men.

'Sorry Alf, you know how it is,' Max grinned, making sure Alfie knew he didn't give a damn about his problems.

Alfie did know how it fucking was. He knew Max was bathing in money. The interest Max charged his clients for taking out loans was eye-watering; so some poor sod who found themselves Berni Flint and couldn't afford to pay the gas would take out a fifty-quid loan with Max and end up paying back five hundred. If they missed a payment they'd be looking at interest on top of interest, or if they were lucky a broken pelvis and a kneecap to show for it – but even having broken limbs didn't see the loan wiped out.

'You see it's the recession, Alf; touches us all. Flaming fucking government are robbing us all blind.'

If he hadn't found himself in this predicament with Oscar, Alfie might've laughed. He doubted Max Donaldson had ever paid any tax in his life. The phone jolted Alfie out of his thoughts and the number flashing on the screen brought him out in a cold sweat; it was Oscar. He switched off the phone and poured himself a drink in the empty club, wondering how he'd find just over seventy grand in the next few hours.

Emmie looked up at the clock; her dad would be home soon and she didn't want him to catch her rooting round his office. Her mother was out shopping which meant she didn't have to worry about her coming back until the shops had closed, and as it was late night opening in Bluewater, she still had plenty of time.

She couldn't find what she was looking for but she knew it was here somewhere. She'd once seen her dad with it and she'd been certain he'd put it behind the large mahogany bookshelf, but it wasn't there now.

Emmie was careful to put everything back as it was. The cigar box slightly angled to one side, the ashtray which she'd bought for him when she and her mum had gone to Paris for the day, and the various pieces of paper all placed back correctly.

She decided to look in the large wooden chest at the far end of the panelled room. Her dad always kept it locked but she knew he hid the key behind the large family photo hanging on the wall which was taken last year. Emmie hated the photo, she thought it made her look fat, but her dad had told her she looked beautiful and insisted on putting it up on the wall.

Opening the chest, Emmie looked round as it creaked and felt her heart thumping. Her eyes opened wide as she saw a wad of fifty-pound notes and a large packet of white powder which Emmie guessed was cocaine. She moved the money to the side and saw the green box she was looking for. She opened it up carefully and breathed a sigh of relief as she saw what was inside: a small silver hand gun.

CHAPTER TWENTY-THREE

It was getting late and Casey knew she had to get up. She'd spent the last couple of days in bed, drinking too much, eating too little and crying in abundance. The hospital had called to let her know Lola had regained consciousness and was asking to see her.

She felt terrible and she was sure she probably looked as bad as she felt. Her mouth was dry and sticky and her nose was blocked from crying but if she didn't get out of bed now, she doubted she ever would. As she turned her head to the side, Casey saw the crumpled letter from her father on the cabinet, and in seeing it she put her head back under the cover wanting to disappear.

Before making up her mind whether she was going to go and see Lola, Casey decided to go and have a drink. Eight double whiskies, two straight vodkas and a pint of lager later, thoughts of not only Lola but also the letter were fading quickly from Casey's mind as she sat unsteadily in Whispers. Casey was unaware she was being watched by Alfie, who was delighted to watch the car crash unfold in front of him, and he decided to speed things up a bit. Picking up the phone behind the bar, Alfie dialled Vaughn's number.

It was open mike night and the club was buzzing. Punters and comedians were packed into the heat of the main drinking lounge, and Casey decided to move closer to the stage as the compere came on to applause and cheering.

'Ladies and gentlemen, for the next part of the evening I'm going to invite any brave members of the audience to come up and have a go; come and see if you've got what it takes to make us laugh. He who dares!'

The audience looked round at each other, seeing if anyone had the bottle to volunteer to go up on stage. When nobody came forward the compere tried to egg them on.

'Come on people, don't be shy. How about you sir? Yes, you with the bald head.'

The man grinned and shouted out a retort. 'Better a bald head than no head mate!'

'You think so? Have you looked at yourself in the mirror recently sir? But then mirrors don't talk – and lucky for you they don't laugh either. Come on somebody, anybody.'

'I will.'

The room turned to see Casey swaying unsteadily up to the stage. There was a round of applause and Alfie grinned, unable to believe his luck or the good timing as he saw Vaughn walk in. This was going to be good.

'Ladies and gentlemen, give it up for the brave lady.'

Casey stumbled over to the mike as the room fell silent. She stood for a few moments gazing up and blinking at the spotlight as the audience started to feel slightly uncomfortable.

Vaughn went to move forward but Alfie held him back.

'Leave her; she's fine, she's just having a bit of fun.'

Vaughn angrily glanced at Alfie.

'Is this why you called me? So I could see her make a fool of herself?'

'I had no idea she was going to do this. I called because I thought you might want to come and have a drink with me and see if we could work things out between us.'

Vaughn pulled his arm away from Alfie's grip, knowing he was lying, and watched Casey with a heavy heart.

The audience remained silent and Vaughn closed his eyes as Casey chuckled to herself, swaying.

'Okay here I go . . . Two goldfish were in their tank. One turns to the other and says, "You man the guns and I'll drive."'

Casey looked out and grinned at the sea of people who stared blankly back at her. Slurring her words and playing with the mike wire as the spotlight glared down on her, Casey spoke in a quieter voice.

'My dad told me that joke. I didn't think it was funny either, but then nothing he did was funny. He wrote me a letter, now that was a joke . . .'

The compere mercifully ran on stage, interrupting Casey mid-flow.

'Give it up for Casey, ladies and gentlemen. What a brave lady!'

The compere pulled her off and the round of relieved applause sounded round the room as Casey waved while she was hustled off into the wings. A tall wiry-framed comedian, equally intoxicated, offered her a drink.

'I take it that was your first time; we've all been through it. I bet you need a drink after that.'

She nodded and knocked back the shot quickly and thirstily.

A further few drinks later, Casey was stumbling out of the back of the club trying to hold herself up against her new acquaintance and oblivious to the fact Vaughn was looking for her. She'd stayed in the room at the back drinking with the other comedians, rather than bothering going through to the main bar.

It was late but the streets were still full of people and Casey watched them in a blur, giggling slightly at nothing in particular.

She felt the man's hands start exploring her body and then roughly go down the back of her trousers. He leant in to start to kiss her and she pushed him away, disorientated and suddenly realising that she wanted to go home. Over the man's shoulder Casey saw someone staring at her and it slowly dawned on her that she recognised him. He continued to stare but a crowd of tourists walked in front of him, blocking her hazy view.

'Casey!'

Casey tried to clear her mind but she found it too hard to focus enough to search out the voice in the crowd.

'Casey!'

She felt as if she was playing a game of cat and mouse; her head was all over the place and she felt sick but eventually through the blur of the street lights, the person who'd been calling her finally walked forward.

'What the fuck are you doing?'

It was Vaughn. Seeing him was like a sobering slap in her face. She felt the guy's hand still halfway down the back of her trousers, and slowly she moved it away as Vaughn held her gaze before turning to look at the man with a cold dangerous stare.

'Listen mate, you've got two minutes to get the fuck out of here, and count yourself lucky you're getting away so lightly.'

'I don't think so *mate*.'

Vaughn, not caring who saw him, punched the man and floored him; immediately becoming annoyed with himself that he'd let his feelings make him stoop to such a level.

'Do I have to repeat myself?'

'Vaughn, leave him alone.'

192

'Means something to you does he? Like the guy at the station?'

Vaughn could hear the jealousy in his voice and Casey was dumbfounded.

'Oh my god you followed me, didn't you?'

For a split second Casey thought she saw a flicker of shame cross Vaughn's face, but it disappeared in a moment and he stood glaring at her, not saying a word, just staring intently and making her feel more like crap than she already did. She could see the mix of contempt and regret in his eyes and after a moment, he turned away.

'Vaughn.' The booze was making Casey unable to form her words without slurring. She desperately wanted him to stop before he walked into the Soho night. She had a sudden fear she wouldn't see him again if she let him go.

'Vaughn, wait.'

He turned round and she could see he was desperate for some kind of explanation for her making a drunken fool of herself on stage and being fawned over by a complete stranger.

Now he'd turned round, Casey had no idea what to say. How could she explain the stranger she was about to go off with only meant she was struggling to cope? He meant nothing, but it was easier for her to destroy herself than to feel the pain.

'I told you not to get involved with me; I said it was complicated.'

Vaughn came up to her and she turned her face away, but he grabbed her arm, forcing her to turn and look at him.

'This isn't complicated, Casey. This is you being the drunken bitch you really are.'

Casey slapped him hard on the cheek and Vaughn clenched his jaw, angry and in unfamiliar emotional pain. She looked at him and knew it was this she'd been trying to avoid; she'd never wanted to hurt anyone but it seemed wherever she went, the hurt she was carrying also destroyed those around her.

'Vaughn.'

It was the only word she could think of to say. She reached out to touch his hand and then watched him shrink back. Casey thought there was nothing like the taste of rejection to sober her up.

'At the station; that was my husband.'

'Christ, it gets better, Casey.'

'He wanted me to sign some divorce papers.'

'And then you thought you'd come and celebrate by getting pissed and picking up some wanker of a guy.'

'It wasn't like that.'

'No? Well it looked like that from where I was standing.'

'I can't explain.'

'No, you can't, at least not to me anyway. I've been a fucking chump haven't I? You've played me like a fucking violin. Well and truly taken me for a cunt.'

'Me? I told you I didn't want to get involved.'

'Well what was that back at your flat if it wasn't getting involved?'

'That was just sex, Vaughn, nothing more.'

She was lying and she hoped he could see it but he looked too angry and hurt right now. It was a stupid thing to say and she knew it. She paused and for a moment she wanted to tell him everything; she wished he'd say something, but all she got was a flicker of a twitch on his right cheek as he continued to stare. Determined not to cry, Casey pulled her coat jacket tight around her as she forced back the tears. Vaughn didn't even reply as he turned away, walking into the crowds of the late night revellers.

From behind she felt someone touch her; she turned round to face Alfie handing her a tissue.

'You don't want to be standing here crying, girl, haven't

194

you learnt by now us men aren't worth it? He'll be back if I know Vaughn. Got a lot of pride has Mr Sadler.'

Casey shook her head.

'Jesus wept, why are women so pessimistic? Trust me. How's about you come with me and I'll cheer you up; after all what are friends for?'

With his hand in the arch of her back, Alfie gently guided her towards his flat, checking to make sure Vaughn had gone. He'd have to leave speaking to Janine about the ticket for another day; it could wait, he had other matters to deal with now. By rights he should be trying to throttle Casey, not fucking her. She'd been snooping into his business and he wasn't happy, but like everything else he needed to deal with it could wait. His cock couldn't, especially when there was a bit of top class cunny to be had.

He'd been right about Casey being a lush, but it hadn't stopped him wanting her, and now Vaughn had seen what she was really like there was nothing to stop him stepping in; in fact sleeping with Casey might even work to his advantage. Vaughn had fucked him off and however petty it seemed, it was his way of getting back at him. Hopefully it would make him see sense and stop him behaving like he'd swallowed a Girl Guides handbook.

He looked down as Casey stumbled and he smiled, thinking how surprisingly easy it was to get women into bed, especially the vulnerable and the fucked-up ones – and Casey was certainly a bit of both.

CHAPTER TWENTY-FOUR

Vaughn wanted to kill someone. He wasn't particular who it was, anyone would do, and he wanted to do it the old-fashioned way. Slowly, and using his hands. He knew it wasn't like him to feel like this: all his life he'd hated the violence which came with his lifestyle and now all he could think about was hurting someone; anyone. He was consumed with rage and had nearly called one of his old associates to go out on a job with them so he'd have an excuse to batter someone senseless.

He was hurting, and he was so unused to it the only way he thought he could get rid of the pain was by hurting someone else. He tried to calm himself down by replanting some roses in his hothouse, but he'd got annoyed when he'd pricked his finger and ended up throwing the pot along with the roses at one of the large window panes, causing a huge crack to appear which had pissed him off even more.

He wanted a large scotch but it was only going to remind him of Casey and the last thing he wanted to do was think of her. How could he have been so fucking stupid? She'd told him herself she didn't want to get involved but he thought after the day they'd made love, things had changed.

No matter what she had said about that night, he knew it'd been special; he'd shagged enough women to know the difference, and all she'd done was throw it in his face. Fucking hell, he was starting to sound like a woman.

Pacing up and down in his state-of–the-art kitchen, Vaughn decided that if this is what love did to you, he was better off without it. He stopped dead in his tracks as the word struck him. Did he love her? Was this what it was all about? If he did, he was a prize cunt for doing so. Alfie had been right about her, though deep down he wasn't certain if he really believed that; but he had to snap out of the way he was feeling. And then it occurred to him what he needed to do; he was going to fuck her out of his system; he was going to get a brass or several, however many it took; he was going to get his brains fucked out good and proper. Convinced it would make him feel better, Vaughn Sadler picked up the phone and called one of his contacts.

Alfie casually glanced over at Casey, who was fast asleep. The night hadn't gone as he'd expected. Stupidly, he'd offered her some red wine and she'd gulped it down more like a whale than a fish. After polishing off the bottle, she'd spent the next couple of hours vomiting her guts out. Eventually she'd passed out on the sofa, where he'd undressed her and put her into his bed. He'd been tempted to fuck her there and then whilst she was out for the count, but as sensual as her naked body had looked, the stench of vomit emanating from her had put pay to his boner.

Now she was sober he knew he wouldn't be getting any action. She'd been contrite and full of guilt in between throwing up in the toilet, and she'd drunkenly rambled on about Vaughn, professing her true feelings for him. All this heart stuff with Vaughn wasn't good for his friend; it was making him soft, and he needed to nip it in the bud before it went any further – but as nothing had happened there was nothing to rub in his face to bring him back down to earth.

Whilst Alfie was chewing things over a thought came to him. Perhaps he'd make Vaughn *think* he'd actually fucked her; it was a way to stop him acting like a Good Samaritan. He knew it was childish, but he was too pissed off at the moment to care.

Ultimately Alfie also knew Vaughn had a short attention span when it came to women; he'd soon get bored of Casey anyway, so no real harm was going to be done. And when Alfie looked at it like that he could see he was actually doing Vaughn a favour, though he wasn't sure his friend would see it that way.

He looked at himself in the large Venetian oval mirror; he was still looking good, and much younger than his age, but he could see the odd line appearing round his eyes and he was certain the stress of the past couple of weeks had caused it. As he continued to inspect himself, he heard Casey snoring lightly and it immediately got on his nerves. He turned round and picked up a pillow, throwing it gently at her head. As Casey started to stir the phone rang; it was Oscar, wanting his money.

'Alfie, first things first, you know what day it is don't you?'

Alfie wanted to tell him to fuck off and stick his money where the only thing that shined was a bum bandit's knob, but he thought better of it.

'I haven't got it yet, but the day isn't over.'

'Sounds to me like you might be struggling. I'll give you till the end of the day, but I'm going to take some insurance out just in case you don't get it, Alf. I'm taking the girls from the club.'

'You can't do that.'

'Oh but you'll find I can, and I have already. Bear in mind

it's you who owes me, not the other way round; besides which there's a party I'm going to take them to.'

'Don't you think that's risky?'

'No. The sort of party this is, no one will be talking. Sometimes it can get a bit wild but that's why Jason pays so well; it's hard for him to find girls where no questions will be asked if they don't come back.'

Alfie had no idea what to say. If he understood correctly what Oscar was saying, then he wasn't happy about it at all, especially as it involved Jason Hedley, a vicious piece of work who'd been pimping since he'd been at school and who'd make the devil look like he had a conscience. But then, what could he do? He owed money and until he paid it back, Oscar was free to run things how he saw fit; it was the name of the game. It was becoming increasingly fucked up and he didn't like it at all, but now he owed Oscar money, he didn't really have any say in the matter.

'Well, it's your call, and we needed to move them from the club anyway; Casey's been asking questions.'

There was a long pause on the phone and Alfie sat down, once again wishing he'd never got involved. He'd thought it was going to be quick easy money, but it was causing him a hell of a lot of grief.

Eventually Oscar spoke.

'She's trouble. Perhaps you need to get rid of our pretty little problem once and for all.'

'No, not yet; Vaughn's put her off the trail.'

'What the fuck is this, Alfie? An Easter egg hunt?'

'Bedtime talk or some shit, but you know Vaughn; he'll not spill the beans. I guess you've heard about Lola.'

'Lola?'

'She was attacked, but it seems she's going to be okay. Apparently Casey found her; I don't know the full story.'

* * *

The moment Casey woke up and found herself in Alfie's bed she felt sick to her stomach. Staring up at the spotlights in the ceiling she was filled with guilt over Vaughn and images of her getting on stage flashed in her mind. Sighing, she turned on her side, trying to ignore the memories of last night's fiasco and hold on to the anger she felt towards Vaughn, because if she could then she wouldn't feel so wretched. Anger was a whole lot easier to feel than regret and remorse.

Hearing Alfie come into the bedroom, Casey closed her eyes and pretended to be asleep.

'Wake up, Sleeping Beauty.'

Casey felt Alfie's hand slide up her leg and she shivered with disgust. She must have had a hell of a lot to drink to end up naked in bed at Alfie Jennings's, though she did remember passing out before anything happened. She supposed that not having slept with him was some small consolation in an otherwise hideous situation.

She wanted to go home and scrub herself clean. Even having to face her squalid bathroom was better than having the feeling Alfie was still on her. Vaughn flashed into her mind and she quickly pushed the thought away.

'Would you mind if I got dressed?'

Alfie grinned at her. 'Not at all; be my guest.'

Casey waited, hoping Alfie would get the hint, but he stayed seated on the cream silk sheets.

'Hello?'

Alfie laughed at her and continued to sit on the bed.

'You weren't so shy last night, Casey. Don't be so coy, I've already seen it all . . . and felt it all.'

'Nothing happened.'

'I know, but I still had to undress you. I was thinking, maybe we shouldn't mention this to Vaughn. You wouldn't want him getting the wrong idea about you, and the last thing I want to do is hurt him.'

Casey nodded her head. She hadn't had any intention of mentioning it to Vaughn, but she was relieved Alfie felt the same way. He no doubt was just as keen to keep this quiet as she was.

Alfie smiled as he spoke. 'Good. We're agreed then.'

He leant back on the end of the bed and stared at her, his eyes twinkling with mischief. Casey suddenly felt sick, and she wasn't sure if it was last night's excess alcohol or Alfie's repulsive manner which was repeating on her. She knew it'd be a standoff with him and she wanted to get home; she leapt out of bed and felt Alfie's burning eyes on her naked body. Casey Edwards had never got dressed so quickly in her life.

After Oscar had put down the phone to Alfie he'd sat quietly, trying to stop his head from pounding. He was in shock. Lola was still alive; he hadn't for a moment thought she'd be found so quickly – he didn't think anyone cared. Things weren't panning out as he'd hoped, but one thing was for certain now, he needed to get rid of Casey and her meddling, sooner rather than later.

Jake Bellingham leant on the edge of his kitchen table opening a can of Coke, unable to believe his luck. Emmie had been on the phone, begging forgiveness.

'I'm sorry Jakey; I got a bit panicky when I said I wanted the packages back. I'll get you the other one you wanted if you want me to; I'll bring it round on Friday.'

Only this morning, he'd thought he was going to have to tell Johno Porter he couldn't come up with all the wares. Not only would it have meant losing any chance of running the turf in Stonebridge Park and becoming a fucking joke, but family or not, he would've no doubt ended up getting the hiding of his life from Johno and his men for messing them about.

He'd been panicking all week about how to tell Johno and he'd put off calling him and ignored his calls through pure fear. When he'd heard what Emmie had to say, he'd had to stop himself shouting for joy on the phone and made sure he played it cool.

'I don't know Em, you've fucked me about too many times. How do I know you're serious? I've moved on.'

'I know I messed up but I'll make it up to you, I promise.'

Jake hadn't said anything for a few moments, feigning indecision, but he hadn't wanted to push his luck either.

'Okay, Friday it is.'

He'd put the phone down and celebrated with a can of Coke and a large spliff. Finally people were going to know who he was; he was going places.

CHAPTER TWENTY-FIVE

'Just tell me who the fuck you were taking grapes to, Jan.'

Janine Jennings stared at her husband holding the hospital car park ticket, and her blood ran cold. She'd no idea what to say and by the looks of his face, Alfie knew it too. She could kill Emmie. She'd told her to throw it away, but obviously she'd just dropped it on the floor of the car, and Janine knew unless she came up with a really good excuse in the next few moments, she was going to be well and truly splattered in it when the proverbial hit the fan.

'Don't know, Alfie love. Maybe it got stuck on my foot or Emmie's foot and we brought it into the car without knowing.'

'Not good enough darling, try again.'

Alfie could feel his blood boiling as he watched his wife lying through her expensive fucking veneers. Before she left the kitchen she was going to tell him the truth. Everything was fucked up; he had Oscar and Vaughn to deal with and now his cunting wife was telling him a load of porky pies.

'You see, I was thinking about it and racking me brains and the date on the ticket is the same date as the day I couldn't contact either of you. I don't bleed once a month, Jan, so don't treat me like a cunt.'

'Alfie, I really don't know nothing about it.'

'Liar.'

'Alf, please.'

Alfie wanted to smash the whole kitchen up. He hadn't felt so enraged in his life. He'd never imagined Jan could stand looking him straight in the eye and lie her saggy tits off.

'See, thing is Jan, I was also talking to a mate of mine and Whipps Cross hospital turns out to be the same hospital as Jake Bellingham was taken to. Funny that, ain't it?'

Janine felt her face flush red. Without thinking she bolted for the door and was surprised to feel Alfie's hands grab her round the back of her neck, dragging her backwards.

'You took my fucking daughter to see that fucking prick didn't you?'

She didn't answer and Alfie kneed her hard in her back. The pain from being winded made it difficult for her to speak.

'Alfie, please – she was so upset.'

'Upset? No Jan, this here is upset. What you see now on my face is upset. Can you see the fucking difference?'

Alfie backhanded his wife across her face, splitting her lip. It was the first time he'd ever raised a hand to her and he felt as much shock from what he'd done as from seeing the horror on her face. The blood and the scream came out of her mouth at the same time.

He looked at her with a face full of rage. She had some fucking front to go behind his back and take Em to see Jake. He could just about understand his daughter; she'd been like a lovesick puppy; but Janine, she was just taking the piss.

He should've killed Jake when he'd had the opportunity. Bellingham would be laughing his fucking head off at him;

204

he'd be a laughing stock. Tough guy Alfie Jennings, who can't even control his family. He should take a leaf out of Max Donaldson's book, he'd got the right idea; he ruled his family like he was fucking Heinrich Himmler.

This time, Alfie clenched his fist and smashed it down in Janine's mouth.

'You're nothing but a stupid bitch, Janine. I've had to put up with your crap too long and I'm not doing it any more.'

His fist came back again and he gave a hard blow to her head. She fell forward, and the sight of his wife lying on the floor with her fat thighs showing and her face covered in blood incensed him as his guilt hit him hard. He bent down and grabbed hold of her hair as she tried to crawl away.

'Where the fuck are you going, Janine? Off to tell some more lies eh?'

Janine's lip was pouring with blood and she blurted out her answers through her tears.

'Alfie, I'm sorry, it won't happen again. I promise.'

'Too fucking right it won't.'

For the next five minutes, Alfie rained down blows on his wife in a sustained attack until he was exhausted. He leant on the kitchen bar and pushed away the guilt of what he'd done and the thoughts of how for a moment he'd turned into his father, by convincing himself Janine had pushed him to it.

The smell of the hospital corridors made Casey lean on the walls to steady herself. She was feeling dizzy, having had nothing to eat, and she could almost smell the alcohol of the past few days coming through her pores.

The nurse on the desk had told her Lola had been moved out of the ICU and onto Cherry Ward, which was on the other side of the modernised hospital.

'Lola!'

Casey walked into the side ward to see Lola sitting up in bed. Her head and nose were bandaged and she had the biggest black eyes Casey had ever seen.

'Bleedin' hell Casey love, you look worse than I do.'

Casey grinned and then burst into tears.

'What is it lovie? I was only kidding, come and sit down here and tell me what's wrong. You haven't burnt down me bleedin' cafe have you?'

'I'm sorry, the last thing you need is me coming in here and adding to your problems.'

'Hey, don't you be silly. I'm better than I've been for a while. Look, they've put me on a morphine drip; I'm in me bleedin' element. I should've been beaten up a long time ago. And they tell me if it wasn't for you, they'd be dancing on my grave by now. I owe you one. And besides, if you don't tell me what's up, you can count yourself fired.'

Casey grinned through her tears; she'd become so fond of Lola and she felt she could trust her. Sitting down on the chair next to the bed, Casey began to talk, telling Lola about everything from her drinking to Josh and the letter and what happened in the club to the visit with Mrs Simms.

After she finished talking, Lola didn't say anything for a while, but then she smiled.

'Bleedin' hell; and I thought I'd lived a life.'

Lola fell silent again and even through her battered face, Casey could see her looking thoughtful.

'I've got the letter on me if you'd like to see it.'

Not waiting for a reply, Casey rummaged in her bag and handed the crumpled letter over to Lola. It was dated January 2009.

My dearest Cassandra,
I'm not sure if you will ever get to read this letter, but
I am going to give it to Josh for him to look after and

for him to judge when the time is right and decide what's best for you, after all, he knows you better than I do now and I trust he will have your best interests at heart and he'll know when you are ready. The last thing I want to do is hurt you any more than you have been already.

I have to start by saying I am sorry, though I know the word will never erase the heartache you have suffered. I never wanted your life to turn out how it did and I have had to watch from afar unable to ease your pain, which is my burden and the consequence of turning my back on you all those years ago.

I pretended to myself I was doing what was right, even though in my heart I knew it wasn't, but it was easier to let your mother make the decisions; it was easier just to get on with my life and deny how I really felt; but not one day has gone by without me thinking about you. I now know I was wrong and should have been there for you, for your child and my grandchild. I should've been there to protect you, my darling.

The time you were in the hospital, I didn't visit you – not because I didn't want to but because I was too ashamed to. By standing back and doing nothing to help when you asked me to, I forced you to give up your child; my grandchild. Forgive me Casey.

The one thing I can do though is let you know the truth. Maybe it will help to put your mind at ease slightly; help you to find your way back from the wilderness I know you are in.

I know for all this time, Cassandra, you thought you'd given birth to a son: in fact you had a daughter; a beautiful little girl called Emmie.

I managed to track her adoptive parents down through an old friend of mine who had some useful *contacts. It's amazing what money can buy, but it was the least I could do; and each year up until four years ago, I wrote to them. Since my illness, I sadly lost touch. Apparently she is thriving and from what I gather she is very much like you when you were little; independent, feisty but also very loving.*

I don't have their address, as my letters were all sent through a third party, but I do have her full name: Emmie May Williams. A beautiful name for a beautiful girl. She lived in the East End of London but from what I understand they have moved now, although I know they had some contacts in Soho – I hope this information will help. If you do look for her, be careful, Cassandra: I don't want you being any more hurt than you already are.

I know if the time is right Josh will have given you this but please don't be angry with him, I didn't tell him what was in this letter, he didn't know about Emmie, the only thing I said was what was written might help you find your child. Of course he was worried you might not be strong enough as was I and though it will be of little compensation for you, remember I always loved you – but I was weak and I know I failed you when you needed me most, I am truly sorry. Enclosed is a photo of Emmie when she was two months old. She has your eyes.

With my deepest love and regret,
Dad xx

Lola put the letter down and stared at Casey.

'My dad died three months after he wrote that.'

Lola nodded and put her hand out to Casey, who carried on talking. 'I went back round to Mrs Simms, but she'd already left for Australia and there was no forwarding address. All this time I've been grieving for my son and all along it was a little girl. It feels as if my whole life has been a lie. I'm so angry with Josh for not telling me that he had a letter for me, I know he was probably doing what he thought was best but I can't find it in me to forgive him. One thing he was right on though: I should've left well alone. It hurts more now than it ever did.'

'Emmie May Williams. Well, well, well. Little Emmie May.'

Casey looked at Lola as if she'd gone mad as she sang her daughter's name, cackling with laughter.

'Oh don't look at me like that, Casey; it'll take more morphine than they're pumping into me for me to lose my mind. What you need to do is put the lid back on that whisky bottle you like to keep so handy and start pulling yourself together, because I think I might just know who you're looking for.'

CHAPTER TWENTY-SIX

Oscar parked his black Mercedes and felt excited; so much so he was managing to ignore the pulsating pain in his head. Nesha had taken the girls to Bow and the last phone call he'd taken had pleased him no end. It was all working out perfectly. Parking a few streets away from the flat, Oscar walked slowly towards the address so as not to aggravate his headache.

The block of flats was in the middle of a large housing estate on the north side of Camden Town. The neglected grey tower blocks loomed overhead blocking out the sun, which added to the sense of gloom.

As he walked through the estate, he saw junkies and winos scampering about like rats. By the looks of things, they'd taken over what was left of the children's playground which was full of shit: syringes and used condoms.

He walked up five flights of stairs to flat number twenty-four. He hadn't wanted to take the lift; it hadn't only smelt of piss but it'd had a pool of it in the corner, and he had no intention of ruining his new Gucci shoes.

When he got to the front door, he didn't bother knocking; he could see it was slightly ajar. The flat was quiet and he gently walked through each room, not wanting to make a noise. The kitchen sink was full of dishes and on the table there were overflowing ashtrays and yesterday's newspapers. The bathroom was tiny and the bedroom was full of Aston Villa posters, piles of filthy socks and jeans strewn all over the threadbare carpet.

The one room Oscar hadn't been in was the room directly in front of the kitchen, and the door was shut. Cautiously he stood to the side of the doorway, raised his leg and pushed the handle down with his foot, giving it a tap with his toes to help it swing open.

The body of Jake Bellingham lay on the floor. Standing over him holding a gun was Emmie Jennings, who was just realising she'd just made a bad situation even worse.

'Vaughn, it's Freddie. I've got the info you wanted. Makes for interesting reading; shall I come over?'

Vaughn hung up and threw the phone over onto the exquisite marble bedside table. He missed and it fell on the floor, waking up his Labrador dog, Sammie, who went into a frenzied barking fit.

'Shut the fuck up Sam,' Vaughn shouted at the golden-haired dog, but it made no difference and in the end Vaughn pulled himself up out of bed, closing the door to get a bit of peace.

Pulling on his Ralph Lauren black robe, Vaughn looked at the two women who were naked and stoned out of their heads on his bed. He wasn't sure what time it was but he knew it was gone lunchtime; Freddie wasn't a morning person and if he was offering to come over it meant the one o'clock news had come and gone.

He lit a cigarette, which he'd been trying to avoid doing, but he was angry he couldn't shake the feeling hanging over him. It would've been most men's fantasy to have a threesome with two blondes and two pairs of pneumatic breasts but it hadn't done anything for him. Of course he'd fucked them and had his dick sucked, but he might as well have been working out a page of advanced equations for all the pleasure it'd given him.

Casey was on his mind and even though he hated every inch of her, he still couldn't stop thinking about her. Stepping into the shower, Vaughn turned the temperature to cold, hoping the freezing water would jolt him back to his senses.

Three-quarters of an hour later, Vaughn had instructed one of his men to drive the women back to wherever they wanted to go; he'd also given them eight hundred big ones each for their trouble.

Back in his office, Vaughn was determined not to think about Casey and was trying to convince himself he was interested in reading the story in the paper about more government cuts. He lit another cigarette and saw on one of the monitors that Freddie had arrived at the house gates.

He'd had security cameras fitted over a year ago and now he was able to see all around the grounds and the inside of the house with a flick of a button. Even now, he couldn't be too careful; the world he'd lived in had a long memory and he was quite certain there were a lot of people who'd be happy to put a bullet in his head at any given time.

'Freddie, can I get you a drink, fella?'
'I'll have a Bourbon on the rocks.'
'Talk, I'm listening.'
'Maybe you'll need to have a drink first; I know I certainly do.'

Vaughn smiled at Freddie; he'd been around as long as he had. Freddie had never been a face or worked a turf but he'd been vital to his and a lot of other people's businesses.

He was a paper man; he found out facts, and whether it was information on clients, punters, coppers or MPs, Freddie constantly came up with the goods. Over the years he'd helped him out on lots of matters and all the info had always been spot on.

Vaughn knew Freddie liked a good quality Bourbon, so he let him drink it in peace and waited for him to talk.

'The man Casey was with at the station is called Josh Edwards; he's Old Bill. Detective Sergeant Edwards; works in Vice up in Birmingham and he's married to Casey, but apparently they're getting a divorce.'

Vaughn's mind was racing: fuck! She'd been telling the truth about the divorce, but for some reason it still felt like a betrayal. It surprised him to hear she'd been married to the Old Bill; she seemed the least likely candidate to be the wife of one of the boys in blue.

'Fuck, fuck, fuck. How could I've been so stupid?'

Vaughn shouted the last part and Freddie, unconcerned at the outburst, helped himself to another large Bourbon, though this time without the rocks and a much more generous glassful than he'd been originally served.

Vaughn gathered himself together.

'But why did she end up here?'

'Well, she walked out on Josh and the marriage about eighteen months ago; seems she was always on the tipping point, one of life's lost souls, as they say, but she had to come down here because she needed to find her child.'

Vaughn sat down on the green leather Chesterfield in shock. It was if someone had given him a punch in his stomach.

'Jesus.'

'Oh no, I haven't finished; it gets better. Take a look at this.'

Freddie, who always enjoyed the melodrama of a story,

handed over a photograph of Emmie and then a photo of Casey. Vaughn looked up at Freddie, not getting the connection.

'I don't understand.'

'No? Have another look.'

Vaughn stared down at the photos and then the penny started to drop. It couldn't be. Could it? He always knew Emmie was adopted; everyone did except for Emmie herself, which he always thought was the wrong call, but no one dared mention it because Alfie had warned them all years ago what would happen to them if they did, and nobody wanted to end up brown bread at the bottom of the Thames.

Looking at the photos it struck Vaughn why Casey had always looked so familiar. It was as if he'd been looking at Emmie: they had the same eyes; the same beautiful haunting eyes.

Vaughn continued to sit in his office long after Freddie had left him. Casey was trouble and his brain was telling him to stay well away. She'd been right when she'd said it was complicated, but Freddie had told him that as far as he knew she was still in the dark about Emmie; he hoped it would stay that way, especially as it involved Alfie. Vaughn knew the last thing Alfie would want would be for someone to rain down some shit on his little family.

Her drinking seemed to be out of control and she screamed red lights and red flags, but every part of her being had got to him, and he didn't want to let her go. She'd lied, or at the very least she hadn't told the truth, and he detested dishonesty; but then what did he expect? He hadn't exactly told her the truth about his life, and did he really think she'd disclose her past to him just like that, and just because he'd wanted her to?

Taking a deep breath and picking up the phone, Vaughn

dialled Casey's number – but it went straight to voicemail. He didn't bother leaving a message and instead dialled a different one.

'Alf, it's Vaughn. I'm looking for Cass and I was wondering if she's been in the club?'

'No, I haven't seen her in here, but it's probably just as well.'

'Meaning?'

'Oh sorry, didn't I say? She stayed over at my flat last night. Sorry Vaughnie, I thought you two were well over. I would never have gone there if I'd known: you know me, I don't sniff my mates' women, but you saw her; she was handing it out on a plate – and well, I was feeling a bit hungry. Good time was had by all.'

Vaughn gripped his mobile phone and couldn't say anything; he felt his chest going tight and he knew Alfie was enjoying every second of the phone call.

'Vaughn? You still there?'

Vaughn could hear the tightness in his voice as he answered.

'Oh I'm still here alright. Live and kicking, Alf, live and fucking kicking. I better be off; things to do, but I'm glad to hear you had a good time.'

'The best, Vaughnie, the best.'

Alfie felt deflated. He thought he'd feel smug telling Vaughn about the night he'd spent with Casey, albeit an exaggerated version. He'd felt so clever telling Casey it was best they didn't mention anything, clearing the way for him to tell Vaughn what he liked.

By giving Vaughn his version of events first, Alfie was sure if Casey *did* decide to say anything, knowing his friend as he did, Vaughn's male pride and ego wouldn't let him believe her – and if she didn't say anything, he would just presume she was a devious cheating bitch. Either way, Alfie was certain Casey's time with Vaughn was over; he would get rid of her.

Alfie hadn't expected to feel as he did: after all he'd done what he'd set out to do. Granted he hadn't got a fuck out of it, but he'd assumed he'd feel happy. Instead all it'd done was left him feeling sorry for himself.

He'd been friends with Vaughn the moment Connor had introduced them, and his friend had never wronged him in all that time. He loved Vaughn as he'd loved his brother, but he'd never admit that to anyone.

Vaughn always remembered his and Janine's anniversary, and sent luxurious presents to Emmie even when there wasn't a special occasion to celebrate. He'd always watched his back when there were people ready to stab him in it, and in the world he lived in, having a wing man he could trust was a rare thing.

Alfie knew he didn't really have a right to be annoyed with Vaughn for not lending him the money, he'd always had his principles; but he was just fucked off he'd got himself into a mess. There was no reason why anyone should get him out of a situation he'd been warned about.

Opening up a packet of cheese and onion crisps, Alfie's thoughts moved to Emmie. He wanted to talk to her, because he'd been thinking hard and what he'd thought about needed answers. He'd gone over the visit from Scottish Charlie in his mind and the more he thought, the more unlikely it was that Charlie had taken the missing packages; impossible in fact. Janine had sworn it wasn't her and after the kicking she'd received, which he still shuddered to think about, he was sure she was telling the truth. So it only left one person: Emmie.

'Well where the fuck is she?' Alfie spoke harshly and glared at Janine for a moment before averting his eyes. Her face was cut and swollen from his actions the day before and he felt thoroughly ashamed of himself; not that he'd admit it for one moment, or ever say sorry: it would not only give Janine the upper hand but also the idea she could take the piss.

He took another quick look at her and saw her lip was double its normal size and she was hunched over on the chair, holding her stomach.

'I dunno where she is, Alf. She said she was going to go and see Maria but it's a good bloody job she ain't here. It'd kill her to see me like this.'

Alfie turned away; he could tell Janine was laying it on thick to get a rise from him but he wasn't going to fall for it. He stayed silent and let her talk.

'Perhaps she did come in, Alf, and saw you doing this to me. Have you thought of that?'

He hadn't, and the panic rose in his throat. He knew when he'd seen his own father beat up on his mother, how it'd left him feeling, and he never wanted Emmie to feel like that or look at him the way he'd looked at his own father.

He'd always scarpered the moment trouble had started at home and never stayed around long enough to watch the final knockout. He'd always gone to stay with mates or slept rough; anything was better than seeing his mother being knocked around senseless, screaming for help, and being powerless to do anything about it.

Life was different today; it wasn't safe for young kids to be mooching round on the streets, especially for a girl.

'We need to call her friends.'

'Some bleedin' chance. I can't do anything like this, can I Alf?'

That was the last straw for Alfie. Janine was taking the piss now and it wasn't any longer just about him; it was about his daughter and her whereabouts, and nobody was going to put Emmie's safety in jeopardy. Leaping angrily towards his wife, Alfie grabbed hold of her face hard – but not hard enough to hurt her again.

'Listen Jan, if it makes you feel better, I am sorry for what I did to you; so fucking sorry you wouldn't believe. I'm down on me fucking knees I'm that sorry, Jan, but do not take the fucking piss out of me. Emmie should be home by now and she's not and I need you to get your finger out of your saggy arse and help me track her down. Do you understand me?'

Janine Jennings's face was a few inches away from her husband's and she could smell the crisps he'd eaten. She'd never seen him so passionate and sincere about anything in his life and she'd certainly never seen the fear which was now in his eyes, nor the tears spilling down his face.

'Okay Alf. I'll help you. I'll see if I can contact any of her friends.'

Midnight came and went and Oscar hadn't heard from Alfie, but it didn't worry him: he was satisfied with what he had. The girls were safely with Nesha and he was going to give Jason the nod for the party. It'd worked out better than he could've ever imagined; every single penny earned from the girls from now on was going directly in his pocket. The alarm clock had rung on Alfie; he'd shot himself in the fucking foot not coming up with the goods in time because everyone in their line of business knew there was always a comeuppance.

Oscar knew Alfie fucking up had worked out better for him. He was now the sole owner of the women, but better still, he'd hit the jackpot and he was going to enjoy playing finders keepers. It'd show Alfie and everyone else that trying to take advantage of his good nature was a very bad move.

Making two cups of cocoa in the spotless stainless steel

kitchen, Oscar put extra sugar in the red mug and took it through to his new house guest.

'Drink this, it'll make you feel better; but it's hot, so don't burn your tongue.'

Emmie Jennings trembled. Even though the heating was on and she'd a thick duvet wrapped around her shoulders she felt as if her body was made of ice. Her head was all over the place and she couldn't quite work out what had happened in Jake's flat.

When she'd first got the idea of phoning Oscar, she'd had to get his number out of her dad's phone. She'd worked out the PIN lock on it which hadn't been hard to do as he'd used her date of birth. She'd nearly chickened out calling, but then she'd seen her dad moping around, something he only did when he was worried, and she knew there was no choice but to call Oscar.

Emmie hadn't known how Oscar would react to her call but he'd been kind and listened to what had gone on with her and Jake and the letters she'd found. She'd confessed about the packages, telling him how it'd been all her fault and not her dad's. She'd expected him to explode but he'd told her not to worry and to meet him behind Tottenham Court Road.

When they'd met, he'd taken her to Starbucks and he'd nodded sympathetically and offered her tissues when she'd cried. He hadn't said much at first but then he'd come up with a plan; a plan which had scared her, but Oscar had told her it was the only way to get her dad out of the trouble he was in and get back the packages she'd given Jake.

It'd only taken her a few minutes to decide. She'd got her dad into the mess and now she needed to be prepared to do anything to help get him out of it. She was terrified but it was the right thing to do; the *only* thing to do.

Oscar had asked her lots of questions and then somehow

she'd ended up telling him about the guns her dad kept hidden away in the house. Oscar had told her to take one of the guns she didn't think her father would miss and then he'd arranged to meet her at Jake's flat.

'Emmie, are you sure you can do this?'

She'd nodded, but her heart was racing and she'd felt dizzy and had to sit down.

'You can back out, Em, but then what's your dad going to do eh? You wouldn't want anything nasty to happen to him would you? Are you sure Jake's expecting you?'

'Yes, I said I was missing him and had changed my mind about bringing him another package.'

'And he definitely bought your story? We don't want any fuckups do we?'

'Yeah, he believed me alright.'

Emmie had felt terrified, especially when she'd put her hand in her pocket and felt the small steel gun.

'Billy will meet you there, and I'll be right behind you.'

But Billy hadn't been there and neither had Oscar. The door of Jake's flat was slightly ajar and she'd walked in without even thinking of closing it behind her, with the gun tightly gripped in her hand. She hadn't wanted to think about what she was doing because if she had, she knew she would've backed out; so she kept Jake out of her mind and her dad in it. When she'd gone into the lounge, she'd frozen in fear and started to back away. Jake was already lying there, with his eyes wide open.

'Give me the gun, Em.'

Oscar had appeared from nowhere, giving her the fright of her life and nearly causing her to pull the trigger. He'd come up behind her in the flat and taken the gun from her trembling hand. She hadn't been able to take her eyes off Jake just lying there with blood running out of his ear; she'd wanted to run, wanted to scream, but she'd been unable to do anything. Her heart had raced but she, like Jake, was motionless, and she hadn't known what to say.

'You did well, Emmie.'

'But I didn't do it; he was here on the floor already, I swear.'

She'd turned to face Oscar who'd smiled and stared at her intensely before going over to Jake's body with the gun in his hand.

'We want to make absolutely sure now don't we?'

'Please Oscar, you have to believe me, I didn't do it.'

'Whatever you say; but you know as well as I do, the only reason why Jake Bellingham's lying here is because of you.'

Oscar grinned at her and then he'd bent over the body and put the gun against Jake's head at close range and pulled the trigger, blowing a hole as wide as Emmie's fist into Jake's skull.

She'd screamed hysterically as bits of Jake's brain splattered over her clothes. The room had spun round and she'd seen the framed poster of Stan Collymore, Jake's all time favourite player, in front of her, splattered with blood. Oscar had put his gloved fingers to his lips to tell her to be quiet before he'd led her out of the flat and driven her to one of his homes.

'Your cocoa's going cold. You need to get it inside you; don't want to send you home with a cold.'

Emmie felt sick. All she could see in her mind was the gaping hole in Jake's brain. Stupidly she hadn't thought it'd be so real. How many times had she and her mum watched *CSI: Miami* curled up on the settee? But it wasn't like that: there were no ad breaks or any opportunities to turn over and watch something different; instead there'd been the pool of Jake's blood, almost black in colour and nauseatingly sweet-smelling; a potent coppery stench which Emmie thought she could still smell. Then there'd been the pulp, the muted grey flesh, the blood-flecked pieces of Jake's brain that had sprayed onto her.

Looking back she knew she should have called her Uncle Vaughn; he'd always been so kind to her. When they'd hung out, she'd always had so much fun and he made her feel special, which she didn't feel very often. She hadn't called him because she'd been afraid he might tell her dad, but that would've been a whole lot better than what she'd got herself into.

'I'd really like to go home now, Oscar.' Emmie spoke in a small frightened voice.

'I don't think that's sensible at the moment. Trust me though; you'll be home before you can say bang.'

Oscar laughed and looked at Emmie shaking on his couch, wrapped in his large duck-down duvet. She'd been such an easy target; a gift. He hadn't been going to leave it to chance or a stupid schoolgirl, so he'd arranged for Billy to pay Jake a visit just before Emmie was due to arrive.

Billy had done well and it'd been over in a matter of minutes; a sharp instrument through Jake's ear and through to his brain, which wouldn't be picked up at the autopsy after he'd used the gun to blow a hole in Jake's head. Billy had managed to find the packets of heroin as well, which Jake had stupidly hidden at the back of one of the kitchen cabinets.

They'd watched Emmie go into the block of flats and he'd given her a few minutes before following her. She'd played right into his hands; she'd given him the gun. He'd blown a hole in Jake's head, frightening her. By the time he'd finished fucking with her head, Emmie Jennings would be putty in his hands.

She hadn't seen his *pièce de résistance* when he'd kicked the gun under the couch; she was too busy screaming and wallowing in self-pity, looking for comfort from him. It'd worked out perfectly: so well he'd had to bite down on his lip to stop himself laughing out loud.

Oscar took a sip of his drink; he was enjoying every moment of this. It wasn't about the money. At first it had been, but it was about so much more than that now. He was going to show the great Alfie Jennings what it felt like to fall, and he was going to show Vaughn he'd made a very big mistake to think he could fuck with him. The one thing both Alfie and Vaughn had in common, their one Achilles' heel, was Emmie; daughter and goddaughter respectively. And it would be their love for her which would be their ultimate downfall.

Finishing off his drink Oscar knew the best part was yet to come: the fireworks hadn't even started, the games were just about to begin; his revenge was about to be taken.

CHAPTER TWENTY-SEVEN

Casey's head was all over the place. She couldn't believe what Lola had told her. Her daughter was almost within touching distance. Of course she wasn't a hundred per cent sure it was her but Lola had been certain that the name 'Williams' was Janine Jennings's maiden name, the same Janine Jennings who was married to Alfie and the same Janine Jennings who'd looked at her like scum in the restaurant. It was incredible, and if she'd read it somewhere she wouldn't have believed it herself. Alfie Jennings of all people.

But now the problem was to know what to do. It was stupid: all these years of waiting and she hadn't actually planned what she'd do. Of course her heart said to go charging in but she knew that would be wrong; she didn't know even if Emmie knew about being adopted, but even if she did there was no saying she'd want anything to do with her, and the last thing Casey wanted was to mess up her daughter's life. She would need to think very hard before she made any decisions.

For some reason Casey thought of Vaughn. She wanted to talk to him. Not about this; she'd certainly keep this to herself, but she had a sudden urge just to hear his voice, though she wasn't so sure he'd want to hear hers. She hadn't really had many friends in life and there was something nice about having someone there. Bracing herself she dialled his number.

'You're some fucking sort of joker calling me up, Casey, you know that? You should take a spot at Alfie's club, I'm sure he'd be amenable; after all, you two are well acquainted.'

'What's that supposed to mean?'

'Nothing.'

'Why are you behaving like this? If you've got something to say, just say it.'

'I'm saying nothing.'

Vaughn hated phone calls at the best of times; he'd rather face the person, especially when he was having a barney with them. He wanted to see Casey's lying face and see if there was anything resembling guilt on it.

He wasn't going to mention he'd found out about her being Emmie's mother; that was something else entirely. He needed time to get his head round that and tread very carefully. His problem with her was Alfie, and what he'd said about them spending the night together.

Everything Alfie had told him hadn't mattered: he'd still wanted to give them a chance; they could've taken their time and worked everything out over time. He would've been happy to help and support her in any way she'd needed; he would've given her everything he had, as well as giving her something he'd never thought he'd give to any woman – he would've given her his heart. But it was too late now, and he was determined not to wallow in it; it was pointless, it was over, she and Alf had seen to that.

He sighed, trying to compose not just his anger but mainly his jealousy whilst picking off a dead petal from the small potted rose on his desk. He was trying not to become childish by being mean to her, and he had to admit he wasn't doing a very good job of it; but he was hurt – it'd knocked him sideways and sent him reeling to hear about her and Alfie, and hearing her voice on the phone sounding so bright and fucking breezy just added to his misery. He guessed he had no right to dictate to Casey who she could or couldn't sleep with, but Christ almighty, sleeping with Alfie Jennings was certainly a massive kick in the balls.

'I didn't call for an argument.'

'Well what did you call for, Cass?'

'Just to say hello; nothing else.'

'Well you've said it now.'

He could've kicked himself; his hurt was getting the better of him and he was being a prize jerk, but he found it so hard to keep his mouth shut when she started to feign fucking innocence. He'd kept hundreds of secrets; ones if he ever opened his mouth about would mean a lot of men would be in a lot of trouble. He had no trouble keeping those secrets, no problem keeping schtum; but for some reason Casey turned him into a male version of Janine: a total gobshite.

'I don't know what's got into you. I understand you're still angry about the other night and I'm sorry, really. I'd had a bad day and I shouldn't have had so much to drink; I'll be the first one to admit that and hold my hands up. It's no excuse I know, but I'm sorry. Can you forgive me? And as for the stuff with that guy, nothing happened . . .'

'Which guy Casey? Which one of them?'

'I'm sorry . . . ?'

'Look, I really don't want to talk about it any more. It's done; finished.'

Casey wanted to talk about it some more but she knew when to leave it. She didn't want to try to defend her bad behaviour and through guilt become defensive and say things she might regret. She'd actually hoped Vaughn would've forgiven her making a fool of herself with the guy in the street. For a moment it crossed her mind that maybe Alfie had mentioned her crashing out at his flat, but they'd specifically agreed not to, and why would he? Vaughn and Alfie were friends and she was sure he wouldn't want to hurt Vaughn by telling him, though really there was nothing to tell; it would've taken a whole brewery and then some for her to ever contemplate sleeping with Alfie Jennings.

She knew Vaughn was a proud man and she didn't expect that he would forget her drunken behaviour, but she'd hoped he would've heard the sincerity in her apology and they could be friends again. The tone in his voice, however, told her he was far from over it, and certainly not in a forgiving mood. 'Well, I'm sorry to have bothered you, Vaughn.'

Casey put the phone down, leaving Vaughn full of frustrated anger; most of all towards himself.

'Two fucking days! What the hell am I supposed to do?'

It was nearly eleven at night and Alfie was pacing up and down in the all-white front reception room. Janine sat on the handmade Italian leather couch and watched her husband despairingly, as desperate for news as he was.

'I fucking told you to keep a better eye on her, Jan. If anything happens to her, I'm blaming you.'

'Me? How the fuck do you work that one out, Alf? She's run away because she found the letters.'

'I told you to get rid of them. Did you not think she'd find them eventually? Fuck me Jan, how stupid could you be to keep a box of letters from her real grandfather and not think it was a bleeding time bomb waiting to explode?'

'I wanted to keep them for her when she got older, to show her she wasn't given up because she wasn't loved.'

'When did you become a fucking social worker, Jan? Who

says she ever needed to know? Who says we were ever going to tell her? I certainly wasn't. She didn't need to know, Jan, because things like this happen; she runs away.'

Janine looked at her husband. He'd always been determined Emmie would never find out about her adoption and he hadn't wanted to listen when she'd said she didn't think it was a good idea, so she'd left it.

When the yearly letters had started to come from Emmie's paternal grandfather via a third party who'd been part of arranging the initial adoption, she'd written back to let him know how Emmie was getting on; she felt it was the least she could do. There had not only been a sense of longing in the letters to know his granddaughter was safe and happy, but also a sense of regret that things had turned out the way they had. They'd touched a chord with her, and she hadn't been able to ignore them and just throw them in the bin.

Alfie hadn't been too happy about it and he'd told her to get rid of them, but she'd kept them to show Emmie when she was older. She'd never imagined she'd find them.

She'd discovered the box of letters at the bottom of Emmie's wardrobe – she hadn't even known they'd gone from where she'd hidden them – when she was looking for Emmie's address book to phone round her friends to see if they'd seen her.

Everything had fallen into place. No wonder Emmie had been moody and distant: she'd discovered after all these years that they weren't her biological parents; they weren't who she thought they were and she wasn't who she thought she was. Essentially they'd been lying to her, and no doubt she didn't trust her or Alfie any more. The kid must have been really screwed up, and Janine prayed they'd find her soon so they could start picking up the pieces for her.

Alfie was still pacing and was beginning to rant at her again, breaking her off from her thoughts.

'And whose fault was it eh? Tell me. Who was the one who took our daughter to see Jake?'

'She's probably with him.'

'And that's supposed to make me feel better is it?'

'No, but I'm sure that's where she is. Where else can she be?'

'You've tried all her friends?'

'She didn't really have any, Alf; not from what I can see. I looked at her Facebook account and most of what I read on Emmie's wall was from those nasty bitches at school spouting their poison about her. I'm telling you Alf, when I see those girls I'll break their fucking necks. Only nice thing was what Emmie had written about Jake, you know, the usual teenage love stuff. So I reckon they'll be together; I'm sure she's with him.'

Alfie roared loudly, kicking the vase of lilies over onto the white carpet, furious at what he was hearing.

'How can you be so sure, Jan? Have you spoken to him?'

'No.'

'No, because fuck knows where he is. And if Emmie is with him, then that means fuck knows where she is too. So you see whatever crap you're coming up with, it's not helping is it? So do me a fucking favour, darling – keep it shut, because you're wrecking my head.'

Janine knew Alfie was being torn in two, but so was she, and she wished for once they could come together instead of tearing each other to bits.

The hammering on the front door made Janine and Alfie stop arguing and look at each other, seeing other's fear in their expressions. Alfie's face drained of colour and he prayed it wasn't going to be bad news about Emmie.

'Do you think it's about Em?'

Before Alfie could answer, they heard the sound of the front door being smashed in. Janine screamed, running behind

229

the couch as dogs and dozens of police ran into the house, shouting instructions for everyone to get down.

The reception room filled up with police in their riot uniforms and it became a blur for Janine as she continued to shriek and watched her husband get kicked in the base of his back and taken down on the floor.

Alfie's hands were pulled behind his back with force and he cried out. The handcuffs were placed on him whilst the Alsatian dogs barked wildly.

'Alfred Victor Jennings, I'm arresting you on suspicion of the murder of Jake Bellingham. You don't have to . . .'

Alfie shouted as his rights were being read out to him. The tallest of the policemen put his foot on the back of Alfie's neck, pushing his face into the thick wool carpet, but it only added to Alfie's anger.

'What about my daughter? What's happened to Emmie, was she with him? Jan, Jan! Call my solicitor and call Vaughn, try to find out what the fuck's going on.'

CHAPTER TWENTY-EIGHT

Pentonville Prison on the Holloway Road was one of the few prisons Alfie Jennings hadn't seen the inside of until now. In the past he'd been kept on remand at Chelmsford Prison prior to being sent to one of the clinks in the North of England, which in his mind was done with the sole intention of making it awkward for his family to visit him.

They'd brought him through the cream-walled building of Pentonville and placed him on A Wing, where they kept first nighters and did inductions. Within twenty-four hours they'd moved him to C Wing for the remand and convicted prisoners, and although Alfie had been in and out of prison more times than he could remember without checking with his brief, this was the first time he'd ever been banged up for something he'd no part of.

'The gun found in Jake's flat has your prints on it, Mr Jennings. We are charging you . . .'

Alfie had looked at his brief incredulously as the DI charged him with the murder of Jake Bellingham. He wouldn't have minded being celled up if he'd pulled the trigger and wiped the smug smile off his face: it was a risk he was always prepared to take when he crossed the line; but he'd been nowhere near the flat. Hell, he didn't even know where the boy lived, because if he had, he'd have been right round there to wring Emmie's whereabouts out of him.

When they'd showed him the bagged-up gun, he'd been so shocked, even the detectives questioning him saw the genuine surprise on his face; but Alfie knew it didn't matter to them if they'd felt up the wrong guy for the murder, as long as they'd finally got their hands on him. That was all that mattered.

He had no clue the gun was even missing; he seldom got it out and he couldn't recall a time when he'd actually used it, apart from scaring the shit out of piss takers. The moment he saw it, Alfie knew he was being framed, but what he didn't know was why.

'I don't want to see her.'

Alfie lay on the top bunk of the metal-framed bed in his cell, staring at the tiny pin holes in the ceiling.

'You could at least make the effort, Jennings; they've come all the way to see you. You're lucky to have a visitor; there are some guys in here who never have a visit.'

'Then you can get her to go and visit them. I told you, I don't want to see her. I'll see him, but not her.'

The prison warden sighed and rattled his keys impatiently, waiting for Alfie to get up and follow him down to the visiting room. He could see the screw wasn't going to take no for an answer, so after lacing up his trainers, Alfie followed the warden out of his cell and through the locked doors of the wing.

C Wing's ceilings were high and airy, with wide steel netting hanging from the first and second floors which went from one side to another, in an attempt to stop the inmates trying to commit suicide by jumping. Most of the cell doors were open and as Alfie walked through he saw the respectful nods from other prisoners who were standing on the landings or wandering about aimlessly in their prison-issue striped shirts and blue trousers.

The visiting room was full. Teas and coffees were being bought at the snack bar run by the Mothers' Union volunteers and at the back of the room Alfie saw the tall figure of Vaughn and next to him, with a handful of tissues, was Janine.

'I don't want to see her.'

'Turn it in Alf, she's cut up about this and she wants to see you. By the look of her boat race, I think you owe her.'

Alfie glanced down at Janine and noticed her face was still very badly bruised; her eye was turning a yellowy black and her lip was still double its size. Standing in front of Vaughn, he felt very ashamed of himself.

'Alfie please, don't be mad at me.'

Janine Jennings blew her nose hard and Alfie decided if he ever got out of this mess, the first thing he was going to do was file for divorce; even if she took every penny he had.

'Fine, stay then, but don't fucking try to talk to me; the last thing I need is you jabbering ten litres of shit in my ear.'

Alfie sat down on the faded red plastic chair and turned his attention to Vaughn. He was relieved to see him and thankful he hadn't deserted him.

'Good to see you, thanks for coming.'

'How are you bearing up, pal?'

'My head's wrecked to tell you the truth. I pay my brief thousands and he can't get me bail. I don't know what the fuck's happening, Vaughn; it's a mess.'

Vaughn leant over to Alfie and whispered to him.

'Did you pull it?'

'No, wish I did. I should've finished the cunt off when I had the chance, but it wasn't me. Have you heard anything about Emmie?'

'Nothing mate. I've got some of my men looking for her and Janine spoke to the Old Bill again; but she's not a minor any more, she's sixteen, so they're not going to do anything in a hurry. Like the rest of us, they think she's just run away.'

'I'm not so sure she has; something doesn't feel right.'

Vaughn shrugged his shoulders and looked down at the floor, kicking an empty paper cup under his chair.

'I dunno; Janine's filled me in about what happened with the letters and maybe she's just licking her wounds like any kid would.'

Vaughn wondered whether he should tell them about Casey but decided against it when he turned to Jan and saw her burst into floods of tears again.

They all sat saying nothing for a few minutes, contemplating their own thoughts, and it was Alfie who finally broke the silence.

'I need you to find out what the fuck is going on. I've been well and truly stitched up.'

'Any thoughts?'

'I can think of a hundred names but at the same time, I can't think of any. Why Jake? Who knew about him? And who could get the gun and stitch me up like that?'

'Lots of people knew about Jake – the whole of Whispers saw you slap the Bellinghams about. It wasn't a secret.'

'But what about the gun? Who had access? Jan? Me? It's fucked up; I reckon the police took it when they came to arrest me; wanted to put me in the frame.'

'Back in the day maybe, Alf, but they can't get away with shit like that now. I know you won't like what I'm about to say but have you thought about Emmie? She had access.'

Janine, who'd been sitting quietly listening, sat up straight and spoke through gritted teeth at Vaughn.

'Emmie? You taking the fucking streak, mate?'

'Calm down, Jan. Listen, you both might not want to

hear it, but think about it for a moment. Alfie slapped her boyfriend about . . .'

'He wasn't her boyfriend,' Alfie interjected angrily.

'He was to *her*, Alf. You slap him about, stop her seeing him and she's mad with you, wants to teach you a lesson, then to make matters worse she finds the letters and thinks you've been lying to her all this time and runs off. Makes a lot of sense to me.'

Alfie didn't say anything straight away; he'd been thinking Emmie might be involved in the gear going missing, for whatever reason, but this? This was something else entirely.

Not wanting to think Emmie could be mixed up in it all, Alfie spoke aggressively to Vaughn.

'Are you having a laugh? How does it make sense? She's not going to shoot someone just because I fucking said she couldn't see some guy; she's a kid for fuck's sake.'

'Come on Alf, what were we both doing at her age?'

'We were different; she wouldn't shoot him if she cared for him like you say she did. She's not going to pump a bullet in his head. Fuck, Vaughn, she's not some deranged American school kid. She's a sweet caring kid; you know that.'

'I know, and I love her as much as you guys do, but maybe things got out of hand. Who knows? It happens Alfie, look at the news; it's all out war with some of the kids today. And what else have we to go on?'

'I'm not buying it; Emmie wouldn't do that to me. There's no way she would set me up.'

Alfie looked from Vaughn's face to Janine's hoping for some reassurance from either one of them.

'There must be another explanation, and what we need to do is find her and find her fast.'

When visiting time was over Alfie stood up, still ignoring Janine. He knew it wasn't her fault but it was easier to direct his anger at her instead of at himself. He slapped Vaughn on his back and spoke, clumsily wanting to make amends with his friend.

'Have you seen anything of Casey?'

Alfie watched Vaughn narrow his eyes at him. What he had intended to say was that nothing had happened with Cass, but at the last moment he'd changed his mind when he'd noticed Janine listening with her crow ears. He didn't want to give her any more ammunition than she already had when he did divorce her. Also, he needed Vaughn to be on his side, and letting him know he'd been lying about him and Casey sleeping together might not go down well; Vaughn wasn't the sort of man who liked people playing games.

Looking at the hostility on Vaughn's face, Alfie definitely decided it was best to keep his mouth shut and let him continue to believe Casey had let off; at least this way, Vaughn would fully concentrate on helping him, rather than be distracted by a bit of useless pussy.

Outside Pentonville, Vaughn was trying to comfort a distraught Janine.

'He'll be fine, Jan.'

'I'm not bothered about that selfish cunt, Vaughnie. It's my Emmie I'm worried about. If what you say is true, she'll be afraid to come back; because I know Emmie, she hasn't got a bad bone in her body: if she has done anything like that, it'll be killing her.'

Vaughn was about to say something when his phone rang.

'Yes?'

Vaughn listened carefully to the phone call and nodded his head without saying a word as his heart sank. After the phone call, he glanced at Janine.

236

'Everything alright, Vaughn?'

'Yeah, everything's fine.'

But as Vaughn helped Janine get into his car he realised things were far from fine, and the phone call he'd just received confirmed that. As he began to drive he realised his hands were shaking.

It'd been two hours or longer and Emmie was starting to get cramp. She was huddled up in the back of a large van with four other girls whose eyes looked dead, and who had said nothing since they'd set off.

Emmie didn't know where she was going but terror gripped her, not least because she was powerless to do anything about what was happening to her.

Oscar had shown her to one of his bedrooms on the night they'd come back from Jake's flat. Emmie hadn't wanted to stay and had told him countless times she'd like to go home but he'd told her to wait till morning.

'Trust me, it's better this way. Get some sleep, and tomorrow things will work out exactly as planned.'

She hadn't argued because she'd been too tired, but when she'd woken up and tried to go to the bathroom the door had been locked from the outside. She'd banged on the door until Oscar had come and opened it, dressed in a black dressing gown over tracksuit bottoms and a t-shirt.

'As you know, your dad owes me thanks to you, Emmie, so you'll be staying with me until you've worked it off. If you behave yourself, you and I shall get along just fine.'

'Please, let me go home; I'm begging you, please. I know if you tell my dad I'm here, he'll do anything to get you the money. He'd sell the house, his properties, whatever it takes – please Oscar, just call him.'

She'd broken down into tears, crying hysterically and shaking. Oscar had looked at her coldly as he leant on the polished wooden doorframe, then he'd slapped her hard round her face.

'If you don't want trouble, Emmie, you need to stop all the noise; I don't want to get a headache.' She'd nodded her head and bitten down on her hand to stop the wails coming out.

She'd been kept in the room for a couple of days and although she'd been brought food, she hadn't been able to eat anything. Each time Oscar had come into the room with a tray or a drink, she'd begged him to let her go home, pulling out clumps of her hair in desperate frustration. He'd hit her twice more and the second time her nose had bled; she'd spent the next couple of hours curled up in the corner of the room.

And then tonight Oscar had unlocked the door holding a light blue dress and told her they were going somewhere.

'Put this on, and no more hysterics, Em. The place we're going to tonight, I want you on your best behaviour. As long as you listen to exactly what I say you'll be fine. You might even enjoy it.'

Emmie was chilled to the bone as she sat in the flimsy dress Oscar had made her wear, the draught from the van doors whipping round the back of her neck. She could feel every bump in the road, and she thought if she didn't do something to try to distract herself, she'd start screaming again; and Billy, the man who was driving, scared her more than Oscar did. The other girls hadn't whispered a sound, and Emmie needed to hear them talk and to stop staring into nowhere as if they were the living dead.

'I'm Emmie.'

They looked at her with hollow eyes and didn't move a muscle. They simply continued to gaze blankly past her, as if she wasn't there. It was all too much for Emmie and she burst into tears and started shaking.

'Please, talk to me, I need you to. My name's Emmie.'

The women looked at one another before the dark-haired one spoke very quietly, in broken English.

'Name is Sanja, name her is Ljena, her Kaltrina and her is Ariana.'

It was clear now to Emmie the women didn't speak much English. She didn't know what else to say, so she just smiled at them, wiping away her tears. She put her head down and she felt her arm being touched. When she looked up, Ljena was wagging her finger side to side, signalling her not to cry.

The van suddenly came to a stop, sending Emmie and the women flying forward, and they all looked at each other fearfully as they heard the van door being unlocked. The icy air billowed in and they shivered together, all united by the cold and terror.

'Get out.'

The man who'd been driving stood next to Oscar and spoke harshly, not giving the girls a chance to move by themselves before he aggressively started pulling them out. He went to grab Emmie but Oscar intervened.

'Billy, leave this one to me. I don't want her touched unless I've given the say-so.'

Oscar nodded his head to Emmie, who struggled out of the back, feeling the cramp in the back of her legs.

'Remember what I said; listen and you'll be fine.'

'Oscar, why are you doing this to me?'

'Me? I'm not doing anything. Alfie owes me; the packages weren't in the flat like you said they'd be. You lied, Em. So instead of Daddy having a nasty accident, which I'm sure you wouldn't want, this way you can pay off his debts. Anyhow, all this, it's not so very different to what your dad does. See those girls there? They belong to Alfie, or they did do before the little matter of the money he owed me arose. Your dad bought them and then shut them in a room, just

239

like I'm doing to you, so I hardly think he's got a right to talk, do you? As they say, what goes round comes round.'

Emmie couldn't believe what she was hearing; but then, why not? Her dad had basically lied to her her whole life, so why wouldn't this be true?

'You're wrong, he wouldn't do that.'

'Oh you're such a silly girl. If I showed them a photo of him, they'd know who he was; in fact they know him in more ways than one, if you know what I mean?'

Emmie put her hands over her ears, bringing home to Oscar how young she was. He pulled her arms away.

'Whether you believe it or not, it doesn't make much difference; it's all true.'

He laughed loudly and Emmie shuddered.

They crossed the small uneven track and started to walk along a path which took them into the woods opposite. Oscar was at the back with a torch and the driver of the van was at the front. It crossed Emmie's mind to make a run for it but she doubted she'd get very far, and if she was caught it might make Oscar angry. He'd already warned her to do exactly as he said, and perhaps if she did, he'd keep his promise and let her go home soon.

Shivering, she looked round at the darkened woods, feeling the slippy ground under her cream ballet shoes. She suspected they were quite far out of London, but as the van was windowless, she'd no clue which way they'd gone.

The trees hung so heavily, the branches interlocking with each other, Emmie doubted the path got any sunlight at all during the day. She stumbled over a tree root and put her hand onto Kaltrina's back to steady herself as the path led deeper into the woods.

Her feet were wet and hurting from the cold and once more she questioned how she'd ever got herself into this predicament. She couldn't stop thinking about what Oscar had said about her dad owning the girls. She didn't know what to believe any more, she felt as if she was going mad, but if it was true, her dad wasn't who she thought he was; it made him a monster. The thought made her panic and she turned round quickly.

'Going somewhere Em?'

Oscar lifted the torch up and the light silhouetted his face, making him look like something out of a horror movie.

'No, I just want to go home.'

She could hear the rise in her voice as fear hit her and her heart started to palpitate. Her body started to go into spasms, jerking her knees backward and forward. Just as Emmie thought she was going to lose total control, she felt a hand take hers; it was Kaltrina.

'Emmie, sshh.'

She looked into the woman's eyes, and even in just the torchlight, Emmie was able to see her urging her to carry on walking. As the group moved on again, Emmie had to stop and vomit.

A few minutes later they walked into a clearing and Emmie saw a huge house lit up in front of her. The driveway was full of cars and she realised they'd walked the back way. In the distance, Emmie could see people going into the imposing front door of the mansion.

Oscar pushed them forward and got out his phone.

'It's me; we're all here.'

Within a few minutes a person cloaked in a floor-length red robe and a golden Venetian mask walked towards them. He spoke, and his voice was muffled.

'Follow me. Everybody's waiting.'

CHAPTER TWENTY-NINE

'I need your help.'

The call came as a shock. It was the last person Casey had thought she'd hear from, but she was secretly pleased. Although she didn't want to admit it, she'd missed hearing his voice, and was grateful the terse phone call they'd had the other day wasn't going to be their last conversation.

'Sure, if I can do anything, but what's this about, Vaughn?'

'Listen, I'd rather not talk on the phone; can you meet me? There's a bar in Greek Street called the Tavern; meet me there in an hour.'

Casey changed into a pair of faded boot cut jeans, a V-necked pale blue jumper and a beige jacket, quickly checked her hair and rushed out of the flat.

It was getting chilly, and as Casey still had fifteen minutes to spare she walked the long way round up Wardour Street and along to Soho Square, marvelling at people sitting outside having their coffees, determined to flout the British weather.

By the time Casey arrived, her toes were frozen in her battered brown cowboy boots and the warmth of the bar was a welcome departure from the cold London air.

In the far corner of the bar, she immediately saw Vaughn

sitting in a small alcove with a bottle of red, two wine glasses and two large glasses of water waiting on the table.

'Hi, thanks for coming. Let me take your coat.'

'I'll hang on to it for a moment if you don't mind and wait to warm up a bit. You've intrigued me by your call, what's it all about?'

'First, I need to know if I can trust you.'

Casey stared at Vaughn and picked up her glass of wine, which Vaughn had just poured, and then decided against it, picking up the glass of water instead. Vaughn raised his eyebrows at Casey but didn't bother asking questions.

'Yes, of course. I thought you'd know that. What's this all about?'

'Look, this isn't a social chat, don't think I'd be sitting here with you if I had a choice, Casey. But since our conversation the other day something's turned up.'

She was a little taken back by his abrupt manner but she chose to ignore it.

'Like what?'

'Alfie's been arrested on suspicion of murder.'

'Oh my god! When? And who?'

Vaughn watched Casey's reaction and couldn't help but feel jealous at her obvious shock. It was clear to him she had feelings for Alfie and it pissed him off. He gruffly asked her a question which he'd had no intention of asking her but he couldn't help himself.

'Are you upset?'

'Upset? I'm shocked; I was only with him . . .' Casey trailed off, stopping short of what she was going to say.

It was like a kick in the balls for Vaughn to hear her nearly admit she and Alf had spent the night together. He just about managed to stop himself from exploding into a jealous rage; it wasn't why they were here. He had to keep focused and stop acting like a lovesick schoolboy.

243

'He's been charged with the murder of Jake Bellingham; but he didn't do it.'

'How do you know?'

'Because he told me.'

'Oh, he told you he didn't do it and you believe him just like that?'

Casey's voice was hostile, which puzzled Vaughn.

'There's no reason he should lie to me, Casey; it's no big deal.'

He shrugged his shoulders and Casey launched into a verbal attack, her voice a loud whisper.

'No big deal? A man's been murdered and you think it's nothing.'

'I didn't mean it like that. It's just Alfie is who he is. It's where he comes from. And besides, I had a phone call.'

'From who?'

'From Oscar; he told me Alfie didn't do it.'

'How does *he* know?'

'Because he did; or rather his guy did, and he just finished it off.'

Casey sat staring; it was all so shocking – these were the sort of things that happened in movies, and she couldn't quite get her head round it all. There was no way she'd expected for a moment Vaughn was going to tell her something like this, and she wasn't entirely sure she wanted to know.

'Then you need to call the police.'

'I'm afraid it's not as simple as that.'

'No wait, don't tell me; it's the law of the world you live in. Am I right? A whole group of alpha males wanting to take the law into their own hands?'

Vaughn stared at Casey as she pulled off her jacket, irritated by her attitude.

'You're right, the world I live in people don't bring the

244

Old Bill into their business, they sort it out themselves; but there's more to it than that this time.'

'Oh please, enlighten me?'

Casey glared at Vaughn scornfully.

'Has anyone ever told you, Casey, you can be a real bitch?'

Casey prickled, she didn't like him to think of her like that; but how the hell did he expect her to behave? He'd just informed her Oscar had killed a man and Alfie was in prison for it, yet he thought she would sit and smile. She was way out of her depth and it frightened her. Casey didn't have the first clue how in the space of a few short weeks she'd gone from looking for her child to spending time with a person who thought murder was no big deal.

Every part of her told her to run, to go back up North to relative safety – and yet here she was, ignoring all her screaming instincts, because as much as Casey didn't want to admit it she didn't want to lose Vaughn. That thought frightened her nearly as much as what he had just told her.

'What do you want from me?'

'I need your help. Even if I wanted to, I couldn't get the police involved, because Oscar's got Emmie.'

'Emmie!'

Casey dropped the glass of water she was holding and it shattered all over the tiled floor of the restaurant. Vaughn could tell by Casey's expression she knew Emmie was her daughter. When Casey spoke, he could hear the terror in her voice.

'Oh my god.'

Vaughn paused and lowered his voice to a whisper.

'I know who you are; who Emmie is to you.'

Casey shrank visibly back into the padded chair.

'I don't know what you're talking about.'

'I think you do.'

The colour drained from Casey's face and her head whirled round.

'How . . . how . . . how long have you known?'

'Not long; I got one of my sources to find out about you for me.'

'How could you do that? More to the point, why would you do that?'

Casey suddenly felt nauseous, and she ran out of the restaurant as quickly as she could. She could feel the tears running down her face as the cold air hit her. She was about to run down the street when her arm was grabbed hold of in a firm grip.

'You'll catch a cold, Casey; here, you forgot your jacket.'

Casey snatched her jacket from Vaughn and tried to sniff away her tears, avoiding his gaze.

'I'm sorry Cass.'

'Just tell me why. I told you I didn't want to get involved with you, but you still felt the need to go digging in my life – and as messed up as it is, it's still my life. You had no right.'

'I said I'm sorry, Cass, but you have to understand that I had to know who you were and if you were hiding anything – but I never for a moment guessed it would be this.'

He paused and tilted his head to one side, which emphasised his handsome face. 'I had started to fall for you, Cass, and I didn't want any nasty surprises; my heart couldn't handle it.'

Vaughn took Casey's face into his hands, cupping it up towards his, letting the light drizzle of rain fall on it.

'We need to find Emmie, and I need your help. Well, Josh's actually.'

Casey looked stunned and pulled away.

'Josh? You are *unbelievable*. You really have dug around.'

'Please Casey, just hear me out. Oscar said he'll kill Emmie

246

if the police or anyone else find out, but I think he'll kill her anyway; it's just a game to him. I need help from someone who might have contacts and know what they're doing, but more importantly someone who hasn't got any ulterior motives. I can't mention a word of this to anyone I know so I was hoping perhaps you'd ask Josh to help, especially as . . .'

'Emmie's my daughter.'

This was the first time those words had really sunk in. It was bittersweet. Casey had spent her whole life dreaming about being able to talk about her child, but to talk about her in such hideous circumstances was no dream; it was a nightmare.

'Yes Casey, so will you help?'

'I don't know, Vaughn. Are you sure it wouldn't be better to contact the police in London, do things officially?'

Vaughn shook his head and spoke harshly to Casey.

'She may be your daughter, Casey, but I love her too and I can't risk anything happening to her. Oscar's involved with the Albanians and they wouldn't think twice about killing Emmie either if they felt the heat was on.'

'The Albanians?'

'Oscar and Alfie were involved with them. They were trafficking the girls; it's big money. The girls in the club . . .' Casey's mind fixed upon the emaciated girls and the clearer those images became the more scared she felt. Her voice trembled as she spoke.

'You said it was nothing.'

'I know I did, I know, but what was I going to say? I was trying to sort it; I wasn't happy with it either. I put my feelers out and spoke to Lola . . .'

'Lola? What's she got to do with it? Jesus, please don't tell me she's involved too? Not Lola.'

'No, not exactly. Oscar was forcing her to feed the girls heroin to get them hooked; she didn't want to do it but she

247

had no choice: she was terrified. I went round to talk to her to get some information and . . .'

'Oh god, it's because of you she's in hospital.'

Vaughn looked at Casey harshly.

'No, not because of me, Casey, because of Oscar. He must've found out she was talking and went round to put a stop to it.'

'Do Alfie or Janine know any of this?'

'I haven't told them about it, and I haven't told them about you.'

'I think you should; you have to. God what a mess. If only she'd stayed with me . . .'

Casey trailed off and rubbed her head, suddenly feeling an overwhelming sense of panic.

'You know I can't take this in; I have to go.'

Casey turned to walk down the street and she heard Vaughn shout behind her, but she didn't turn round; she needed to think.

The rain was beating down heavily on the window and Casey put her pillow over her head, but no matter how tight she held it the problem wasn't going to go away. All she could think about was her beautiful daughter.

Sitting up, Casey knew it was pointless trying to sleep; the tossing and turning was just waking her up more. She picked up her mobile, which was on the floor next to her, and pressed the quick dial button. It went straight to voice-mail and Casey sighed, leaving no message. She got up wearily and pulled on her clothes.

Back at his house near Virginia Water in Surrey, Vaughn Sadler couldn't sleep either. In the end, he'd gone into his hothouse to prune some of his roses, in the hope it'd have the calming effect he needed.

Oscar had told him to wait and do nothing until he called again, but he wasn't going to allow him to dictate what was going to happen; he needed to do something because Emmie's life depended on it, and he doubted if he sat back and waited that Emmie would be alive to see her next birthday.

He couldn't do this on his own, and sadly when he sat down and thought about it there were few people he could trust. He needed to keep this as quiet as possible and sometimes gangland London was like a women's beauty salon; full of whispering and gossip.

Had he been surprised Casey had walked away? He wasn't entirely sure. She'd reacted badly that he'd been looking into her background, but it must've been a shock to her to hear about Emmie.

When he'd seen her walking into the bar, he'd wanted her. But when he thought of her the image of Alfie's hands all over her body came into his mind and was like a bucket of cold water being poured all over him.

One thing she'd been right about though was the need to tell Janine about Oscar, Emmie and Casey. He wasn't sure about telling Alfie: he knew what it was like to be locked up and unable to do anything about things which were happening on the outside; it was a one-way ticket to frustration which could only lead to madness. Being locked up twenty-four seven was hard enough at the best of times, let alone when there were issues you needed to deal with beyond your control.

He thought he'd leave speaking to Janine till morning; she needed to get as much sleep as she possibly could because after what he was going to tell her, he doubted she'd even be able to close her eyes. He'd drive down to see her at first light: face to face would be better, especially as he'd a strong suspicion how she was going to react.

Vaughn walked through the hothouse, examining the roses

249

he'd neglected lately. He heard Sam start barking again in the background and at first he chose to ignore it, picking wilted leaves and buds off the pale pink roses. After a few minutes of listening to the yowling, he marched through to the main house to see what all the fuss was about. As he entered his study, where Sam was running round in circles, he heard the front gate buzzer go and on the monitor he saw Casey looking wet and dishevelled.

'Hang on a sec, I'll drive up and get you.'

Vaughn grabbed some keys and rushed out to the grey Aston Martin parked in his vast driveway. It took less than a couple of minutes for him to get to the large black steel gates, but he didn't want Casey to have to walk to the house in the pouring rain.

'Jesus girl, you don't do things by half do you? Get in, why didn't you call me?'

Vaughn guessed from the look she gave him that she'd tried but had just been unable to get through. He smiled apologetically as he pulled up at the house.

'Sorry, signal's not always great here when there's a storm on.'

Inside the warmth of the large reception room, Vaughn lit the bespoke fireplace, more for effect than for anything else. He hadn't asked what she was doing coming to see him in the middle of the night but he hoped she'd come to help.

Turning to Casey, he wondered if he should offer her a drink, but he hesitated. He hated seeing her drink. He'd never just seen her stop at one, and he hated what she turned into when she was drunk.

'Do you want me to make you a cup of tea or coffee? I've no idea how to use the coffee maker in the kitchen, but I can make you an instant one.'

'Something stronger would be nice; and if you've got some dry clothes I could put on that would be great.'

Vaughn gave a tight smile as he poured a small measure of brandy into the glass before going to get something dry for her.

Casey came back from the bathroom in the cream Dolce and Gabbana tracksuit Vaughn had given her, having taken off her wet clothes. It swamped her frame but she was grateful to be dry. She sat down on the chair and looked at him intently.

'I need to know everything. I can't ask Josh to help if I don't fully know what's going on. Josh is somebody I can trust with my life and I want him to know all the facts so we don't put him in danger.'

They held each other's gaze for a moment before Vaughn took a deep breath and started to tell Casey about the goings-on in the club, about the girls and about Oscar and Alfie.

A couple of hours later, they both felt exhausted.

'I'm going to see Janine tomorrow, tell her about it, or as much as she needs to know; maybe it'd be good if you came. Get some sleep here and we can go together.'

'Okay; and I'll call Josh.'

She stood up and followed Vaughn up the stairs to a different bedroom from the one she stayed in before. At the door they stood inches away from each other, and after a moment, Casey leant in to kiss Vaughn; but he pushed her away. He could see the hurt in her eyes, but as much as he wanted to make love to her he couldn't; not after she'd spent the night with his friend. He gave her a quick kiss on the top of her head, and turned and walked away.

CHAPTER THIRTY

Emmie was terrified as the gold half-mask was placed over her face and she, along with the other women, was forced to undress in full view of Oscar, the driver and the man who'd come to greet them in the red robe.

As Emmie stood in the middle of the stone-floored room trying to cover her naked body with her hands, she tried to think of her cat, of her friends, of the day her dad had taken them to the funfair in Southend and her mum had got stuck on one of the rides; anything other than the horror of her reality.

She was handed a white cloak by Oscar and put it on quickly, clutching hold of the front to keep it closed, hoping not to expose herself any more than necessary. She watched as Oscar put on his mask and she shivered, partly with the cold and partly from Oscar's cold eyes staring at her through the slits of the mask he wore.

'This way.'

Oscar pushed the women forward and they followed through to a long darkened corridor with tall gothic narrow windows. They walked barefoot along the cold stone passageway until they came to a stop at a set of heavy wooden doors and waited in silence for the man to unlock it. Unnoticed in the dark, Kaltrina squeezed Emmie's hand, silently trying to give her some courage.

Through the door was a huge ballroom full of about two hundred people wearing different Venetian masks: silver masks with halos of feathers; complex baroque-style ones; gold full-faced masks decorated in multicoloured crystals, and one which filled Emmie with panic.

She'd learned about the mask in history; it was called the Medico Della Peste – the plague doctor; and chillingly it was associated with death. It was brilliant white with a long beak of the same colour, and round eyeholes circled with crystal discs which created a shimmering effect, but for all its detailed craftwork the mask was full of menace: and whoever was wearing it, was staring directly at her.

Although all the other masks were different, Emmie noticed the people in the room were all dressed in the same floor-length red velvet robes. On any other occasion, she would've marvelled at the luxury of the room and the dazzling masks, but as she stood there in the moment, she felt she was surrounded by evil.

The room was ornately decorated. Purple ornaments and tapestries adorned the walls along with black velvet drapes falling into heavy folds on the wooden floor. Candles and candelabras illuminated the room, the shadows dancing along the walls creating a playground of mystery and decadence.

At the far end of the room, there was a raised platform and almost as soon as they'd entered, a man wearing a full black mask stood on the stage and rang a bell.

'Good people, the moment has come. The witching hour has begun.'

His voice sounded like an invocation, and after a moment he raised his hands to the ceiling and let out a loud cry. Emmie sensed her body jerk, wanting to bolt, but her feet were incapable of moving and she felt the reassurance of Kaltrina's hand holding hers tight. The party guests stood to the sides, parting the room and leaving only the young women standing huddled together in the middle.

Emmie's legs shook and she struggled to see clearly as her eyes filled with tears behind the mask. One of the men in the room, wearing a silver mask with black feathers and wearing a grey trouser suit under his robe, walked slowly towards them and took hold of Ariana. She cried out, sinking to the floor in panic but she was dragged away by two other men, screaming.

One by one, the women were led away in different directions, followed by a small group of men and women, until it was only Emmie left standing alone in the middle of the room. She looked to her right and she saw the masked figure of Oscar, whispering to the plague doctor. After nodding his head, he came towards her.

Behind the eyeholes of the white mask, Emmie could just make out the man's eyes, dark and intense. He pulled her and she stood firmly, refusing to go. He stood for a second, looking at Emmie through the slits of the mask before grabbing hold of her head. The man didn't talk as he led her out of the ballroom.

Emmie was crying loudly, nearly on the verge of hysteria as she was pulled down a long corridor with doors on either side, passing a room which had loud screams coming from within. Unlike the others, nobody followed them, and Emmie was alone with the man.

'Please, let me go, please. I'm begging you.'

The man ignored her as they stood outside a room at the end of the corridor. When he opened it, Emmie leapt backwards into the man who gave her a hard shove forward. Her eyes opened wide in horror as she saw a large oak four-poster bed covered in red satin. On top of it lay an array of bondage gear. Handcuffs, hooks, whips and metal studded objects were neatly placed on top of the cover and Emmie let out a scream as the wooden door closed behind her, muffling out the sound of her cries.

Emmie's body was shaking so hard that for one moment she thought she'd wet herself from fear. The lights were dim and flickered out a red eerie glow, casting long shadows on the walls.

She stood in the middle of the room trying to get her eyes to adjust to the darkness. The sudden silence of being on her own only added to Emmie's fear; not knowing what was going to happen, yet waiting for the unimaginable to begin.

As Emmie's eyes started to become accustomed to the light, her body jolted back in panic as she realised she wasn't alone. She realised the dark moving shadow in the corner wasn't a shadow; someone was sitting there, watching her.

She screamed and instinctively backed away, but there was nowhere to go as the shadowy outline of the person stepped towards her into the dimmed light.

'Sshh my darling, sshh.'

He reached out a hand and stroked Emmie's bare arm, making her recoil, but he grabbed her hard, drawing her closer to him as her body shook in cold terror. His voice was muffled but excited as he spoke through the tawdry mask.

'I'm not going to hurt you. Daddy won't hurt you.'

Emmie started to scream hysterically.

'You're not my dad, I want to go home.'

The slap across her face took her off her feet, sending her sprawling across the floor.

'Now then that won't do; Daddy doesn't like naughty girls. Bad things happen to bad girls.'

He bent down and stroked her back and Emmie once

more struggled to get away in the confines of the locked room.

'Where are you going? There's nowhere to run. Don't make Daddy cross now, baby girl.'

He grabbed Emmie and pulled her tight against his body, and she immediately could feel his erection; she squirmed but even though the man only came up to her height, he was too strong for her, and overwhelmed with dread and hopelessness, Emmie began to cry; deep shameful sobs.

'Hey now, Daddy's not cross any more.'

The stranger began to kiss Emmie's face but stopped at her lips, instead tracing her mouth with his fat pudgy fingers.

'Lie down.'

He raised his voice when he said it and Emmie heard the threatening tone. Trembling she got onto to the bed, keeping her back towards him.

'Turn over.'

Slowly, Emmie turned onto her back and lay exposed and naked as the man took his clothes off and sat on the bed next to her.

'Please don't, please.'

Emmie turned her head to the side as she begged her masked tormentor. She felt his hands on her again; stroking her body, making her nauseous with every caress. She heard his heavy breathing and felt his hot breath through his mask as he leaned into her closer, and then she heard him start to hum before the sound turned into a gruff song which she'd sung at school when she was younger. With horror, she recognised the song. It was 'The Teddy Bears' Picnic'.

He stopped and Emmie turned her head towards him.

'Tell me you love Daddy.'

Emmie hesitated a moment before speaking, wishing she was back at home with Alfie and Janine. She felt the man shake her, wanting her to answer him.

'I love you.'

'Daddy, say Daddy.'

'I love you . . . Daddy.'

'That's right, that's a good girl.'

The man's fat hands left Emmie's body and she turned her head quickly away as he started to groan and pleasure himself.

CHAPTER THIRTY-ONE

'What the fuck are you telling me?'

Vaughn sat next to Casey in the Jennings's huge conservatory, feeling very uncomfortable as he watched Janine have a meltdown in front of him. He'd known she wasn't going to take the news about Emmie and Oscar or Emmie and Casey lightly, but he hadn't dreamt he'd have to sit watching her roller-coasting from one emotional dip to another. The range of emotions Janine was displaying shocked him; she was switching between crouching down and wailing loudly, her hands covering her face, to pacing up and down effing and blinding at the top of her voice. He wasn't great at dealing with women's emotions at the best of times, let alone when they were in crisis; it was taking all his self-control not to run for the door.

'Tell me it ain't true, Vaughn. Tell me none of it is true.'

All he could do was nod his head as she knelt by his side clinging onto him, tears streaming down her face.

'Maybe we should get you a doctor.'

Casey spoke up for the first time and as Janine turned to look at her with her narrow eyes, she regretted it straight away.

'A quack? You think I need a bleedin' quack, lady? What I need is my girl back. *My* girl, not yours – she's mine and always will be.'

'I know, and I'm not trying to take her from you – I just want to help you get her back.'

'Well don't even try it. You had your chance all them years ago but you gave up your rights. And let me tell you another thing; if you think you mean anything special to Vaughnie, think again! You're just one in a line and believe me, it's one big fucking line.'

Vaughn glanced at Casey and smiled at her apologetically; Janine had always had a big mouth, especially when she was scared or upset, but it suddenly dawned on him how ignorant she actually sounded and how much her bluster would hurt Casey.

'Turn it in, Jan, will you? For your info, Casey isn't just another one; she means something to me.'

'Yeah, like toilet paper to an arse.'

'Button it, Jan. It's not Casey you need to be worrying about, she's going out of her mind as well; we all are.'

'And that's meant to make me feel better? You're having a fucking giggle.'

'I'm sorry, Casey, don't mind Jan.'

The apology from Vaughn sent Janine into an apoplectic rage.

'Why are you apologising to fucking Miss Prissy here? It's me who you should be apologising to for bringing her here.'

'Listen Jan, I know you're upset about Em, we all are – but I won't have you being rude to Casey; she doesn't deserve it, she's done nothing wrong.'

Casey touched Vaughn lightly on his knee and spoke.

'It's fine, just leave it.'

Janine stood in front of them with her hands on her hips, her face turning red as her voice came out as a screech.

'Oh, I bleeding get it now! Porking the mother of the year here is more important than anything else now is it? As long as you're getting your leg over that's all that matters hey?'

Sitting there with Casey by his side, Vaughn actually felt embarrassed she was his friend. She was an East End girl through and through, and though he admired that she'd defend her family like an alley cat with a rocket up its arse, she needed to learn when was the right time to fly the flag.

'When you calm down, Jan, I'll come back and we'll talk some more, but I can't speak to you when you're like this. I need Casey and Josh to help me, but more importantly Emmie does. We can't fall apart now. When we get her back we can calmly sit down and talk but until then, I don't really give a fuck whose daughter she is or isn't, or who I am or am not fucking. All I want is to get Emmie back home.'

As Vaughn and Casey stood up to go, Janine started to pace up and down again, wiping her frustrated tears away.

'You're going to go just like that and leave me here all on me Todd. What am I supposed to do now?'

'Calm down, that's what, Jan. I'll call you later.'

Vaughn walked to the door to leave but Janine blocked his way.

'Calm down? How the fuck do you expect me to calm down? For all we know she could be dead by now, and you don't give a shit.'

Vaughn raised his voice to a thunderous level.

'Of course I give a shit, woman; if I didn't do you think I'd put up with this crap from you eh? I'm not doing this because I have to, Jan: no-one's put a gun to my fucking head. It's because I want to and I love Emmie, like you do, like Casey does – I'm not going to let some cunt do anything to her. But don't think for a second I *have* to do anything.'

Janine Jennings had always fought fire with fire and she

260

screamed back at Vaughn with the same raised decibels in her voice.

'Yes you do, Vaughn.'

'That's where you're wrong, sweetheart; I don't, so please don't push it any more than you already have, Jan.'

'But you see you do; because I haven't got anybody else to help me and I've never been so terrified in my life.'

Vaughn sat next to Casey in the dingy wine bar in Lamb's Conduit Street, listening to Adele playing on the jukebox in the corner.

It was getting late and the bar was making him feel worse, but he couldn't find it in him to get up and go. He'd left the Jennings's house shouldering the responsibility of bringing Emmie home safely, but for the first time in his life he felt scared.

On the way back he hadn't spoken to Casey, and to her credit she'd said nothing as he drove like a maniac along the M25, pointlessly swearing at the top of his voice to the other drivers.

He'd parked in a disabled bay, daring Casey to say something to give him an excuse to argue with her. He wouldn't be surprised by the time they went back if it'd been towed away, but he didn't care. In fact, he didn't care about anything right now apart from getting pissed.

Casey watched Vaughn finishing off his sixth straight whisky. She still felt in shock; she hadn't even been able to process Emmie was her daughter and her search had finally come to an end before all this had happened. And then she'd had to face Janine.

She'd watched Janine's face as she blurted out her anger and far from being angry she'd felt sorry for her. Janine had broken down and lain on the floor crying and Casey had nodded to Vaughn to leave them alone, which he happily did, almost running as he fled from the emotional car crash.

She'd bent down to hold Janine and had met with angry resistance.

'Get off me you cow.'

'I'm not your enemy, Janine. I haven't come here to hurt you.'

'Then why did you come?'

'Because I love her like you do and not a moment went by without me thinking of her, but that doesn't mean I want to take her away; I don't. I can see you love her and that's all I needed to know; that she was loved and she had someone to tuck her into bed at night.'

Janine had sniffed loudly before wiping her nose on her sleeve, then her eyes had softened as she'd talked to Casey.

'Me and my big bleedin' mouth; Alfie always said my gob was as big as an elephant's arse. I'm sorry, Casey, I didn't mean the things I said – it's just a shock, it all is. And when I get frightened it's like somebody's pressed the gobshite button in me head.'

'There's no need to apologise, I understand.'

Janine had stared at her and Casey had thought she was going to have another go at her but instead, she'd taken hold of her hand and spoken gently.

'My bark's worse than my bite you know. Emmie will tell you that.'

With the mention of Emmie, Janine had broken down into tears again and Casey had held her huge figure as Janine's body was racked with sobs.

'I think maybe it'd be a good idea if we started again. Friends?'

'Friends,' agreed Janine. 'She looks like you, you know. I'll show you a picture of her; you'd be very proud.'

They'd been at the bar for over an hour now and Vaughn finally talked to Casey, slurring his words as he spoke.

'I feel I'm in over my head.'

'Josh is coming down; hopefully he'll be able to help, I'm sure he will; but it seems so hopeless. I have this terrible feeling.'

Vaughn could feel himself looking for a fight and even though he knew it was wrong, he couldn't stop himself.

'Well that's helpful; thank you for your input, Cassandra.'

'Don't call me that.'

'Why not?'

'Because you're pissed and I don't like it.'

'Oh that's rich coming from you, the lush of the year.'

Casey was hurt and she fought back the tears, but she stopped herself getting angry because she knew Vaughn was hurting as well and this was his way of showing it.

'I know you're angry but please don't take it out on me, Vaughn.'

He stared at her unsteadily in the gloom of the bar and smiled ruefully, suddenly looking deflated. His hair flopped over his forehead and his face was flushed from the effects of the alcohol.

'I'm sorry; I shouldn't be taking it out on you. Are you ready?'

Vaughn grabbed his jacket off the bar and walked out, not waiting for an answer.

Outside, the cold hit him and he put his hands in his pockets. Feeling his phone, he pulled it out and noticed a message. He spoke to Casey as he pressed the voicemail button, waiting for the message to play.

'I'm really hoping when Josh comes down we can start looking properly . . .'

Before Vaughn finished his sentence he stopped and raised his hand as he listened to his message.

'Vaughn; it's Oscar. I'm surprised you haven't got your phone on. Never mind, I thought I'd send you a photo,

263

hopefully it'll remind you to keep your mouth closed. And once I've decided what I want, I'll be in touch again.'

Vaughn clicked off the message and started scrolling into the inbox of his mobile.

'Who was it?'

'Oscar. He said he was going to send me a photo.'

Casey watched as Vaughn's face filled with revulsion as he stared at his iPhone.

'Take a look.'

He passed it hurriedly to Casey and she stood with her mouth wide open in horror as she stared at the photo. It was a photo of Emmie gagged and bound to a bed, a smiling Oscar standing by her side.

CHAPTER THIRTY-TWO

The visiting room was packed with scantily-dressed women all trying to give their other halves an eyeful at Her Majesty's pleasure. Oscar picked the burger he'd had earlier out of his teeth and looked round, contemplating going over to the kiosk to buy a cup of coffee. It'd been a long night and he was feeling exhausted, but he hadn't been going to let lack of sleep stop him from visiting Alfie.

The party at the mansion had gone better than he'd expected and there'd only been one slight hiccup in the night's proceedings. None of the women had put up a fight and made it difficult for the clients to enjoy themselves – though Oscar guessed this was more down to fear than obedience.

Throughout the night, he'd been able to observe the girls and their punters through the peepholes which were discreetly positioned on the inner walls of the bedrooms. It'd been mainly to check the women were cooperating. He'd found no sexual gratification in what he'd seen, as most of the acts they were inflicting on the women were darkly perverse, even by his standards.

The one person he'd been fascinated to watch was Emmie.

He'd wanted to see how she'd cope, but he'd been slightly disappointed to watch the man she was with go easy on her. He'd played being Daddy with her and then tied her up and performed all the usual bondage games, but it'd been tame in comparison to the others.

Around four o'clock in the morning, there'd been a problem with one of the girls. He and the master of ceremonies had been sitting in the kitchen when one of the men had rushed in, still masked, his hands covered in blood.

'Can you come?'

They'd followed him to the far wing of the house to a lavish bedroom decorated in gold and red. At first in the dim light he'd thought the bed cover was meant to be red, but it soon dawned on him it was soaked with blood; Kaltrina's blood.

'She's in the bathroom.'

Oscar had walked into the bathroom and his head had immediately started pounding as he saw Kaltrina lying on the floor. She was naked and had a ball gag in her mouth. Her eyes were wide open and her body displayed bite marks and open wounds from the sadistic whipping she'd received from the clients. Around her mouth, Oscar could see vomit.

'She was face down, so we didn't realise she was choking. Sorry.'

Oscar looked at the tiny man in the grey mask. He could see his eyes looking fearfully through the slits of the mask and Oscar had wanted to laugh at his apology. It was as if he'd been caught spilling milk rather than standing in the bathroom of a 17th-century house with a dead Albanian woman lying on the floor.

He hadn't been perturbed at the loss of Kaltrina, only grateful it hadn't been more than one; it was only a dead whore after all, and the money for the party had more than covered her. Besides, Zahir had already delivered the other

266

women to the warehouse he owned in Wapping Docks, so he had plenty to spare.

He'd sent Billy to the bathroom, leaving him to do what he was paid to do; the cleaning

When he'd got Emmie from the room, he'd been amused that she'd almost been relieved to see him, even though she hadn't spoken a word. Oscar noticed how panic-stricken she'd looked as they'd made their way through the woods and back to the van. They had been halfway to London when Emmie had started having a fit after noticing Kaltrina wasn't amongst them.

'Where is she? Where's she gone?'

The other women had put their heads down, trying to ignore her crying. Emmie had started banging the sides of the van and Oscar eventually had had to lean over and hit her hard in the face, knocking her unconscious with his fist.

He'd decided against taking her back to his flat, and instead had taken her along with the others to Wapping. When she'd come round, Billy and the driver had already carried her upstairs and June, Lola's replacement, had been waiting to bang her up with the best Afghanistan brown money could buy.

'Good to see you; thanks for coming.'

Alfie stood over Oscar with a big grin on his face and sat down opposite him.

'I thought at times like this, you need all the friends you can get.'

'I appreciate it, Oscar, especially after the mix-up with the money. As soon as I get out, you know I'm good for it.'

'Forget it. Something else has turned up; let's say we're all fair and square.'

Alfie scratched his chin. He was puzzled, but wasn't going to argue; he was just grateful for Oscar coming to see him.

'I don't suppose you've heard anything on Emmie have you? I couldn't get through to Jan or Vaughn. You haven't seen him have you? He said he'd get his men out to look for her. You know it's a strange thing but I never thought Emmie would run away; cuts me up to think of her so unhappy she needed to go AWOL.'

'Funny we should be sitting here talking about Emmie; it's what I came to talk to you about. I said to her only last night that I was coming to see you.'

Alfie shot up in his chair, raising his hands in shock.

'Last night? You've seen her? How? Where is she? How is she?'

Oscar laughed at the urgency in Alfie's voice, grinning as he spoke.

'Don't worry, she's being well looked after.'

Oscar sat back triumphantly and slowly it started to become clear to Alfie what Oscar was saying. He felt the rush of blood in his head as he clutched hold of his chair.

'If you've laid a fucking finger on her, I'll kill you.'

Oscar leaned forward with his face inches away from Alfie.

'How? In case you haven't noticed, you're in here, Alf, and I'm out there; and as you was so careless in leaving your gun lying around at Jake's apartment, it looks like you'll be serving a long bit of bird, mate.'

It took Alfie a moment to speak.

'You?'

'Not just me, it was Emmie as well. She took your gun, Alf – and she took your gear. You don't know her as well as you think you do; got a taste for the wild side that one.'

'What do you want? Whatever it is, I'll get it for you and then you can let her go.'

'You see that's where it becomes a problem for you; I don't think I want anything. I'm happy with the way it is.

268

Oh by the way, I've got a photo of her. Thought you'd like to see it; remind you of your little girl.'

Oscar took out his phone and showed Alfie the picture he'd sent to Vaughn. Within a second of seeing the picture, Alfie had leapt at Oscar, grabbing hold of his throat and grappling him to the floor. Alfie felt the prison guards pulling him back, but the image of Emmie lying tied up fuelled his adrenaline. His arms were being pulled behind his back so he used his mouth to bite down on Oscar's ear, drawing blood.

The pain to the back of Alfie's head went right through his body as one of the guards used a baton on him whilst the others managed to handcuff his arms behind his back. The officers dragged him up by his arms and Oscar stood up slowly, feeling the blood trickling down his face. Panting, he spoke as Alfie started to be dragged away by the wardens.

'That was a very fucking silly thing to do, Alf.'

'You won't get away with this, you cunt.'

Oscar opened his mouth wide and laughed scornfully.

'Oh but the thing is, I already have.'

Talksport was on the radio, turned down so low neither Vaughn nor Casey, who were nursing sore heads, could hear it. They sat at Vaughn's maple wood kitchen table, trying to force down the soggy cereal which had been sitting neglected in the breakfast bowls in front of them for the past half an hour while the photo of Emmie played on both their minds, and the enormous task of trying to find her hovered over their heads like an oppressive storm cloud. Josh had said he'd be down as soon as he could but he was held on a case in Newcastle, so in the meantime it was left to Casey and Vaughn.

The rational part of Casey felt they needed to call the police as soon as possible, but she also knew Oscar – and knew what could happen if things went wrong. She was scared. It was all so alien to her; she knew she was completely out of her depth.

Vaughn had said Oscar wouldn't hesitate to go through with his promise of killing Emmie if he got one whiff of them calling the police; and as much as it was a risk them going alone, at least this way there was still a chance of finding Emmie alive, however minuscule that chance was.

Vaughn sneezed and rubbed his temples before speaking, keeping his voice quieter than usual.

'We need to go and see Lola, then visit all the saunas and brothels. Oscar's a creature of habit; he'll be around somewhere close to his old haunts. He needs to keep his businesses running and someone's bound to know something. As much as they say people in my line of work don't talk, that's bull; they chat like fucking parrots.'

'And that's our plan?'

'Well, have you got any better ideas?'

'Maybe we should wait for Josh. The two of us on our own are like Tweedledum and Tweedledee.'

Vaughn stared at Casey then got up and threw his bowl into the sink, splashing the milk all over the black tiles.

'I'm going to get a quick shower and then we need to get off. I suggest you do the same.'

As Vaughn stomped out, Casey pulled a face behind his back, making her feel childish but a whole lot better.

The ladies behind the desk in Hot Vibrations watched the monitor and saw Vaughn coming up the stairs with a very attractive auburn-haired woman.

They could see all the clients coming up on the concealed camera by the door. It was powerful enough to see all the comings and goings but small enough not to be seen by the clients, who demanded the utmost discretion at all times.

Hot Vibrations was just what it said it was; hot. The moment Vaughn hit the top step he took off his jacket, loosening his collar as he grinned at the skinny brunette with the large breasts behind the desk. His hangover was still very much present and what he really would've liked was to have a long slow massage and a lie down, instead of chasing round London.

'Hello girls, long time no see.'

Maureen, the sauna receptionist and one-time brothel owner, gave Vaughn a genuine smile as she walked round to give him a kiss.

'I thought you'd forgotten us.'

'I've just been busy looking after my roses.'

'What can I do for you then? Want me to give your girl an induction?' She nodded over to where Casey was standing looking uncomfortable.

'No, she's not for sale.'

The women laughed and Casey smiled but narrowed her eyes at Vaughn, which he noticed, turning quickly away from her cold stare.

'Didn't think she was; she looks a bit too uptight.'

Vaughn looked flustered for a moment and wondered what it was about the women who worked in the sauna which made them so intuitive. They might not have had much of a mainstream education but they were street smart, and that to Vaughn was more important than any paper qualification.

'She ain't uptight, Maureen; your eyes are playing tricks on you.'

Maureen grinned and poked Vaughn in the chest playfully.

'Never kid a kidder love, you could ping a string on her, she's that wound up.'

Maureen turned to Casey. 'No offence love, I'm only having a crack – Vaughnie knows that. I don't mean harm and if you're with him, I reckon you must be alright. I'm

271

guessing you don't want any servicing today, Vaughn, so how can we help you?'

Vaughn looked at Maureen. He'd once owned Hot Vibrations and as much as the women had been a rowdy crew, he'd found them real and warm, showing him their full loyalty.

'I need to know if Oscar's been in or around. Or if you've heard anything about some girls he's got.'

'I haven't heard nothing or seen him. Mind, if he did, I'd show him the bleedin' door. Nasty piece of work, that one.'

'Would you mind if we spoke to some of your girls?'

'What's this about, Vaughn? Sounds serious.'

'It is, and if I could tell you, you know I would. But I need you to keep your mouth shut about my visit, same goes for the others.'

'You know I will; my mouth will be as tight as my fanny.'

Vaughn raised his eyebrows then laughed.

'Christ, in that case it doesn't fill me with much hope you'll keep schtum.'

Maureen cackled. 'You cheeky fucker. Go on through to the back and I'll send the girls in who know Oscar.'

Casey looked around the small dingy back room and shuddered. The cracked window overlooked Kings Cross station and it seemed a world away since she'd made the journey down to London. The sky was grey and through the cracked window pane she could feel the cold air.

She'd always found the thought of these sorts of places depressing; young women caught up in a trap of selling themselves for money, being used for financial and sexual greed. However, she knew her views probably wouldn't be popular here and a lot of the women would argue that they were the ones in control. The fact that they didn't see having sex with a stranger who paid them less than the cost of a week's shopping as being exploitative was the most depressing aspect of it all.

Vaughn watched Casey pacing around the room and hoped she wasn't taking the moral high ground, condemning the women that worked here. It might not be what he wanted for Emmie but working in a sauna compared to working the streets made it comparatively safe for the women, and that could only be a good thing as far as he was concerned.

His thoughts were interrupted as the skinny brunette from reception walked in first. As she sat on the only available chair in the room, Vaughn saw the track marks on her arm, hidden behind a thick but unsuccessful layer of makeup.

'Thanks for coming to talk to us. I'm Casey.'

The woman stared at her suspiciously and it was obvious to Casey she was hoping Vaughn would be doing the talking. She had thought it might be better that way round, but Vaughn had insisted.

'Listen Cass, I'm no Jeremy Kyle; women are good at all the chat and bullshit. I want you to do it.'

She'd reluctantly agreed, not feeling very confident herself, but wanting to do everything possible to help find her daughter.

So now Casey was faced with a hostile woman not wanting to talk to her. She had to admit she was nervous.

Karen looked at the pair of them and straight away took a dislike to the woman. She seemed closed and brusque and she decided she was going to direct her conversation to Vaughn.

She had a lot of time for Vaughn; he'd not only treated them with respect but he'd never used his fists on them like a lot of the pimps did.

'I'm sorry, I don't know anything.'

'We haven't asked you anything yet, Karen.' Vaughn spoke firmly, stamping his mark and letting her know he wanted

273

answers. But one thing she wasn't going to do was take the piss.

'We're trying to find Oscar Harding, have you seen anything of him?' Casey spoke softly, sensing she needed to try and get the woman on her side.

'Look, I don't know anything. I see him about; we all do, but I haven't for some time.'

Vaughn looked at her and suddenly realised how difficult this was going to be. For once he was on the other side of the questioning and he saw how frustrating it was when you needed answers and weren't getting any. There was an unwritten code in his world which was going to stop people talking. Ironically he'd lived by it all his life and had threatened people with beatings if they opened their mouths, and now he expected them to do something he never had: talk.

'Listen, if Oscar's paying for pussy hush, I'll match it as long as you tell us what you know.'

'What's that supposed to mean?' Karen looked offended by Vaughn's remark and sat up, bracing her body.

'What it means is I don't want any bullshit. I want you to tell me what you know about him. It's essential we find him and I know money is what drives you and I'm not knocking that but if you are part of his setup, I'll make it worth your while to give us the information.'

'What? And end up like that poor cow Lola?'

Casey, who was sitting back and somewhat impressed with Vaughn taking the lead, interjected quickly.

'Please Karen. We're looking for someone who might be in danger.'

Karen looked at her nails and pursed her lips before speaking.

'I know Lola talked to you, Vaughn, about the girls in the club; everyone did, word gets round. Next thing we know she's banged up in hospital. No thanks, I've got a two-year-old to look out for. Now if that's all, I need to get back to work.'

Vaughn looked at Casey and shrugged his shoulders disappointedly as the next woman came in.

After an hour seeing all the women, it became clear to both Casey and Vaughn they weren't getting anywhere. Vaughn turned to Casey as she stood up and stretched her legs.

'I think it's time we went and had a chat with Lola.'

Lola sat up in her hospital bed and tried to whistle as she listened to what Casey and Vaughn were telling her, but her swollen mouth made it impossible for her to do so.

'I'll help you however I can. It's about time Oscar got his comeuppance. It's one thing doing what he does to me but it's another doing it to Emmie. I'm sorry, Casey. I don't know much, but I know there's an Albanian woman who works above the slot machine place on Little Argyll Street and a while ago she brought some girls over from Romania. Don't know what happened to them, but I know she had some dealings with a guy called Zahir and he has dealings with Oscar.'

'Do you know the woman's name above the slot machine place?'

Lola cackled. 'Fucking hell, Casey love, I'm an old brass not a frigging school register.'

Vaughn grinned at Lola, thankful she was willing to talk after getting such a terrible beating.

'Anything else?'

'Well, there's a guy called Jason. He's known for his parties for people with money and I know Oscar has had some dealings with him. Me and Jason go back a long way; he's a vicious lump and there's no love lost between us but he trusts me, knows I've never done him over; if you can find him, I bet you'll find Oscar not far behind him. If you do find Jason you can say Lola sent you. It won't get you into Buckingham Palace but it'll get you into one of his parties.'

Vaughn looked concerned.

'Are you sure, Lola? It's risky putting your name forward if you're talking about Jason Hedley. I've seen him about a few times and he's a dangerous man.'

'I'm a big girl, Vaughnie, I should've spoken up a long time ago. It's about time the likes of Oscar and Jason were stopped in their tracks.'

CHAPTER THIRTY-THREE

Emmie sat on the corner of the thin stained mattress. The other women sat close by, staring into nowhere and saying nothing. The room they were in was vast, with high ceilings and large inaccessible windows at the top, and a bathroom and toilet at the far end. Oscar's men had come in a couple of times to check on the new girls and had brought in food and water but it lay untouched.

Emmie lay down on her mattress trying to push the thoughts away. She couldn't let herself think about what'd happened to her in the manor house; it was too shocking and it'd left her feeling numb. She could still hear the screams of Kaltrina and the sheer terror in her eyes as they dragged her away. Emmie let out a deep sigh; Kaltrina and what'd happened to her was something she was trying not to think about.

The only positive thing to come out of it all was Emmie's resolve to stay alive. When Oscar had first locked her up, she'd wanted to curl up in a ball and half expected someone to come charging in to rescue her, but as the days went on Emmie realised it wasn't going to happen. She decided that resigning herself to her circumstances certainly wasn't going to get her out of there. Like a sleeping dragon had awoken inside her, Emmie was willing to do whatever it took to escape.

What she really wanted to do was group up with the others, but she wasn't sure if she could trust any of them. She could see most of them were out of their faces on drugs and looked like walking zombies, especially the new girls. One of Oscar's cronies had given her a fix after they'd come back from the manor house and all night she'd vomited and had cold sweats.

They hadn't given her any more so far, but she was determined to escape before they did. If they started feeding it to her, she knew it'd be inevitable that she'd become addicted to it and then the only thing she'd be thinking of would be her next hit, rather than how to get the hell home.

The only girl Emmie didn't think looked dead behind the eyes was Ariana. It was a risk talking to her but Emmie thought it might be her only hope.

Shuffling over to her, Emmie sat on the mattress with Ariana.

'You okay?'

Ariana shrugged her shoulders and said nothing.

'If you speak English, please talk to me.'

The woman stared into Emmie's face and gave a half smile.

'A bit. I speak bit and understand lot.'

'I want to get out of here.'

Straight away Emmie saw the fear on her face. It was obvious to Emmie that Ariana had understood exactly what she was saying.

'I don't know how I'm going to do it yet but we could go together. Once we leave here I can call my dad . . .'

Emmie stopped and felt ashamed, remembering Oscar had

told her it was her father who had locked these women up. Emmie resolved that when she escaped she wasn't going to go home; she'd go to her Uncle Vaughn's. As much as she loved her dad, she didn't know if she ever wanted to see him again.

'No, we'll go to see my uncle; he'll look after us, I know it.'

Emmie took Ariana's hand but she gently pulled it away.

'You nice girl but no understand. If I go here, then at my home in Albania, they kill my family and I have daughter.'

Ariana's eyes filled with tears as she continued to talk to Emmie in broken English.

'I no choice. I stay here; my family live. I go leave; my family dead.'

'No, no. We can go to the police; they'll make sure they're alright. They'll keep your family safe.'

Ariana looked at Emmie sadly and touched her face gently.

'You good girl but young. All the time this happens in my country. Police, government, shut eyes. They no can help. Some family no money and sell, some stolen from families but no run out and back to home because Mafia. They kill family and bring back. I love daughter, so I stay here.'

'But you can't, Ariana. You can't because something might happen to you.'

Emmie looked around and spoke in a whisper.

'You could die here; we all could if we don't do something.'

'I no fear die; die makes me free. You try go but careful, yes? You go live for me.'

Emmie burst into tears and laid her head on Ariana's chest. She stroked her head gently as she had to her own daughter back home in Albania.

It was dark, and Emmie didn't know if this was because of the winter nights drawing in early or because it was actually late. After her chat with Ariana, Emmie had quickly scuttled back to her mattress and pretended to be asleep when she heard Oscar's men come into the room. They'd started administering the heroin to all the women and eventually they'd gone to Ariana.

Emmie had watched, utterly terrified, scared to even let out her breath in case she made a noise. A short stocky unshaved man had grabbed Ariana roughly by her hair, pulling her towards him and rubbing his crotch in her face, laughing as she protested. Emmie had wanted to go and help but she was too afraid to even move and her whole body had started to tremble. Getting annoyed with Ariana's struggling, the man had kneed her hard in the face, sending her backwards onto the dirty mattress. He'd yanked her arm out straight and the other man had plunged a needle into her veins.

When all was quiet and the men had gone, Emmie had tiptoed over to Ariana to see if she was alright, but hearing a noise she'd been frightened back to her mattress. Emmie fell into a restless sleep as she tried to detach herself from what she had witnessed.

Sitting up, she looked across to Ariana's mattress to see if she was awake. The bathroom light was still on, and as Oscar had ordered his men to remove the door, the flickering bulb provided enough light for Emmie to see Ariana was still lying down. After a while, Emmie got up and went across to her mattress, speaking in a low voice.

'Ariana. Wake up. Ariana? You okay?'

Ariana didn't say anything so Emmie lightly touched her arm, shaking her gently. Ariana flopped over onto her back and Emmie reeled away in horror as the overwhelming smell suddenly hit her and she saw one side of Ariana's face covered in her own bloody vomit. Her glassy eyes were wide open, staring up at the ceiling, her skin looking pale and clammy

280

with deep stained red blotches on her face and neck. Emmie let out a distressing scream. 'No!'

Emmie grabbed hold of Ariana, pulling her limp body up with great effort onto her lap. She slapped Ariana's face, desperate to see a sign of life. When there was no movement, Emmie put her face onto Ariana's, hoping she could feel her breathing, however shallow; she felt nothing apart from the mucus-streaked vomit from Ariana's face, which now covered her own cheek. The panic rose inside her and this time Emmie shook Ariana violently. 'Ariana, no, please, please wake up.'

There was still nothing and part of Emmie knew it was hopeless even attempting to try to save her: it was clear she'd overdosed; but she was desperate, terrified at the thought her new friend was dead, terrified for herself at being left alone. Emmie sobbed deeply as the mix of her tears and Ariana's vomit ran down her face.

'Please don't leave me, Ariana, please. I need you please.'

Emmie could hear the roaring of her breath escaping from her chest and she turned to the other women and cried out to them.

'Please help me, help me. I need help.'

Emmie pushed Ariana off her lap and jumped up and ran to the other women in the room. Each woman lay on her filthy mattress, not moving and too stoned to care as Emmie shook them furiously. Giving up trying to rouse them, Emmie ran to the locked door and started banging on it.

'Hello! Please, I need your help please. Someone please help me!'

Vaughn watched the street vendor with the stained yellow fingers cooking the hotdog and fried onions.

'Tempted?' Casey grinned at him as she spoke, catching up behind him.

'No, I value my life too much.'

They were on their way to Little Argyll Street to see if they could follow up the information. They'd jumped on the number 73 bus on the Euston Road outside the UCH for half an hour before Vaughn had pressed the button to let them off.

It was drizzling and the walk through the supposedly quieter back streets was hampered with shoppers, tourists and workers making their way home in rush hour.

After ten minutes they got to the beginning of Little Argyll Street and right away saw the flashing lights of the slot machine arcade that Lola had told them about. As they crossed over the road, Vaughn slowed his pace and spoke to Casey warmly.

'You know, you can always talk to me about Emmie. I know there is no "you and me" now, but you don't have to carry it all on your own.'

Casey flinched. It stung to hear Vaughn say that. She'd really thought he'd been going to give her another chance, but maybe the things she'd said to him when she'd been drunk had cut too deeply. When Janine had questioned Vaughn's relationship with Casey, insinuating she was only his whore, Casey had been touched and quietly optimistic when he'd said she meant something to him – but since then, Vaughn had kept her at arms' length. It hurt and it was confusing but she didn't want to fill her thoughts with it now: she needed to concentrate on Emmie. Casey spoke, knowing she sounded terse because she was hurting.

'I'm fine, really.'

They looked at each other, neither one of them knowing what to say next, and walked in silence, mulling over their own thoughts, unable to work out what the other one was thinking.

* * *

All of a sudden Vaughn stopped walking and held back Casey by her shoulder.

'Oh shit. That guy who's just come out of the blue door, I've seen him before at Whispers; he came in a few times to see Alfie. I think he's got something to do with the girls. Come on.'

Vaughn picked up his pace as he followed the man down the street.

'What do you want to do? Shall I trail him and you go to see if our Albanian lady is in residence?'

'I don't know Cass, it's a bit risky.'

'I'll be fine. I won't do anything stupid, all I'll do is follow him, and it's better I do that surrounded by people in the street rather than going up on my own to the slot machine place; we don't know who'll be there.'

Vaughn nodded, he didn't like it but it *did* make more sense than sending her to the arcade where she might be in danger.

'Okay, but be careful and stay in contact.'

Casey acknowledged his words with a wave, quickening her pace to keep up with the man. She turned into Regent Street and had to rush across the road as the traffic lights turned green and the London traffic sped perilously towards her.

She still had the dark-haired man in sight as he pulled his hood tight around his face before he turned down Hanover Street.

The rain was coming down hard and the wind had caught up with it, whirling it around and hitting the faces of the people of London with an unrelenting harshness. The man was walking at such a pace, Casey was banging into people and not really taking much notice of anything else. She passed the Rolls-Royce dealers' on the corner and saw him walk into Hanover Square. Casey looked both ways before crossing the road, but was unaware of the man sitting watching her in the blacked-out car she'd just passed.

Fat Man Cardale felt like his face was about to fall off. The throbbing ache not only encompassed his jaw but the whole of his body. He could taste his own blood in his mouth and was surprised how salty it was. His lip had already swollen up and his front teeth were much looser than they'd been when he'd got up earlier in the day.

The vicious blows rained down by Vaughn Sadler had made him scream out in pain like a girl as he felt his teeth being pushed back by the force of the fist in his mouth. The pain in his eye as it came into contact with the sovereign on Vaughn's finger pierced through him, as if a needle had been thrust straight through it.

Vaughn took a breather and hoped he wouldn't have to do anything like this again. He'd been out of the loop for a while and as much as he missed the adrenaline of his old life, doing what he was doing now showed him how much he actually hated the violence of it all – which was ironic because Fat Man Cardale was lying at his feet, grunting like a wounded animal.

'You have one more fucking chance, Cardale, to tell me the truth or to put it plainly, I'll kill you.'

Terrified and desperate to save his life, Cardale spoke with blood and saliva trickling down the corners of his mouth.

'There's a guy I see from time to time, his name's Zahir; he traffics women into this country, that's all I know.'

'Not good enough.'

Vaughn snarled as he gave Cardale another blow, causing him to hit his head on the sharp corner of the table in the overheated room.

Cardale lay on the dark blue carpet in blood-drenched agony. The pain in his stomach was excruciating and he could hardly breathe. Warm blood poured from the gash in his forehead and over his swollen eyes, stopping him seeing clearly the expression on Vaughn's face, but he heard the menace in his words as he came to kneel down over him.

'You know I don't have time to play games. We can either do it the hard way or the easy way; it's down to you Cardale, but one way or another, I'll find out what I need to know.'

'Okay, okay. Zahir's doing some business with Oscar. He brought some new girls from Albania into the country the other day for Oscar, but I don't know where they are. Everyone knows Alfie begged out on Oscar, but before it all hit the fan Alfie was tight with Zahir as well. Originally they were only going to use the girls for private punters but since Oscar's taken over the running, there's been rumours he's dealing with Jason Hedley and touting them out to parties instead. There's a lot more money in that, and I hear Jason's hosting another one in a few days somewhere in Essex.'

It was like Lola said; Jason Hedley was in the middle of it. He'd actually come across him before. Like Vaughn himself, Jason was a card player, and he knew only too well what a nasty piece of work he was.

Jason was originally from Bristol – though Vaughn had always thought his accent sounded Welsh – and like others before him, had come to London fifteen-odd years ago to make his fortune. Unlike so many others, he'd done what he'd set out to achieve and had become extremely rich.

Jason was one of the most prolific pimps in South East London and ran his girls with barbaric violence. Vaughn had heard none of Jason's women had ever been able to leave his firm of her own free will and still have their facial features intact. Another rumour Vaughn had heard many a time was Jason's liking for very young girls.

The parties he hosted were only for the super wealthy, where anything went as long as you had the money to pay for it. It didn't surprise him to hear Oscar had joined forces with Jason; they were certainly birds of a feather.

'What about the Albanian woman who works here? We were told she ran some Romanian girls from here.'

'June? Tardy bitch did, until she got a better offer. I treated that cunt well and next thing I hear she's gone off to work for Oscar. Some bitches will never stop being ungrateful little whores.'

Vaughn walked back over and felt his knee playing him up again; it'd been a while since he'd given anyone a kicking and he was sure tomorrow he was going to pay for it. He looked down in disgust at Cardale who was starting to moan again in agony.

'And you've told me everything there is to know? Because if I find out . . .'

'I swear; there's nothing else.'

Vaughn watched Cardale's face grimacing in pain and guessed he was telling the truth. Thankful Casey wasn't there to see a part of him he'd thought he'd left behind, Vaughn walked out, certain Cardale wouldn't be uttering a word about his visit.

CHAPTER THIRTY-FOUR

Josh Edwards stepped off the train at platform number five and wondered what the hell he was doing. When Casey had called him and said she wanted his help, he'd been surprised and keen to do whatever he could – but that was before she'd explained the whole crazy story to him.

'Are you out of your mind, Casey?'

'I know, but what other option have we? And you owe me, Josh.'

'I owe you?'

'Yes, all the time you had that letter and didn't tell me.'

'I was only doing what I thought was best.'

'Well, now I'm doing the same. I don't want to lose Emmie before I even have the chance of seeing her.'

'You do know what you're asking me to do, Cass? I could not only lose my job, but I could go to prison as well.'

'I realise I'm asking a lot, but I've no one else to ask.'

There'd been a long pause before he'd answered and against his better judgement, and as he'd always done, he gave in to her.

'Okay, okay. I must be insane but I'll help you. You and your daughter.'

After several phone calls between them, Josh had taken all the names, nicknames and addresses of the people Casey had wanted him to look into. Most of the names she'd given him were well known to the police and had form as long as the New York Marathon. He'd also made calls to colleagues past and present, gleaning as much information as he could.

'You know this guy Vaughn; he's no Mr Kipling either.'

'The cake maker or the writer?'

Josh heard the sarcasm along with the defensiveness in Casey's voice.

'I want you to be careful that's all.'

'Listen, Vaughn isn't my concern, Emmie is. He asked me to help and that's what I'm doing.'

'Okay, try not to bite my head off. I haven't turned up anything that you don't already know: seems they've covered their tracks pretty well; but if it's any help I've managed to get someone to cover me so I'll be on the train tonight.'

As Josh walked through St Pancras station, which was heaving with foreign students all eager to see the London sights, he tried to ignore the voice telling him he was making a very big mistake.

He wasn't due to meet Casey until the morning but he'd decided to come down and spend the night in London and have a leisurely start, rather than having to share the Birmingham to London train in the morning with overtired commuters.

Flagging down a black cab, Josh decided to push the boat out and treat himself to a slap-up dinner. If he could get a table at L'Escargot, he'd go there. It was a rare opportunity to enjoy an evening on his own without having to worry about work or anybody else. He could do all the worrying he liked when he spoke to Casey in the morning.

'I've lost him; sorry.'

Casey sat having a drink in Blue Rooms, a bar off Park Lane. She'd followed the man through Hanover Square but somewhere between South Molton Street and Grosvenor Square she'd lost sight of him.

Besides being soaked through by the sudden downpour, she was also exhausted. When she'd lost sight of the man, she'd taken herself to the bar and left calling Vaughn until now.

There was a long silence on the phone after she'd confessed to losing the trail and then she'd heard Vaughn roaring with laughter, which had immediately got under her skin.

'What's so funny?'

'I'm sorry Cass; I just think it's funny.'

'You had the easy job. I had to battle my way through the hordes of people, not to mention the rain.'

'You're getting old!'

Casey chose to ignore the last comment. 'Anyway, what happened with you? Did you have any luck?'

'Shall I come and meet you? Don't really want to discuss it on the phone.'

Casey picked up her empty glass. She'd stuck to orange juice so far and she really wanted to get home before she was tempted. She felt drained and she was due to see Josh tomorrow. She hadn't told Vaughn he was coming down. She wanted to speak to Josh first before she introduced him to Vaughn and she wasn't looking forward to the introduction; the last thing she wanted was to be in between two very large male egos.

'No, listen; can we leave it till tomorrow? I'm tired.'

Vaughn was disappointed, he wanted to keep things

moving and he also wanted to see Casey but he kept his emotions away from his voice.

'I can come down quickly, I won't stay long, I'd like to get a handle on this.'

'No, really I just need to sleep.'

'But . . .'

'Please Vaughn.'

'Fine, I'll meet you at your place first thing.'

'Can we make it lunchtime? I'll come and meet you. Whispers is still open isn't it?'

'Yeah, Stevie's running it for Alfie. Shall we say one o'clock?'

'Okay, see you then.'

As Vaughn put down the phone, he couldn't help but think Casey sounded guarded.

Casey lay on her bed still fully clothed with her ankle hurting. On the way back from Blue Rooms she'd misjudged the step off the kerb and found herself sprawled over the wet pavements of Leicester Square. Although her flat was only a ten-minute walk away, it'd taken her double that to get home.

In the dark Casey could just about make out the ceiling and she wondered how long it'd be before the large pieces of peeling paper fell off completely. She was trying not to think about Emmie – because when she did it made her blood run cold to think of her with Oscar.

She stretched her legs and drew them back quickly, gasping as cramp hit her left calf, and she rolled about on the bed rubbing her leg.

'Hello Casey, would you like me to help you with that?'

The sound of the words being spoken in her bedroom nearly made Casey roll off the bed in fright. She froze, clutching her calf even though she wanted to run. She tried

290

to tell herself to move but she wasn't sure which way the voice was coming from and she was afraid to run into whoever it was standing in the dark.

Casey's heart was beating fast and she knew she needed to move. She leapt up but her ankle gave way as her feet hit the floor.

'Where are you going, Casey?'

It seemed like the voice was getting louder and coming closer towards her; or perhaps that was in her head, she wasn't sure; it felt like her senses were letting her down, as if she were a trapped animal. Her panic seemed to be emphasising the pain in her ankle and frustratingly, she could feel the tears run down her face.

'I'm over here, Cass.'

It suddenly came to her who the voice belonged to.

'Shall I come and help you up, Casey? You seem to be struggling.'

She didn't want to answer him because then she'd be acknowledging his existence standing in the corner of the room but as she heard his footsteps on the bare wooden floor, she vocalised her fear.

'Please. Please, just stay away from me.'

'And why would I want to do that? I want to know what you were doing following Zahir. You are what my mother would call a meddler.'

The side lamp was switched on, and Casey rolled away from the sudden light to see the face of Oscar Harding. She watched him slowly put on a pair of black leather gloves – and in that moment Casey knew she had to run.

Leaping up she ignored the pain of her ankle and ran for the bedroom door. It took only a split second for Oscar to react and he ran after her, grabbing on to her jacket. Casey turned and hit out, bringing down her hand in a defensive move onto Oscar's forearm. It had the desired effect and he

291

lost his grip as she ran towards the front door, but he was right behind her and somehow he dived for her legs, bringing Casey down hard on her face and splitting her chin open as it banged onto the hard floor. She kicked furiously with her legs and heard him groan as the heel of her cowboy boot caught his nose.

'You bitch.'

She was out of breath as she scrambled on all fours, paying no attention to the splinters going into her hands as she grappled to stand up. It was crucial for her to head for the kitchenette to try to get a knife but as she went towards it, Oscar seemed to read her mind.

'You looking for one of these?'

Out of his pocket he produced a large serrated knife and for the first time, Casey opened her mouth to scream but it did nothing except slow her down and give Oscar a second's gain on her. He grabbed hold of her waist and pulled her towards him as her nails scraped along the floorboards, desperately trying to keep hold of her grip. He overpowered her easily; Oscar was strong and determined and Casey could feel any moment now she'd lose the battle. Giving it one more try, Casey twisted her body and threw her hands up towards his hair and pulled, making him cry out but also making Oscar more enraged.

'Fucking whore.'

Oscar straddled her and pushed down hard on her chest, restricting her breathing with one hand. With the other he held the knife against her cheek.

'There are some things I don't like, darling – and cunts who put their noses in other people's business is one of them.'

Oscar pushed the tip of the knife into her cheek making a small cut and Casey sucked in her breath, biting down on her lip to stop herself screaming.

'I don't know what you're talking about.'

The backhand slap sent shockwaves of pain through Casey, and she felt Oscar grab hold of her fingers and start to bend them backwards.

'Everyone thinks they're a hero until it starts to hurt. If you don't want to end up in a body bag, I'd start talking.'

CHAPTER THIRTY-FIVE

Alfie lay on his bed staring up at the empty top bunk's rusting springs, and sighed. He forced himself to get up, even if it was only to pace about in the tiny cell. Being inside was killing him, not just because this time he was entirely innocent, but because Oscar had Emmie. No one had heard from him for a few days, and to top it off Janine hadn't heard anything more from Vaughn either.

Apparently he and Casey had their heads to the ground. Not that Alfie knew why the fuck Vaughn had decided to pick up again with Casey, but as long as they found Em, he didn't give a rat's fucking arse if a band of nuns were helping him.

Alfie leant on the cell wall, which was adorned with pictures of big-breasted women put up by his cellmate. He felt as if he was losing the plot, and stared down at the floor as he went over the earlier conversation he'd had with his brief.

'I'm sorry, they're not going to give you bail. This is a serious offence.'

'Don't fucking give me all your spiel, I know all the patter, just like I know who set me up. It's the same cunt who's got my daughter.'

'And have you got any proof of this, Mr Jennings?'

Alfie yelled at his brief, sitting in his expensive Savile Row pinstripe suit opposite him, and wondered what the fuck he was paying him for.

'I don't need proof – the fucking toerag told me.'

'It's only hearsay.'

'Are you trying to give me a cardiac? He's put me in the picture and he's got Em and what I need you to do is get me out of here.'

'That won't be possible.'

'What the fuck am I paying you for then? Apart from giving you the monkeys to buy expensive whistle and flutes.'

'Alfie, the police – as you know – have the gun with your fingerprints on it.'

'Course there's bleeding fingerprints on it, because it's *my* gun! I ain't denying that, what I'm saying is I didn't pull the trigger. Ballistics didn't find a jot on my fingers did they?'

'No, but not finding a trace of gun resin on your fingers isn't conclusive evidence you didn't fire the shot. You could quite easily have worn gloves.'

'Whose side are you frigging on, mate?'

'Yours of course, but it's not a matter of sides; the police have got physical evidence and that goes a long way. You've got a record, Alfie, and there are witnesses you had a fight with Jake's uncle in your club. The police think it was a revenge killing.'

'Trust me, if I was going to do a revenge killing, I wouldn't have just shot him in the head; I would've fed his own fucking balls to him.'

'A word of advice. When it goes to trial, Mr Jennings, you should try to refrain from speaking like that.'

Alfie had banged his hand down on the table in the private visiting room which was allocated for legal visits.

'Am I talking double fucking Dutch here? This can't go to trial; it'll be the perfect excuse for them to finally bang me up. I need to get out of here so I can prove I didn't do it.'

Alfie had seen his brief take a quick glance at his watch before he'd shuffled his files, getting ready to make a move to go. For the first time in his adult life Alfie felt desperate, and he heard the anguish in his own voice. 'Oscar Harding is the man they want; not me.'

'Mr Jennings, we'll do all we can, but I'm not sure if it'll be enough.'

Josh Edwards's enjoyable evening started to fade into a distant memory as he stood shivering outside Casey's flat in Dean Street and pressed the door buzzer hanging precariously off the wall.

He pushed all the other bells, but got no reply from any of the flats.

Another hour in the cold passed and Josh had finally had enough. After a quick look round, he gave the peeling white door a hard shove with his shoulder. Two kicks and one shove was all it took for Josh to force it open and he walked into the warmth of the stairwell gratefully.

He was furious with Casey and hoped there was a good explanation why she hadn't bothered answering her phone or the door. It was bringing back painful memories of the past.

He remembered the months prior to her disappearing, how she'd go off for days without contacting him and then turn up just as he was at the end of his tether, stinking of booze and refusing to tell him where she'd been. It'd hurt him deeply to see her in such a state but it'd also hurt how she'd dismissed his feelings entirely.

Josh shook his head as he walked up the stairs and refused

to think about those times which had caused him to take compassionate leave from work. Not that Casey had known; she'd already vanished by the time he needed any help of his own.

Josh continued up the bare stairs, burying his thoughts back where they'd come from and wincing as the stench of urine assaulted his nostrils. The walls were filthy and the paint was peeling off, exposing the crumbling plaster underneath. Empty cans and bottles were on every landing piled up in the corners. Josh didn't want to judge but it was hard not to, especially as Casey had been so fastidious back in their home in Birmingham, always having a gentle nag at him to pick up his socks and underwear off the bathroom floor.

Perhaps it was a sign of how far she'd fallen; he could never have imagined Casey living like this – but then, he didn't know her any more.

At the top of the stairs, Josh hammered on the door. There was no answer, and he knocked again just as hard, but this time with his foot. It was her who had called him to come and help and now she wasn't answering. Fury was an understatement.

'For fuck's sake.'

He muttered to himself and took out his phone to call Casey again. His phone connected and he could hear the ringing of her phone from the other side of the door. He clicked it off and called her name through the door.

'Casey? Open up. Cass?'

Again, there was no answer; and apart from not wanting a wasted journey to London, he desperately needed to use the toilet after drinking three large coffees in the hotel.

Josh gave a heavy side kick to the door, forcing it easily open.

'Cass?'

He walked in tentatively; he didn't want to give her a fright, and it felt intrusive coming into her flat in such a manner. He looked in the bedroom and saw her brown bag, and it gave him hope she hadn't gone very far. The bedcovers were all over the floor and the sidelight lamp was still on.

He decided to wait in the living room for her to come back. If she was angry at him for forcing his way in, she'd just have to understand he couldn't be expected to wait out in the cold or in the filthy stairwell. He wanted to make himself a cup of tea to warm himself up, but first he needed the toilet. Opening the only other door in the flat, Josh stopped in his tracks.

'Holy shit.' He spoke out loud in shock and horror and quickly closed the door again. He was desperate to go to the toilet and as Casey wasn't back yet, he decided to take a piss in the kitchenette sink. As disgusting as that might be, it was nothing compared to what lay behind the bathroom door.

Vaughn sat in Whispers and chuckled a few times, more out of politeness than out of him actually finding anything closely resembling humour. The club had started to do lunchtime gigs but from what Vaughn could see it was a waste of time. The only other people besides himself in the club were the other comedians waiting apprehensively, though Vaughn couldn't see quite why they felt the need to be nervous as the place was devoid of customers.

Vaughn toyed with the idea of ordering another drink but changed his mind when he looked up at the neon clock and saw the time. Casey was late and it pissed him off. He hoped she wasn't lying in bed nursing a hangover.

'Can I get you anything else, Mr Sadler?'

Vaughn didn't bother answering and stormed out, nodding

a respectful greeting to the bouncer on the door, and headed towards Casey's flat in Dean Street.

Vaughn didn't need to bother pressing on the buzzer to be let in, as the door was already open. He marched angrily up the stairs to her flat.

'Cass?'

Her front door was slightly ajar and Vaughn walked in. He came to a sudden standstill to see the person he recognised from the train station, standing with his cock in his hand having a piss in Casey's kitchen sink.

Casey slowly opened her eyes and for a split second thought she was still in her flat in Dean Street – but then the pain in her face and her hand began to throb and Casey remembered where she was.

She started slowly to sit up and felt her cheek stuck to the pillow with dried blood. As she sat up straight, the room began to spin and Casey had to lie back down, holding her hand and nursing the overwhelming pain in her fingers.

Last night in her flat the pain Oscar had inflicted on her had been so intense she'd passed out and had only come round for a moment or two as Oscar and a stocky man leant over her as she lay on the floor.

Casey realised her fingers were bandaged neatly with lint and a homemade splint. She had no recollection of them being attended to but guessed the track mark on her left arm might have something to do with the reason she had no memory and why she felt so dizzy.

As she lay on her side, Casey heard footsteps and closed her eyes quickly, feigning sleep and bracing herself for whatever Oscar had in store for her. Her leg was touched lightly but Casey continued to keep her eyes closed and hoped her body wouldn't betray the terror she was feeling.

She lay holding her breath nervously but then heard the person begin to talk.

'Hi, are you alright? I saw you being brought in last night. Do you speak English? My name's Emmie.'

Casey jerked herself up in shock and surprise and sat with her mouth wide open as she took in Emmie. It'd been sixteen years since she'd glimpsed her being carried away and now here she was in front of her.

She looked at Emmie's long tumbling hair, the same silky hair as the lock she treasured, and her soft skin, her bright eyes and turned-up nose. Casey found her love was as strong as the day she'd given birth to her. She leant forward and held her.

'Oh my god, Emmie! Thank god I've found you.'

Casey didn't miss the irony of her own words. She watched Emmie's face light up.

'OMG! I can't believe it, you're from here.'

Casey laughed; it was hardly how she'd expected their reunion to be, but whatever their predicament, it couldn't take away the fact she was finally looking into her daughter's eyes. She held her a little longer and then spoke, taking in every detail of Emmie's face.

'I'm Casey by the way and I'm a friend of Vaughn's.'

'Are the police coming? Are we going to get out of here?'

'No, not yet, but there are people who are doing everything they can to find you.'

Casey saw Emmie's face drop and she began to shake.

'Why aren't the police looking for me? It's because of my dad isn't it? He's a part of this.'

Emmie's voice became high-pitched and Casey put her hand gently on her knee, immediately grimacing as the throbbing in her fingers was exacerbated by Emmie taking hold of her hand.

'No, Emmie. Your dad's worried about you, so is your mum; we all have been.'

'If they're so worried why aren't they sending the police to find me? I can't stay here; I can't.'

'Sshh Emmie. I'm going to be honest with you; Oscar made a threat and told us if we went to the police he'd kill you. We all thought it was better this way.'

An astonished look crossed Emmie's face and her eyes filled with tears. 'How's it better? No one knows where we are and Oscar's mad, he frightens me. Since I've been here two women have . . .'

Emmie shook her head and covered her face with her hands, letting the tears fall between her fingers.

'What Emmie? Two women have what?'

'It doesn't matter, I don't want to talk about it; I can't.'

The anger rose up inside Casey; enraged Oscar had traumatised her because he wanted to play a sick power game with Alfie. She put her hand on Emmie's head and sat quietly, waiting for her to talk again.

'Can I ask you something, Casey?'

'Anything, sweetheart.'

'Is it true my dad bought these women?'

Casey looked round and saw a number of women still asleep, lying on thin mattresses and covered only in stained sheets. She looked back at Emmie and wasn't sure what to say, but then she saw the pleading look in her eyes, wanting to know the truth, but afraid of it. She looked so vulnerable and there were times honesty wasn't always required.

'No, darling, he didn't.'

Casey could almost feel the relief coming from Emmie and knew she'd done the right thing. If they were to escape, Emmie would have plenty of time to learn the truth about Alfie Jennings.

'Emmie, I'm going to do everything I can to get us out of

here and I know Vaughn will be looking for us. Whatever happens from here I will never leave you again.'

'Again?'

'I won't leave you.'

Casey smiled at her and Emmie replied in a whisper.

'Oscar told us there was going to be another party in a couple of days and I can't go through that again, I can't.'

Emmie's voice cracked and Casey held her in her arms, ignoring her own discomfort.

'If it's the last thing I do, I will get us out of here.'

Emmie's tears spilled onto Casey's chest and as she sat rocking her, she hoped to hell she could figure out a way of getting them out of there alive. There was no way she was prepared to lose her daughter again, not now she'd found her – and she certainly wasn't going to lose her to a sadistic gangster like Oscar Harding.

CHAPTER THIRTY-SIX

The two men stood staring at each other, both knowing who the other was but neither of them wanting to say anything. It was Josh who made the first move, suddenly feeling very exposed, standing with his dick in his hand.

'Hi, I'm . . .'

Vaughn cut him off angrily. 'I know who you are, but what I want to know is what the fuck you're doing here? Casey didn't tell me you were coming down today.'

Josh ignored the hostility.

'Good to meet you too, Mr Sadler.'

Vaughn was taken aback by the jealousy rising up inside him and turned to leave; there was no way he was playing fucking piggy-in-the-middle with Casey and her on/off husband. He knew he was coming down and he appreciated it, but she hadn't told him it was going to be today. It had given Vaughn a nasty surprise to see that Josh was obviously so at home in Casey's flat that he was taking a piss in her sink. He knew he was being hasty but at that moment he couldn't help himself; he would catch up with Casey later. He didn't need to feel like a jealous prick, and it was distracting him from thinking straight. The best thing he could do was leave them to it and go and find Emmie on his own.

'Tell Casey thanks but no thanks, I'll sort it out without her.'

'Wait, where are you going? *You* were the one who asked me to get involved.'

Vaughn stared at Josh, hating him for being Old Bill but hating more the thought that Casey had once been in love with him.

'Exactly, so I can't understand why she treated me like a bleeding blind man and kept me in the dark about you coming today.' Vaughn stopped and had a painful thought. He glared at Josh and spoke coldly. 'Or did you come here last night?'

Josh looked on. He hadn't liked what he'd found out about Vaughn in the police files and he didn't like what he saw now, but if he was going to help Casey and Emmie he needed to put his personal feelings aside. He decided to ignore Vaughn's question, aware of what he was getting at.

'Do you want my help or not? Because believe me, I'm happy to get the train back to Birmingham.'

Vaughn snarled at him. 'There's only one thing worse than the Old Bill and that's the Old Bill with a fucking attitude.'

'Look Mr Sadler, to say I'm on your side is stretching it a bit, but I'm certainly on Emmie's and Casey's side and you're not the only one unhappy with this.'

'Yeah well, it would've been nice to have been told you were here.'

'There's one thing you have to know about Casey. She's very much her own woman, and once she's decided to do something, then she'll go right ahead and do it.'

Vaughn sensed the jealousy rising inside him again and

he spoke with as much hostility as he could conjure up in his voice.

'I didn't fucking ask you that, mate, so do yourself and me a favour and keep it buttoned until Casey comes back. Where's she gone anyway?'

Josh looked at Vaughn. If he thought he could push him around, he'd definitely got the wrong man. Ignoring him again, Josh sat down tentatively on the filthy looking couch, moving a pile of clothes to make space.

'An answer, preferably today would be good. I'll ask you again; where has Casey gone?'

'Listen, Mr Sadler, I'm sure in your line of work you're used to people jumping at your every word – but I'm not one of those people. It'd be good for you to remember that.'

Vaughn had an overwhelming urge to pick up the kettle and do some damage with it but he swallowed hard and dug his nails into his hand instead. As Vaughn controlled his anger, he sat down on the kitchen stool and spoke to Josh again, this time without letting his feelings show.

'Neither of us want to sit here staring at each other, so if you could tell me when she's due back, I'd appreciate it.'

'I don't know. Contrary to what you think I didn't stay here last night. I was supposed to meet her this morning – she wasn't here, but her phone is, so I guess she hasn't gone very far. I let myself in.'

'I was supposed to meet her at one o'clock in the club.'

'So I guess she's gone AWOL. She hasn't changed. Listen, I really haven't got time for this, I'm going to go back to my hotel. If you see her get her to call me, but tell her not to leave it too late, as if I'm not needed here I'll get a train back to Birmingham tonight.'

Josh got up from the couch, and kicked a pile of dirty laundry out of the way. About to vent his frustration again on the dirty shirts and trousers he looked down to get a good aim but stopped when he saw a splattering of fresh blood over the floor and on some of the nearby clothes.

Josh quickly got down on his knees and found more droplets of blood on the floorboards. He looked up and saw the look of anxiety on Vaughn's face.

'When was the last time you heard from her, Vaughn?'

'Last night. We went into the West End to see someone but then I saw a man I knew from the club and she followed him.'

'What! You let her go on her own?'

'She was fine. I'm not going to put her in danger. All she was doing was seeing where he went. She lost the guy and I offered to meet her but she told me she was going to come back here and get an early night.'

Josh was only half listening as he continued to survey the room. 'Over there.' He pointed to more specks of blood near the kitchenette units. 'I don't think we should jump to any conclusions, Vaughn; she could've had a nose bleed or something, especially if she'd been drinking.'

'A nose bleed? Are you having a fucking cackle, mate? Something's happened to her; I know it. Her phone's still here and she was supposed to meet you this morning and me at lunchtime.'

'It doesn't mean anything; it's what she does.'

'No, she wouldn't do it to Emmie. She wanted to help, there's no way she would just go off without telling either one of us.'

'You obviously don't know my wife, Vaughn.'

Vaughn turned on Josh angrily and started to shout, trying to ignore the panic inside him.

'I don't give a fuck what she used to be because I know what she is now, and I'm telling you she wouldn't do that to Emmie. She lost her daughter once and she isn't about to do that again. Her phone is still there and so is her bag and

306

it doesn't take a motherfucking genius to know something bad has happened.'

Vaughn stopped shouting, suddenly feeling emotionally defeated. 'I'll only say this once, Josh, but if there was ever a time I need help, it's now. There are two people I love in trouble and I would happily bet everything I've got that Oscar Harding has something to do with Casey not being here. I'll do anything it takes to find them and I need to know, are you with me?'

Josh stood in stunned silence, amazed at the emotional outburst and Vaughn's declaration of love. All he could do was come up with an answer which sounded as if it was a line from a bad movie.

'You bet your life I am.'

CHAPTER THIRTY-SEVEN

Standing in the windowless grey waiting area of the prison, Vaughn checked his mobile for the umpteenth time. He'd attempted to phone Oscar but it'd gone straight to voicemail. He'd been tempted to leave a message, warning Oscar if he laid a finger on Casey he'd have no alternative but to find him and kill him; the problem was he was only ninety-nine per cent certain Oscar had Cass and leaving a threatening message wouldn't help.

He looked across at Josh fidgeting with his jacket buttons and decided to go and talk to him.

'Can I ask you something, mate? I'm curious. What were you doing pissing in the sink?'

'Have you seen the bathroom?'

Vaughn said nothing and smiled to himself.

The prison officer waved them through to the main visiting room where he saw an unshaven Alfie sitting at one of the tables.

'Nice one Vaughn. Good to see you. Who's this?'

'Josh Edwards; he's Casey's husband.'

Alfie was lost for words. What the fuck was going on? He looked at Vaughn, who shrugged.

'Are we playing happy fucking families now?'

'No, Josh is going to help me – or rather, help us – find Emmie, and now it seems Casey too; he's Old Bill.'

Josh shot Vaughn a biting stare; they'd agreed in the car not to tell Alfie who he was but he'd spat it out at the first opportunity.

Alfie stood up from his chair in astonishment and saw the prison officer walk towards him, thinking there was going to be more trouble with prisoner 17181. He hurriedly sat down again, not wanting another spell in solitary.

'Have you shat your marbles down the bog, mate? Bringing Old Bill in here and to me? Do you want everyone in here to think I'm a grass?'

'Listen, I don't like it any more than you do, but we need him.'

Josh sat up straight from the hard prison chair, somewhat offended, and spoke to them both.

'I *am* here.'

Vaughn looked at him and was about to open his mouth but Alfie got there before him.

'Shut the fuck up.' Alfie turned back to Vaughn. 'Listen Vaughn, this ain't happening.'

'You've got no say in it, Alfie – especially now Oscar's got Casey. And may I remind you, if it wasn't for your dealings with Oscar, we wouldn't be where we are now.'

Alfie rubbed his head. It was so fucked up he didn't know where to begin. He sat and looked round the room, seeing all the other prisoners with their loved ones and asking himself for the hundredth time how he'd ever got in such a fucking mess.

'You need to tell me everything. If you know of any of

Oscar's cronies you need to tell me; I need names. It's the only chance we have of finding Emmie.'

'You having a bubble? You want me to be a grass as well as sitting here rubbing shoulders with a fucking monkey? I need to get out of here and find him myself.'

Vaughn stretched across the table and grabbed hold of Alfie's striped collar.

'Fuck the code, Alfie, and for once, fuck your ego. If you think you're going to sit here and not tell me about Oscar and his cronies, behind bars or not, I will fuck you up more than you are already. There is no way in hell I'm going to let anything happen to Casey or her daughter.'

Casey was feeling rough. The heroin had made her body break out into clammy sweats and her hands were starting to shake, but as much as she wanted to put the way she was feeling all down to what had happened with Oscar she wasn't going to kid herself: she knew the signs of withdrawing from alcohol and prayed it wasn't going to affect her ability to support Emmie. She *had* to stay clear headed – it was their only chance to work out a way of getting out of there.

Casey looked over at Emmie, who was pacing up and down in an attempt to lessen the boredom and hold on to her sanity. Emmie had told her some of what happened at the party and it had confirmed Casey's worst fears.

The other women in the room hadn't roused enough to communicate with them – if it wasn't for them walking zombie-like to the bathroom, complete with dead eyes and sallow skin, Casey wouldn't have even known they were there.

If they did have a chance to escape, she doubted she'd be able to take them with her, they were so out of it on heroin. If she did find a way out for her and Emmie, they'd only have one chance and she couldn't afford to blow it. It seemed

310

callous but there wasn't much she could do. Casey sighed and lay back on her mattress. There was no doubt in Casey's mind that Jason and Oscar would be planning another party. Time was running out for Casey to get them out of there alive.

CHAPTER THIRTY-EIGHT

Jason Hedley grinned at Oscar before letting out a large burp. He'd got indigestion from the korma chicken curry he'd eaten late last night and it was repeating on him more times than an episode of *Friends*.

'I was impressed, you came up with the goods – and from what I hear Billy did a good job cleaning up.'

Jason glanced at Oscar in the mirror and leant forward to pick out a bit of chicken from his tooth. With his boyish face and twinkling eyes, he'd always looked younger than his years, helped by the fact that his body was in peak condition, with a year-round tan from sun beds and trips to Majorca.

Giving himself a last check in the mirror, he turned his full attention back to Oscar, moving towards the large south-facing window to sit down. He'd bought his flat for cash two years ago for just over two million and it suited him down to the ground. It was situated close to Hyde Park and from his back bedroom, he could see the walls of Buckingham Palace; it was certainly a long way from the run-down estate he'd grown up on in Bristol.

'So are we still on for the party, Oscar?'

'Absolutely; but I was hoping to renegotiate the price.'

Jason stopped admiring his manicured nails and stared at Oscar. That was the problem with easy money; people always wanted more. Oscar's women had been good and what he'd seen he'd liked, but they weren't worth anything more than he'd paid for them the first time round. It wasn't as if their pussies were suddenly made out of gold.

'I'm sorry Oscar, I'm already paying full whack. So, no can do I'm afraid.'

Oscar looked round the luxurious apartment and decided Jason was taking the piss. He'd sorted the girls out for him without so much as a grumble last time and had come away one down, not to mention that stupid bitch Ariana, who'd screamed all the way through the party then had corpsed on the smack back at the warehouse, making him have to pay Billy more again to do a cleanup. He didn't dispute the money was good, but it certainly could be better and he was determined to get more.

'I appreciate what you pay, I really do, but your clients want something special and I provide it. Surely that counts for something?'

Jason wondered why Oscar couldn't see what a good thing he was on to and what a fucking fool he was being. One thing Jason hated with a vengeance was greedy people – and Oscar Harding's love of money was going to fuck him up one day, but for the time being he needed him. Jason narrowed his eyes and stared hard at Oscar. As soon as this next party was over with, he'd find someone else to provide the goods.

'It counts for a lot, but I'm not going to pay over the odds, Oscar, just because I appreciate what you do; I'm a businessman. And a word of advice: no one likes a man coming into their castle and demanding their gold.'

'Jason, we're friends, so I wouldn't like to have to tell

you my girls won't be coming and put you in an awkward position with all those clients who've paid for their slice of utopia. To see you getting a reputation as a man who breaks his word would be dreadful, because I know how difficult it would be to find women like mine at such short notice.'

'Are you trying to blackmail me, Oscar? Because you and I both know what a foolish mistake it would be.'

'Blackmail? Now that's an ugly word. I was merely expressing my concern for your reputation, which we both know is everything in this business.'

Jason licked his lips. Oscar had his bollocks in a vice and they both knew it. There were over two hundred people all coming to the party, who'd paid over ten grand apiece to attend.

'Fine, I'll add another three grand a head.'

'Make it five and we've got a deal.'

Jason grinned, without the smile hitting his eyes.

'Four grand and that's my final offer.'

'You drive a hard bargain, Jason; but okay, four grand it is.'

Jason shook Oscar's hand, hoping one day instead of shaking his hand he'd be breaking it, and then he'd show him what a hard bargain really felt like.

Vaughn read the headlines of the *Evening Standard* and slammed the paper back down in the news stand.

'Anything interesting?'

Vaughn was about to snap Josh's head off but his lip started to throb and he started to feel very sorry for himself. It was a stupid thing he'd done.

'It was a stupid thing to do back there.'

Josh echoed his thoughts and it annoyed him immensely, mainly because he was telling him what he already knew.

'When I want your opinion, I'll ask you for it.'

'Even you can't think it was sensible.'

'Fuck me, what is it with you? So I made a mistake in telling Alfie?'

'A mistake – is that what you'd call it?'

No, it wasn't what he'd call it but as Vaughn clambered into his Range Rover with his face throbbing, the last thing he was going to do was admit what an idiot he'd been in telling Alfie that Emmie was Casey's daughter. He shuddered at the thought of his stupidity.

'Come again?'

Alfie had stared at him over the prison visiting table, not quite sure he'd heard correctly.

'Casey's daughter. Emmie is Casey's daughter, Alf.'

It had still taken Alfie a while to react; he could see Vaughn's mouth working and he could hear the words, but he couldn't comprehend them. It was too shocking to take it seriously.

'Is this your sick way of winding me up, Vaughn?'

'No; it's the truth. I didn't know myself until recently.'

'And you think you're going to start playing happy families with my daughter?'

'It's not like that, Alf.'

Josh had looked on at the two men and as he looked at the twitch in Alfie's cheek he'd started to count in his mind how long it'd take for the full eruption to take place.

Alfie put his head in his hands and held it there for a moment as Josh got up to thirty-two.

'You bastard, I bet you've been laughing your heads off at me.'

Alfie's fist had come flying up as he kept his head down; it had made perfect contact on Vaughn's lip, splitting it open and knocking him backwards off the plastic chair. Immediately Vaughn had scurried up and leapt on Alfie, his fists pummelling in all directions.

The prison officers had blown their whistle trying to stop the fight but it'd had the opposite result and had set off a domino effect of violence amongst the other inmates.

A tall Asian man who had a score of his own to settle dived on the man opposite him, encouraging a cacophony of furious shouts of anger amongst the remaining prisoners in the visiting room.

Vaughn grabbed hold of Alfie's arm quickly; he could see the guards were on their way. He twisted it round his back, pulling it to the point of breaking, and slammed Alfie's head on the floor.

'Listen to me you prick, I didn't know about Emmie, no one wanted to hurt you. I shouldn't have said it but you need to start talking.'

'Get the fuck off me.'

'Not until I get some names.'

'No chance.'

Vaughn slammed his head down again on the concrete floor.

'You and I both know you love her; we both do. Give me some names, Alf, don't be a prick because you'll regret it later.'

Vaughn saw the backup officers run into the room and he knew any moment they'd be dragged away.

'Jason Hedley, you need to speak to him.' Alfie winced in pain as the officers pulled him away. 'Wherever he is, you'll find Oscar and Emmie.'

Vaughn opened the window in his Range Rover and decided he was going to buy a packet of cigarettes. After the guards had arrived, they'd all been frogmarched into another room whilst the prisoners were taken back to their cells.

They'd waited for over an hour in the tiny locked room before they'd been eventually let out by two flustered looking

316

prison officers. It'd been a hell of a wait as there'd only been two chairs in total, even though there'd been over thirty visitors crammed in.

In the chaos of the visit, he hadn't heard his phone ringing and had missed a call from Oscar. He braced himself before listening to the message.

'I'm disappointed not to get hold of you; I was rather looking forward to having a chat. Thought you might be missing someone? Don't worry, she's in safe hands. I'll be in touch but I thought I'd send you a picture. This is becoming rather a habit don't you think?'

Vaughn took a tentative look in the photo messages inbox and saw a glimpse of Casey, bound and gagged like Emmie was. He groaned angrily and flung his phone on the dashboard.

'Fuck, he's got her. I knew it but Jesus, now it makes it real.'

'We need to speak to the police, Vaughn.'

'We can't. Oscar has his fingers up a lot of people's arses; you couldn't survive in this game if you didn't. The minute we step into a police station, he'll get wind of it. There are plenty of bent coppers about who are happy to mow the lawn on you if it means them getting a couple of holidays abroad each year. We need to go and see Jason Hedley – his name is the one which keeps cropping up. Somehow, you need to persuade him to let you go to the party he's hosting.'

'What about you?'

'No, Jason and I have crossed paths too many times. No one down here knows you, so it'll be perfect. All you have to do is use your acting skills and persuade him you're desperate to have some perverse pleasure and let him know Lola sent you.'

'I don't know, it sounds chancy.'

'That's because it is.'

* * *

In every brothel they'd driven to, Josh had got the same answer from the overly done-up receptionists with their caked-on makeup and cleavages which would make a priest sweat.

'Sorry treacle, I haven't seen him. He turns up when he wants. I only work here; I'm not his keeper.'

'Fine, I'll leave my number and if he comes in, please get him to call me.'

The receptionists hadn't even bothered to look up.

'I think we're hammering on brick walls, Vaughn.' Josh sat back in the passenger seat as he drank a watery coffee; he knew it would be doubtful they'd come across a man like Jason Hedley so easily. Men like him only were found if they wanted to be.

'I just got a call from my old buddy. I think we're in business.'

Without warning, Vaughn sped off, causing Josh's hot coffee to go spilling onto his lap.

Vaughn sped through the back streets of Islington, passing the Moorfield Eye Hospital and onto the City Road roundabout before turning left at Pitfield Street, then finally into Ashford Street.

Vaughn pulled up outside a disused block of offices and switched the engine off.

'I hope you can play cards, because you're off to the casino.'

Vaughn opened the glove compartment, pulled out a brown padded envelope and handed it straight to Josh.

'There's twenty thousand big ones in there, I want you to take it and make it look like you know what you're doing. Give the impression if you lose it, there's plenty more where it came from. Excuse my pun, but if you play your cards right and Jason *is* in there, he'll come to you like flies gather round shit.'

'You're kidding, right?'

'Just go in and act normally.'

Josh didn't answer. He looked out of the tinted black car window, everything telling him to get out of the car and leave the Met to deal with it. His career would most certainly be on the line if anyone got wind of what he was doing. It was unbelievable to him how a couple of phone calls from Cass had turned into him being passed twenty thousand pounds by an infamous gangland criminal, albeit a retired one.

'I thought you said you were with me. Not having second thoughts?' Vaughn spoke to the back of Josh's head as he gazed out of the window. For someone who was supposed to be a detective he had the balls of a fucking gnat. What Casey had seen in him, he didn't know. Anyone would think he'd asked him to take out the President of the United States rather than go into a private casino and spend twenty grand of someone else's money.

'I need to think; problem with that?'

Vaughn actually had a great big steaming problem with that but he held his tongue. A few moments later, just as Vaughn was about to lose his patience, Josh spoke.

'Okay, tell me exactly what you want me to do.'

Josh hadn't thought he was dressed appropriately to go into a casino in his dark blue jeans and white shirt, but Vaughn had insisted as long as he had the members' card it wouldn't be a problem. Vaughn had been right; the laid back atmosphere and casually dressed punters made it feel less like a casino and more like a pub.

The decor of the casino was very understated, with plain cream walls and a thick red carpet specked with grey. The only feature which separated the place from any other social venue was the punters sitting down at the tables with large wads of cash piled in front of them.

Josh decided to go to the roulette table in the centre rather than showing himself up playing cards.

'Lay your bets.'

'I'll have an outside bet. Five hundred on black.'

Josh placed some of Vaughn's money on the black and watched the ball whirl round, clattering over the tilted circular track running around the circumference of the wheel. Although he was there for purposes other than to enjoy himself, he couldn't help feeling a flutter of excitement in his stomach as the ball slowed down and bounced over the coloured numbers. He could feel the tension from the other punters round the table who'd placed inside and outside bets ranging from fifty pounds to double his.

'Red 18.'

The sigh was audible from the others as the Japanese croupier called out the result and Josh was conscious of his shoulders dropping in disappointment.

'Bets again gentlemen; rolling in one.'

'Three thousand on red.'

Josh decided to go along with Vaughn's advice and give the impression of not caring about the money; and really there was no reason he should – he doubted it was earned by good honest work: but he couldn't help feeling guilty. It wasn't in his nature to be frivolous with money and he didn't enjoy the idea of wasting it, no matter who it belonged to.

'Like a flutter, I see.'

Josh turned, rather startled after being so engrossed in the action on the green felt table, and saw he was almost shoulder to shoulder with a man whose teeth seemed to have been blasted with Dulux Brilliant White. The overpowering smell of expensive aftershave hit him and Josh moved to the side slightly, feeling rather uncomfortable having his personal space invaded.

'It's a fool's game, but a rich fool's.'

'And which one are you, a fool or a rich man?'

Josh went along with the game.

'I'd probably say a bit of both.'

'I prefer cards myself. Do you play poker?'

'No, never bothered learning. I thought seeing as I was going to lose my money anyway, what's the point in spending hours learning to do it?'

The man laughed and then reached out his hand to Josh to introduce himself.

'Jason Hedley.'

Josh was already prepared with his introduction. He shook Jason's hand and smiled.

'Good to meet you Jason, I'm Kelvin Armstrong.'

Jason nodded towards the roulette table and grinned as he held Josh's hand in a firm grip.

'Looks like lucky number seven isn't shining on you today, Kelvin.'

'Perhaps not in cards, but maybe in other matters. You're a hard man to get hold of, Jason – I've been looking for you. Lola sent me.'

CHAPTER THIRTY-NINE

Oscar splashed water over his face as he relaxed in a bath full of bubbles in his large white marbled bathroom. His plan was coming together better than a bishop with a whore. He'd wanted to show Alfie not to fuck with him, and now he was going to fuck with Alfie instead. He was going to bring him and his whole empire down. As for the almighty Vaughn Sadler, it was fun to see him chasing all over London as if he was a fucking kitten after a piece of string. He was going to destroy him and leave him a broken man.

Everything was falling into place. The money, the women and the reputation, but especially the party. He was looking forward to seeing Casey squealing like a pig. Since she'd been on the scene she'd caused nothing but trouble. If it wasn't for her, his ex-wife Lola would be pushing up fucking daisies; and for that Casey was going to pay.

He would stand back and watch as the sick and the perverse acted out their darkest sexual fantasies on her and he'd laugh when she bled, pleading for him to tell them to stop. Oh yes, pretty little Miss Casey would regret ever putting her nose into his business.

Holding his nose and leaning backwards, Oscar submerged himself under the hot water with a large smile on his face.

Josh stood in the hothouse, watching Vaughn re-plant a small pink rose bush. It was not what he had been expecting to see when he agreed to come back to Vaughn's house.

It'd gone surprisingly well with Jason, and for a man with such a fearsome reputation he'd been very open about the party the minute Josh had talked about Lola sending him.

'So apart from gambling, what other vices have you got?'

'The same as any other man.'

'I don't know what any other man's vices are, Kelvin. I know my own, but I wouldn't presume to know yours.'

'Where's this going, Jason?'

'Just curious to know how you like to spend your money.'

'Well as I said, I was looking for you – surely that tells you something?'

'Perhaps but I'd like you to spell it out. I wouldn't want us to have any crossed wires, would I?'

Josh had instinctively sensed it was important to play on Jason's overblown ego.

'I met a guy called Rainton when I was serving a three for GBH in Strangeways and it turns out we had the same taste in women. He mentioned Lola and after I got out I decided to go and see her and she told me you were the man who could make things happen; she said you would sort me out. I've been out for a while and I've been asking around a bit, but you weren't an easy man to find.'

Josh had stopped and watched Jason mull over what he'd just said. It was usually risky having an alias; in his experience they nearly always could be torn apart, but Kelvin Armstrong was as strong as an alias got. He'd used it when he was working undercover last year on a case involving underage girls working in a prostitution ring, and his department had made sure it was watertight.

'I know Lola but I don't know anyone called Rainton. When were you serving?'

'Came out in June. Served all my time at Strangeways.'

'Rainton?'

'Sam Rainton. He knows you. Anyway, no matter.'

'No, hang on, why don't you leave me your number and let me have a think about it.'

It'd been an hour after he'd left the casino that he'd got the call from Jason. Josh had supposed he'd got someone to run a prison computer check on Kelvin Armstrong and his fictitious cellmate, and like magic the names would've popped up, confirming to Jason what he'd said was true.

'We've got a party next month, I'm sure you'll like it.'

'I heard you were hosting one sooner than that.'

'Well, not everything you hear is the truth.'

'Whatever the price, I'll double it. I'm in the mood for a good time; it's been a while.'

Josh had waited, saying nothing and waiting for Jason to make the next move without seeming too keen.

'What if we say thirty Gs?'

'A bit steep, but I think I can manage it.'

'Okay, meet me at the Grosvenor House Hotel in the tea room at two. Bring the money and later on someone will call you with the details.'

'I have to take back everything I said about you or thought about you, Josh; I'm impressed.'

'I think we should inform the police.'

Vaughn slammed down the flower pot and faced Josh angrily.

'Listen, we know Oscar's providing the girls for the party,

which means he'll be there. What we don't know is if Emmie or Casey will be – and if we do anything hasty we may never get them back.'

'If they are there, we call the police. That's the deal, Vaughn. I'm not going to this party if I don't get your word.'

Vaughn pushed his face inches away from Josh and poked him in his chest.

'I don't like your attitude.'

'At this stage, Vaughn, I don't care what you like and what you don't like. You can't do this without me and I won't do this without that promise.'

Casey stood in front of Emmie and smiled weakly; she was worried.

'Are you okay?' Emmie faced her, looking anxious. Casey knew Emmie wanted her to be strong and assure her everything was going to be fine and as hard as the pretence was, Casey was determined to do just that.

'Think it must be the food; not exactly haute cuisine in here, I might even complain to the chef.'

It raised a smile from Emmie.

'Are you ready to get dressed?'

Emmie nodded and Casey saw her lip quivering as she tried to fight back the tears.

'Listen to me, Emmie, I will do anything I can to make sure we get out of here but I need you to be brave for me. Can you do that?'

'Yes, I'll try.'

'Good girl, now put this on and I'm going to pop to the bathroom.'

Casey leant on the sink in the bathroom fighting back her own tears; there was no way she could let Emmie see her like this. She wouldn't let herself think about what lay ahead. Emmie had told her more about the party and as much as going to this one might be their chance to escape, it could also quite easily be their undoing.

'Casey, we're waiting for you.'

Oscar's voice boomed menacingly and Casey quickly splashed water on her face. Her face still hurt, as did her hand, and as she looked in the mirror, she saw the dark circles under her eyes. Not for the first time, she closed her eyes and said a prayer.

As she walked out of the bathroom, she saw Oscar's men with some drugs paraphernalia in their hands. Oscar saw Casey looking at it and he spoke with a mocking grin on his face to her and Emmie.

'None for you girls I'm afraid. I want you to be able to feel every moment of your time here.'

The back of the van was as uncomfortable and cold as it'd been the first time round but the difference this time was most of the women now knew what was in store for them. Emmie gripped tightly on to Casey's good hand; the sense of terror was almost palpable.

'Oh isn't this sweet; holding hands like little fucking Bo-Peep.'

Casey cut her eye at Oscar as he leaned over the front seat and tapped her on her knee. During her dark heavy drinking days she'd come across and slept with a lot of men, but she'd never met anyone who'd exuded anywhere near as much evil as Oscar Harding did.

The women sat on the metal floor of the van, huddled up to give each other comfort and warmth, tightly packed together with their heads down in their laps to stop the cold air hitting their faces.

Casey was shivering and she couldn't stop her whole body trembling however hard she tried; she'd never felt so cold in her life.

'Get ready ladies.'

Oscar spoke as the van slowed down, running over rough ground, swaying the women from side to side.

'You okay, Emmie?' Casey whispered.

Before Emmie could answer, Casey felt a hard swipe to her head and she shrank back in pain as she realised Oscar had hit out at her.

'Don't take the piss, Casey. No talking and no fucking stirring the ranks.'

Casey said nothing and waited for the back doors to be opened by the driver. She scrambled out of the van stumbling on the impractical shoes Oscar had given her to wear. Her dress was short and flimsy and the breeze of the night whipped up the bottom of her hem, exposing her thighs to the freezing night's temperatures.

Casey glanced at the other women standing in similar dresses and as much as they were cold too, Casey could see the distant look in their eyes from being drugged up on heroin.

There was part of Casey which envied their continual drugged-up state, being numb to the horror of the reality around them, but she also knew there was no likelihood of any of them escaping if they were stoned.

The path was dark and the wind howled round the tops of the trees as the rain beat down on the twisted branches. It was pitch black apart from the moon which was beginning to diminish behind the hazy night clouds and only the light from the torch guided them through the woods. Casey shuddered from the bitter air.

It took ten minutes of unbearable cold and wet for the group to arrive at the sprawling estate.

'Is this the same place you were before, Em?'

'No, it's not. I'm scared, Casey.'

'I know sweetheart, but just do as they say and you'll be fine. I promise.'

Casey had no idea if Emmie would be fine but empty words were all she had to give her. They walked a bit further to a large gravel drive full of cars and smartly-dressed people milling about, and waited for Oscar to make a call.

A few minutes later a man dressed entirely in black and wearing a white mask came over to them.

'Glad to see you made it, Oscar.'

'My word is my honour, especially as you crossed my palm with gold.'

Oscar laughed loudly as Jason Hedley stared at him with hatred behind his mask.

Vaughn parked his car down the long country lane and turned off the lights and engine. It was freezing cold and looking out into the dark black void of the night brought home the enormity of the situation they were in.

'Are you ready?'

Vaughn shuffled round to face Josh wearing a white mask. The person who'd called with the details had instructed him to be clothed in all black and to wear a half mask which had to be white.

'Yes, I'm ready as I can be. I'll call you when I'm in there; and Vaughn, remember what I said. If Emmie and Casey are there we call the police.'

Vaughn nodded, watching Josh as he opened the car door and walked into the dark of the night.

The man led the women down the stone-tiled corridor, Casey and Emmie following behind. It was cold in the house and they could see their breath, but it was far warmer than outside. The corridors were lit with large black candles; ornate rugs decorated one side of the wall and gilt-framed

328

paintings of Cartwright's countryside hung on the other.

They walked through a large room with furniture covered in dust sheets which led into a small room with a small barred window.

Jason studied the girls and walked up to Emmie, who was shaking from the cold, as well as through fear. He took hold of her golden hair and ran it through his fingers before he stroked her face with his hand. He spoke through his mask to Oscar.

'Bit of a change of plan. I'll take these ladies to their rooms, and I want you to stay here.'

Oscar was about to argue but he guessed this was Jason's way of showing him he was still pissed off for having to pay out of his arse for the girls. If it made him feel better to make him sit in a cold bare pantry room, so be it. He had big enough balls to take it; after all it was him who was laughing all the way to the bank.

'No problem. I'll make myself comfortable.'

Oscar gave a tight smirk as Jason led the girls out of the room.

The house gave the impression of being made up of long dark corridors and corners and their footsteps echoed along the stone walls as they walked. Jason stopped at a carved oak door and knocked. It was opened by a person wearing a mask. Emmie screamed then tried to stifle the high-pitched noise escaping from her mouth by clamping her hands over her face.

Casey closed her eyes as Jason handed over the first woman to the group of people waiting in the darkened bedroom clad in their sinister disguises. Ljena's drugged-out silence gave way to screams of terror as she was forcibly pulled into the room by the perverted men and women waiting to act out their twisted fantasies on her.

Emmie started to cry along with the other women and

Casey would've been happy to join them in their tears if it wasn't for the fact her mind was racing with panic. She hadn't expected the house to be so impenetrable. The windows were small and barred, the stone walls were thick and the doors were heavy and dense. With each passing moment, Casey thought it was less and less likely they would ever be able to escape.

Eventually only Emmie and Casey were left, and Jason led them to a white wooden door. It was opened by a tall man who took one look at Emmie and reached for her, but Jason stopped him.

'Not her; she's mine.'

He pushed Casey forward and she turned to Emmie, who had a look of terror on her face that mirrored how Casey was feeling. Emmie reached to hold Casey's hand and started begging.

'Please Casey, please, you promised me you wouldn't leave me. Please don't leave me, don't let them take me!'

The words Emmie screamed out were profound; evocative of Casey's feelings from the past and mixing with the terror of the present. She tried to reassure Emmie but she was unable to speak, traumatised by Emmie's screams as the door shut behind her.

Josh heard the scream coming from somewhere in the house above the scream of the woman in the room he was standing in. He didn't want to watch as the man next to him – who'd introduced himself as Pete as if they were at the regatta in Henley – undressed the woman, who was begging them in broken English to stop.

He slipped out of the room and into the candlelit corridor. He'd lost his bearings as he'd come in; they'd been led up so many staircases and round so many corners and through different doors, he didn't know if he was at the front or the back of the house.

They'd been instructed by the masked guide not to leave their rooms, but it was the only way to try and see if Emmie and Casey were in the house. Besides, he felt sick at what he'd just seen. He couldn't stand there and watch the woman being violated and do nothing.

Josh walked slowly down the corridor, pushing himself into the shadows, hoping not to be seen. There were several doors leading off the walkway but as he couldn't hear any noise coming from behind them he decided to keep on going. Part of him hoped to find Casey and Emmie and the other part hoped they weren't here; he couldn't bear to see them in such horrific circumstances.

He knew what Oscar looked like, he'd seen the police photos; but he suspected he'd also be wearing a mask to mix in with the sinister perverted clones. Luckily no one knew him, so if Josh did bump into anyone, as far as they were concerned he was just Kelvin Armstrong.

He came to a door with noise coming from behind it and he turned the doorknob and pushed, bracing himself for what was on the other side. He saw a young woman surrounded by a group of people in masks the same as his. Josh could see she was as helpless and as fearful as the woman he'd left with Pete, but she wasn't Casey and she wasn't Emmie and he needed to find them. He shut the door quickly, praying he could come back with some help.

There was a set of stairs at the far end of the second corridor leading down to the basement and Josh slowly walked down them, feeling the mouldy air attacking his lungs. The floor was slippery and Josh stepped carefully, putting his hand out to steady himself against the freezing cold wall.

His senses were on heightened alert as he moved further into the darkness.

There was a noise to the left of him and he froze, not wanting to make a sound. Even though it was cold, beads of sweat made their way down his masked forehead and his breathing was staggered as he stood motionless against the wall. He heard the noise again and slowly crept along to the end of the dark corridor, his heart pounding. Josh shut his eyes for a moment and took a deep breath to steady his nerves.

Slowly, he leaned his head round the corner.

'Oh my god.'

He saw Emmie, naked, tied against the wall and he ran across to her; he could tell she was going to scream but he pushed his hand hard against her mouth and tore off his mask with the other.

'Don't say a word, Emmie; I'm here to help you. My name's Josh.'

The panic in her eyes told him she didn't believe him and probably thought it was part of the same sick game.

'I'm Casey's husband and a friend of Vaughn's.'

He spoke quietly and quickly as he fumbled with the leather ties binding her arms and legs to the metal rings on the wall. He finished untying her foot and hurriedly took off his black jacket and put it round her shoulders. She was trembling and seemed rooted to the spot but he needed to get her to move, fast.

'Emmie, we've got to get out of here.'

She didn't respond and he shook her gently and then held her close to him in a warm embrace.

'Emmie, is Casey here?'

She nodded and Josh started to guide her towards the stairs of the cellar.

'I'll go and find her, do you know the way out?'

'Going somewhere?'

Josh looked up and saw a man walking down the stairs. He couldn't see his face but he recognised his voice; it was Jason.

CHAPTER FORTY

'Fuck.'

His phone said no signal and Vaughn couldn't help but
think Josh had tried to call. His thoughts were speeding off
at all different angles and he wasn't sure what to do. If he
left the car and they came back, what then? If he went to
the house, he might easily be spotted. He couldn't help
thinking Josh had been right when he'd said it was a stupid
idea to come out here on their own. The fucked-up thing
about it was now that he was ready to call the police, he
didn't even have a signal to do it.

Five more minutes. He'd give him five more and if Josh
hadn't come back then, he'd go and look for him. Vaughn
didn't know if it was the absolute darkness which was
making him nervous or the fact he didn't know what was
happening, but he felt more anxious than he'd ever been
in his life.

The time went by and Vaughn left the keys in the ignition,
deciding it was unlikely the car would get nicked; but if Josh
did come back with the girls and he needed to get away in
a hurry, the car would be waiting for him.

He didn't have a torch, only his cigarette lighter, and he

wasn't entirely sure where he was going. They'd driven past the gates of the vast driveway leading to the house the party was being held at but he didn't want to go the front way; he'd be seen by security and stopped straight away.

The brambles caught on his jeans and Vaughn found himself stumbling over the twisted roots of the trees sticking out of the muddy ground. The rain was coming down harder and it was bitter as the wind cut into his face. He pulled out his mobile from his pocket, but it still showed no signal and Vaughn swore out loud as his foot caught in some ivy root, sending him headlong onto the ground.

Oscar was getting restless in the room and tried to call Billy to make sure he hadn't fallen asleep in the car. He sighed when he saw there was no signal on his phone. That was another problem with being in the countryside; you couldn't ever get a signal when you needed it. Another reason for him to hate poxy fucking rural areas. He stood up and decided to have a look round the house. He didn't care what Jason had said; if he wanted to leave the room, he would. No one told Oscar Harding what to do, least of all a man who looked like he'd nicked his teeth from the nearest race horse.

Emmie screamed as Jason walked down the stairs and ran behind Josh who pushed her to one side.

'What the fuck is this, Kelvin?'

'Get out of my way, Jason; I'm taking her with me.'

Jason laughed and pulled off his mask.

'We don't do party bags. Punters don't get to take the girls home.'

Josh faced Jason, who stood only a few feet away in the dim light. He could hear Emmie crying and his eyes darted to see if there was anything he could use as a weapon. He'd known he was going to get frisked when he came into the house, so he hadn't brought anything to protect him.

Jason sneered.

'No one takes the fucking piss out of me.'

In a flash, Jason took out a steel blade from his inside pocket and stared at Josh in fury.

'Josh!'

Emmie yelled in panic as she saw the blade and Jason looked puzzled.

'Josh?'

'That's right – my name's Josh, and any minute now the police are going to be here. So I'd put down the knife if I were you.'

Josh thought he saw a flicker of hesitation in Jason's eyes but it was soon replaced by an ugly dark look.

'Well in that case, I better make this quick.'

Jason stabbed at Josh with the blade and he staggered back to the wall, clutching his stomach.

'Run, Emmie!'

He looked at Emmie as she stood staring in horror at the dark blood pouring through his fingers. He thought she wasn't going to move, but after a second she ran, pushing past Jason who tried to grab her. Taking advantage of the moment, Josh took a swipe at Jason with his fist, knocking him into the wall as he hit him square in the jaw.

Jason stood up and this time drove the knife into Josh's leg as Josh grabbed him round the neck. They both fell to the wet stone floor. The knife dropped and Josh scrambled to get it but his injuries slowed him down and it was Jason who got there first.

'You cunt, I'll kill you!' Jason screamed stabbing Josh in the face as he tried to protect himself with his arms. He cried out in pain but the sound was cut short by the blade slashing the corner of his mouth, pouring red warm blood onto the stone floor.

Jason Hedley stood above him and laughed, before turning to find Emmie.

Emmie ran along the corridors in her bare feet trying every door. She couldn't see properly from panic and each corner she turned she half screamed as she imagined running into Jason or, worse still, Oscar. She saw stairs everywhere but she knew it was pointless going up them; she needed to stay on the ground floor if she was going to try to get out.

Turning a corner she saw the long corridor they'd walked down on the way in. She knew at the end of it there was a side door to the outside but she'd no idea if it'd be open or not. She thought of her new friend Casey and she knew she'd want her to be brave and try to get out and find help.

The middle door of the corridor creaked and Emmie could feel the tears running down her face. She tiptoed down the passageway and she saw the white door in front of her. She wanted to run but she couldn't afford to make a sound. She continued to walk quietly as she passed two closed doors. The door seemed so far away even though it was only a few feet in front. There was one last door to pass and Emmie couldn't hold back any longer; she ran.

She was telling herself to hurry as she tried to unlock all the bolts on the door; she needed to go faster. The bolts came undone but when she tried the door, it wouldn't open. In a desperate attempt she rattled the handle but it still wouldn't move and all Emmie could do was start to sob again.

The bloodcurdling shriek coming from the inside of the house made Emmie retch and once again she attempted to shake open the door. She could hear footsteps heading her way and they were becoming louder and heavier. She was trapped. At the other end of the corridor she saw Oscar and she let out a terrified shriek.

'Emmie Jennings, I'm surprised at you.' Oscar's voice was full of menace as he walked towards her, making Emmie shrink back. He was only a few inches away when he reached out and began to touch her face. Emmie jerked her body back and screamed, as the door suddenly opened and she was flung backwards onto the cold ground outside. Oscar, attempting to grab hold of her, fell on the ground as well. Emmie scrambled up as quickly as she could but found her leg being held by Oscar.

'I don't think so.'

Oscar shouted as Emmie stamped her other foot on Oscar's nose, making him release his grip enough for her to free her leg from his grasp. Not looking back, she ran into the dark of the woods.

She could hear Oscar close behind her as she ran, stumbling along the path in her bare feet, breathing hard, her heart racing uncomfortably. Emmie knew she needed to get off the path, otherwise she'd be a sitting target for Oscar; he was so much faster and stronger than her, and it was only a matter of time before he caught up.

The combination of the steep ditch and the brambles had her falling down on her front, the sharp thorns tearing with unforgiving ferocity into her skin.

'Emmie, stop playing games because it's really starting to fuck me off,' Oscar snarled from somewhere close by. 'I'm coming to get you.'

She was covered in mud and her bare legs could hardly support her. The rain was thrashing down, making it unclear what direction his voice was coming from. She saw a stream to her left and she waded through it, sucking in air as the ice water numbed her already freezing body.

On the other side she tried to scramble up, slipping as she climbed up the steep bank. She made one last effort and pulled herself to the top with the help of some overgrown foliage.

Emmie staggered along, panting heavily. The side of the wood she climbed into was darker than the other side and she could only see inches in front of her. She stopped for a moment to catch her breath but as she did so felt an arm grab her. She started to scream but a hand clamped over her mouth. Terror took over as she tried to strike the figure but she was being overpowered and the grip round her middle was getting tighter.

'Emmie, stop; it's me.'

All the fight left her body and she felt the hand being released from her mouth as she turned to face her Uncle Vaughn. He held her tightly and his anger flared up as he realised she was naked apart from the jacket she was wearing.

'You're safe now. But Emmie darling, I need to know where Casey and Josh are.'

'I don't know. A guy called Jason attacked Josh, I don't know what happened but he saved me and told me to run. I don't know where Casey is but Oscar's in the woods somewhere.'

Vaughn thought for a moment then looked at Emmie.

'I need you to do something for me.'

Oscar's nose was in agony where Emmie had kicked him. The little bitch wasn't going to get far and he'd teach her a lesson. The only way Alfie Jennings was getting his daughter back was in pieces in a little bag.

He walked a bit further, being careful not to fall in the

slippery mud. He didn't want to keep walking into the night and he stood still for a moment to see if he could hear anything. To the right of him he heard something rustle. He turned his head slightly and he heard it again.

'Emmie, it's pointless running.'

He heard her voice clearly coming from the darkness.

'Stay away.'

'I'm afraid I can't do that.'

Oscar moved towards Emmie's voice and saw her standing by a large tree. He laughed as he moved towards her.

'Who was a very silly girl to try to get away from Uncle Oscar?'

'I don't know, Oscar, you tell me.'

Oscar physically jumped as Vaughn's voice came from behind him. He turned as Vaughn's fist hit him straight in the face, shattering his nose.

'Take a last look round, Oscar; it's the end of the line for you.'

Vaughn produced a jagged knife from his jacket and in one move, expertly slashed Oscar's throat.

Vaughn slipped through the side door of the house as described by Emmie and made his way through the corridors. He wanted to find Josh, but first he needed to find Casey. He'd been out of the game for a while but his instincts came back to him: his senses were on heightened alert.

As he carefully walked along the dimly lit hall, he began to make a vow; if Casey *was* alright he'd show her how much he loved her, he'd show her . . . Vaughn stopped himself, pushing the thoughts to the back of his mind. There was no room for emotion, it would only lessen his senses. He needed to be alert; he couldn't think about anything else apart from the job he had to do: get to Casey before it was too late.

Vaughn squeezed the knife in his hand as he went up the back stairs, and opened the first door to see a woman being violently molested by a group of men. Fury flooded through his veins and he yelled out in anger.

'Get the fuck away from her.'

He brandished his bloodied knife making the group of people run screaming to the corner of the room. Vaughn walked towards them and sneered.

'Take off your masks.'

They hurriedly took their white masks off, revealing their faces. Vaughn looked at them and saw normal looking people who indulged in abnormal activities. He wanted to beat them to within an inch of their lives but he knew it wouldn't help; their injuries would eventually heal and they'd still be left with the darkness inside them.

'Do not touch her, do you understand?'

They nodded, faces full of fear, and Vaughn ran out of the room feeling more on fire than he'd ever been in his life. He kicked open the doors to the rooms and found groups of depraved people enacting their sexual fantasies on young, haunted looking women. He felt sick to his stomach and he knew he needed to find Casey quickly.

It seemed as if he'd looked in every room but as he ran into the last corridor, he heard his name being called.

'Vaughn!'

Casey shouted out when she saw Vaughn. Jason had heard the commotion and had dragged her out of the room. She'd tried to fight but he'd held a blade against her throat. She didn't know where he was taking her, but then she'd seen Vaughn running down the far end of the corridor and had taken her chance to call his name.

Jason held the knife tighter against her throat and she could feel it drawing blood as it cut into her skin.

'Let her go, Jason, there's nowhere for you to run.'

Jason smirked and did a sideways kick, opening up the fire exit door to the roof. He pulled Casey with him through it as the rain lashed down.

Vaughn charged down the corridor and stood in the doorway for a second as he watched Jason pull Casey nearer to the edge. He could hear the sound of sirens in the distance as he made his way out onto the roof.

'Jason.'

Vaughn's voice didn't carry as the storm continued to pick up pace. The rain battered his face, stinging his skin. He could see Casey and Jason a few feet away but he couldn't hear what Jason was saying.

'Jason, let her go.'

He saw him smile as he pointed the knife at Casey, trying to force her to walk backwards towards the edge.

Casey's mouth was dry and she could almost hear the blood pumping round her body. Jason was now holding the knife to her chest, trying to force her back. If she stepped back any further she'd fall off the roof; the wind was blowing hard and she was already struggling to keep her balance.

'There's no place to go, so you might as well get it over quickly, Casey.'

He laughed as she looked at Vaughn who was standing motionless but poised near the roof door. They exchanged looks and in that moment she knew she had to take her chance.

She lunged at Jason who instinctively slashed at her chest; she felt the pain but she ignored it as it gave her time to sidestep away from the edge. Vaughn ran forward and grabbed hold of Jason who stumbled, knocking into Casey who fell backwards, scrambling madly to hold on to the broken rail.

She was holding on but she felt her bad hand giving way

and she couldn't grip the rail with just one hand; Casey closed her eyes, waiting for the inevitable to happen.

As her good hand began to slip she called out, terrified. 'Vaughn!'

The hands that grasped hers weren't Vaughn's; as she looked up she saw Emmie's face concentrating to find the strength to save her. Casey could feel Emmie's clasp slipping away and she heard her call out in alarm.

'Help me, I'm losing my grip! She's falling!'

Casey's fingers began to leave Emmie's and she knew in a moment she was going to fall to her death. She screamed, but instead of falling she felt herself being tugged back up. Through the rain she looked up and saw Vaughn holding on to her. He pulled her easily up, back onto the roof, hugging her and Emmie tightly as the rain powered down.

Casey gently broke away from Vaughn's hug; she looked at him with a glint in her eye as she spoke.

'What kept you?'

Vaughn laughed out loud and was grateful for the rain disguising the tears of joy and relief pouring down his face.

'The police should be here soon.'

Emmie spoke to Vaughn as they walked arm in arm to the upstairs corridor.

'Then that's me out of here. It'll be better that way.'

Casey nodded her head as Vaughn wiped his knife and put it away in his pocket. She looked across to the lifeless body of Jason Hedley lying on the roof. His throat had been slashed.

EPILOGUE

Emmie sat in the warmth of Vaughn's sitting room with Sam curled up on her lap wagging his tail as her mother chatted ten to the dozen opposite her.

'I'd have let him bleeding rot in that prison if I were you, Emmie. How the hell I could've spent my life at that bugger's beck and call, I don't know. Only good thing, Em, about the whole bleeding business is there are no more secrets.'

Emmie smiled at her mum. She never thought she'd be grateful to hear her mother's chatter or enjoy watching her eat her way through a huge bag of cheese and onion crisps but she knew now she'd never want it any other way.

Emmie had been questioned by the police about the party but she'd kept her mouth tightly shut. They'd found Jason's body straight away but it'd been another couple of weeks before they'd found Oscar's body, which had already begun to badly decompose.

The case was still open but Emmie doubted the police would be able to charge anyone. The world they lived in was tight knit and people didn't talk unless, as her dad had always said, they wanted brains on walls. The Albanian women had been taken to refuges. Emmie hoped they'd eventually be able to go back to their own country without fear of reprisals.

She'd also made a statement to the police telling them it was Oscar who'd killed Jake, and the solicitors had told them the CPS would probably drop the case against her dad. He'd got bail and was allowed back to his flat in Soho as long as he adhered to the bail conditions set out whilst he waited for the CPS's final decision, which her uncle had said was really just a matter of course. Her Uncle Vaughn had told her there was no way they'd pursue her dad on the murder charge; the CPS just liked to make people sweat. The most he'd get charged with would be possessing a firearm without a licence, which her uncle had told her with a good brief and the right amount of pressure leant on the right people, he'd get off.

But as much as she was pleased her dad wasn't going to go down for a crime he didn't commit, Emmie knew she didn't want to see him again now she'd said her goodbyes.

She'd gone to see him after he'd been released from Pentonville Prison. Emmie had walked into Whispers and seen her dad sitting at the empty bar drinking a bottle of Stella. To Emmie he'd looked like a broken man. She could see he could still turn on the charm and his cheeky smile, but Emmie had thought it felt desperate and his eyes seemed to have aged.

When she'd walked into Whispers his face had lit up and he'd wolf whistled at her as he always had done when she'd walked in a room. She remembered how it used to make her feel special, but now it only made her feel sad.

'Hello darlin', glad you could come; your old man's been missing you.'

'I've missed you too.'

He'd smiled and stroked her face, taking in how surprisingly well she looked after her ordeal.

'It's good to see you, Emmie. I'm glad you didn't come and see me when I was inside, I wouldn't want you seeing your old man banged up like that. I was thinking maybe we could go to Harrods, have a bit of a spending splurge to put a smile back on your face. What do you say, babe?'

'No thanks, Dad. I've actually come to say goodbye.'

'What you talking about? Don't tell me you're off to see your cousin Lucy in LA? Bleedin' hell, Em, you've just got out of hospital; do you think it's wise? I bet your frigging mother has something to do with this.'

Emmie had looked at her dad and her heart had broken. She loved him so much, but after what she'd been through and seeing what he'd indirectly put the other women through she couldn't have him in her life.

'No Dad. I'm saying goodbye to you. I love you and always will, but I don't like you or what you do, and I can't have you in my life.'

She'd seen tears in his eyes for a moment and then his face had hardened.

'Is this because of the stuff with Casey? Because let me tell you, it might be her bleedin' DNA bobbing around in your body, but that's all it is, Em; DN fucking A. I'm your dad; it doesn't change a flipping thing.'

'I know it doesn't; I'll always see you as my dad and you know I love you, but it's not because of that; it's *you*, and what you do, and what you stand for.'

'Fuck's sake, Em, what did they do to you? Shove a frigging Bible down your throat? Come on babe; it's business. How the fuck do you think I paid for all the designer clothes you and your mum wanted? All the holidays to America, not to mention the school fees and the big house – they didn't appear from nowhere.'

Emmie had said nothing but it'd hurt to see her dad still justifying his actions after everything she'd been through.

She'd kissed him on his cheek and walked away. The tears had streamed down her face and hadn't stopped until she'd got home as she'd listened to him pleading for her to go back.

She was happy now; her Uncle Vaughn had told them she and her mum could move in with him after they'd gone back to the family house in Essex to discover her dad had changed all the locks.

The moment she'd walked through his front door, she'd immediately felt at home. Emmie knew there was a long way to go to get over what she'd been through, but she felt safe, and ironically it was the first time in her life she hadn't hated who she was. What had happened had changed her, she'd had to grow up overnight and she knew she'd never be the same again – but that was fine with her.

Vaughn smiled and walked out of the room, leaving Janine to chat ten to the dozen to Emmie. He'd invited them to stay as long as they liked. He'd wondered if he'd regret his invitation but it was the best decision he'd ever made. All his life he'd kept relationships and women at a distance but now he had three women to look out for, and three to look out for him.

He walked into the master bedroom and stood for a moment as he watched Casey asleep in his bed.

After he'd rescued them he'd left Casey and Emmie at the house and made his way through the woods and back to the car before the police had arrived. He'd done what he needed to do and he hadn't been going to wait around for a medal. He certainly hadn't been going to wait around to get a life stretch.

He'd half expected to find Josh at the car waiting for him, and when he wasn't he'd stayed there until dawn hoping he'd appear, but as each minute had ticked by and the sun had begun to rise Vaughn had known something had gone terribly wrong. He'd been tempted to stay and continue to wait but he'd known all he would be doing was kidding himself; he'd been in the business long enough to know if a person hadn't arrived back by sunrise, they were never coming back. He'd got in his car and driven slowly home.

And then a couple of days later he'd got the call which had made him laugh out loud.

'Mr Sadler, I was hoping you'd bring me some grapes; and maybe some of those flowers of yours which you seem to be struggling to grow.'

He'd walked into the hospital unit and seen Josh lying all tubed up and looking like he'd been hit with a ten-tonne truck; but he was alive, and for some reason that had made Vaughn very happy.

'You look like shit.'

He grinned as Josh managed a smile and he sat down on the chair next to his bed. They'd sat watching the football together on the television, having come to a silent understanding.

Casey had called from the hospital where they'd kept her in for a few days for the injuries she'd sustained. He hadn't gone to visit her; he'd wanted to keep a distance in case the police were sniffing around her.

When she'd been discharged, he'd sent a driver to bring her to him, and he had no intention of letting her go. But Alfie had been another matter. He'd known he'd been released from prison, but he'd been surprised to get a call from him.

'Vaughn, it's Alf.'

He'd hesitated before he'd greeted him, not quite knowing what to say.

'I wasn't expecting this, Alf.'

'I haven't had a chance to thank you.'

'I don't want your thanks, Alf; I didn't do it for you.'

'I know but I want to do something for you. Being banged up and all the shit with Emmie gave me time to think. You know the thing with Casey and me . . .'

'Stop, I don't want to hear it, Alf.'

'I think you will; nothing happened between us. I took her back to my flat, and all she talked about was you and then she passed out on me. I was pissed off with you about the money, so I made you believe I'd fucked her.'

Vaughn had been shocked beyond belief at Alfie's revelation, but he'd also been more relieved than he'd ever been before. He loved Casey no matter what, and maybe he was wrong, but knowing she hadn't actually slept with Alfie made it even more special. All that time he'd treated her badly and pushed her away for something she hadn't done and didn't even know about; no wonder she'd seemed confused by him.

'I can't believe you did that to me.'

'Don't start getting on your high and fucking mighty, Vaughn, I was doing you a favour.'

'And how do you make that out?'

'She's a lush, and no better than the brass who stands at the end of my street every night.'

'Enough, Alfie. What's wrong with you – even after everything you still don't get it? I love her and hopefully I'll get the chance to spend the rest of my life with her.'

'You've been eating fucking marbles, mate, you've gone soft.'

'Maybe, Alf, and you're entitled to your opinion; but for now I don't want to hear it and I don't want you around my life.'

'You can't cut me off.' Alfie sounded panicked.

'I can, Alfie, and I'm going to. I love you, god knows I

do. I made my promise to Connor and I'll stick to it, so if you ever need me, Alf, you know where I am, but for now I've got to say goodbye.'

With that, Vaughn had clicked off his mobile before deleting Alfie's number from his phone. If Alfie wanted to get hold of him, he knew how.

Walking back out of the room, Vaughn closed the door quietly behind him, smiling at Casey curled up in his bed.

The minute Casey heard the door shut, she opened her eyes, truly happy for the first time in years.

She'd been terrified when Janine had said she was going to tell Emmie about who she was – the thought of being rejected by her daughter was too much to bear.

'What if she hates me once she knows who I am, Jan?'

'She won't. How could she? You saved her life, and apart from that, you're her mum; well, one of them anyway.'

Casey had squeezed Janine's hand, she was so grateful for her emotional generosity. When Emmie had walked into the room, she could feel her legs shaking.

'We've got something to tell you.'

Emmie had looked worried and had glanced at Janine as if she'd done something wrong. Janine had spoken to her softly with so much love in her voice.

'Sit down baby; there's a bit of a story you need to know.'

Janine had told her story and after she'd finished Casey had been too scared to look at Emmie. But then she'd felt someone sit next to her on the couch and take her hands: the same soft hands which had helped save her from the roof.

'I knew you were special.'

Casey had looked up into her daughter's eyes as Emmie spoke the words to her. 'Thank you for coming back for me, Mum. Grandpa said in his letters that you'd always loved

350

me and not a day would go by without you thinking about me.'

They'd held hands and Janine had burst into tears, running over to join in on the emotional reunion.

From being lost for so long, Casey had now gained a wonderful family and found her daughter. Emmie was going to be part of her life from now on, as was Janine and even Lola, and Casey was more than happy to share her life with them all. She was going to get help and work her way through her demons with Vaughn by her side. She was ready to start to live life again, and not just exist. Turning over in the bed, Casey smiled as she realised she could finally stop running. What had been taken, she'd found.

Thurs 15th March 2012
Happiness at last

The End

Read on for an exclusive extract of Jacqui Rose's
new novel, out in 2013.

PROLOGUE

2008

'*If any of you know of any just cause or impediment why
these two people should not be joined in Holy Matrimony
ye are to declare it now or forever hold thy peace.*'

*They turned to look at the man in the front pew leaning
to one side as he slept; his mouth slightly ajar and his fraying
grey cap pulled over his eyes. His stiff brown collar jacket
was pulled up tightly round his neck in an attempt to stop
the cold winter's draught giving him a chill. Behind him a
small woman in her mid-fifties sat with her head down,
engrossed but unable to solve the crossword in the paper.*

*They were strangers to them who they'd never see again,
but that's what they'd needed today; people who didn't know
where they came from and who didn't care. It hadn't been
difficult to find two witnesses to sit in the draughty church
for the twenty minute ceremony, certainly not when they
were being paid three hundred pounds to do so.*

A moment passed; silence remained, save the light snoring

from the man and the echoed scratching of the woman's pen on the paper as she worked out clues.

'You can now give her the ring.'

Taking a deep breath he glanced at the vicar for the first time before nervously scrambling into his pocket to retrieve the simple platinum band. Traditionally it should've been the duty of the best man to hold the ring, he knew that, but neither of them had wanted to risk having someone there they knew; someone who just might talk.

As he pulled out the ring, his fingers touched the cold steel of the hand gun; something he always carried, especially on days like today.

'Got it.'

The vicar nodded, wearily continuing with the ceremony, giving the impression he'd rather be somewhere else.

'Those whom God hath joined together, let no man put asunder.'

They smiled at each other anticipating his next words.

'Then I now pronounce you man and wife.'

Outside the rain was starting to come down hard but it didn't matter to them. What mattered was the moment; the moment which they knew couldn't last. Almost in unison they took off their wedding rings, placing them into their pockets; it was unlikely they'd be able to wear them again.

They held each other's stare then turned away, not looking back as they walked separately into the chill of the late November afternoon, longing for the day when it'd be safe for them to be together.

CHAPTER ONE

'Bleedin' hell.' Maggie Donaldson swore loudly as she jumped out of the way; she narrowly avoided being hit by a china tea cup whizzing past her head as she opened the front door and stepped into the hall. She watched, slightly bemused, as it smashed against the garish lamp in the corner, tiny fragments of blue china showered down, as if a sudden cloud burst was taking place in the cramped hallway.

Using the back of her red scuffed heel to shut the battered front door, Maggie's bemusement slowly turned to anger as she looked around the gloomy hallway, listening to the raised voices. She sighed loudly, pushing out all the air in her stomach as she did so.

She'd been away for just over a year and somehow during that time she'd convinced herself things would be different. It'd been stupid to do so, she'd even known that at the time, because violence in her family was like a thirst; as recurrent and necessary as other people's cups of morning tea.

How many times as a child had she cowered in bed listening to the screaming arguments, the crying and the slamming of doors before making sure the coast was clear to creep quietly downstairs to comfort and tend to her mother's injuries?

The brutality hadn't just stopped there: it'd touched everyone with sadistic cruelty, twisting and coiling itself around the heart of her family. Maggie could count on one hand the times she'd been hugged as a kid, but she'd lost count of the number of black eyes she and her siblings had received growing up in the Donaldson household.

She'd only managed to survive her mother's visits to casualty, her father's drunken rows and the daily terror she'd seen in her sibling's eyes by having hope; hope that one day it'd all come to a full stop. But as Maggie Laura Donaldson looked at the discoloured silver cutlery strewn all over the floor and the mismatched tea set thrown about the hall like hand grenades in a battlefield, it told her all she needed to know: her hopes were as taunting and hollow as ever. Only a miracle could change things and Maggie knew miracles didn't happen in the Donaldson household, not even small ones.

Standing with weary resignation in the newly painted kitchen doorway, Maggie watched as her father-armed to throw another porcelain bomb at her retreating mother-spit out his venomous words.

'Jaysus fucking Christ Sheila, if it's the last thing I do, I'll have your blood on my hands, woman! I'll happily do time for you. Look at me like that again and see what happens. I swear on the Virgin Mary, I'll...'

Interrupting her father's furious rant Maggie spoke, her voice filled with the hard edge of coldness she'd learnt from him.

'Hello, Dad. This is a nice welcome home, ain't it? It's good to see nothing changes; home sweet bleedin' home.'

IN CONVERSATION WITH
JACQUI ROSE

Where does your inspiration come from?
Well, *Taken* was inspired by some of my own experiences, but on the whole I'll hear something or see something that I'm passionate about and for whatever reason it'll touch my heart. Then that will trigger an idea in my head and, whether I want it to or not, it'll start forming a storyline. Then characters start popping out of nowhere, wanting me to tell their stories and the only way to get rid of the constant dialogue in my head is to write it down!

Have you always wanted to become a writer?
Yes and no. I've always loved writing and as I little girl when I knew I had to write a story for homework I'd get butterflies in my tummy from the excitement. The idea of losing myself with characters I'd created and going anywhere I wanted in my stories made me happy beyond words, but I assumed writing was for clever people, people who went to University, so I never even considered it as an option. But as I come full circle in my life, I feel I've finally found what I'm supposed to do and wonder how I could've ever doubted it.

What's the strangest job you've ever had?
I suppose it would be working in a transvestite shop doing makeovers. My day would be spent transforming the men who came into the shop into their female alter egos. So I'd start off with Ralf and within a couple of hours I'd magically be with Rachael. It'd

Marкульт .

be a total makeover, from choosing their underwear right the way through to their wigs from the huge store cupboard there, but I couldn't begin to tell you how many arguments I had trying to explain that most women really don't care if their underwear matches with their handbags! But I loved every moment of it.

When you're not writing, what are your favourite things to do?
This is another difficult one. Because of the situation I was in, for a long time it seemed as if I went around with my eyes closed, shutting out the world, but now my life has changed so much that everything fills me with interest and wonder, whether it's going for a simple walk, jet skiing, riding, meeting with friends or fishing off the Brigg. As long as it makes me feel happy and safe then it becomes one of my favourite things.

What is a typical working day like for you?
I'm very disciplined. I have a strict routine which even her majesty's forces would be proud and envious of. I take my children to school, go to the gym for strictly ninety minutes, have my cup of tea out in the garden whatever the weather, try to stop myself from tweeting the most tedious of things and then precisely on the stroke of eleven thirty, I start to write, not stopping until the clock strikes four when I go to pick up my children again, only for it to begin again the next day. I love every moment of it.

Have you ever had writer's block and if so how do you cope with it?
No, I've never had writer's block, quite the opposite. My head is so full of characters letting me know they want their story told, it sometimes gets to the point where it wakes me up at night and I'm like, 'Okay, okay, enough already. I'll write about you.' Names come into my head and I write them down knowing there's a story behind them but I don't know what it is until I let my characters lead me along their path.

Do you have any secret ambitions?
Yes, I really, really want to do investigative television documentaries, a kind of female version of Ross Kemp; I like what he does, his show don't pretend to be anything clever, it is what it is and I like that, somehow it just works. The idea of doing a weekly radio phone- in show also appeals to me, but only if I had a co-presenter!

358